THESE MARVELOUS BEASTS

THESE MARVELOUS BEASTS

THE COMPLETE FROST & FILIGREE SERIES

NATANIA BARRON

To All the Beautiful Monsters

The monster never dies.

— Stephen King, *Cujo*

PART I
FROST & FILIGREE

BEASTS OF TARRYTOWN

I met a lady in the meads,
    Full beautiful—a faery's child,
Her hair was long, her foot was light,
    And her eyes were wild.
- *La Belle Dame Sans Merci*, by John Keats

She was a gordian shape of dazzling hue,
    Vermilion-spotted, golden, green, and blue;
Striped like a zebra, freckled like a pard,
Eyed like a peacock, and all crimson barr'd;
And full of silver moons, that, as she breathed,
Dissolv'd, or brighter shone, or interwreathed
Their lustres with the gloomier tapestries--
So rainbow-sided, touch'd with miseries,
She seem'd, at once, some penanced lady elf,
Some demon's mistress, or the demon's self.
- *Lamia,* by John Keats

"You're a woman with a brain and reasonable ability. Stop whining
and find something to do."
    -- The Dowager Countess of Grantham

LYNDHURST

These sorts of stories inevitably begin with a mysterious moment, some great, unexplained event. The scene is set, and the narrative begins apace.

This story, however, breaks with tradition. It starts with an invitation to a party, a little light gossip, and the promise of new neighbors. Hardly the demesne of the supernatural. But do not be put off. There shall be plenty of magic as our tale unfolds.

You see, for the two heroines of said tale, the ordinary is the extraordinary. In every way measured against humanity, these women are unusual to the extreme. They possess all the skills expected of women of birth, and are yet not women of birth in the traditional way. They are older, wiser, and stranger than their peers, yet possessed of abilities and persuasions to both delight and terrify.

Yet, in the unlikely instance that someone should stumble into their garden, their appearance would not, perhaps, be enough to raise alarm. They sit together, across a heavy iron table, positioned behind one of the largest mansions in Tarrytown, New York. Shade is provided by way of an enormous wisteria canopy. The two women sip tea out of delicate cups with an ivy and rose intertwined pattern, little rivulets of steam rising and eddying.

One is tall and lean, her face unmarred by time yet displaying a visible hunger in her lines. Perhaps it is her fiery eyes, an amber brown hue, or the shocking pale of her skin as it transitions to the full, inky curls about her brow. Either way, she is lovely by many measures, despite the pallor, and she dresses a la mode, down to the scalloping on her heels and the slant of her hat. These days she goes by the name Vivienne du Lac.

The other woman, Nerissa Melusine Waldemar, is shorter, rounder, with a plainer look to her features. Her eyes could be blue or grey or green, but never in a striking way. Her chin is a bit weak, her brows disrupted by a pair of spectacles. The hair atop her head might once have been arranged well, but now tumbles half-heartedly down one side. Her dress speaks to practicality, limned with mud about the hem, and something dark remains under her fingernails.

There are enough clues within these descriptions to give a close observer pause. It is cold, yet the wisteria blooms. As long as the women talk, their tea does not get cold. The woman with the tousled appearance wears no shoes, and now and again her grimy toes peek out from beneath the hem of her dress. The substance beneath each slivered moon of her fingernails is certainly blood.

From the front—and, indeed, all other angles of the house—this little garden oasis is invisible. For the world around them is wreathed in winter snow and wind. Yet here, in their little enclave, no frost or flake dare invade. This private garden is for these two friends, and them alone. Their mundane tea time, though clearly accentuated by a most vexing magic, is possessed of a deep calm and comfort, the quiet of two women known long to one another.

A third figure emerges from the house itself, a manservant of sorts. He is swarthy in appearance, dressed in the custom of a butler, with a long, single braid down his neat beard. He is broad of shoulder and light of step; so light, in fact, that he does not appear to walk so much as he drifts. Yes, where his feet touch the ground is a rather curious blur, a smudge of topaz and light where a pair of shoes ought to be. It is almost enough to be a distraction from the earrings he wears, thick and gold and marvelous, dangling almost to his shoulders.

When the man—if he is so—approaches, giving a most regal bow, the pale woman stands. "Barqan," she says, "Nerissa and I were just discussing our new neighbors. Have they yet called?"

Barqan comes up from his bow and says, "No, Lady du Lac. I've only now just received the post, and while the Villiers have sent a most impressive invitation, the rest is sadly bereft of communication from the Rockefellers."

"I told you they wouldn't call," Nerissa says, pushing up her spectacles with one hand and then peering down at her dirty foot, as if to examine it. She frowns at what she sees and then straightens, taking in Barqan's figure. "And you're not even trying to conceal yourself. It's shameful."

Barqan raises a neat brow and presents the letters to Lady du Lac. He does not, as is his habit, entertain Nerissa's admonishment.

"He doesn't have to conceal when he's out here with us," Lady du Lac says sweetly, taking the proffered letters and rifling through them quickly. "It's the least we can do considering his continued indenture against his will."

"You seem to have plenty use for him," Nerissa says.

"That's only because I can't seem to break the bond. You know I find slavery abhorrent," replies Vivienne, clicking her tongue. "You promised me you'd find answers."

"Well, it isn't as if I don't have other work to do. Every time I bring it up, you seem to have another reason we need to keep him around."

"It would be foolish to send him out to pasture while we figure this all out."

"I'm still here," Barqan says drily.

"You're always here; that's the problem," Nerissa says, pushing away from the table. Her manner is like a farmhand getting up from milking the cows. "I've got to go visit the goats," she says to Lady du Lac. "Viv, make sure you don't let warm holiday greetings get to your head. You promised: One. Single. Party. That is all."

Vivienne stands across from Nerissa, clutching the invitations close to her chest. Other than a twitching finger, she is a figure of ice and snow. The intricate lace on her shoulders almost fades into her skin, looking more like Fey tattoos than clothing.

"You are not allowed to tell me what to do," Vivienne says.

Nerissa laughs as she passes Barqan. "Of course I'm *allowed*. You just don't ever listen."

A faint flush of red creeps upon Vivienne's cheeks. It does not make her look healthy. It makes her look monstrous, especially the way it accentuates her strange eyes. "We agreed on two parties this year."

"That was *last* year. We've progressed firmly into nineteen eleven," Nerissa says, as she retreats up the steps to the long porch, one of their servants opening the way for her—or else just through the power of the enchanted door. "You're getting forgetful in your old age, my dear."

"But I have three dresses already," Vivienne whines. It's a piteous sound.

"One party. Choose well," Nerissa replies.

She does not look back to see Vivienne glaring at her, but knows full well the look.

~

B efore the tale goes much deeper, it is essential to understand a few important things about Vivienne and Nerissa. As far as either of them knows, they are immortal. Nerissa is perhaps a century older than Vivienne, but neither knows for sure. Those first dark decades of their lives are somewhat clouded with a mutual thirst for blood. It took a long time—many lifetimes in the most literal sense—to rectify that debt. It is far more difficult for Nerissa who, unlike her friend Vivienne, is far less human.

But to say either of them is human is a stretch. Is a serpent any less a rock than a wolf? No, of course not. A human being may very well be defined by their extremely limited existences and their uncanny ability to tease out art and meaning in such short a span. Neither Vivienne nor Nerissa think much like human beings, though one might say that over the years they have gone a bit human*ish*. Especially Vivienne, who has always been drawn to people and their lives and rules. It gives her the illusion of warmth in her state of permafrost, as Nerissa is fond of calling it.

Vivienne is not the only one of her kind, but one of a dying race. Many have heard of the Fey, or the Fates, and she is certainly related to both of them. More properly she is a *night sylph*. In her youth, she was known for wooing young men and then driving them mad once they discovered she was not, in fact, human (this is very traumatic for men, especially those in the age of chivalry, for whom powerful women were ever a source of terror). It is in her nature to fall in love, however, and while she has learned some ways to curb her most deadly tendencies, it is not unheard of for her to fall off the proverbial wagon now and again.

Nerissa, meanwhile, is more reptile than human being. However, she is able to change her appearance to suit any will. Most of the time she looks as she does now—a barefooted and rather untidy woman of middling age who would be more at home in a library than a vast manse like their current residence (which Vivienne calls *The Joyous Guard*.

Nerissa finds this name ridiculous, as most of Vivienne's human obsessions. She has yet to get over the fact that she could not woo Launcelot from Guinevere and has named the manse in his honor. The place is called Knoll, properly, or else Lyndhurst, and it is a fine enough name.)

In specific terms, Nerissa is a *lamia*. Unlike Vivienne, she is the last of her kind. This is owed to the fact that most were killed during the previous century, often mistaken for vampires during the last Purge. It was due to Vivienne's social connections and Nerissa's own reformed behavior, no longer subsisting on human blood and, instead, turning to her flock of goats, that she was glossed over. Lamias are far more trusting of mankind, or at least they were before the Purge, so they came to a most gruesome end.

Now that the world has turned, another century passed, and the Americas established beyond a backwater trading post, Vivienne and Nerissa—after long centuries in England, Russia, China, and Japan—came, at last, to New York City itself. Finding the rush of such a place a bit too much to handle and their fortune better suited elsewhere, they relocated upstate to a town on the Hudson called Tarrytown, on the suggestion of a friend, one Anna Gould, who happened to be enduring a most horrendous divorce. Rather than stay in her family's abode, she hired her friend Vivienne to keep after the place herself. Ms. Gould doubtfully knew the true nature of Miss du Lac and Miss Waldemar, but, as so many before her, she found Vivienne near impossible to argue with. And given the option to live in a Gothic manse, Vivienne spared no effort.

Much of Nerissa's work, however, is tied up in the business of maintaining such a property, though it never will be hers entirely (a strange side effect of her kind is the incapability of ever owning land or property). Vivienne is all dreams and delights, while Nerissa is habitually left with the dregs. It had been Vivienne's idea to build the "painted garden" as she calls it, a kind of mirror to the Fae realm in between the walls of Lyndhurst itself, a memory of the lives they once lived giving up their native world for this. Both have ever been creatures of both worlds, but the Fae realm is far behind the times of fashion and sadly lacking in blood nourishment.

As Nerissa walks the long corridors of the ridiculously large mansion—it is honestly one of the most befuddling and insulting recreations of the Gothic she has ever seen—she thinks about the goats and about her distaste for the djinni Vivienne has masquerading as a manservant. It's a touch too precious, she thinks, and invariably a giveaway. He does not like doing what he is told and often lets things slip under the guise. It's happened before, their discovery, and it's never ended well. The agreement is to stay on at Lyndhurst for at least five years, and while only one has passed, it has felt like an eternity. The socialites of Tarrytown and its surrounding cozy towns are nothing if they aren't insistent on parties and soirées and galas and events, all which disgust Nerissa.

Human food makes Nerissa downright ill. Especially fruit. To her, they always smell half rotted. Why anyone would want to stuff slimy seedpods down their gullet is beyond her, but Vivienne absolutely adores human food. It doesn't make a difference whether or not she eats it, as her energy is simply gained by being around people, a kind of latent vampirism that does little harm in small doses but can be deadly in large.

Nerissa has no such luck. She knows she's cranky because she hasn't had much in the way of food, but in this forsaken palace, it takes so long to make the trip from the garden to the pasture.

The groundskeepers know to leave Nerissa alone to the goats, and she picks times when she knows they won't be around. The younger one, Jim, has been looking at her a little oddly, but most of the servants simply discuss her as being the "eccentric sister" when it's plain to see for anyone with a pair of eyes that the two mistresses of the house are not related.

Still, Nerissa feels her worry lessen slightly as she approaches the flock. She consented to a pair of boots on her way out, but as soon as she nears the paddock, she shirks them off and climbs the gate and sits among the goats for a bit as they paw around her. Despite her frequent feedings, they are not afraid of her. She doesn't kill them after all, and based on skills learned while in Africa, she knows how to bleed them with minimal pain and maximum harvesting.

She only feeds off the females, of course. The rams are too aggressive and kept in another pasture, their blood muddied and unsavory to her palate. Today it's Millie's turn to give the gift of nourishment to Nerissa. The ewe is two years old by now, Nerissa reckons, and full of vigor. She does taste best.

Taking Millie by the bell, she walks her to the little stable where she goes about her "scientific" work, as she's told the staff. She's given explicit instructions to be left alone, despite their curious glances. After the first few months, however, and tasting the first slaughter, they did not ask further questions. A fortunate side effect of Nerissa's feeding is surprisingly tender and less gamey meat. While no self-respecting elite would deign to eat such sub-par meat, the servants at Lyndhurst had absolutely no qualms regarding its swift consumption.

To feed, however, Nerissa cannot continue the facade of her human form. Practicing magic while absorbing life is almost impossible. One cannot both sneeze and drink at the same time, after all. The goats see her change, but it doesn't appear to unnerve them. Most of them have moved on now that they understand Millie is to be selected—one might say in their primitive capabilities, they have rallied around the lamia as followers of some ancient goat deity—but a few remain behind, nibbling weeds at the edge of the shed and peering toward her every now and again.

She disrobes and prepares to change, still petting Millie and preparing her.

Were a human being to see Nerissa change, as very few have, they would not remain so composed as Millie and her sisters. Her skin shifts in a thousand little undulations, myriad little plates rising in patterned scales about her face and down her arms. Where there were two arms and two legs, a most common arrangement for *homo sapiens*, there are now four arms—each with black claws upon three fingers—and a long tail more akin to a dragon or large lizard than a snake. There are some smaller appendages that sprout from the sides, under the dress she wears, that might prove helpful for some basic locomotion, but judging from the sheer musculature, they are likely unnecessary.

Her face and hair shift as well, her eyes going black—not just the color of her eyes, but the sclera as well—and widen to the size of a horse's. Nerissa's hair loses its soft, loose quality, and each individual strand becomes thicker, like limp algae. She is not ugly by lamia standards to say the least. Should any number see her, they would compliment the blood red of her teeth and the glistening mucous on her lips and ears and nose. These are desired characteristics and, it is rumored, in their heyday many went to great lengths to appear such a way, supporting a small cosmetics industry in Ancient Greece.

But to Nerissa, who has known so few of her own kind, she sees her own hands, all four of them, and shudders. The talons, the scales. These are elements of her body she has grown ashamed of over the centuries. Humankind fears these things. Those of cold blood, those of rough skin. Though she can shift into any shape imaginable and has lived the life of men and women a dozen times over, she must always be this way to feed. She must always face her true self, in all its sticky, inhuman glory.

The talons are, at least, ideal for extraction. There is that one vein, common in many domesticated creatures. The Maasai use an arrow, Nerissa uses her talon, to puncture the vein and drain the blood. By the time this happens, Millie is in a daze. Nerissa suspects it is her eyes. In the dark, her own are similar to the goat's, curiously shaped hourglasses just faintly darker than the black around them. Perhaps goats see it, too.

When, at last, Nerissa emerges from the shed, having made sure that Millie is sufficiently recovered, she is back to the guise she wears most days. This is as human as she gets. She chooses the details of eccentricity, not because she must but because it helps her get into character. It also means she is forgiven for avoiding some of the trappings of her sex—shoes, extensive petticoats, that sort of thing—and can be excused when she lapses.

Now that she's sated, however, she realizes how awful she's been to Vivienne. This is what happens when she waits too long to feed. Ideally, she would feed every day. But now she stretches out her feedings to thrice weekly, making sure to feed strategically. When she was younger, and far more active, the food was a necessity. But this soft life of dinner parties and gardening does not quite require such gluttony.

Yet it has been getting more difficult to maintain the abbreviated eating schedule. Goats are not as nutritious as humans, even with the special diet she has developed for them. And she must rotate through the herd to get ample feeding. In the back of her mind, she begins to worry that she may need to consider a new kind of beast. Goats are easy, but she doubts something larger like a cow would be so manageable. Going through two goats a sitting would be difficult, but so would changing the arrangement with Lyndhurst.

Nerissa is so engrossed in her thoughts that she does not notice the shadowy figure emerge from the side of the shed. The figure is slight, cloaked, and swift moving. When Nerissa turns slightly to check on Millie one last time, the figure is gone, and while she senses an odd shift in the air, she thinks little of it and, instead, simply keeps on her way toward the main house to apologize to Vivienne.

A WINTER'S BALL

Vivienne spends most of the next week planning for the ball at the Villiers' mansion. While they are not her favorite family of note, they do have one of the larger properties and are known to invite a mix of foreign dignitaries, artists, and occasionally a more bohemian sort to their parties. George Villiers, the patriarch of the family, was something of a world traveler in his time, and generally accepted to be a gregarious and generous man with a penchant for making friends in and out of society with his charm. This extends, of course, to those of the gentler sex, for whom he is also generally accepted to have appetite. His wife, Lady Edna Montague Villiers is that pale, fragile kind of woman so often found in such circles, too concerned about her own diminishing health—much of which can never be corroborated by doctors, but always by palmists and soothsayers (none of whom are authentic)—to see what's going on right beneath her own roof.

To Vivienne, such concepts as fidelity feel very old fashioned. Having lived through a number of court situations in her time, and outlived every last one of her mortal lovers—or killed them, same difference—she finds the simultaneous shock and awe of matters between the sheets to be tiresome.

No, what truly excites Vivienne du Lac about parties is the clothing. Since the first moment she set her eyes upon a human being, she knew in an instant that clothing, that fashion, connected her to them in a way it did none of her sisters. They are mostly happy to frolic in their natural forms, to weave weeds of water and air, flower and frond. And in a rather basic, primitive way, she supposes that is alluring. Sylphs have a reputation for treating nudity as a kind of art. Aside from their paleness, they do look very human indeed, yet suffer none of the unfortunate side effects of aging. So ever-curving breasts and unmarred skin make for a good show.

But Vivienne adores materials. Patterns. The play of light on thread. She is quite good at her own handwork but has to play down her talents lest she attract too much attention.

Her formula for success is simple: find a willing accomplice, typically a relatively little-known designer from Paris or the closest city, and strike a deal with them. She provides a healthy stipend and extensive notes, drawings, and schematics for each and every dress. All credit is relinquished, of course, and once they learn from her craft and approach, they are free to use it elsewhere.

That said, the week before the ball is a dizzying maelstrom of samples, measurements, and fittings. She is even allowed to dress Nerissa, to her extreme distaste, because they agree to show a unified front. They can't endure the gossip of a grand gown and a horrible one together. It would raise too many questions.

Living in secret has its own great challenges. But Vivienne has discovered, over the many years of her existence among humans, that character covers up many ills. While she has not lived in this part of the world for quite some time, she knows this kind of people well enough. Especially those from the city. And the Villiers' party will be filled with the elite, and by extension, the most fashionable in the entire hemisphere. She simply cannot miss such an opportunity.

"Are you certain about this?" asks Mr. Pender, the clothier most recently employed by Vivienne du Lac. He is a short, thin man, with an even thinner mustache. He favors stripes and shiny buttons, and he generally doesn't argue with her.

But Vivienne already knows this is the point with which he is going to struggle. The colors are unusual—lavender and white and black fur—but he does not question. The accessories are unusual—raw mother of pearl and natural shapes instead of square facets—and Mr. Pender accepts with smile.

It is simply the length, or lack thereof, that takes Mr. Pender aback.

"Trust me," Vivienne says, smoothing her hand across the top layer of her dress, a slightly darker shade of purple than the sheath below. "In a year or two, it will be all the rage."

"But—do you not think it's slightly inappropriate?" he asks, with some difficulty. And then he adds, "You don't think you'll be cold?"

Vivienne, of course, remembers her earlier days, in particular her wooing of many a knight and her favorite outfits comprised simply of strategically placed orchids.

She smiles anyway, patting Mr. Pender on the shoulder. "You forget the black and white fur caplet. It will keep me more than warm."

"But the dress. Your *ankles*."

"My ankles will be fine, sir. You needn't worry. Or are you so concerned for your reputation that you would give up the sum I have set aside for you?"

Vivienne doesn't need to look at him. She feels his energy, feels his sensations and heat like moving webs all around them. It's an ancient dance, and many men have tried—and failed—to take the lead. She will not kill Mr. Pender, not yet anyway, but she is strong enough still, and wise enough now, that she is able to twist his thoughts just so. He won't love her; she never could tolerate that sort of thing. But he will trust her, and that's halfway there.

Mr. Pender looks to make an argument, but then all the fight goes out of him and he says no more.

The rest of the planning goes without incident, and Mr. Pender is even amenable enough to finishing the work on Nerissa's dress, which is nowhere near as beautiful but just as short.

When they finally arrive at The Drummings, the Villiers' mansion —known locally as the Rookery for the ever-present ravens atop its spires, or Droppings, due to the unfortunate side-effect of the avian guests—the drive leading up to the front entrance is a mangle of broughams and carriages and frustrated valets. For the average partygoer, the weather is a horror: wind and drizzle have made the affair both soggy and frigid, casting uncomely splashes of red and snot across many a fair face in attendance, man and woman alike. To think of all that work dashed because of a cruel twist of climate.

Nerissa and Vivienne never have to worry about such inconveniences. For Nerissa's part, she can look however she wants, so long as she does not reveal her true face. For Vivienne, she is always flawless. Her skin does not age, nor needs embellishment. Her dark hair and glassy eyes could not have been better shaped had they been carved in marble.

"Oh, look, it's Lady Olivier," Vivienne says, peering out the window with a crooked smile. "She's fallen into a puddle, and she's beating her footman about the head with her purse. And by the sound of it, she's stashed the entirety of the family's jewels in it. The poor man." The way she giggles, however, reveals her true feelings on the matter.

Nerissa fiddles with the sleeve of her dress. The whole contraption is ungodly uncomfortable. How is it that Vivienne manages to find one horrid dress after another with levels of such mind-boggling engineering for the sole purpose of tormenting her? Nerissa knows well enough that maintaining human form—any human form—is difficult as it is. One's original form does not simply vanish into the aether. It must be cleverly hidden and maintained over a long period of time. She still has extra arms and a long, serpentine tail. It is only through her skill and concentration that she keeps them concealed.

"Sometimes I think you want me to lose my glamor," Nerissa says, pulling Vivienne away from the window. "And don't gawk. You'll draw attention."

"Of course I will. That's the whole *idea*," Vivienne says, stifling a giggle.

When they finally reach the entrance, it is quite clear that the poor Villiers have done a very poor job of planning for the weather. There are not enough servants to manage the thick coats. The marble steps are slick, and while some effort has been made to throw salt, it's still perilously slippery. Neither Vivienne nor Nerissa have any trouble navigating, of course, but they make a show of looking as if they are in need of help to avoid raising any eyebrows. They have both learned to do this instinctively, a kind of chameleon act around humans.

Nerissa prepares herself as they present their cards to the footmen. Even in the chaos, it is time for the ball to begin; in fact, well past time. The smell of rich food reaches Nerissa just as their names are called, and she takes a few deep breaths, hoping that she can keep her wits together in the presence of so many frenzied human beings. She is rarely tempted these days to drink of them, but when they get excited and angry, she finds her tastes return in flashes.

Vivienne has no such difficulty, nor such concern. The center of this space is her very element. Angry or happy or afraid, it matters little to her. Just being among the crush of the crowd infuses her with a glow she is otherwise lacking. Her stony features brighten; her hair shines brighter. She is prepared to make her entrance.

The anticipation is almost overwhelming for her. As the heavy doors open—so thickly laden with holly, ivy, and juniper that for a moment it is as if she is walking into a hidden forest—her heart races, her pulse beats inhumanly fast. The feeling is not nervousness. Her body is not built in a way to experience such human emotions. But it is the thrill of the hunt, the promise of satiety, that so pushes her forward.

It is her favorite moment, when all eyes turn to her. When she, above all others, is held up as the ideal. A point of jealousy, a point of adulation. Like a goddess of old.

Except something happens.

Something wrong.

When her name is called, it is called wrong: "Lady Vivienne du Lac" and then, in the din, everyone is looking *through her* because they call another name, louder, and everyone has hushed.

They are not paying attention to her.

"Miss Christabel Crane!" comes a booming voice. It seems that someone has found a megaphone.

Vivienne is unceremoniously ushered away, Nerissa separated from her before she can object.

But just long enough that she can glimpse the face and form of her foil. A small girl, barely into womanhood, but graced with every measure of loveliness treasured in this time. Long, pale curls piled upon her head with precise twists and turns looking both refined and just tousled enough. Her face is sweet and her lips fresh. But the dress is truly the point of attention. Vivienne knows with but the merest glance that it is from the hand of a familiar rival, Jeanne Paquin.

Ah, still. The dress!

It did not rely on any kind of trick or gimmick, for the dress, while not cut in any unusual way, looked as if it had been painted with albino peacocks. A living painting. The material shimmered through each and every feather, and as she walked past Vivienne, it seemed that the birds moved their heads ever so slightly.

And still, there is more. The dress is merely half of the trouble.

On young Christabel's arm is none other than Vivienne's old paramour, Worth Goodwin, the son of the Questing Beast herself, may she rest in peace. Perfect, brilliant Worth Goodwin. Tall and clever, bright as the summer sun. Both the opposite and complement to Vivienne, and her greatest folly.

She stands confused, thinking him dead for a very long while now.

$$\sim$$

The last time Nerissa saw Worth Goodwin, it was 1850. He was to go off on an adventure to locate one of the Exigents they were ever fighting, a kind of Fey creature gone mad with evil and vice. Different from Aberrants who were dangerous but less conscious; a minotaur to a bison, respectively. But that last time, over long cigarettes at the William Blake in London, it was as if they had not all shared a house together for a hundred years, nor had they worked together to track down ancient artifacts with the power to destroy Britain and, indeed, most of the continent as well.

Nerissa and Worth were a good team. A marvelous team. Until Vivienne fell in love with him. Until the two of them began feeding off each other's powers and hating each other. It wasn't a good situation for either of them. Worth needed to be wanted, to be hunted, and Vivienne needed to hunt. Both creatures woven of supernatural threads and should have been kept apart. Nerissa was worried they would destroy one another, and with the world in such short supply of beings as wondrous as they…

She didn't exactly destroy their relationship. But she nudged it in the direction of utter annihilation. Enthusiastically. She conspired with Worth to get him out of the country and assume his demise. It was easier that way for Vivienne, who would continue to follow him if she knew the truth. Lying to the sylph was surprisingly easy to do once Nerissa got the hang of it.

Besides, jealousy over their relationship was making her scales go flaky.

Now, seeing the look on Vivienne's face, however, Nerissa realizes that all her work was in vain. Vivienne would always love Worth. The idea that she could have prevented such a thing seemed utter folly now. How could she have ever thought she had the power to prevent him from coming back?

She thought they had an arrangement. There would be words.

But then, no. Nerissa calms herself down. She can feel her skin going scaly, and losing her sense and her disguise would help absolutely no one.

The panic subsides. Worth Goodwin is with another woman. And by the way she is casting loving glances up at him, he is no simple escort. Does the young girl have any idea how old he is? Likely not. Human is perhaps his most favored form, but a Glatisant, he can be any animal he wants. Nerissa is generally limited to the humanesque, though once she managed a satyr. It is as uncomfortable as one might imagine.

Now, Viv.

Vivienne. Yes. She is not happy. She is frozen.

Nerissa must reign in her glee, must compose herself. Because while it is terrible to see Worth Goodwin, it is not terrible to see him with another woman. It is, in fact, delightful.

Unless it inspires Vivienne to go into a blood-soaked frenzy. But it's been at least a hundred years since she's done that, so...

"Vivienne," Nerissa whispers, taking her friend by the arm. She is frigid to the touch, all the warmth and vitality of the event draining from her upon seeing Worth. "Let us go see what sort of canapés they have over here. I'm told that their vol-au-vents are amazing."

"I want to go home," Vivienne says, and begins to sink back toward the front door. She does not look at Nerissa. She does not seem capable of getting her eyes away from Worth.

"He's just a silly... creature," Nerissa says, hesitant to use the word "man" since it is far from an accurate description. They are close enough that such words will not get caught by those around them. "Let him to his... whatever it is he's working on."

"But I thought he was dead in Brazil," Vivienne says, dreamily.

Nerissa winces, as that is more or less what she told Vivienne. And more or less a fabrication. Their sundering was a long time ago, and the details a bit fuzzy, and Nerissa may have expanded on some details a little beyond the realm of the factual. The truth is that she knew Worth was miserable, but she was tired of hunting Aberrants. So, she stole Vivienne's ledger—a remarkable book containing the details of the work of Waldemar and Goodwin, meticulously illustrated and annotated—and sent it off with Worth in exchange for his freedom. He did go to Brazil, at least briefly.

"I'd thought the same thing, died hunting orchids and..." Nerissa says, hurriedly. "Oh, look. It's... ah... Mrs. Bod—Bodding—er," Nerissa tries, but she really has no capacity or desire to know the names of the elite of Tarrytown and New York City proper. They are but spirits on a similar course, but brief interruptions.

"Rockefeller!" Nerissa hisses, and at last, this gets Vivienne's attention, and the attention of most of the people around them.

The impropriety is at last enough to cause Vivienne to turn on her friend, grab her by the arm, and escort her away from Christabel Crane, whomever she may be, and toward the canapés.

~

O nce, Worth.
    Once upon a time, Worth.
Once upon a time, Worth and Vivienne. Together. Entwined. Strangers to the world, supernatural beings of curious, heavenly form. They were happy. And furious. And constantly rutting. To say nothing of all the arguing, though that was part of the passion, too...

But Vivienne doesn't remember the last part in that moment. When she beholds Worth Goodwin for the first time in nearly a century, her thoughts aren't of the fights, the trysts, the jealousy, the lies. They are, instead, full to bursting with reminiscences of certain smells—olfactory being one of her strongest suits and most connected to her memories— redolent of coupling and frolicking and general mischief making. Worth always brought out the devious side of her, and she in him.

The sense of elation lasts just for a short jolt of time. As mentioned before, Vivienne is not human. She does not experience emotion, or indeed, time, in the same way as a human. Her emotions are layers, and often she gets tied up in one or another. It is difficult for her to feel her way through the layers once she has ventured down into them. And once she understands that Worth Goodwin is not simply attending to Christabel Clare, whomever she may be, she descends quickly into cold madness. Jealousy is a guaranteed venture into the deepest chill of her soul.

This is the state Nerissa calls "permafrost," and it's a helpful state for Vivienne, at least from a purely defensive standpoint. She becomes nigh impervious to the slings and arrows of the world about her. Her body temperature drops, her movements slow. She is no less lovely, but much more deadly. Those human*ish* components of her body diminish significantly, and her ability to make calculations where human life is concerned goes along with them. Which rarely ends well for anyone, let alone Vivienne herself.

Which is why Nerissa is essential to her overall reformation. The good years have been consistent with her around. The lamia is even less human*ish* than Vivienne, and yet she has a great deal more intuition about her. Perhaps, Vivienne wonders in one of her deep-down layers, it's because she doesn't feed off people in the same way. She doesn't know them immediately, feel them about her like a pressing wave. She has to reach out to read the signals.

"Vivienne, listen to me, please," Nerissa is saying at her.

Vivienne discovers she is now sitting upon a gaudy settee in a rather dark room. There is a window open somewhere, and she can hear the rain pattering on the roof. It smells of stale old people and musty clothing, and she'd rather not be in such a place. But it is the sort of location Nerissa always seeks out. The dark and the dank.

"I listen to you far too much, if you ask me," Vivienne replies, batting at her friend. "You told me he was dead."

Nerissa takes a deep breath and backs away, her scales shimmering for a moment before they're hidden beneath layers of her glamor again. Vivienne thinks it's a shame, though she's never mentioned it, because she's quite lovely when she's in her natural form. But that would be unwelcome. Nerissa has told her time and again over the many long years of their friendship that her natural state is abhorrent, and telling her otherwise would just be confusing.

"Most likely dead," she says in reply to Vivienne.

"I loved him."

"You were bad for each other."

"But so delicious," Vivienne sighs. "He didn't even look at me. I don't know what to say to him."

"Well, you best consider. You almost caused a scene, you know. Mrs. Yarborough nearly passed out when she touched you. You could have taken down half the party with your antics."

"Antics?" laughs Vivienne, the bitter edge to her voice like a cold knife. "You can't honestly tell me that... he's just... that it..."

"You've been in a state for an hour," Nerissa says. "An *hour*. After all this work for this ridiculous party, you freeze up, and I have to half drag you up the stairs."

"I am in disarray, but I have composed myself," Vivienne replies, brushing her hair with her fingers, preparing to re-enter the fray. She must steel herself. If Worth sees her in such a weak state, he will assume her frail and pining, and while that may be true in the realest sense when it comes to him, it cannot be. She must be better.

"Because I took care of things."

"Why?"

Nerissa pauses a second, giving Vivienne the look of disappointment, before saying, "Because that's what I always do."

"Oh, come now. You act as if these things happen all the time. You know very well that I've been on very good behavior since Worth..."

"Yes, that's what frightens me."

"It looks like he's got his hands full as it is, and..."

Vivienne feels him before she sees him; she always does. The huntress knows her prey, even when she's been wronged. She smells him, tastes the words on his tongue before he utters them in the doorway. She is only surprised she didn't sense him earlier.

He enters the room, and with him comes the smell of the deep forest, of home. Copper and dirt and growing things, wet fur and a thousand memories at once.

He is so handsome, down to his very essence, and Vivienne wants nothing more than to surround herself in him once again.

But his look is cold, focusing more on the lamia than herself. How one can cause physical pain with a glance? It is most unfair.

"Regardless of what it may have looked like, I am here to see you," says Worth. "Both of you. It's been a long while."

Worth is limned in dull light from behind, his dark brown hair cast slightly auburn. It is a familiar face he's wearing now, much like the one Vivienne met when they were first introduced. The one he wore when he and Nerissa were in business together, if it can be called such a thing. Waldemar and Goodwin: monster hunters. For a while it was an interesting collaboration, and she did enjoy working on the ledger of their adventures and finding an outlet for her alchemical hobbies, but...

Nerissa hisses, the sound echoing off the walls of the small room, breaking her thoughts. What would one call this place? A foyer? A closet? Some anteroom to the balcony, perhaps. Whatever container she's been put in, Vivienne is momentarily taken aback by the sound her friend makes. It's a sound she has not heard in a very long time, and it reminds her of tastier meals than the canapes at tonight's festivities.

Vivienne doesn't have time to process her surroundings further, nor does she concern herself with memories of bygone days, because seeing Worth this close throws her down a few more layers of emotion, not yet into the permafrost but to a crackling tundra just above it.

"That's hard to believe," says Nerissa. "You look like you've had your hands quite full."

"I assure you, my intent is pure," Worth says, looking genuinely hurt. Pitiful creature, but too damned handsome for his own good. "But where are my manners? It's been quite some time since we've seen one another, and I was under the impression that you two were off to take a significantly less visible existence."

"Whoever told you that?" asks Vivienne, finding her voice, though it is a little meeker than she'd like. "Circumspection and gossip. You know I never like being out of the limelight."

"Except when you're wanted for murder," Worth points out.

"That was a long time ago, and not the entire story," Nerissa interrupts. "And for the most part, you are right. We have been keeping a low profile, inasmuch as we have not been working in the same capacity as we did once, when you were part of my business."

"*Your* business?" asks Vivienne. This is a strange way of saying things, but she senses that, yet again, Nerissa is playing at some invisible territory game with Worth. They were ever at each other's throats before, but to say that the business was Nerissa's alone is quite a blow. To both of them. Vivienne was essential to keeping them funded, to helping the access the strange and arcane. She might not have accompanied them on every mission, but...

"That's precisely why I came here. Well, once I heard rumors of a pair of women that met your descriptions taking up residence at Lyndhurst. I haven't been in New York long, you see, but my friend, Ms. Crane, has a request to make of you, and I promised to make introductions," Worth says, taking a tentative step forward.

"Ms. Crane can ask us herself," Nerissa says.

"Oh, yes, she will," says Worth, "but I first wanted to prepare you, of course, for the matter at hand. There is a detail of rather immense importance."

"Where have you been?" asks Vivienne, the words coming out of her mouth before she can stop them. She is bobbing between the permafrost and the frozen tundra, then down to the fire at her core. He isn't even looking at her. He's addressing Nerissa. He's half ignoring her. What madness is this?

"Who is this Ms. Crane?" asks the lamia. "Your new paramour?"

"She is no *lemman*," says Worth. "That's what I needed to explain. I have to tell you how I got here, how I found you, and..."

"But why did you leave?" Vivienne asks, her voice high and pining. "Why did you leave in the first place? Did I make you so miserable?"

There would be time to answer this question, Vivienne knows, if the world were a fair place. But she is a supernatural being, one whom even the earth does not seem to understand.

From below them, in the main hall, there is a sound like gunfire but lower. It reverberates, causes Vivienne's ears to ache. It reminds her of their bygone days when Worth and Nerissa would sometimes take their work home, or else they traveled pathways between Fae and the Grey, what they called the world of mortals.

Worth curses lowly. "Prepare yourself," he says. "They may have deep pockets, but their wits are shallow."

He takes Vivienne's arm, his hands warm through his gloves, the energy of him flowing freely into her so perfectly and completely she almost cries out.

"I'm perfectly capable of defending myself," Vivienne says, making no attempt to free herself of his touch. "Please, what is happening?"

"Something bad," is all the Glatisant offers. "Please. You must focus. You must not kill them." He looks pointedly at Nerissa.

"No promises," the lamia replies smoothly.

"Nerissa, please," Vivienne says curtly. Except she knows Nerissa cannot focus well in a frenzy. Too much blood and there would be no controlling her, no matter how reformed.

Worth grits his teeth and gazes at Vivienne, deep circles like bruises under his arms. The look in his eyes is sharp, concerned. People downstairs are panicking. The walls of the Rookery shudder again.

But then, there is something else.

Something darker.

Vivienne senses it has been here the whole time, but with the shock of what happened in the room, it has slipped away. Something shifts, slides away into the night, a dark creature moving below with speed and power. Vivienne feels its negative presence, sucking in the energy she has claimed as her own.

"What is that?" she muses, half to herself.

"You felt it?" Worth asks, blanching.

"It's leaving… it's… it's gone," Vivienne breathes, shaking her head to dispel it like a bad dream. "I didn't realize the danger we were in until it had left."

Worth looks visibly relieved, but then he winces. "They're coming. Brace yourselves. They may not know how to behave."

"Do you remember how to fight?" Nerissa asks Worth from across the room. Clearly, she's come prepared because she's carrying that silly silver knife she always manages to sneak on her person. As if she *needs* a weapon. She is a living tool of destruction. And lies, it appears, considering their present company. Lies and knives are nearly the same thing.

Worth nods, but Vivienne senses he's nervous. But that could be the echoes from below. Servants are running every which way, platters falling to the ground. The walls shake again, sending plaster and dust into her hair and across the shoulders of her gown.

This is enough to send her into action, and, with Nerissa in the lead, she follows along into the breach.

OUROBOROS

When the world was younger and people more accepting of strange beings, Nerissa was often told that she was an exception of her kind. Many lamias were known, she had heard, for being blinded by love and wanting that they were easily caught with a bit of fresh blood or the promise of a warm body. While there were certainly times in her life where such a temptation might have garnered her attention, she, nonetheless, prided herself on rising above the stereotype. As a feared creature, she knew that humankind often portrayed her sort in bold strokes so as not to be faced with the truth: that they are inferior in nearly every manner known. From their incessant need to breed and excrete, to their ever-changing rituals and religions and rules, human beings are short-lived and even shorter-minded.

Perhaps that's why they taste so good. Less time to get gamey.

That thinking, however, would get Nerissa killed. She had spent years training that part of her brain to resist the call of human blood, and until she sees the scene in the Villiers' ballroom, she is confident in her practice.

The source of the noise is an explosive of some sort, designed to propel glass shards in every direction. And as a result, human blood is everywhere. Women are dripping in it, their arms and shoulders streaming the stuff. Men are wiping it from their foreheads. No one appears mortally wounded, but the shrapnel has shredded quite a few guests to the point where they look strewn in red ribbons.

And it smells so delicious, Nerissa can hardly stand it. Even though she's aware this is likely a trap.

She feels Vivienne behind her, hears someone cry out. She knows she's slipping, can't hold… she will eat, finally, what is not goat blood and…

"Another explosion!" someone cries, just before it happens.

It's a perfect diversion, and Worth pulls her so violently around her waist that she flies back with him, bursting back through a pair of doors. She fights with him because she hates him and knows she can't win because he is the Glatisant, and she will never let him have Vivienne. Because he doesn't deserve her, and Nerissa does.

"Come now, Nerissa. We must behave," admonishes the Glatisant. She wants to rip out his eyes. It would be most satisfying. Eyes are her favorite part.

They struggle through a dark hallway, blessedly free of people save for a few servants who pretend to look the other way. They have been well trained. Vivienne is reining in her power, but Nerissa can feel it building. Yes, yes. This is what she is hoping for. Perhaps if Vivienne lets go, they will be able to leave this dreadful place and start again somewhere else. Somewhere warm. Without corsets.

They twist and turn into a storeroom and begin to fight in earnest, Nerissa fighting back both Worth and the mounting fury inside her. So much human blood! She wants to get through him to get a taste and, in that moment, will do anything to attain her meal.

It isn't the first time she's fought Worth, but he's holding back. Neither of them are letting go entirely. He doesn't feed on people. His power is a strange, intangible thing. He does not need to live off human beings in such a way, and as such, has always kept far from Fae.

But Nerissa senses that he is expecting this, somehow. Had been trying to warn them. It's hard to remember when all she can think of is draining people of their lifeblood.

In her moment of weakness, Worth clobbers her across the shoulders well and good, and Nerissa tumbles forward into a high cabinet stocked with glasses and platters. They rain around them, clattering off her body as ineffectual as rain. Though she does not yet appear a monster, her scales are tougher than iron and still exist beneath her glamor.

Nerissa sees an opening and goes for Worth's side, hoping to sink her claws into his skin but coming up empty as he writhes away. He's deadly fast and dances away as if her steps are choreographed.

But the angrier she gets, the clearer she understands Worth's weaknesses. It's his disguise that is weakest. It stems from a thumb-sized organ in his chest, and it works to refract and bend light and sensation. His human form is real and functioning, but only so long as the pressure point is unharmed. A good thwack around the center, and he's bound to go down. She rises up on her back tails, wonderfully strong, and roots herself into the ground prepared to deliver the blow just when he's least expecting—

Nerissa is about to get the rise on him when Vivienne stops everything. It's a talent she has. Her permafrost is usually contained, but she can express it with surprising alacrity given the right circumstances. While fisticuffs don't become her—and she's reticent to fight considering the risk it runs to anything with a pulse—she is strikingly good at them.

Then the world stops abruptly at an icy command, and Nerissa and Worth are frozen together in a hideous pastiche; he, part jaguar, gazelle, and bison, and she ripped entirely through her dress and protruding her tails halfway down the hallway. Vivienne will be most furious that she burst out of her vestments.

Vivienne, for her part, rises in a frosty column, ice in her wake like the delicate veil on a bride of death. Nerissa is ready for the inevitable tide of stinging icicles—this is not the first time Vivienne has had to separate the two—but her power stops, a wave of warmth blasting into the room, enough that Vivienne falls to her feet, but not enough to thaw the Glatisant and lamia.

Then lights kindle. Doors slam. Nerissa can feel a dozen presences or so cluster around them; Vivienne groans something incomprehensible in Fae.

"You see, I told you they were the real thing!" says a voice, crackled with age.

There are hushed words of praise and amazement. Laughing, too.

"Well, it is as we thought. Welcome, friends, to the Circle of Iapetus. We welcome you into our mysteries and implore your help." A second speaker.

The voice comes from a tall man, stern of face but not quite yet aged into palsy. This is not, Nerissa thinks, Mr. Villiers, who as she recalls is merely a winter or two away from death (with what can only be described as frustrating irregularity; sometimes she is able to ascertain the future of various mortals, and for some reason, Mr. Villiers is on her list).

Neither Worth nor Nerissa can speak, but that's due to Vivienne's spell, though it is lessening. Nerissa begins to calm herself, to steady her hearts and slow her blood. Outright attacking Worth might not have been the best course of action, but she did enjoy it.

"Please, Ms. du Lac," says a young woman, coming from behind the first speaker. It's Christabel Crane. "I implore you to release your friends and let us parlay with you. I promise, we mean no harm. I hoped Mr. Goodwin had a chance to discuss the matter with you."

Vivienne, Nerissa knows, is currently living her nightmare in the bold contrast of a Caravaggio painting. Not only is she revealed to this rag-tag group of mortals as a wretched witch—her hair white strewn about her head, her nails long like icicles, her breasts bared for all to see—but she has also torn her dress.

It's about time, Nerissa supposes, that someone has figured them out. She is both relieved and annoyed, but then, she hasn't been trying that hard. Barefooted women gallivanting around cavorting with goats are bound to attract attention at some point or another, after all. No matter how precious Vivienne is about such things, Nerissa is always the weaker in terms of presentation. A snake is a snake, after all.

With a deep breath, Vivienne drops her pale arms, and when she does so, both Worth and Nerissa fall to the ground. Worth uses the opportunity to shift back into his human form, though he is regrettably lacking clothing. Nerissa, however, decides to abstain from any glamor at the moment, in a kind of silent protest. Though she is the most talented of the group, she is glad to save her energy. That, and now free of her corset, she is hesitant to even whip up a semblance of the confounded contraption. She casts the remnant of her split garment to the side and hisses.

Nerissa isn't yet convinced that biting off a few heads won't be in the cards this evening. And it's been so long since she's had a good draught of the carotid.

"I made the attempt to speak to them in a civil manner," says Worth, breathless, "but we were interrupted before I had a chance."

"You took too long," says an old woman with the air of a vulture. Vivienne would know the name, but Nerissa can't be bothered with such details. The crone would be sour to eat judging by the yellow stains on her fingers and around her mouth. Not to say the elderly are generally less tasty. Quite the opposite. She's always enjoyed a little mellow to her marrow.

"*I* took too long, madame?" asks Worth, looking quite offended, his body flushing red in response. "I'll have you know that I took half the allotted time."

"They hadn't even brought out the canapes yet," Vivienne says dreamily. She seems a bit dazed, and that does not sit well with the lamia.

"That was a dangerous prank," Nerissa says, and her voice is rough in her throat. She sounds practically feral, and she'd forgotten how good it is to use her regular voice. "People could have died." *Should have died.*

"They didn't," the first man says. "Most of the blood was already in the device before it went off. We were very careful."

"And your plan was to, what? Unveil us to the whole of New York elite?" Nerissa asks.

Christabel looks mortified at the behavior of her fellow mortals, and she presses in front of the very talkative man, saying, "Mr. Rockefeller, are you telling me you detonated a blood bomb?"

"I was doubtful," he says, looking pompous as ever, "that these creatures would perform as expected."

"We are not circus clowns," says Nerissa, glaring at Rockefeller so much he actually blanches.

"If I had known you had plans to detonate such a device, I never would have risked it. Such blood could have caused a frenzy, and none of us might be standing right now if it hadn't been for these reformed creatures." She turns to Vivienne and offers a wan smile. "Truly, your restraint is quite admirable."

"Well, no one *died*," says Mr. Rockefeller, puffing his chest and no doubt offended that this young woman is scolding him so, unwilling to give compliment to the monsters. "And it will be the talk of the town. Every scar will be a story!"

"I told you they were the real deal," the old woman says, jutting her finger at the lamia. "But would anyone believe me? No, of course not."

"No one actually thought it would work," another says. "We've never had such beings in our presence like these."

"But that was quite a show!" the old woman says says with a laugh, gaze perusing every inch of Nerissa's body.

"I still can't believe what I'm seeing. That tail—what are those, ah, made out of, if I may ask?" Rockefeller says, hesitant.

Nerissa seriously considers devouring the man whole, and enjoying the look on Vivienne's face as she does it, when Christabel answers for her.

"You absolutely may *not* ask. As it is, I am beyond appalled at your behavior. First, our guests have been told that it was a pair of errant coffee urns that went ballistic, but I promise you that if such an event happens again, we will not be able to cover it up so easily. We are fortunate that the house is decorated in so much red velvet," Christabel continues. "Secondly, this is the Villiers' home, and our presence has ushered in thousands of dollars in damages."

"All press is good press," the old woman says.

Nerissa finds this a disgustingly American concept.

"For all the wrong reasons. I will have to undertake a letter writing campaign and work to pull every string available to ensure this does not happen again. If anyone crosses, you know the consequences," Miss Crane says with the authority of a politician or preacher. "We have much, much larger issues at hand. Unexplained deaths. Mysterious disappearances. If we prattle on long enough, whatever stalks us now will have plenty of time to eviscerate us—and shame on us only."

Well, now. Nerissa can certainly understand what Worth sees in this mortal. She is commanding, though small. Rockefeller frowns and turns away from her, and then Christabel regards the three unusual "beings" as she so aptly put it, with as bright a smile as she can manage. For a slight thing of no more than twenty, it's impressive. She lights up the room, even Nerissa has to admit that.

"We are imploring you for help," Christabel says sweetly, looking Nerissa straight in the eyes—no small feat. Many men have wet themselves upon seeing them, blood red and streaked with green as they are. "Mr. Goodwin was intended to ask you first, before any other methods were…" She takes a deep breath, steeling herself against the stupidity of her cohort. "I fear we may have made so grave a mistake in this misstep that there is no going back."

~

Vivienne finds her voice, at last, but it is a far away, strange thing. She knows, on one layer of her emotional consciousness, that she is the best person in matters of discussion with human beings. Worth is too forgiving of them, and Nerissa too distrustful. But she is still too shocked and thrown off by the scent of blood to react as quickly as she once did.

31

"We have seen far worse," she says at last, which is far from the truth. They have been surprised a few times in their long years together, but never once in public with such an audience. Truly, the level of stupidity exhibited by these specimens is far beyond the pale.

Crane. She respects that woman under all her layers of disgust. Something familiar about her. The way she talks, that manner. But why?

But the Circle of Iapetus? What nonsense. It's been a long time since she's stumbled her way into a mortal cult, and she never much liked them to begin with. Such a sad sartorial palette with dark robes and tacky headdresses.

"They're just very excited to see you—as you are," Christabel says, though there is no thrill in her voice. In fact, judging by the response, Vivienne has the distinct feeling that she is more or less unimpressed. "You will pardon their staring. Our order has studied your kind for a long time, and seeing you as you are is rather delightful."

"Usually she likes it when they stare," Worth says drily.

Vivienne ignores him. "You could have simply come for tea. In that case, the likelihood of human dismemberment would have been significantly diminished."

"Yes, I realize that now, except these good people here wanted proof, and while I hoped for a more toned down reveal, courtesy of Mr. Goodwin, that did not go as planned," Christabel continues. Now she's smiling, and it's hideous and Vivienne hates it, especially because of the way that Worth is looking at her. Why does the woman have to be clever *and* pretty? The combination is too much to bear, really.

"Was this beast not enough for them?" asks Vivienne, gesturing to Worth.

To his credit, he does not rise to the bait.

Vivienne decides that she cannot spend another moment in such a state, and so she shivers slightly and re-arrays herself more acceptably. The dress, she can do little about. But a bit of mist and some frost around her middle make a good enough facsimile to cover the barest parts of her body. Unlike Nerissa, she is limited in her transformations, but she does the best with what she has.

This, of course, elicits some expressions of awe from the limited audience, which helps Vivienne regain her composure, shattered as it has been. Her fear does not manifest as one might expect; it is really more of a simmering rage, though colder than the deepest Siberian snow. It is good to bask in awe, and it helps soothe her. The attention more fully on her is akin to a lizard sitting in the sun. Direct application without shade is preferred. And Christabel is in danger of being the pesky tree in the way.

Since no one is saying anything, Vivienne tucks one of her loose tresses up into the twist atop her head. "Well, since you went through all this trouble and have not only outed us both but sincerely mortified us in the presence of our peers, I suppose this must be very important."

For the first time, Christabel looks unsure. She draws herself up to her full, yet somewhat limited, height, and says, "Yes. The Circle of Iapetus was begun as a joint venture between my great-grandfather and his paramour, carried on by her afterward not only through her children, but also through their progeny."

There is a great deal to consider in the woman's words, but Vivienne begins to put it together.

"Now I know you who you remind me of," Vivienne says, extending a long finger toward Christabel. She does not quite touch her cheek, but just close enough, letting the long nail linger just a moment past discomfiture. "You're a Van Tassel."

"And a Crane. Great-grandmother ensured that there was no mistaking where her firstborn was from." Christabel sighs. "But that part of the story is so often left out. It's easier to believe it was just a bully, after all, that won in the end, and not poor Ichabod. But they were all changed that day—my father argued, for the better. Through Katrina and her husband knew the identity of their firstborn's father, they kept it secret for a generation until the family was sufficiently moved."

"This is all very impressive," Nerissa says, clearly feeling to the contrary. "But you've gone and destroyed any semblance of a cover we had. Our hope was simply to live our lives in peace, and now that is quite impossible. We will have leave."

"No, no, please," Mr. Rockefeller says. "It is of the utmost importance that you hear us out. Lives are at stake—more than have already been spent."

~

Nerissa had never been in a situation that, once revealed, people actually wanted to continue to remain in close proximity to her. A young woman, in fact, is looking rather admiringly at Nerissa's scales, an occurrence which has certainly not happened in all her long life. She was made, by whatever mad god or goddess or happenstance, to be the very opposite of what humans desired.

But, she supposes, there is one in every crowd.

"We are an ancient order, revived from the Romans," Mr. Rockefeller says, clutching his chest. He pulls out a small amulet with a flame-wreathed hammer upon it. "The symbol of our order. A secret order. We have ever guarded the flame of mortality."

The symbol is made of iron, which, of course, makes Nerissa's teeth ache. Clever. They know enough just to be dangerous.

"A literal flame?" Nerissa asks, still unconvinced, and truth be told, growing a bit bored with the pageantry. How ancient could this order be?

"Well, no," says Christabel. "Perhaps once there was—that brought by the son of Iapetus, Prometheus. You see, we are the intercessors between the realm of the supernatural and the realm of the mortal, the Fae and the Grey as you call it. My great-grandfather Ichabod was a lifelong scholar of witchcraft and the occult and was able to re-shape the Circle before his untimely death."

"You will have to clarify that at some point," Vivienne points out wryly. No doubt she has her own version of what happened in Sleepy Hollow. "But that is a diversion. This wouldn't have anything to do with the presence I felt just before the explosion, would it? Something dark and… reaching?"

"Yes," says Rockefeller. "It appears whenever we gather. Drawn by our very presence, it seems. A true sign of our favored state, I believe. The first time it showed up, it killed Lord Dunbreen, his body a mangled mess afterward. Thankfully Christabel recognized the mark, brave girl that she is. Her parents, you see, were also victims."

"We are quite used to the pain of carrying the burden of the Flame," says the old woman. "We all carry scars." She holds out her hand, the blood still crusting across her papery skin.

"The creature didn't hurt anyone tonight. That was the result of your ballistics and sincere lack of judgment," says Nerissa. "It seems you may have confused monsters."

Now the humans are thoroughly upset. They all begin talking at once, and Worth is trying to say something, but instead, they just all end up speaking over one another and going red in the face.

Vivienne catches Nerissa's eye a moment and gives her a rare, but tired, smile. It has been a very long time since they saw one another face to face this way, and the circumstance is both embarrassing—that they were captured in such a way—that they almost begin laughing at the same moment.

But no, they need no words. For the moment, they will let everything play out as it should.

"You do not have to help," says Christabel. "But it might be prudent."

"You are going to tell us that you've some relic of a weapon known to destroy people of our ilk, and if we don't help you, there will be a price," Nerissa says, taking a step closer to Christabel. To the girl's credit, she does not move, though every last one of the other humans do. Nerissa continues. "Or perhaps, you will think to blackmail us, to out us to the public. You can be certain, we have seen worse, and we will not be bowing to your requests."

She is very proud of her little speech. It's not often that the words align themselves so rightly in her mouth, but as Vivienne appears incapable of speaking for herself, and Worth appears lost as ever, she decides it's up to her.

But that's when she sees a smile on Christabel's lips.

"You see," the young woman says, "while there are a number of people of your abilities, though admittedly few in this general area, the decision to reach out to you and your companion was quite beyond my power."

Nerissa knows right away that something is amiss, and that something is almost certainly Vivienne. They have not always lived together, and there are very large gaps in their friendship—whilst they were arguing or falling out of line or simply sick of one another—and a big gap coincides precisely with this insane business about Ichabod Crane, and the beginning of this Circle of Iapetus nonsense. Humans and their asinine cults and clubs and religion. It's enough to make Nerissa jump at them and bite their heads off.

The inclination is so strong in fact that she licks her lips and takes a step forward. Or, rather, tries to, when one of the younger men puts his hand on what is presumably a hidden dagger or firearm—so lacking in creativity, these people.

She cannot summon her power.

Nerissa realizes that the Circle of Iapetus has, indeed, made a circle around the three esteemed creatures of advanced ability. And they are all holding their amulets...

And it seems to have an impact on them all.

Worth looks as if he's going to vomit, and Vivienne looks absolutely deflated.

How did such a thing happen so fast? Just enough iron. Just enough blood.

"Vivienne," Nerissa says. "Tell me you don't know anything about this."

Vivienne is not the one to respond. It is, of course, Worth. "My dear, Vivienne knows everything about this. She's the one who started it, after all. Don't you recall, my dear? It was a glorious winter."

THE TINES THAT BREAK

There are many troubles with living a long life, especially when the majority of those around you do not. Vivienne has always found that people, those of the human variety, tend to blur together after a while, rendering her memory a bit iffy to say the least. It is one of the reasons she has always insisted on traveling as much as possible, even though it is difficult for her to do so—she, in particular, does not care for warm climates as they disagree with her frosty nature—because what little variation occurs among humans is best experienced by expanding one's geography. There are only so many Johns and Janes and Marys one can keep in mind, after all.

And this fatal flaw, of course, is where she finds herself. Standing in the center of these laughable Circle of Iapetus converts, she is too entrenched in permafrost at first to allow for the details to sink in. Christabel Crane, for instance. Katrina Van Tassel was her great grand-mother some ways back, and yes, Vivienne had been her friend. A very good friend.

Worth was there, as well.

But they were so distracted and oaths just didn't seem... permanent.

"Katrina Van Tassel aided me in a time of need," Vivienne says slowly, doing everything in her power to avoid Nerissa's gaze. It's not as if she doesn't know the precise look she's getting, anyway. Being friends and companions for the better part of a millennium means being able to communicate emotions like utter revulsion and betrayal without so much as a glance. "And I agreed, that should she need a favor in return, I would provide my aid."

"You must understand, Lady Du Lac," Christabel says, her voice taking on a reverent hush, "that finding you has been a long time coming. I am not the first Crane to seek you out, and as such, the atrocities we are now facing grow more serious every day."

"Atrocities?" asks Nerissa. She's hissing again, and Vivienne would like to tell her to cease those bestial vocalizations, but now is not the time for such admonishment.

"You must feel very proud of yourself for finding us," Vivienne says. "But I am quite sorry to say that I do not know the terms of the agreement, and I am afraid without my recollection..."

Before she can even finish the sentence, a young man standing close enough to Miss Crane to be almost inappropriate begins reading from a scroll.

On this day, dated the sixteenth of February in the year of our Lord Eighteen Hundred and Twenty-Six, I, Vivienne du Lac, solemnly swear an oath of debt to Katrina Van Tassel and all her descendants. In return for a boon, I shall grant...

"Enough," Vivienne says. Yes, she remembers now, and any flailing around the matter won't delay the fact that someone has outsmarted her. It is nearly enough to make her consider freezing these humans. She could do it. But living her life without hunting human beings has been so much more enjoyable than when she couldn't stop destroying them. It's not their blood that she wants, it's their hopes, their dreams, their thoughts. She wants them to love her, and her alone.

It is clear that Worth and Nerissa both sense this change in her, for they move slowly toward her.

"This creature that hunts us does not just thirst for human blood," Christabel says, continuing as if Vivienne's refusal is inconsequential. "It desires, we think, your sort as well. Worth came to us with his friend, Yvan Tousignant, who may have been killed by this creature; we, too, have lost many, as Mr. Rockefeller said, including my own parents who delivered me here to Tarrytown."

Nerissa glares at the Glatisant. "Oh, the beast helping a maiden in distress. Quite poetic."

He looks affronted. "Yvan was a dear friend, and one of us, a vampire by classification. You know not of what you speak; this danger is a threat to all of us."

"It all just seems rather convenient."

"When Christabel came to me with this difficulty, I mentioned that I worked with you, Nerissa, and that we were a good team when it came to destroying Aberrants," says Worth. "I have looked into the issue myself, but I fear I am incapable of dealing with Aberrants of this magnitude on my own. I thought I would have to go through great measures to find you again, but then I heard rumor of the eccentric new tenants at Lyndhurst, and I had to reconnect... even if it meant dragging up old... difficulties."

Vivienne winces at that name, Aberrants. She's never liked it. Not all creatures of power can manage to contain their wits over long years and, once long ago, Worth and Nerissa were particularly good at tracking them down and destroying them. When they could not be rehabilitated, of course. Though that was very difficult to do. It had only worked once or twice, and even then, not for long.

But she misses Worth. She misses his smell and the way he always checked himself in the mirror when he took on human form just to make sure he got all the details right—which, it should be noted, he most certainly did—and she longs for that time they had. Those beautiful years of intimacy and, perhaps, love. As close as she has ever come. He doesn't look at her that way any longer, doesn't reach out for her. But at the very least, he has only become more beautiful with age.

"What kind of creature is this?" asks Vivienne. "You say 'Aberrant,' but I do not think you've got the entire picture. Aberrants don't generally go after the Fey."

"This creature is unlike anything I've seen before," says Worth. "I have never seen it, but what it did to Yvan defies explanation. I cannot speak of it in such company, but trust me when I say it is of the utmost importance."

Vivienne always has trusted him. That is ever her problem.

～

"So what is your decision?" asks Christabel.

Nerissa tries not to hiss but does not do a very good job at it. Something about the Crane girl makes her want to gnaw off her own arm to get away.

Worth looks pale and uncomfortable. He is still naked. Nothing is quite so comical to Nerissa as the naked male human body. So clownish in the fiddly bits.

"I did promise," Vivienne says weakly when no one speaks. By the way she's looking at Worth, Nerissa is well aware the assumption is that he will be part of whatever Aberrant hunting they will be doing.

And even if Nerissa wants to refuse Vivienne, which she does down to her narrow bones, her heart is a traitor. For Nerissa is fond in the way Romeo pined for Juliette, fond in the way Cyrano longed for his Roxane. For the poor lamia, this pursuit is quite in vain, but it makes little difference. In her heart of hearts—of which she does have three—she knows that refusal will get her exactly nowhere. One glance from Vivienne, one pout, and she will be undone.

Of course, the whole business would be significantly more tolerable were that that hideous Glatisant not mixed up in the thing. Nerissa has yet to puzzle out exactly why Worth is involved. But she will. Once she's feeling better and her guts aren't wiggling like worms and her three hearts have stopped flitting about so helplessly.

"Yes, you did promise," says Mr. Rockefeller, a grin spreading on his face. "You signed it in your blood after all, Lady du Lac. And as I have always said, blood tells. Whether it is in our lineage, or in our hands."

There is an air of superiority to the man, and Nerissa decides she won't even bother to eat him if she kills him. Just leave him to the carrion birds while he's half alive, perhaps, so that they can slowly devour his innards in their way, drawing out his demise in long, red-ribboned agony.

"But I cannot ask my friends to be part of this," Vivienne continues. She raises her chin and looks every inch a queen of ice and snow. "I beseech you to let me to the task and allow Nerissa and Worth to be on their way."

"I wouldn't hear of it," says Worth. "Nerissa and I are the ones with the experience, as I have told Miss Crane time and again. Forgive me, Vivienne dear, but your forte has never been in tooth and claw. Whilst we were working partners, we undid many an Aberrant knot. You are somewhat unpredictable."

Nerissa is infuriated that Worth beat her to the punch, but her words never come out so honeyed.

"We had a partnership," Nerissa says. "And we have a partnership now, though of a different kind. I wouldn't let you to the vultures alone."

"Then it is decided," Christabel says, the tension in her eyes and gait relaxing.

Nerissa watches Vivienne as she continues to hold on to her brightest glamor, what she can manage with dampened magic. Iron in its pure form, without the rest of the composites of blood, is a pox to all Fey creatures save a few, pure, few. It is said to be the enemy of corruption.

"We are somewhat stymied," Vivienne admits, gesturing to the circle about them. "I'm afraid at the moment, we won't be of much use."

Mr. Rockefeller makes a dismissive gesture. "We must contain the threat while we can. But I have something for you."

He reaches into his jacket pocket and produces a large, gold-embossed envelope. "You are all invited to our holiday ball Friday next. The creature will more than likely appear there, and we expect you to neutralize it before any blood is spilled. My wife has gone through great toil to organize the event. You are, of course, more than welcome to come before the event to get an idea of the layout of the place."

"That would be helpful, yes," says Vivienne, quietly, brushing her hands over the ornate invitation.

Christabel makes a signal, and the members of the Circle of Iapetus all lower their hands; some begin walking away.

Vivienne almost decides she doesn't detest the Crane woman when she turns to Nerissa and says, "Thank you. All of you. Your assistance is most appreciated. And please, bring that djinni of yours along. I have a feeling he will be most useful."

AN INVITATION TO DINE

B ack at Lyndhurst, Vivienne sits alone in her bedroom holding the beautiful, gilded invitation from Mr. Rockefeller. It is handwritten, the lovely scrawling script speaking to an artistic heart, or else a person of exceptional breeding. Her name, or at least the one she uses, is written most strikingly. The way the leading capital slides into the double n has always looked balanced to her, and though it has never looked so gorgeous, she finds she is most empty inside whilst gazing at it. Having a human name makes her no more human, and her run-in with Christabel Crane and the Circle has left her chilled. And quite sad.

Worth has promised to call, to discuss more details. To help, as he says, to elaborate on some details of what might be considered confusing in this matter.

Since they returned from the ambush, Nerissa has done everything in her power to keep a distance. And Vivienne doesn't blame her entirely, even if her reaction is a bit over the top. Then again, that sort of reaction is par for the course where the lamia is concerned. Her anger is rare, but when it flares, it is unlikely to be sated save with large amounts of blood. Which explains why the servants were discussing just how many sausages they could get out of half a flock of sheep who mysteriously appeared on their property, bled and ready for butchering. Nerissa is never subtle in her anger.

Still, Nerissa has never wanted to be human.

Even if she has always loved them more than Vivienne.

It is she who convinced her that Aberrants and Exigents—those who knowingly went about murdering human beings *en masse*—were best kept at a distance and, when proved too dangerous, to be killed. She would never admit it, but the lamia hated living among the Fey. The Grey has always suited her better.

Still, the gilding is so beautiful on the card. Yet, somewhat dimmed due to the facet the sentiment is not genuine. It is a *concession*. It is payment. It is only on account of her monstrousness that it has been given.

Vivienne doesn't cry, but her layer of sorrow feels very close. It is quite akin to the permafrost, perhaps adjacent and sometimes intersecting, like strata on the earth.

She turns the invitation over in her hand, noting the address. And that is when she realizes her fatal error. The man within the Circle of Iapetus is not even John D. Rockefeller, but his lesser brother William. The spark of joy left at the invitation extinguishes.

What horrid creatures.

Nerissa rarely visits Barqan if she can help it. He makes her feel lesser just by existing, knowing that she's got a debt to pay to Vivienne that she hasn't fulfilled. If it only weren't so complicated...

But for the sake of their current situation, she must speak with him, even if she doubts it will be fruitful. The Circle knows about him, and it's her job to make sure he isn't exploited. The magic that lurks beneath his enslaved exterior is dark and unpredictable, and he's always been a wily one, willing to wait far longer for revenge against his mistress than one might guess.

As she makes the walk up to his quarters—a small bedroom overlooking the private garden, far from the other servants—she decides that his inherent lack of blood may be the reason she doesn't trust him. While her blood may be neither warm nor red, it is still extant. He is a being of smoke and magic and, while bound, always seems to be on the teetering edge of either madness or fury.

Barqan slides through the door before Nerissa can even knock, materializing with a grin on his face, knowing full well how much such shows of trickery bother her.

"Greetings, mistress," he says, making a show of shimmering before resolving into his human guise. It is convincing enough that the rest of the staff think him just exotic rather than unsettling. "I thought I heard your distinct slither, but thought I must be in a dream. You would never sully yourself by seeking my company on purpose."

"Circumstances are dire," Nerissa responds. "I assume Vivienne has spoken to you."

"About the Circle? Indeed."

Down the hall, the clatter of lunchtime goes on. Lyndhurst is always host to guests of the owner, and it is never quiet in the servants' quarters.

"And you're not concerned?" she asks.

"Their charms do not harm me," he says, his eyes flashing blue a moment before settling. "A lovely side-effect of enslavement. A stronger magic ties me to my mistress, and therefore, I am unaffected."

"You haven't been around them."

"That much iron?"

"*Old* iron. The kind of thing we were trying to find our way around years ago."

"Pity that it doesn't work on the djinn," he says, holding up a cuffed wrist. It tinkles faintly, on a frequency impossible for humans to perceive. "As superior beings, we require far scarcer elements to weaken us and make our scales slough off."

"I know you have no love for me, Barqan," she says. "But in this, we must work together. Vivienne has promised a boon to these people, but I fear there is more danger than she is aware. She is clouded by her admiration of—"

Barqan interrupts with a word the lamia has not heard in many centuries. Dark and wicked and precisely what she had in mind when describing Worth. A word for humans, and other inhabitants of the Grey, that does not bear repeating.

"I see we have a mutual dislike of Mr. Goodwin," she says, somewhat gladdened.

"I do not trust a beast that can never be truly caught," he says. "It is against the laws of our kind."

"Our kind?"

"Regretfully, I must agree that we are of a similar ilk. The Glatisant does not feel… familiar."

Nerissa relaxes a bit. This is the longest conversation they have ever had without devolving into name-calling and fisticuffs. She had promised

Vivienne on her life that she would do anything to prevent such altercations, even if it meant pretending that the djinni did not exist at all.

"You remember when Worth and I worked together. You remember what we did," she adds. "I am not his friend, but we did have a good go at being decent colleagues for a while."

"You sought and destroyed Aberrants and brought Exigents to justice. Even if you might have been considered one of those at various points your life. I suppose it's a matter of perception." He grins so sharply his teeth might as well be daggers.

"Yes. I suppose that is more or less true. Rehabilitation is possible for some of us. Especially those unable or unwilling to make our homes in the Fae."

"At the cost of the goat population this side of the great Mississippi."

They both laugh, together, and it feels good. She has never laughed with Barqan. The opportunity for humor has never crossed her mind. He is a wily djinni who, she is nearly certain, is patiently plotting her death. And perhaps Vivienne's, too. But they both abhor Worth Goodwin, and that is a most promising beginning.

"If you help me in this," Nerissa says, "I will make sure you are released at the nearest convenience." Making the words causes her a great deal of personal nausea. It's the only bargaining chip she has with him.

He perks up at this, rising at least six inches off the ground before settling again. The chains around his chest glow momentarily under his weskit, then dull again.

Before he can speak, though, Nerissa continues. "If you help. If you aid us in this—both in destroying the Circle and Worth, and above all, preserving Vivienne's good name, we will do right by you."

Worth arrives late, as always. The sun is just setting and Vivienne has tried to burn the invitation at least six times. She feels herself slipping into her introverted state, that level of her emotions where she seeks an audience with none but herself. There she is free from argument and disruption, and she can more properly heal herself when ruminations of sorrow become too close.

But Worth's presence distracts her before she can drift too deeply into that quiet, for she hears him walking about outside her door.

"You may come in," she says, casting her voice into the hall, as she is able to do. It is an old sylph trick, and one she rarely uses these days save for distracting the staff when she is trying to be clever, or else not wishing to be discovered.

Worth does not need to be invited, per se. Vivienne leaves the door open for him because she wants, in her heart of hearts, for him to seek her out.

The door opens softly on its hinges, and Worth enters the room. He is dressed in his resting attire, a long white robe lined in silver floss, silk trousers, and warm slippers. This is all show for him, considering his true body is covered in all manner of fur and scale. But, as with many other vainglorious creatures, he adores the show of it. Even if he has utterly forgotten his shirt underneath. Vivienne does not mind the view, glamor though it may be.

"Thank you, Lady du Lac," Worth says, all grace and civility. "I feared you would bar me from entrance considering our less than cordial meeting."

"What is this?" Vivienne asks, taken aback by his most ridiculous manner of address. "Lady du Lac? I am no more a Lady than you are a djinni. And speaking of which, I cannot seem to find him. He is ignoring me. Which, I thought, was against the rules… Why are you looking at me like that?"

Worth takes a deep breath. "I admit, I am, as always, enchanted by your presence and utterly uncertain as how to proceed."

"Now that you bring it up, parading about a pert hussy with less class than a Boston donkey was not the ideal first impression after this dreaded absence, no."

"You mistake my relationship with Miss Crane."

"I never mistake that look," Vivienne says. "It's the one you used to give me."

"I did not come here to talk about our past trysts, Vivienne, nor current dalliances. I came to talk about our business arrangement," Worth says, but his body language speaks otherwise. It is very difficult to disguise both one's bestial self and one's bestial desires. Knowing that she still holds such power over him gives her a most overwhelming sense of satisfaction.

Vivienne is already wearing her most revealing shift, the one she found in Paris with the décolletage to her navel. Since she looks, more or less, human, she has very little need to drape herself in such finery, but she is always bolstered by the power of her form in various states of undress. She knows Worth is particularly fond of her stomach, and she reaches a hand there to touch the soft, cold skin. He always reveled in her chill touch.

"I seem to be missing a shirt," Vivienne says softly. "You'll forgive my mistake."

Worth tries to make a few words with his mouth, but he just frowns.

"The cat got your tongues?" she presses, knowing the full count at four, and every one as talented as the next.

"You are most inappropriate."

"You used to like that about me."

"Vivienne, this is a serious matter."

With a pout, Vivienne lowers herself down onto her bed, crossing one long leg over the other and casting her head back so her black hair spills down her shoulders. She has taken great care to position herself just so, to remind him of her most expert talents.

"You are a serious bore," she says, closing her eyes. Her charms don't work directly on him, but she imagines what it would be like if she could compel him. "But if you want to know my thoughts on the matter, I have plenty of them. Including that I see you to be quite the turncoat against your kind and, if I didn't find you so absolutely devourable, I wouldn't have even allowed you in the room."

"You know I can get in," he points out, "if I really want to."

She ignores this little detail and continues to speak. "As I see it, I have been hoodwinked into helping these ridiculous mortals one last time. My sincere hope is that they will come to their collective senses soon enough and realize, as they did in London when we were last in business, that it's best to keep us out of their troubles, even if Aberrants are involved. That you conspired with them to out us is unforgiveable."

"There is more to this. I couldn't tell them because I am working undercover. I wasn't even trying to expose the Circle; I was trying to avenge the death of someone dear to me."

"Are you saying you were a double agent?" Vivienne tries not to laugh, but it is a most laughable concept.

"Something to that effect."

"Nonsense. Subterfuge is your worst skill. Even worse than your croquet. Your very nature is to be true to yourself, even if that is an ever-shifting menagerie."

"They've got your ledger, Vivienne."

This piques her interest. She had thought it lost, assumed it was burned in their Paris house fire of 1899. Once Worth left Goodwin and Waldemar, she had no use of it, anyway. Just a litany of the details of their adventures, annotations, and the occasional alchemical dalliance.

"They must be lying. That book was destroyed," she says.

"No, I... stole it."

"Worth!" She is genuinely shocked.

"I took it with me when I left. I was hurt. You'd... hurt me, darling. But I knew it was important work; I kept it secret for a long time until I found someone who I thought could aid me in the research, finding antidotes to iron and the like."

Vivienne doesn't believe for a moment that he stole it. The convenient theft is too riddled with Nerissa's signature to be much of a consideration.

"The notes have details about a great many things. How to kill Fey, for instance. What we used to subdue them."

"Someone had to keep track of things. I wasn't completely useless, as you make me out to be. After all, if it wasn't for me, you'd have had a sincere image problem."

"The uniforms, you mean?"

"When fighting evil, it does behoove a person to look the part."

"They were rather uncomfortable."

"Fashion is pain, my dear. And you couldn't very well go looking like two wandering werewolves, could you?" Vivienne scoffs. "You're not the only one with a reputation to uphold. I couldn't very well be associated with the two of you looking so indecent. I see that you still have a rather lacking approach to fashion. Tell me, did Christabel dress you?"

Worth stutters and says nothing, so Vivienne continues.

"But we weren't talking about my sartorial contributions to the cause, no. We were speaking of my ledger."

"We were," says Worth, his tongues finally working in concert. "We were speaking of the ledger."

"I can't see why you're so concerned," she says. "It's written in *daemonic*. Even if, as I'm assuming, it's found its way into the wrong hands, no mortal can read it."

"Yes, but they are close to figuring that out. Christabel's is a mind like no other I've known, and I think she may be learning the language. I need to get it back... to protect all of us."

Vivienne sighs. "I already said I would help you."

"I have a personal stake in this," Worth says. "You need to understand. I can't lose you both..."

"And who are we talking about, now?"

"A young vampire by the name of Yvan. Quebecois by derivation. We'd been traveling the Appalachians together when we arrived a bit outside of Tarrytown to find..." He trails off, wincing. "Christabel mentioned him earlier. I just didn't have the heart to explain it."

"Were you making a terrible pun about stakes, just then?" Vivienne asks.

"No, that was..." He shakes his head, caught in her web again. A deep breath follows. "Yvan is dead."

"Maybe he looked at your excuse for fashion and perished at the thought."

"Vivienne. He was a healthy vampire. Sane and solid. But he went Aberrant overnight. I had to..."

Vivienne understands. Being creatures such as they means they understand innately what can happen when an Aberrant goes on a rampage. "You killed him. You had to," she says.

"I did. He went for a walk and came back to our cabin. And when he returned, he was already half mad. He made me promise I would find Christabel Crane, that she would lead me to answers. She has, though added a few more queries to my list, and I know the Rockefellers and the Circle are somehow involved, and when I realized you were here, I thought it expedient to make introductions."

"You could have called on me in a civil manner. After years of hearing nothing from you, there are significantly less risky approaches, you know."

"I wrote. You didn't answer."

The mail.

Nerissa.

Or Barqan.

Or both.

Damn them to the last circle of Hades.

"Still, that was an overwrought gesture, the bloody party," Vivienne says, taking in air slowly and deliberately to calm herself. "It was a great shock, and the night did nothing for my complexion. Nerissa could have snapped."

"But she didn't, and that's important. You see?"

Vivienne does not see and has half a mind to push him out the door herself. "I honestly don't see why you couldn't have just come for tea."

"They wanted proof you weren't Aberrants. So, I allowed for a test. You need to trust me."

"I can't without understanding, Worth. You're going to have to give me the details."

Vivienne has had enough of talk. It is a pale imitation of communication between them, and she is fairly certain that Worth has warmed to her at least a little bit. The idea of seeing his lover in detail does not appeal much to her, but there is no use asking him a thousand questions when he is capable of simply showing them to her.

When they were younger, and in love, they shared this mental projection together, creating little sub-dreams where they could share in memory and creation. A sacred, psychic space. She and the Glatisant, it seems, have similar workings in terms of their mental capacity and strength. It's not something she's ever been able to do with Nerissa, though she has tried. Worth would blame it on her lizard brain.

The look Worth gives her is full of hope.

"You want me to show you?" he asks, tentatively like a child.

"Of course," she says. "It's all I ever want from you." Which is not entirely true, but it's a good place to start.

It isn't until his skin touches hers that she remembers, that she really feels the grief of missing him for so long. She used to think that they were made for each other—he, the prey, and she, the huntress—but in the ensuing years apart, she began to doubt that.

When his hand approaches hers, she recalls immediately, and with striking detail, how it used to be. The blending of their bodies, their true bodies. Her fingers, skeletal and frosty; his, an ever-shifting glasslike framework, insubstantial and moving from reptile to mammal to avian and back again. His fibers meet her fingers, like branches reaching out toward the sun. Each strand of him twists into her arm, moving quickly up her frame until it finds its way up to her temples, forming curlicues around her temples.

Then, the story begins...

YVAN

I t's a matter of living smartly in New York, that's what Yvan always
says. No one will know who and *what* they are if they are smart
enough. There are enough places they can go to get food—enough
volunteers—that so long as they can blend in, there will be no challenges.
During their time in Canada, it had not been so difficult. Fewer people to
run into, and by nature, Yvan's work—he is a kind of arctic botanist by
trade—requires a certain level of solitude.

But with his recent book completed, and no sign of the *moly* he sought
together with Worth, they decide to make the trip to New York to see
some of the academics in the area with whom they had correspondences.
Yvan is always more trusting of human beings than Worth is, but then he
blends in more easily, especially among the educated, cloistered away in
their studies and offices, scarcely different than the reformed night
hunter vampire himself.

Yvan Tousignant is in every way a perfect complement to Worth. He is
outgoing and naturally friendly, charismatic and genuine. Like Vivienne,
who Worth is still reminded of every day, Yvan seems to flourish in the
company of people, wanting to please them and be part of their society.
Hence his most baffling obsession with botany, a peculiarly solitary
endeavor.

"Imagine what good I could do in this field in the span of my lifetime,"

Yvan tells Worth the first night they meet, atop a London hotel in the spring. They very quickly fall in love.

And how could they not? Yvan is, despite every literal indication to the contrary, very much *alive*. He moves and talks and expresses himself with a kind of Gallic intensity, his dark eyebrows up and down the pale lines of his brow, his hands a frantic ballet of movement.

Worth has never met a dead being so full of life and passion. Most of the vampires he has met during his long tenure are either Gothic hangers-on or Byronic creatures leaning toward orgies, excess, and tacky home furnishings. Which is welcome now and again, but damned difficult to manage in the long term. One can go through only so many chaise lounges.

But Yvan does not have a home. He is a nomad, a traveler, an adventurer. Working with Nerissa, years ago, Worth had a similar kind of connection—not to her personally, as he found her repugnant physically —but to the work itself.

It had been Vivienne who destroyed any semblance of balance by insisting he settle down and engage in a facade of domestication. Still, he has kept Vivienne's notes since the sundering of their relationship, and her meticulous categorization of flora and fauna in the supernatural realm prove most helpful in their studies. He considers it a parting gift from Nerissa, and one of the most valuable items in his possession.

Living with Yvan makes him happy. Down to his toes, it makes him happy. The road calls to them both, and side-by-side they explore the corners of the world still left to mystery. They fall in love with the land, and with each other; they understand more about who they are and why they exist. Now and again they discover an Aberrant or a mystery otherwise impossible to puzzle out, but it is all dealt with in time and Worth is content.

Sleepy Hollow is as quaint a place as it sounds, but the idea of creatures of their mettle living among the average gentry is not well accepted. But Yvan has friends, he promises, who will keep them safe from harm, or at least from persecution. Most do not believe that monsters like them exist, and those who do are quite certain none of them are reformed in the least.

They take up separate apartments, lest they heap yet another grand scandal upon themselves, and Yvan spends his days resting and recuperating and his evenings meeting with the academic elite as far away as

New York City. It's important that Worth stays his distance during this time, so he does. But he is greatly lonely.

This is when he discovers the names of the two women recently moved in to Lyndhurst in nearby Tarrytown.

Of course. He knew something felt extra chilly about this place.

Despite his work to very diligently avoid the two of them, Vivienne and Nerissa are within a half hour's stroll. The lamia is of less a concern, but Worth knows if Vivienne sees him, she will be both furious and betrayed, and he can't explain to her exactly what went badly with them, but he knows it to be true. He loved—loves—her, but in a desperate, wanting, perpetually unsatisfied way. They bring out the worst in each other—she, her capriciousness; he, his narcissism—and their years together were marked with such overwhelming sadness and dismay that the mere thought of seeing her again makes him feel nauseated.

When at last he tells Yvan about it, the vampire initially shrugs it off. He has come into contact with a young scholar named Christabel Crane, who has been hinting to a sort of secret cadre among the elite of Tarrytown and the surrounding boroughs. As it stands, Yvan is more interested in this than anything else. It is rumored they have, in their possession, a great many antique books, and one that may hold the key to the *moly* he has sought for so long.

One late night as they sit together in Yvan's quaint parlor, Worth brings up Vivienne again, and this time, the vampire reacts with anger.

"Do you expect me to feel jealous, is that it?" Yvan asks, rising from his seat to angrily pour himself a glass of wine. "Really, if you keep going on about that fickle creature, I'm going to have to drag her here by the hair so you do the deed done yourself. Apparently you aren't satisfied with our current arrangement, *maudite*."

Worth is so taken aback by the language coming from his lover that he takes a moment to respond. He is in his natural form, preening the fur on his hindquarters near his hooves, delicately, in order not to show his face. Though his face looks the part of a snake—it is, in reality, more akin to the great Komodo dragon—it is surprisingly expressive. But truly a detriment in terms of grooming. Whatever god had its hand making his body must have been well and truly drunk, for the fangs and tongue of a reptile do very little to smooth mammalian fur. It takes ages to get it right, and while he may have four tongues in total, they are rarely in agreement.

"I was simply stating," Worth manages at last, turning from his work, "that Fate seems a cruel mistress to bring us within such close proximity. It is no surprise that the winter is so bitter cold this year, what with the Queen of Frost herself holding court."

"There you go again," Yvan mutters. *"Caulisse."*

"No need to get so vulgar."

"Dare you call me vulgar, after the stories I hear of that woman! Yet here you mention her, flatter her, as if she wasn't the most damaging creature you ever came across."

"I told you, our relationship is complicated. But it's her meticulous notes that have helped us in our studies. Without her book, we might never have—"

"Yet she is so damned woven into your brain that you can't stop talking about her. I honestly don't know what I would do if I saw her."

"It's best we keep you separated, Yvan. For the good of all of us. She's powerful, though she looks fragile. A bitterest cold that will wipe your soul clean."

"I *have* no soul." The way Yvan says it, Worth understands the threat and decides it best to refrain from bringing up the fair sylph again.

~

It does not get easier. Yvan stays out later and later, arriving dangerously close to dawn on more than one occasion, meeting with Christabel Crane. He calls her odd, yet fascinating. Worth grows more and more concerned for the vampire, but when he brings up the issue, Yvan shuts him out and says he is being possessive.

This is not the creature he fell in love with. Without the open road between them, without the promise of adventure, their differences are so much clearer. Worth wants to get to know the lay of the land, to discover the patterns of the town. He spends hours plotting the comings and goings of millers and bakers and merchants, noting the strange habits of errant husbands and housemaids. He finds it so curious that they would live their lives so in the open, so easily left to discovery. Yvan, however, wants nothing to do with anyone else in Sleepy Hollow. He wants only to speak with the Circle, but despite his better efforts, he is never truly allowed into those secrets.

They fight. Many times. When Worth makes a passing comment about seeing whether or not Nerissa Waldemar might be a good resource, the vampire flies into a jealous rage. Worth is not physically hurt—his blood draws substance from the air and sun, much like a flower, and no amount of loss would cause his death—but he is bruised within. Yvan leaves in a fury.

Then, after waiting up all night, Yvan does not return home to his apartment. Beyond exhausted, Worth falls asleep on the chaise lounge in the vampire's parlor and sleeps right through the day. The sunlight refreshes him, but so deep his melancholy that he slips into a near hibernation.

A scratching sound awakens Worth, and he quickly draws up his glamour. He is so used to doing it in moments of discovery that the act is more of a reaction than conscious. He pulls on a nearby bathrobe and listens at the door, unable to find the tie and instead leaving the garment displaying his most natural human state, if it can be called such a thing.

Leaning into the door, Worth senses the urgency behind it. It's a skittering, whimpering sound. Like dog nails scrabbling on the floor.

Then a moan, and a curse: "*Caulisse.* They took the book... wretched woman... Aberrants... ledger..."

Two things wind through Worth's mind: one is that he knows the sound as Yvan's voice, the other is that he did not sense him. A Questing Beast always knows the feeling of his captor. His scent, his presence, his unique energy imprint. It has always served him well and alerted him, even when sleeping.

But it isn't working.

Then there is the matter of the ledger. They have spoken at length of its value, all whilst avoiding the subject of its author. He must be desperate to be bringing it up.

When he opens the door, he understands why.

Yvan is covered in boils and scratches. The sun is not up, but even so, those burns are different—he had seen them once when they timed an expedition wrong. These are hideous things, purple and black, cracking on the top like burnt custards left too long in the oven. He is stripped naked, black blood seeping from his marvelous, pleading eyes, in slow trickles down the lines of his face.

Moving faster than any human could, and resuming his natural form, Worth encircles the vampire and sweeps him into the apartment, wrapping his body around him as if warmth would help a creature already dead.

"Yvan, listen to me, breathe deeply," Worth says, not knowing what else to say. Vampires don't breathe, exactly. They take in air when they want to, to smell or to express a more humanlike exterior, but it isn't necessary.

"Get it out," Yvan says, his dry, cracked lips pulling taut over blood-speckled teeth. He flails, fingers going back to whatever he was working on before. "It's inside of me! I need to let it out!"

His chest. Yvan wants to break into his own chest.

"There's nothing there. Just whatever it is that makes up a vampire's heart."

"My heart is broken. I need to get it... out and... fix..." Yvan renews his efforts, thrashing, long arms fumbling and scratching his own skin.

Worth pulls Yvan tighter, but the vampire is suffused with energy. He is writhing, his hands and nails going for his own chest with such pure power that no matter how strong Worth tries—at least without dismembering his lover—he cannot prevent him from doing so.

It is a gritty, grisly business. The floorboards creak and char with the energy between the two, skin flaying off the vampire's chest as his nails dig deeper and deeper.

"Love, stop, please," begs Worth, shouting from his hideous mouth, four voices at once. The hart, the leopard, the snake, the lion. There are other words, but no script could put them in a legible semblance.

It is pure sorrow, pure angst, and grief. At last, unable to stop the vampire lest he destroy him himself, Worth unravels around Yvan and pulls back, blue tears falling from vermillion eyes.

To watch such a thing, a creature searching for some hidden meaning, mad and rending, is beyond any horror Worth has yet witnessed, and there have been many. Never has he seen a creature work so hard to destroy himself.

Yvan manages, at last, to worry his hand through his chest completely. He pulls out a rib triumphantly, the bone cracking brightly in the evening quiet. The look on the vampire's face is both of wonder and horror. As he pulls his hand out, bloody black to the wrist, triumphant, he frowns immediately. There is nothing there but the remnants of a heart, shriveled and dark, old veins once living snapping off and splattering against his face. It does not pulse, but it twitches, and then a bright stream of light comes from it, twisting away and out the window.

"I couldn't help you," Worth says. "I'm sorry."

Yvan laughs shortly, spraying blood across the room. It stinks of offal and worse, staring at his heart. "Why, what a sight," he says. "I do have a heart after all."

Then, Yvan falls. It only takes a moment for the body to decompose, the long pause of a few hundred years finally culminating. By the time Worth stumbles his way to his lover's corpse, it is but a dark stain upon the ground.

INTO THE BREACH

What horrendous company these human beings are, Nerissa thinks, as she skulks back to the room she has adopted since they began this miserable Tarrytown adventure. She smells sweet and fermented, like a cherry spoiled in the sun, but she doesn't notice because she's forgotten how drunk she is. Alcohol is, generally speaking, a detriment to most sharp minds, and to lamias perhaps most of all. Something to do with their blood composition.

So, she muses on her situation darkly. She had wanted to go to the city proper, certain that the best way for monsters to stay out of sight would mean finding a population large enough in which to hide. But Nerissa loved the idea of living in one of the large houses in the country, and once she got on with the planning, there was no stopping it.

And now Worth is here and ruining the little peace they made for themselves, a calm stillness that passed through her hands like water over rocks. The very people she spent so long trying to help—mostly because of her antiquated appreciation for their arts and culture—turned on her. She knew you couldn't trust wealthy people. That was why, in their previous business, she and Worth never took a penny for their work. It was all pro bono. People who could pay always wanted more than they billed, and it is too exhausting to keep up with.

Nerissa does not wish to speak with Vivienne, but they were both expected at the gala party at Rockwood, William Rockefeller's home. It would not do well to ignore the summons. And there is much planning to do.

That, at least, she and Vivienne can agree upon. Nerissa makes it her goal to avoid Vivienne, apart from formal summons to gather in the drawing room together along with Christabel Crane and a few of her Circle cronies. They would have to be transparent about their dealings, of course, but once it is over, Nerissa is absolutely certain that she will be leaving Tarrytown, Lyndhurst, and all the inane goings on of the New York elite for good. If Vivienne wants to stay, that is her prerogative.

After calling the meeting, Nerissa is purposefully late. And she decides to dress as commonly as possible, knowing such behavior will bother Vivienne immensely. It is perhaps childish, but Nerissa has lived with the sylph long enough to know each and every one of her pithy complaints, and dirty hems and out of date clothing are nearly as intolerable to her as men with unkempt mustaches and books arranged out of alphabetic order. It's the little things, really.

As soon as she opens the door, she feels her high spirits, fueled by willing disobedience, darken immediately. Worth and Vivienne are so close they are practically entwined. Barqan is standing stiffly by the window as if keeping an eye on the entrance to the house, but is probably just catching a nap. Christabel and her cultists—a fellow named Smythe and a middle-aged woman named Mrs. Bellemains—are drinking alcohol from fancy glasses and laughing.

Laughing.

"I'm glad someone can find levity amidst the gathering doom," Nerissa says, making her way rudely past the Circle and toward Vivienne and Worth. "It's best not to let such evil possibilities ruin our fun."

"Hello to you, as well, Nerissa," Worth says drily. "We were wondering if you were going to show up. Considering you arranged the meeting, we expected you to be here when it started."

"I was a bit detained," Nerissa replies, turning to check and see if Barqan is, indeed, asleep. He is not and gives her a sympathetic look.

"An hour is a bit more than detained," Vivienne says, refusing to make eye contact, "even for you."

"Well, the point is that we are all here," Christabel says, injecting herself into the conversation. She is positively ebullient, and as a rule, Nerissa despises ebullience. "We have been making conversation in hopes that you would join us to add your expertise."

Nerissa snorts in a most delightfully impolite way, takes the glass of wine from Mrs. Bellemains, and drinks it in one quaff. It's terrible stuff. Brandy, she thinks. But she is quite convinced that playing the part of a monster is her best approach, even if it is simply a creature with terrible manners. There is no doubt that social taboos hold as much gravitas as actual bloodshed among these people.

"*My* expertise?" Nerissa asks, considering the bottom of her glass before putting it on the windowsill—not, she knows, the ideal place to put it, but the closest flat surface and, therefore, her decision.

Did she have much to drink beforehand? Now that she has the brandy rolling down her throats again, she remembers that, yes, she has been enjoying the one spirit she quite likes, *port*. She found an impressive store of the stuff in the wine cellar the day before. She finds that rolling back the narrative of her day results in more than a few gaps.

"You recall when we were in business together," Worth says slowly, deliberately, as if Nerissa is an imbecile and cannot understand twenty languages and speak seventeen. "In England. Our work, to find the Aberrants. To help people."

"Ah, yes, the good people of Lower Kent," says Nerissa, waving her arm in the air so close that she nearly takes off Mr. Smythe's glasses. "You mean those halcyon days where we worked for the good of people who needed help, not those who were willing to sacrifice the lives of their friends and family to out a trio of uninteresting monsters?"

An uncomfortable silence ensues, only interrupted by a forcible burp provided by the lamia. She has practiced a long time to get the sound and shape of it just right, as burping is not inherent in her kind, whose bodies are more accustomed to slow feeding and thereby need very little in the way of air expulsion.

The effect, and the look of horror on Vivienne's face, is worth all that work, however. Nerissa has been saving it up for quite some time, this surprise act of defiance. While she considers all concepts of human rudeness to be just a matter of perspective, or else a side effect of over-breeding, Vivienne has followed the rules of etiquette every day of her life since learning of them.

But this is one expression beyond the sylph's ability to cope. Rather than utter words or cast magic in her direction, Vivienne simply grabs Nerissa by the elbow and ushers her out of the room. Were she not well past the point of inebriation, the lamia would be well equipped to resist such an assault on her person, but given how the floor is sloping both away and behind her, and she isn't entirely sure how she ended up in that room in the first place.

Once the two are down the hall, Vivienne pulls Nerissa into a small anteroom and locks the door. The hinges rattle as they freeze slightly, and even in her sorry state, Nerissa registers that her friend is furious.

Good. That is her aim.

"I don't even know what to say to you right now," Vivienne says, pinching her nose. She is dressed just one degree from formal, the only indication she has not gone all the way in the tilt of her hair and the absence of jewelry.

"Say that we'll leave," Nerissa offers, shrugging. "Say that we will take Barqan and go to Prussia, where he is from."

"Persia," corrects Vivienne, "and you must truly be lost to the world if you are suggesting doing anything with Barqan."

"Right now, I like him more than I like you," the lamia replies, going to push up her glasses, but realizing too late that she never bothered to put them on. "A great deal more."

"This is about Worth, isn't it?" Vivienne asks.

"This is about Worth, isn't it?" parrots Nerissa, making her hand into a little puppet and then giggling. The noise escaping her sounds foreign, as if her insides have been replaced with a boiling tea kettle.

Vivienne says something very unkind in French, and given a regular day, Nerissa would have retorted in High German, a language she always felt most at home in. But instead she just stares back at the sylph and snorts.

"You are so blind to it," Nerissa says at last. "You are so damned obsessed with trying to please them that you would do anything, even sell me out."

"I did no such thing. You don't have to do this. I tried to speak with you, to explain what I know now—about Worth and Yvan, his lover."

That word is enough to cut through the haze, and Nerissa feels her legs go out from under her, and she slinks into a large jacquard chair.

"I don't have lovely eyes," she says, thinking of the Keats poem. It's one that they read together every year, that and his *La Belle Dame Sans Merci*. For a mortal, he understood some aspects of their being quite well. "I have horrible eyes. The Romantics always wanted to find something beautiful in their monsters, some lingering shred of perfection amidst the ugliness. But my eyes are blood red and black-pupiled. And I am, and always will be, repulsive."

"What if you didn't have to be?" asks Vivienne, kneeling before her friend and putting her hands on her knees.

The touch is enough to send the lamia's hearts fluttering, the three little organs playing a counterpoint dance about each other. It's enough to distance her from the mass quantities of alcohol coursing through her body, to still her into a kind of stunned silence and then, perhaps inevitably, a sense of shame.

"I don't know what you mean," Nerissa says. She does not ask Vivienne to remove her hands. Her own are trembling.

Vivienne's eyes are deep violet, such an impossibly perfect color. How could she be such a beautiful monster? What gifts.

Vivienne explains Worth's story about Yvan, telling the lamia as quickly as possible about the events recently unfolded.

"We believe that they may have harmed Yvan to get the ledger—or that the creature we're trying to fight is somehow connected to it. He wanted to become mortal again. That's what the *moly* was for. Worth didn't understand until I explained it to him. It may be that, coupled with his research, we are on the brink of discovering the key to mortality."

The realization of what Vivienne is implying sends Nerissa to her feet, nearly unable to retain her human guise, so deep is her revulsion.

"Are you... you think that *I* want to be a human?" the lamia asks. "That I would give up all that I am, every fiber of my being as knit by the gods, to... to pass as a human being?"

Vivienne blanches, shaking her head. "I didn't mean to imply that you are somehow lacking, my dear. It's only that you've seemed so miserable for so long, and I thought perhaps it was the years wearing on you. The continued distance."

"Do not mistake my sorrow for your unhealthy human obsession."

"But, Nerissa, please. I want to understand what makes you so miserable."

Nerissa laughs brightly now. "You! *You* make me miserable. And you can write that down so you don't forget it while you're chasing baubles and making small talk with millionaires, all of which will shatter and die."

It is Barqan who materializes through the wall. He is showing off, and normally Nerissa would chide him, but she's no idea how much of the conversation he's heard. Not that it matters; he knows her heart well enough. But that's the least of her problems for now.

"Barqan, I did not summon you," Vivienne says sharply. It is not often that she speaks to him in such a manner; usually she is careful and sweeter than she should be.

"Perhaps not. But my mistress is in distress, and I am compelled to help."

"What is it?" Nerissa asks sharply.

"I hear that the Circle is aware of my presence, and therefore, this is most intimately my business," Barqan says. His eyes are glowing a muted green. Unusual. Nerissa doesn't know what in the heavens that could mean, but she takes it as an ill omen.

Vivienne frowns, trying to go for the door to leave. How is it that she's the one acting the victim now? Barqan bars her way, however.

"How did they find out about me?" he asks, more directly this time.

"I don't see how that has to do with anything," she shoots back. "You are both wasting precious time. Regardless of our individual thoughts on the matter, we have to get this business done. Then we can decide what we are going to do."

"There may be other things they know," he says. "Methods of freeing me. There are texts, some thought lost to time, but if they exist..."

"My concern," Barqan says, continuing as if Vivienne has said nothing at all, "is that if they are able to break certain bonds between the supernatural and the mortal, that they may be able to do the same for me. The version of myself, as presented to you now, is but a mere reflection of my abilities. You know this. Were I to be unwittingly released, outside of your control, I would not have hold on my faculties. The end would be bloody indeed, both for you and for your human friends. The ledger has some rather impressive details on your attempted work to free me, I recall."

Yes, there is much to fear in the djinni. There has always been an undercurrent to him, a restlessness, and her debt to him is at the center. She has kept him in chains too long. There is an air of inconstancy in his very being. His shackles transform him into a lie, a living lie. A power awaiting release. Lamias can hide, it is well known, but their true nature is always there, just below the surface, hiding behind a mask. To look upon Barqan is to see a vessel containing an object of unimaginable power.

"Then you will stay here," Vivienne says simply, her frozen smile unwavering. "I will simply tell them that your presence is needed elsewhere, and you won't be attending the ball."

"If the threat is as great as you make it out, though," Nerissa says, "we're going to need every power we have. And Barqan has always been handy in a fight."

"Regardless, we must find my research and any sign of what Yvan was doing—and, hopefully, do away with whatever threat is attacking the Circle."

"You don't think it's Yvan, do you?" asks Barqan.

"That was my first inclination—some soul transference—but the first haunting happened before Yvan and Worth even arrived in Tarrytown. So it is unlikely," Vivienne says. "Nerissa, dear, what do you think? Will you help me?"

Nerissa sighs. There is no true way out of this ordeal. As much as she would like to abandon Vivienne in this hour of need, she cannot help but feel moved by Worth's story. While it would be delightful to call it a hoax, she knows his abilities well enough. During their years together, they would often meld in the same way, he opening up his mind to hers to play back memories. The connection could not be forged.

Yvan is dead, as well as two important Tarrytown figures connected to the Circle. It is personal. Once, she was fond of Worth; once, she relied on Vivienne's alchemy to help them in their pursuit of Aberrants and Exigents, and her accounting to understand the connected threads. The idea of abandoning her to fend for herself made Nerissa's head pound.

Or maybe that is all the port. It is honestly hard to tell.

"I suppose you'll get your second party after all, Viv," Nerissa says, shaking her head. "You do tend to get what you want. That much I've learned."

SOIREE

Despite the difficulties of the last few days, Vivienne du Lac can't help but feel excited about the prospect of a second ball. While this get-together has all the pomp and circumstance of the Villiers', it is in a bigger house, with more impressive guests, and the menu is the talk of the town. It is said that scarcely a wedge of cheese could be found between Tarrytown and New York City. The Rockefellers have more pull in terms of culinary influence than any family in the area and are not accustomed to hearing the word "no" in any capacity.

Yet, through all her excitement, Vivienne is bothered by the circumstances around the event. She did get her way, in the long run, and part of her is most pleased with the outcome; getting her way is almost as delightful as ruining a soul in the old days, and it is a much safer replacement.

But now, Worth is distant. He loved Yvan, and he is still mourning the man, and this opportunity to confront this beast is a chance for revenge.

And Nerissa. Vivienne's emotions sit on a very thin, nearly transparent level as she brushes her long hair in the mirror and stares through it. It is a calm place, but it is a precarious one, set between passion and fury. One tip up or down and she will be most difficult to deal with. The way the lamia looks at her, it is as if she were saying so much more. As if the quiet creature, so brilliant and so damned mysterious at the same time, has found someone worth fighting for. Vivienne is almost flattered.

65

"You didn't yell at Mr. Pender anywhere as long as you usually do," Barqan said, materializing through her room, unannounced. He takes a glance at the silk dresses upon the bed, which are, in the grand scheme of Vivienne's wardrobe, almost boring. The high collars are an interesting touch, but otherwise, they are unremarkable.

"I wasn't in the mood for screeching," Vivienne says with a sigh. "You, of all people, should understand that. I am being squeezed out on every side by those I counted dearest."

"Perhaps because this situation is precarious," the djinni offers, going to work hanging the clothes and accessories to Vivienne's specifications. "For all of us. Even me. And I'm typically prepared to stand on the sidelines. Having to participate in this business is unsettling for me, to say the least."

Vivienne notices nothing unusual about the djinni, save for his recent obsession with voicing his opinion in a most grating manner. She had never noticed how his voice seems to come from more place than one, and it is, for the first time, just the tiniest bit unsettling. Her powers do not work directly on the djinni, and they never have, and she's always enjoyed that lack of concern.

"You're looking at me strangely," Barqan says, his back turned to her.

"I have a question for you, if you don't mind," she says. "A couple, actually. If you wouldn't mind me asking."

"When have I ever disobeyed a command, madame?" he asks.

She cannot think of a time that he has, yet this conversation feels like undiscovered territory. As if it is the first time they are meeting. Yet they have been together for a hundred years.

"When you are around me, Barqan, what do you feel?" she asks.

"Irritation," the djinni says.

"No, I mean more specifically."

He pauses a moment, considering. "*Intense* irritation."

"I mean, from a supernatural sense. You are a being of curious make, as we are. But you are suffused with more magical matter than all of us combined."

"I am not sure what you are asking, madame," he replies. "I am not interested in flattering you. You get enough of that with everyone you come into contact with."

"Barqan, you are being frustrating," Vivienne says.

"It is the curse of being insubstantial."

Vivienne crosses the room to get a better look at him. "Show me your real form. As best as you can. I don't want to see the finery and the costume. If I didn't ask you to dress the part of a footman, how would you look?"

"I don't see that this serves any purpose. These games you play grate on me, madame, if you permit me to be honest."

"I do not. That's insulting."

"I am not sorry."

Vivienne grits her teeth, remembering what it felt like once to drown three knights in a bog after they competed for her hand over the course of a month, their bodies wasted to near nothing. In her darker days, this was her favorite method of killing. Consuming their sad energy in their last moments is a special kind of joy, the flavor so nuanced and complex, something so difficult to share with the non-soul sucking contingent.

"From a magical point of view, you know how sylphs work, I presume, or at least how I do," Vivienne says.

"You feed off organisms' energies the way plants feed off the sun's rays, or at least, if the plants slowly destroyed the sun during their course of feeding. It is similar to the Glatisant. But colder."

"Yes, but with you, when I reach out to you, I get no response. I can try and pull you all I want, but there is an empty void. Like a cold current in a room."

"The djinni are older, darker, than you imagine, madame."

"You said that if you are freed in an unorthodox way, you could go mad."

"I would most certainly. Without my shackles, I would gravitate to my mistress. The pent-up fury of a thousand years, the sleeping rage just beneath my surface."

"And by unorthodox you mean…"

"Worse than old iron."

She sighs. It is a risk, but one they must take. "You didn't answer my first question, but perhaps I was asking wrong," Vivienne says. He is never straightforward, though usually honest. Brutally so. "You always seem to find me, Barqan. How do you do that?"

"Your voice," he says. "Your very breath. As I am commanded, all others are but shadows to me, and you are a candle in the dark."

"Be sure to find me when I call," she says. "We have a fight before us, and I need you close by me."

"Yes, madame. Of course. I know no other way."

SOLSTICE AND SOLACE

At last, the day of the ball at Rockwood dawns, and every village in the nearby area is brimming with gossip and rumors. It is strange enough that Christabel Crane has resurfaced, claiming kinship to the local madman of myth, Ichabod Crane, but the weather has gone most strange, as well. The local farms know well enough what kind of ill omen that can prove. The morning of December the nineteenth rises in a mist, a thick and soupy business, which delays deliveries and perplexes travelers. Old Mrs. Nox gets so turned around trying to get to her last dress fitting that she does not find her way back until the day after the event.

Vivienne and Nerissa, however, fare better. At least in terms of scheduling. The lamia is not, in any stretch, over her love of the sylph, even if she has convinced herself otherwise. Her days are spent feeding and taking long walks.

Vivienne, for her part, continues to focus more on the logistics of the event than the pageantry. One of the concerned housemaids even sends a doctor in to see her, which is more than laughable, but serves, at least, to allay the fears of the mortal staff when the pale physic declares that "no illness in heaven or earth" affects the lady of the house.

Worth finds the lamia on the day of the event because he knows her quite well, despite their ensuing years apart. She has to eat; it is a biological imperative. And he is aware that interrupting her in her feeding state is both dangerous and stomach-churning. Having worked with her for many years, he is well aware of the risks.

So, he waits until she is finished and surprises her on her exit from the barn, the sound and smell of goats emanating from behind her.

"Worth," she says, without inflection, not looking up.

He's always been certain that she can sense him before he arrives and has long wondered if they share some common genetic component. If so, it may be one of the reasons they were such a good team.

"You didn't used to hate me so much," he says. "In fact, there was a time where I counted you among my greatest friends."

Nerissa snarls at him, then seems to think better of it, drawing her hands down each side of her face in an attempt at composure. It is cold outside, but there is no guarantee they will remain uninterrupted. Lynd-hurst is always alive with the many souls who keep it going from day to day. In that way, Worth reflects, it is like a giant clockwork beast. The building itself is a kind of creature composed of a thousand little bodies doing their jobs. Not so different, perhaps, from a beast made of four monsters.

"You know when that changed," Nerissa says, though said in a lighter manner than Worth would expect. The lamia is tired. "And I helped you escape what could have been a very unhealthy relationship."

"I shouldn't have left her the way I did," he admits.

"It wasn't *my* idea."

"No, but you did what you thought was best for her. And for yourself, perhaps. I was an interloper. But for the time we had together, we did great things. And I think we could, still."

"I have no time for turncoats. Especially in matters of the heart."

This is intriguing. Such passion from the lizard.

"I have no desire to pursue Vivienne, if that is where your concern lies," he says gently, knowing how delicate he must tread. "I understand how you feel for her. And had I known, from the beginning, I would not have pursued her then, either."

"You see, therein lies my disgust," Nerissa says, flashing her natural teeth. They are bright and sharp and, in their way, lovely. Worth has always appreciated glimpses of her natural being; it makes him feel less abhorrent to the world. "You do not want her. You had her, you let her go, you have moved on with your life. You hurt her and scorn her and flaunt other women around her, and still she loves you. It is a most cruel thing you have done to her, Worth. And you have taken her from me, forever."

This is a surprising turn of events for Worth. He has never thought of his relationship with the sylph in such terms. For once, he is without a word. All four of his tongues are incapable of forming the right reply.

"Yes, it *is* quite a terrible thing," Nerissa says. "But, as we stand, her life hangs in the balance. And though you claim not to love her as you once did, you are still her friend, I hope."

"I will always be her friend. And I will always love her. But there exists a point between two people where the maintenance of the relationship is a detriment to the happiness of one or both of its participants. She is many things, but capable of meeting my particular needs, perhaps not."

Worth can tell that these words do little to allay Nerissa's ire. She looks away from him, brushing new-fallen snow off her sleeves. The lamia has dressed hastily, and the precipitation is filling the wrinkles of her clothing in a pattern like lightning. Worth cannot tell how much of her is figment. She is strongest after a feeding and, therefore, her magic at its pinnacle.

Nerissa frowns, shrinking down into her muffler. "I wish I could dislike her. I wish I could detach myself from this fondness. It has burned inside of me for ages, Worth. And I thought that coming to Lyndhurst, spending time together in retirement, away from the prying eye of the rest of our sort, we could connect in ways we had not been able to before. But now I see I was being dull-witted."

"Vivienne wants one thing more than all else," Worth says, starting to reach out to put his hand on Nerissa's shoulder and then thinking twice of it. "To be accepted."

The words slide off Nerissa's scales for the most part, he can tell, but a few of them stick. Some of them are too true to ignore. Perhaps that is the great gulf between them, not the unrequited love of self, but that of their very natures, Worth wonders. The lamia is difficult to understand, that much is true, but her love—and near obsession—with Vivienne is, at least, dependable. It always has been. And perhaps that is the most difficult part, watching Nerissa realize just how impossible her infatuation with the sylph is, how utterly at odds their natures.

"She didn't used to be like this," Nerissa says at last. "She was once so…"

"Free?"

"Proud was the word I was looking for," she says, almost a whisper. "Of what we are."

"And now, no longer."

"She and Yvan both sought the key to mortality. Perhaps we must learn to let them to their choices. If we love them."

Black tears streak down Nerissa's face as she nods. "I suppose there is a time we all must choose. For my part, I have something specific in mind."

Worth can't help but smile. They worked together long enough that these discussions always have had their own subtext. "What caliber?" he asks.

ARTILLERY AND ARTERIES

Nerissa has always been fascinated with mortal weaponry. From cannons and crossbows to the more sophisticated firearms and ballistics, their pure alchemy has always amused and enticed her. It is a rather brutal way to go about killing Aberrants, and she's aware of the strange irony involved, but destroying those of her kind—regardless of their state—with her own magic has ever made her uncomfortable. Both she and Worth agreed, in their days doing business together, that their abilities should only be used for the finding and apprehending of Aberrants, not the killing and disposing.

Worth, for all his propriety, has always encouraged this behavior, and Nerissa is reminded of just why they worked together so long when she sees his reaction to her trove.

The shed serves a dual purpose for the lamia. Since she arrived at Lyndhurst, and knowing Vivienne's distaste for human weapons, she's kept her cache locked away in a series of custom-made chests, cleverly hidden behind the tack. Most of it is organized in an old dental cabinet, ideal for the smaller, more delicate mechanisms. She still occasionally finds bits and pieces of dental equipment and dentures, but more often than not, they come in handy for small repairs.

So when Nerissa opens up the first drawer to reveal a magnificent assortment of both familiar weapons and new models, Worth draws a breath of awe.

She is quite proud of the firearms, mostly because they are improvements upon the original designs. Back in their early days fighting Aberrants, they were lucky enough to have a weaponsmith of their own. A goblin by the name of Chester, to be exact. He was happy to do the work for them in exchange for wine and a roof over his head, and over the years, he came to accompany the team on occasion. Ultimately, the drink did him in during a visit to Scotland; the proliferation of whisky proved too difficult for him navigate with his explosives. A rare case of goblin combustion.

"You kept everything," Worth says. "It's all pristine."

Nerissa watches as he draws his hands over the shotgun he'd christened "Malice" and notices his hands are shaking. She wonders, not for the first time, why she couldn't have simply fallen in love with him and have been done with it. They always had so much more in common than she and Vivienne. One can never underestimate the power of a mutual appreciation of complex firearms, after all.

"We will have to be discreet," Nerissa says. "We will be under a glamor, and the more irregular our forms, the more challenging blending in."

"Alas, no Malice, then."

"Likely not. But you forget, Malice had a little sister. Mercy."

She feels the smile before she realizes it's on her lips. For some reason, she does not bury it. Instead, she lets it spread, the warmth whorling down the front of her, like a current of sunlit water in a pool.

Mercy is a small weapon, but marvelously made. Some would call her a Derringer, but that is a gross simplification of a weapon designed to debilitate creatures of immense size and power. Its charges are few, and perilous, composed of a many-layered bullet designed by Chester himself to deliver both a low electric shock, generally enough to incapacitate even Level Three Aberrants. But then comes the poison layer, comprised with one of Vivienne's own recipes, both neurotoxin and poison combined. To an average human being, it would be certain death; to an Aberrant, it's enough to shock them into sleep for a long time.

Worth takes Mercy in his hands and audibly sniffles. It appears that Nerissa has, inadvertently, struck a chord with Glatisant. It makes her mildly uncomfortable, but also rather amused.

"It's been a long time since I felt anything but hunted," Worth says at last. "With Yvan, there was a sense of pause, a sort of escape from it. But when I hold Mercy in my hands, when I am well accoutered, I feel as if I am not only doing right by myself, but I am stronger."

"Dangerous, perhaps, to lend that much power to anything outside of yourself," Nerissa suggests, not at all certain she likes where this conversation is going.

Worth sighs, taking Mercy's holster and worrying his fingers over the leather. "I know that, Nerissa. But what I'm trying to say, however ineffectually, is that I miss working with you. I know you wanted me out because of my connection with Vivienne, and I don't fault you for it. But I think we could have worked things out better. If no one hunts the monsters, is anyone safe?"

"I'm not sure who the monsters are anymore, Worth. I just know that if what you say is true, and if what Vivienne is planning is true, we've got to protect ourselves. And that's why I've kept this arsenal all these years."

It's a bit of a lie. She and Barqan kept letters from Vivienne, did everything in their power to keep them apart. But she knew that, eventually, it would all come around again. The connection between those two was just too powerful. And now her own foolishness with the ledger meant their lives were all in danger. She should have just let it play out, but jealousy had worried its way so deep into her heart she didn't know how to cope. Those blessed decades alone with Vivienne were supposed to be time for them to grow together, time for her to show the sylph just how much she was desired and wanted. Instead, they fell into a life of lazy human indulgence and boredom.

"You don't miss Waldemar and Goodwin?" he asks.

She doesn't want to admit it. She doesn't want the words to come out. But it's like something in her has broken these last few days. As if centuries of protective layers have sloughed off and gone, leaving her raw and exposed.

"I'm tired of hating you," she says at last, which is the closest thing she can manage to an apology. "Let's wreak a little havoc, shall we?"

Worth grins. "By all means, milady. The pleasure is mine."

The night before the gala at the Rockefeller house, it snows in Tarrytown. It's a perfect, light snow, the kind that dances by windows, luminous flakes clustering like icy fairies in the lantern light. Everything is hushed as the snow falls, just enough to be beautiful without causing distress for travel, and even the animals in the town bow to the silence in the world around them. When Nerissa goes to feed from

Flossie, her second-favorite goat, there is no complaint to speak of. After she is finished, she sits in the open rafters of her barn and watches the snow fall, thinking of Vivienne.

~

Christabel Crane summons the courage to visit Lyndhurst alone. The last interaction with these creatures left her more than a little confused, but also doubtful of their help in the matter. She trusts Worth because he is, by nature, built to please. It's the lamia, in particular, that discomfits her. She needs assurance. Her reputation rides on it, her legacy.

And Worth has not called on her in person. He has kept a great many correspondences, but he has been at Lyndhurst since their last meeting. They have not spoken of their last time together, nor of their harsh words.

The djinni meets her at the front door, opening it before she can even manage to knock.

"It is a strange time for a woman to be out by herself," Barqan says to her. He has made no effort to hide his nature, his feet nothing but a blue mist on the ground. The rest of the staff appears to be away, most of the windows unlit in the expansive mansion.

"I wish to speak to the ladies of the house," Christabel says. "About tomorrow's plan. My... investors are concerned."

"I have yet to figure you out, Ms. Crane. But I will," the djinni says.

"And how will you do that?" she asks, unsure to what he refers.

"You are not what you seem."

"And what do I seem?"

But Barqan is silent, though he lingers for a moment too long to be comfortable, and then vanishes. It is unsettling and leaves a feeling like wiggling worms in Christabel's stomach. But she waits, nonetheless, clapping her hands on her arms and wishing she had packed an extra pair of socks. Her feet are half frozen to the ground.

By the time Vivienne appears at the doorway, Christabel is thinking in such detail about just how many layers of clothing would be required to gain her some measure of warmth that the sylph's appearance doesn't merely shock her, it almost makes her laugh.

Vivienne is wearing a long robe of sheer fabric, and nothing else. Her thin, pale body appears impervious to the cold, her black hair streaking down her breasts and curling ever so slightly at her waist.

"Hello, Christabel."

"Lady du Lac," replies Christabel, lips trembling but her voice still strong. She has made it a habit not to show fear in front of these people. A lifetime of living among such creatures has helped in some respect. Vivienne is different, though. She is older than the vampires and Fey common to Sleepy Hollow. Though the Horseman might give Vivienne a run for the money if he wasn't avoiding her.

"Won't you come in?" the sylph asks.

"I don't want to inconvenience you," says Christabel, giving her most luminous smile, the one that her father once told her could convince an angel to work for the devil.

"That has never been of concern to you before, my dear. Why should you start?" Vivienne asks, showing her teeth in a wide grin that can only be described as hungry.

"I fear we have gotten off on the wrong foot—"

"Oh, you dear mortal child. We have gotten off on the wrong plane of existence," says Vivienne. "But that is neither here nor there. Our mutual affection for Worth Goodwin keeps me from gutting you on these very steps and scattering your entrails from here to the Bowery. It would make such a lovely contrast against the snow."

The threat is not idle, and Christabel can taste her fear on her tongue. She breathes deep into her belly, urging her heart to calm. It's a practice she learned as a young child when her mother would parade her out in front of the scarier neighbors in Sleepy Hollow. *Never let them sense your fear*, she told Christabel, *for they hunger for it.*

She must admit, however, that she has never seen a creature quite the like of Vivienne du Lac. The very air around her crackles as if infused with ice crystals. Though she is naked for all intents and purposes, there is not a single line of her out of place. Her nudity is, in some strange way, precisely appropriate.

"May I come in?" Christabel asks when Vivienne does not.

Vivienne gives no verbal agreement but tosses her head with a clear lack of concern. Since she does not bother to close the door in her face, Christabel assumes that she is to follow her into the house.

The cavernous mansion is very dark, very damp, and very cold. Unlike the other great houses in the area, Christabel hears no indication of movement: no clanking of plates and cups, no sweeping of floors. A cold blue light illuminates the path around Vivienne's feet, just enough to ensure that Christabel doesn't fall into an errant piece of furniture or accidentally molest a statue.

At last they come to a room with a red carpet and red velvet walls lit by a series of brass lamps. Christabel recalls similar decoration in one of the rooms in Kiquit, but it's hard to remember. After a while all the opulence blurs together. Coming from relatively simple means herself, such excess is distasteful.

Vivienne, still avoiding any mention of her lack of clothing, arranges herself on the sofa and begins to comb her hair. It is such a simple action, yet both inappropriate and perfectly orchestrated that all Christabel can do is stare at her for a while.

"You know I could have Worth if I wanted," Vivienne says. Her strange, icy eyes don't meet Christabel's, but instead stare off as she pulls the teeth of the comb through her hair. They look like little bony fingers.

"I don't doubt it," Christabel says, "but I believe you are mistaken. Worth and I... we were courting, for a time, but it became quite apparent to me that I would not be able to provide for him in the way that he needs."

The creature stops her meticulous combing and turns to face Christabel, her eyes unblinking.

"Provide for him? Why, he isn't some winsome waif with nowhere to go," Vivienne says. "He's quite capable."

"He's still mourning Yvan," Christabel says softly. "And you. You know that, too, I think."

It's hard to say these things out loud because, of course, she loves Worth Goodwin. From the moment they met, he implied as much: people have a habit for falling in love with him; it's just his nature. At first, she didn't understand what he meant, but in time, the pieces started to come together.

The admission, however, does not register any emotion or physical change in the sylph. She stands in one fluid motion, the silk dress pouring down her form with a whisper across her cold skin. Christabel knows it's cold without touching it, though she isn't sure exactly how. Being around the sylph makes her tired, drowsy, as if she's had a little too much wine.

Slowly, slowly, Vivienne approaches Christabel. She's a good head taller than her, and when they are toe to toe, she must look down, her hair curtained around her angular face. She looks more like a tree than a person in that moment, some machination of fauna and shadow. Vivienne stares Christabel down, saying nothing. She breathes long, soft breaths, more like half whispers.

Christabel is transfixed; she can see the power in Vivienne, sense it in her bones. Yet there is enough within her to resist.

Vivienne stretches out one long finger, her smooth nail tracing a line down Christabel's cheek and then withdrawing sharply.

"Who are you?" the sylph asks.

Christabel blushes, her guard suddenly crumbling. "I am but myself," she says, taking a step back.

"But do you even know who that is?"

"I… don't know what you mean."

"Don't you?" Vivienne asks with a light laugh. Whatever she has seen in Christabel has given her a lively glow about the cheeks. "I could taste you and find out."

"I should be going," Christabel says, wondering how on earth it has gotten so late. "The coach will be wondering where I've gone off to."

"Do you think you'll have the fortitude to survive tomorrow?" Vivienne asks, returning to her chaise. In a moment, she resumes brushing her hair, looking as intentional as a painting.

"I promise to do my part. Your help is much appreciated, but you must understand we also have a contingency plan. If things go awry…"

"They won't," Vivienne says simply. "Or at least, not on our account."

With this last word, her eyes flick back to Christabel.

Then the sylph says, "You may go."

And Christabel does.

BEAUTIFUL TERRORS

"The dress is simple because you are simple," says Vivienne, standing before Worth, Barqan, and Nerissa on the evening of the Rockefeller gala.

By the measure of any other eyes than hers, the dress is far from simple. The design looks painted on by hand, watercolors splashing across silk in green and blue hues blending into one another in an almost organic frenzy. The material is gauzy and shimmering, shot through with streaks of silver. The edges are trimmed in a sharp, delicate lace edge, vanishing to points like teeth at their peaks. And there is a series of buttons, polished mother of pearl, which is the simplest portion of the outfit.

Nerissa supposes, by Vivienne's standards, the resulting gown is plain in that it is absent of much embellishment beyond the pattern and material.

"In the off chance that we need to use Barqan's full form," Vivienne explains, "you will need full range of movement."

"The last time I was freed, I ate an entire brothel. Sad little stringy things, I recall," the djinni says, almost wistfully. "I do hope your plan works. This design may not be enough."

"It is all we have," Vivienne says. "And I've adapted one for myself, as well."

"We could run away," Nerissa says. "Slightly less messy, I'd think."

"We could," Worth says, "but that would only delay the inevitable."

"But at what cost?" Nerissa asks, thinking again of Christabel and her beautiful starlit eyes, and wondering if they aren't all simply bewitched by a talented human being. How ironic.

"We need to find out what happened to Yvan," says Vivienne, looking pointedly at Worth, for the first time her eyes hinting at pity there. Then she looks at Nerissa, and there is actually hurt registering in her face. Shame, perhaps. It is only a moment, but enough to make Nerissa's heart leap at the thought. "So it doesn't happen to any one of you."

Ah, that last bit. It cuts sharper for the fact that it came upon the edge of hope. Nerissa is reminded, yet again, that Vivienne desires to be human, to be accepted. And more and more she is building walls between them: so it doesn't happen to any one of *you*. Not us.

Worth hears it, too, judging by the set of his jaw. It's why they've had to have their own plan in all this business. They cannot rely on Vivienne, not with her plans to take the journal; they cannot trust their lives—and the lives of the guests—to her whims.

It is why Barqan is so important. And why Nerissa must, at last, let him go. For she knows the words, and she has known for some time. But she had been hoping to save it for the right moment, that time when it would be a gift to Vivienne, a peace offering. A present. Except the longer that she held on to the knowledge that she could free the djinni, the less she believed that Vivienne wanted him gone in the first place.

And it is so difficult to find a good footman these days, anyway. At least he is good at that job.

"You're all clear on the agenda, then?" Vivienne asks. She has never taken the lead on an assignment before, always preferring to stay in and keep blood off her dress, but Nerissa has to admit—in spite of her rising anger—that she's got a knack for it.

Vivienne walks back and forth before them, her skirts swishing at her feet as she paces, her hands clasped behind her back. Every bit the commander.

She pauses to look Barqan in the face. His eyes smolder, and for a moment, Nerissa glimpses the monster beneath. "My friend, if we are successful, I swear on all my past loves that I will find the key to your freedom."

Is Nerissa imagining things, or does the djinni glance her way for a brief moment? Is he aware of her thinking?

The lamia's thoughts come short, however, when Vivienne stops before her, cupping Nerissa's cheek in her long, cold fingers. Every scale on Nerissa's body comes to attention—each one tuned to sense changes in temperature and humidity—as the sylph reaches out to her. It is the most intimate they have been in an age, and seeing her so close now, all else in the world fades to the merest touch.

And in Vivienne's eyes...

Pity.

It is worse than hatred. It is worse than anger. It is rejection on the harshest of terms.

"When this is over," Nerissa says, just as Vivienne moves on to Worth. "I'm leaving."

"I know," Vivienne replies, not looking back.

Nerissa hears their interchange, understands they say words to one another about love and fealty and the many years as friends, but it matters little. She has waited too long to explain to Vivienne how she has pined for her; if there ever had been a chance, and now she doubts that was ever even the case, it has long since evaporated.

"This is what comes of silence," she hears the djinni say beside her. "You give the sylph a chance for the dramatic, and she will, of course, take it."

~

Nerissa keeps quiet in the brougham as they approach Rockwood, avoiding looking across the seat to Vivienne. Barqan and Worth are in another carriage, likely ensconced in the same deep quiet. She has never known them to endure one another long, but given the circumstances...

"You look lovely, Nerissa," Vivienne says softly. "I just wanted to tell you that."

Nerissa fumes inwardly, then cools. Waves of love and hate wash over her in direct dissonance to one another. She says, with effort, "Thank you."

"You're still mad at me."

"I *said* thank you."

"You're never grateful unless under extreme duress or all-encompassing rage," Vivienne points out.

That is a valid point.

"And you don't compliment me unless I look human," Nerissa replies.

It's another hurtful truth, but at this point, what matter is it? She's already riddled with barbs from the sylph.

"You never show me anything other than human," Vivienne replies, smoothing the fur about her collar with an errant hand. "It's hard to remember these days that you are anything but a woman, if slightly more frazzled and less put together than the average."

The two women fall into this kind of discussion, or used to, quite often. It is a comfortable tension between them, the silences between words full of other modes of communication far too complex to manage in the limited language of the English. No, that is not fair: no language, living or dead, could come close to satisfying this interchange; it is best left off the pages, for every attempt to do otherwise merely adds to the mire.

They do not apologize. They do not make amends. They simply recognize in one another faults too deep to ignore. It is a stalemate of enormous proportions, neither creature willing to bend or move to the side for the other. The lamia does not profess her love for the sylph, and the sylph does not let open even the slightest indication she might return the feeling.

"I suppose that is that, then," Vivienne says, taking one last glance in her mirror compact to check her face. The color of her lips is blood red, but not a line out of place.

"Be careful that you're not too confident," Nerissa warns as the brougham comes to a stop. "Lives are at stake."

"When we're involved, lives are always at stake. It's only a matter of precision and self-control."

These are the very words Vivienne first spoke to Nerissa, finding the lamia glutting herself on diseased soldiers in a bog. She had seemed so poised, so full of control, yet bubbling with power just below the surface. The sylph promised to help Nerissa rise to a better calling, a place reached by ethics and her duty as a long-lived creature, not governed by a continual thirst for blood and entrails.

It took a long time to wean herself off the entrails. And now, Nerissa watches Vivienne across the way and wonders if this is where it all ends. If all those broken, beautiful, delightfully flawed parts of their relationship are about to end.

The wind swirls the dusty snow from the eaves of the immense home, passing back and forth in the lit lanterns and electric lights like pulverized diamonds. Yet, somehow, Nerissa feels it is colder within the walls of the carriage.

~

V ivienne never had a mother that she can remember. The entire concept of a mother, or indeed of having children, is a foreign one to her. She has seen innumerable births in her tenure upon this earth, and she has always had respect for mothers and motherhood, but never felt drawn to it.

Yet, as she scales the steps of Rockwood, she finds herself thinking about children. Specifically, if she or Nerissa could ever have them. Do lamias hatch from eggs? It would make some amount of sense. Perhaps they are born half-formed, squirming from their waists down like baby snakes.

Worth had brought up childrearing once, but Vivienne had laughed at him and then tackled him again, playing with his tongues the way she knew would shut him up without argument. Had he truly wanted children with her? Was that why he left? Could two beings of such natures even procreate? Is that what Nerissa wanted?

Even the appearance of Mrs. Dunnett, leaning over so far her breasts are one whisper away from abandoning her corset altogether, does nothing to brighten her spirits. Usually it would send her into such fits of joy that she would spend at least a half hour recounting the absurdity.

She hasn't made up her mind about tonight. If she stumbles upon a cure, some way to rid herself of her abilities, her essence, she would very much like to see what happens. Barqan and Worth have warned her of the danger: such a combination of conjuration and alchemy could kill her outright. Though not a mortal by standard definition, all creatures and monsters can die given the right circumstances.

"Why, Lady du Lac," Mrs. Dunnett says, coming up sharply, her gelatinous orbs settling back into place. "I'm glad to see you here. I wanted to thank you for the suggestion of Master Pinkering; he's done such lovely work on my dress, and I had no luck until you made mention of him, and…"

Mrs. Dunnett drones on as they walk together into Rockwood, and Vivienne doesn't notice the myriad decorations or the lovely draperies at all. Instead, she is wondering why in the world she ever looked for the approval of a woman like this. How beneath her it is to do so. And why she should even bother saving such a person.

~

The soiree commences. Worth and Nerissa and Vivienne blend into the gathering crowd with ease, over a thousand years of talent between the three of them, and spend the first hour enjoying hors d'oeuvres and wine, making small talk, and in the case of the lamia, enumerating a mental list of who she will eat first if this all goes badly. One must have an exit plan, after all.

Vivienne finds it most difficult to enjoy herself, the impending doom notwithstanding, and she is at a crossroads of conscience. Vivienne is not without depth; it must be stressed that her life as it is has been so much longer than the span of the average lifetime. Once her adherence to the old art of alchemy was as fickle as her love of fashion and culture now. One must reinvent oneself many times over, after all, to make the passing of the years more tolerable.

She watches the soirée as if from a distance, no longer focusing on which dandy to entice or win over. She takes no notice of the high-ranking politicians and military officials. Vivienne is thinking of two things and two things alone: her alchemical journal and the impending arrival of the beast.

"I call it the Beast of Tarrytown," comes a voice behind her, as if knowing her thoughts.

Vivienne startles to see Christabel Crane beside her, bedecked in a dress white as snow, casting the young woman's skin in a kind of pearlescent contrast. Her piles of pale hair have been arranged most fetchingly, and Vivienne cannot help but feel both pale in comparison and envious of the woman's style.

"You do, do you?" Vivienne asks, collecting herself as much as possible. "And what do you think it is?"

"A hunter. No, a hunger. I've been studying this a long time, though I may seem young to you. I believe it is a kind of collective Aberrant."

"Have you told Worth your theory?"

"I have. But he is doubtful of my thinking on the matter because he believes the work he did with Ms. Waldemar to be complete."

Vivienne glances across the room at Worth, who is dancing with a young woman dressed in a green gown two winters out of fashion. Must be one of the poor Monterose girls.

"And thereby negating all the work we did," Vivienne finishes. "It would be very difficult for someone like Worth to accept. He takes the burden of the world upon himself; he always has."

"A martyr, yes. In many things," Christabel says with a sigh. "I only hope that when all of this is over, he can forgive me for dragging him into this business. Though the arrangement was mutual, he has much more to lose."

"We have our plan," Vivienne says. "I am confident in it."

"I will signal you as soon as it's time."

"Providing this Beast of yours shows up."

"Oh, it always does." There is a note of sadness to Christabel's voice. More to investigate at a later date, providing they make it out intact.

"You'll have to excuse me, Ms. Crane, but I have a dance card to keep up with," Vivienne says, and makes her departure.

She scans the room, going over the plan again. She knows that the Circle has a room within the walls here. She'll just need a good excuse to get out into the fray.

Vivienne takes a few steps into one of the darker alcoves and immediately feels the pressure beneath her feet change. Her mouth goes dry, her hands tremble. Again, that sense below her. Christabel had called it a hunger, and now it is stronger than she sensed it at the Villiers' house. It is growing, wanting.

Vivienne closes her eyes and prepares to make a short journey.

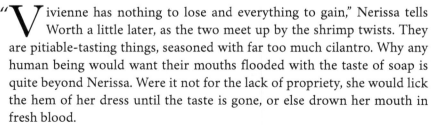

"Vivienne has nothing to lose and everything to gain," Nerissa tells Worth a little later, as the two meet up by the shrimp twists. They are pitiable-tasting things, seasoned with far too much cilantro. Why any human being would want their mouths flooded with the taste of soap is quite beyond Nerissa. Were it not for the lack of propriety, she would lick the hem of her dress until the taste is gone, or else drown her mouth in fresh blood.

"I wouldn't be so fast to discount her," Worth says. He looks surprisingly calm considering the situation and what is at stake, and it bothers Nerissa to no end. She does not get nervous; it's not in her nature or her nerve endings. But Worth has always functioned as a gauge for her to know how to feel. She has missed him on that account, at least.

"I never discount her," Nerissa hisses.

A portly man with a terrible toupee approaches Nerissa, extending a hand with papery yellow skin. He is the kind of man inevitably drawn to her: old, married, and thinking that her bespeckled visage is in need of rescuing.

"Might you humor me with a dance, mademoiselle?" asks the would-be suitor.

"I'm afraid that my friend Ms. Waldemar is morally opposed to dancing," says Worth, stifling a giggle. This is not the first time such a situation has presented itself.

And perhaps that is the reason that Nerissa grabs the old man's hand and takes him to the floor, because she is tired of being predictable.

Dancing with the old man is not any stretch of fun. He says his name is Count something—Fescue? Farthing? She decides that it's Count Fundus—and he has a great deal of money, a dying wife, and a young heir who seems to have no interest in finding a wife. Would she be interested, he wonders?

And for a brief moment, Nerissa contemplates vanishing into the life of a young heiress to Count Fundus's line. Unattractive, perhaps, but full of talents her spouse could only dream of. Granted none would end up with childbirth, but there were always unwanted babies around waiting for the taking.

Her thoughts are cut short by someone tapping her on the shoulder. It's one of the Iapetus cultists, as she's taken to calling them, the man with the mustache—Rockefeller himself. He looks drunk already, judging by the blossoms on his cheeks, though that could be purely hereditary.

"I regrettably must demand Ms. Waldemar's attention," says Rockefeller.

Count Fundus looks genuinely crestfallen, likely having taken her silence for consideration of the matter.

"I hope you will find me once your duties to our host are satisfied. I do think that young James will find you delightful," Count Fundus says as Rockefeller leads her away.

To his credit, the host does not try and touch the lamia. Most men, she has found, are naturally repulsed by her, save the old and infirm and desperate. At least, when she casts her negative glamor. It's another story when she wants to be desired, but those tales are for another telling.

"Christabel sent me a note," Rockefeller says, eyes shifting side to side as if in suspicion of everyone within a ten-foot radius. "There is a disturbance in the wine cellar."

He says it as if he is delivering the news of a dead relative.

"That should be easy enough to contain," says Nerissa, reaching out to try and sense Worth and Vivienne as she is wont to do. Oddly, they are not progressing in the same direction, but rather in an opposite manner.

"It is a very large wine cellar," says Rockefeller.

"I will need our footman," Nerissa says, trying to think through her concern. "Mister Barqan."

"Of course, of course. He will be brought to you post haste."

"And Worth and Lady du Lac," she says evenly, no more concern in her voice than if she were reading the grocery order.

"I have given them instruction to enter from the servants' quarters. We have two entrances to the cellar, you see. The disturbance appears to be in the middle, and that is of great concern."

"Why? Is the house structurally vulnerable there?"

"Why, no. It's where we store our best vintages."

LA PETITE MORT

When Worth arrives at the servants' entrance to the wine cellar, he spots Christabel right away. She looks ghostly, pale against the shadowy stone walls, wisps of her delicate hair moving just so in the breeze. She has ever been a beauty to behold, a kind of exception to her kind. While many women have tried to get his attention over the centuries, she has been the only one to hold it, even if for a brief amount of time.

"It's through there," she says, pointing ahead. The doors shudder, heavy and reinforced with iron. Christabel carries a delicate key around her wrist.

"I'm ready," Worth says.

"Where is Lady du Lac?" Christabel asks, without turning around to see.

"She had to attend to a… quick matter… she should be joining us presently," Worth says, not very eloquently. For reasons he cannot fathom, the woman has a habit of making him feel entirely unprepared for human speech, let alone the complex and brilliant thoughts of his own kind.

"If she's looking for her journal, I have it right here. I really hope that isn't the case because I don't think we'll be able to take care of this creature without her," Christabel says, her voice distant, echoing slightly in the cool damp of the cellar.

"I am a terrible liar," Worth admits freely, knowing full well that any attempt at the alternative will land him in even more trouble. "I am incapable of weaving untruths before you."

She sighs. Her disappointment is bitter enough to tinge the air with sharpness.

"I thought I could trust you," she says at long length, brushing an errant hair from her brow, her small fingers dancing above her eyebrows in perfect elegance. "I thought you understood."

There were many things about Christabel that Worth does not understand. He wants to explain that to her, but again, his words fall to ash in his mouth.

"Vivienne and Nerissa are like me. They are fickle like me. I've spent decades trying to protect people from the likes of this creature before us, and I promised you that I would do just that. I have not changed my stance on the matter, I assure you."

"Yet you allowed Vivienne to leave your sight, knowing full well that she, unchaperoned, will be up to no good in this place. You say that you are like them, Worth, but you have been lied to. You are not like them. They are hunters. They are blood drinkers. You have never been such a thing... you beast, you chimera."

Worth shivers. He has never told her in exact terms of his naming or kind. He had hoped to avoid it, simply cast himself off as one of the lesser Fey. With their remarkable tendency to procreate with anything willing, such a claim is not out of the realm of possibility.

But he is rarer than that. In all the measure of the world, there had ever only been two Glatisants; his mother and himself. What parentage he had besides is forever a mystery, but he is no chimera. He is more.

"I am the Glatisant. I am the Beast, and I am the Quest," he says, and for one brief moment saying it out loud to a mortal is remarkably satisfying.

It does not, however, have the intended effect. Christabel just looks terribly sad, her eyes pinching at the side, making her look for a moment a hundred years older than her tender age.

"Beasts, every last one," whispers Christabel.

As if in answer to her, the creature in the cellar moves behind the door. It is a noise that demands attention, and yet its form is difficult to discern. The sound is both shuffling and slithering, yet like a thousand pounds of sand sifting through a giant sieve, stacking up high enough to hit the skies.

They both move to open the door without speaking to another, and

Worth is momentarily quite proud of himself for reacting in such a way. It reminds him of his days with Nerissa, when no danger was too great together. But why should he feel such a way with Christabel? There isn't time to contemplate, alas.

The heavy doors swing open.

The beast, at last, emerges.

For Vivienne, when glancing a kind of psychic preview to the creature, she had felt a void of power, a darkness as she described it. But we must remember that Vivienne is no average creature. Light and dark are measures quite different to her. She called it a shadow.

Worth is shocked to see the beast is not a deformed creature or horror. While he can sense that its intent is vicious, its form does not match. For all its beauty, its presence is like a rain of acid all around him.

But the beast can only be described as beautiful. It is filamented, a dizzying swirl of strands of light high and wide as the cellar itself, which is no small space. Yet Worth has the distinct suspicion that were they to find themselves in Westminster Abbey, the creature would have no trouble expanding to accommodate such a size.

Upon each long stalk rests an eye, or else a whorled pincer. Thousands of them, looking and grasping. But no mouth to feed.

It is a glittering mass of beauty, emitting the most terrible of noises—like scratching and sand shifting, but on a scale greater than he had ever heard—and while he can sift through all the creatures he'd captured and done in during his lifetime, there is no clear point of entry to categorize this being.

He turns to Christabel to say something, or else gauge her thoughts on the situation, but she is moving away from him as if being pulled by an invisible hand.

Like Barqan, her feet do not move as they should have across the ground. She is slipping forward like a chess piece directed by an invisible hand, and as Worth watches, he notes that the great creature of light twists and reaches toward her, new little tendrils reaching out in filigree and curlicues, a sight both beautiful and horrific.

They wanted her all along.

It made perfect sense to Worth in that moment, and he chides himself for missing it. They all know there is something unique about the young woman, something clever and pure and bright. All the strange occurrences happened after she arrived, which happened to be at the same time of Yvan's death. It had been convenient enough to distract him.

He pulls out Mercy and takes a deep breath, trying not to concern himself too deeply with the fact that Christabel is being pulled inexorably toward a very likely doom.

Then Nerissa appears, and the world becomes even more interesting.

~

Vivienne walks slowly, in shadows, through the expansive Rockefeller house, taking note of the details around her. It's much too garish for her tastes, a strange amalgam of aesthetics, acquired for the sole reason of displaying wealth, and not with the care and precision one should when undertaking the adornment of such a home. It's a shame, really, that people of such wealth hire people to decorate for them—she has been approached many a time for her services, and most times turns down the business—because one's home ought to be a further extension of one's soul.

She has never had a home. As far as she knows, she is incapable. In the same way that vampires cannot bear too much light, she cannot claim any building, land, or waterway as her own.

This is why Nerissa is so mistaken. It is not that she wants to be human, exactly. It's that, by extension, she will have a place of her own. Deep inside her, all these long centuries, she has felt a deep longing, a need to belong, physically, to the world around her. It is why she has spent so much time on the frivolous pursuit of fashion. She adorns her own temple, her body.

The Circle keeps an enclave within the house, and Barqan, in his clever way, has discovered the location while they caroused. With his ability to move quietly and almost transparently, he can shift easily between planes and between rooms.

She stops in one of the chapel-like outcroppings along the hallway, checking for voices, sensing as deeply as she can. Reaching out her frost, she concentrates, penetrating the large building around her, digging deep to sink tendrils into every nook and cranny, to find her friends.

But she cannot.

The shadow below them is too large.

Vivienne frowns, pulling back, just as she hears a voice, familiar, from down the hall.

It is Mr. Rockefeller and the old woman.

"...so damned cold up here," says the woman, her voice sharp as knives.

"How you could build such a large house with no hope of actually maintaining a consistent temperature, I have no idea, son. You've brought the look and the feel of old drafty English castles."

Rockefeller clears his throat. "There must be some kind of draft somewhere. I will be certain to alert the architect. We paid him far too much money to deal with such..."

But the old woman hushes him, and they both fall silent.

Vivienne doesn't have to breathe if she doesn't want to, so she stills herself completely. Had she the gifts of Nerissa, she could blend in as almost anyone or anything; were she the Glatisant, she would be all charm and desire. Instead, she must dig deep into the permafrost and think cold, silent thoughts, reach into the darkest of her places and think like stone and glaciers and...

"Must be the wind," Rockefeller says at last.

"You're sure you have this under control?" The old woman sounds surprisingly vulnerable, nervous almost.

"Yes, we know what she was after. We've removed it from the equation. If she tries to get..."

Vivienne sends little flakes after Rockefeller. It's a practice she has not done for some time, as it is very powerful and highly risky. One flake, inhaled, is all it takes for her to understand the mind of a man. She sends her little minion his way, and through a kind of psychic water bond is capable of knowing his immediate thoughts. It doesn't work, however, among the keen-eyed or in large rooms—far too much space for error.

The flakes look as if they're coming from one of the large windows, and she adds a little flair to the effect by rattling the windows. As expected, Rockefeller himself goes to shut the window as Vivienne slinks away, and it is relatively easy to position the flakes after him.

He coughs a few times. "Infernal drafts!"

Then Vivienne sees more deeply. Understands more truly. Rockefeller is not a bad man at heart, but few who commit evil ever are. He believes that she and Worth and Nerissa are monsters to be dealt with; but that is not his final prize. He fancies himself capable of catching the djinni.

The creature below is not... is... Vivienne can't see it through his eyes. But he is not afraid of it.

And then there is something else in his mind. Something familiar. Something he is passing to Christabel, making her frown.

Vivienne's own journal.

It takes a great deal of concentration not to break her cold spell, not to push the boundaries of her bond to break the man. She could do it, and he might deserve it.

But vengeance wastes time, and if she is to get out of this business without ruining her shoes, she's going to have to warn Barqan and the rest. Their plans of preventing the djinni from utter devastation are more important now than ever.

~

Nerissa has seen strands like this before, just never on such an enormous scale. Twice during their travels in Persia, she and Worth stumbled upon these curious creatures after neutralizing ifrits. She has always maintained that they are celestial residue, a kind of aftersoul, left behind when the body is no longer capable of withstanding the rigors of death.

In some ways, they remind her of Worth's connecting tendrils, his ability to sink his consciousness into other creatures. Except that aura is a kind of blue, a cold but welcoming wavelength.

Here before her, the light is pink and yellow, undulating and twisting in what could only be described as agony. And it's all toward a particular source.

That Crane girl.

"It's always the pretty ones, isn't it?" Barqan says drolly.

He has already changed out of the appearance of a butler, and Nerissa realizes how long it's been since she's seen him in his azure and silver glory. His eyes, lips, teeth, and hands are all metallic in appearance, as if they were dipped in quicksilver. But just at the edges of the silver, a deep kind of topaz—almost translucent, but not quite—takes over. He looks a bit like an igneous rock, if it were six feet tall and handsome as the day is long. It is not the first time that Nerissa looks upon him and wonders what their relationship would have been like had she had an eye for the male form.

"Vivienne tried to tell me something was off with the girl," whispers Nerissa. "I chalked it up to jealousy, but now I see that I am mistaken."

"Vivienne has a habit of behaving a bit unpredictably in matters of the heart; yes, I felt the same way. But now, clearly, we are both in error."

"Worth isn't doing anything."

"He's not terribly good in a fight unless he's got clear direction. I should have been with him, but Vivienne ordered me to be with you. And

93

I'm afraid I cannot go against her orders, regardless of how ill-advised I find them."

Nerissa shakes off her glamor, every last vestige of humanity. It is so rare, this experience, that she shivers, wondering if this is what human beings feel when they are naked. The air of the place is charged with an electric tinge, and she feels it against all her scales, taking in the subtle reverberations around her.

"These filaments," she says to Barqan, "they are not easy to entrap. First we've got to distract them from Christabel."

"I don't understand why you wouldn't simply let them take her."

"Vivienne swore to protect her, and considering that the pestilent sylph the closest thing I have to family, I consider it my burden to bear, too."

Barqan does not sigh, as it is not the kind of expression he is fond of making, but the shrug of his shoulders makes it clear he finds such a promise rather beneath him.

He asks, "So, your thoughts on distracting it?"

Nerissa thinks for a moment. Traditional Aberrants and Exigents simply respond to their favorite food. But in this case, it appears its favorite dish is Christabel Crane, and as much as Nerissa would appreciate watching the fragile little bird be shredded to bits of confetti, she realizes from a strategic point, it may not be advisable.

So, she takes a deep breath and measures the distance, considers the room, and reaches into her pocket.

"We wouldn't need much fire to start this," she says, "at least, a little bit of a distraction. Then we can figure out what to do with… the rest of this."

"I could be useful."

"Barqan…"

"Mistress."

Nerissa winces at the use of the term. "I told you not to call me that."

"I avoid when possible, but you know this is truth. Vivienne is not here, and may not arrive, and if so, your plan must adjust. I can help, in my full form. But the key to these shackles lies within you."

It's strange, how a little lie can go so long. When the djinni was gifted to her, it was the lamia who impressed upon him, not the sylph; for the gift was for Nerissa from the sultan, not to Vivienne (who has always been very much enamored of the man). But Vivienne was so delighted with the idea of having her own personal djinni, that instead of ordering the djinni to her own will, Nerissa commanded him to follow Vivienne. Which is why, years later, when she ordered him free and it didn't work, Nerissa chalked it up to a faulty spell, a different kind of djinni for whom the rules were different.

But to free the djinni—who is unquestionably useful, even if a terrible colleague—meant telling Vivienne the truth, admitting her lie, and losing the very window into the world she so desperately wanted. The djinni reported back to the lamia whenever she needed.

"I don't think we'll have to resort to such things," Nerissa says, fiddling with the flintlock on her favorite piece of artillery. "Or at least, unless there is no choice. Now come, Barqan. Give me a bit of fire. Let's arouse the beast. Then you protect Vivienne. At all costs."

～

There were exactly three occasions in Worth's four hundred some-odd (it gets difficult after a while to count) years that he presented himself fully in the view of human beings. On most accounts, he is given the attributes of animals most feared: lions and lizards and snakes and griffins. However, this is simply the arrangement he most often presents. The truth is that a Questing Beast, our Glatisant, can present in whatever way he prefers, of any array of genders or design. We call him *he* because *he* has felt most comfortable embodying the characteristics of a male during most of his lifetime, but that does not mean he is restricted to such things. He well knows that the masculine outward appearance affords certain liberties and privileges less easily attained by those like sylphs and lamias who are, for all intents and purposes, more or less anchored in their true forms as females.

But as he sees Christabel pulled inexorably forward and senses Neris-sa's transformation, he does not need to pull upon masculine energy. It is too combative at times, too alpha versus beta. And considering the bulk of this filamented beast, he needs to draw about himself something more protective, more maternal.

He takes the hyena for his first choice as his hindquarters, well known in the world for her most aggressive and territorial presence—larger than the males and more sexually dominant—with quickness and reflexes he much understands.

For the front paws, he desires a weapon of massive power, and so he takes from the most remarkable of North American creatures, one he saw many times with Yvan, the grizzly bear. He is meant to rend and destroy, to slice and separate, to stun and overwhelm, and there is no creature more elegant and destructive than the grizzly bear mother in such circumstances.

The third choice, which will reside along his back and tail, goes to the dragon, a beast almost entirely hunted to extinction. For his purposes, it is a dragon of the Northern Tundra, its ridged scales and tail full of venom, and a most delightful secondary defense should he be cornered.

Lastly, and this is always the most important, he must choose something for his head. While there are always four tongues involved, one's head is usually a point of focus. He must present something both terrifying and useful. It has been a long time since he has incorporated such an amalgam, and there are many good selections among the animal kingdom. A rhinoceros would provide him good protection and a strong weapon; the elephant both tusks and a spare appendage; a scorpion would get points on simply the horror of seeing a small creature so enlarged.

But no, there is but one choice for him. It is ancient and reduced to myth in some places, but this enormous eagle of mega fauna proportions is ancient—both scaled and fitted with a most ample beak. The wings are a secondary addition, as well, and combine most fetchingly with the dragon scales. The golden beak is really just a bit of flair, but ultimately, the result is most impressive.

Once he has assembled his form, he rears up to his full height. In most circumstances, this would be considered most impressive, but due to the scale of the filamented beast before him, it is less than effective.

Still, he lets out a cry, fire ensuing from his mouth thanks to the upper lung capacity of the dragon, a green, thin flame that corrodes the stone above them. It is a warning.

And so it begins.

～

Nerissa lets out her keening wail, a scream she has held in for almost five decades, and is both elated and filled with dread. It awakens the true beast within her, which lay dormant for too long. Or long enough. It is so difficult to tell when the battle glory descends.

Guns are no longer useful, and they never would be against such a creature. But she must try.

Her tails leave a sticky trail behind her, but she picks up impressive speed, teeth bared, as she twists and pulls darkness around her. This ability is at the center of her power, to bend light and shadow, and it dims the filament as she approaches.

No sooner has she come within striking distance, however, than she is thrown back into a high collection of Pol Roger 1877, worth at least three hundred dollars a bottle. Mr. Rockefeller will be most displeased, but then again, he is the one who appears to continue to invite the thing into his presence. Having a soirée at his house seems ill advised, to say the least.

She does a brief calculation of the total cost in her head and laughs shortly, just before the shards of glass enter her back and fill her with stinging whir. It is enough for her to lose her grasp a moment on all things real and shake the stars from her head.

But this is one of the strange things about lamias. Like many predators, they find an inordinate amount of pleasure in pain, particularly that attained in battle (clearly one can derive that from her relationship with Vivienne). Now that her own blood is spilled—it is a metallic gold, for those most curious, since it must warm and cool with her lizard-like body —what humanity she might have claimed begins to slip further and further away.

Now, she must destroy the creature at all cost. For all she knows, she may have been fighting this thing since the beginning of the world. It matters little.

Even if it means she is bound to lose.

Vivienne appears in a wave of frost, riding it ahead like some ice queen out of a song—which is not to discount the possibility that she has been exactly that—down the steps to the cellar and into the fray.

She sees Worth, resplendent in his creature vestments, and she has never loved him more; she sees Nerissa, flailing against the filamented monster within—so large, and so impossibly overpowered—and she has never wished another's safety so ardently.

"Barqan!"

The word comes from her without thought, and he appears, smoke and silver and glowing figure, hovering right before her.

"Mistress Vivienne," he says.

"Guard me."

Hands out, her body now unadorned but for skin and a delicate filigree of frost dancing about her more unmentionables, she calls every inch of permafrost to herself. It starts slowly at first, a kind of groaning in the ground, a warning. If you have ever stood upon a frozen lake and provided just a little too much weight, you know the noise. A deep, cold, bone cracking. Except, with Vivienne, this goes on far longer than one might expect in a natural circumstance. It reverberates and echoes, sending ice crystals up into the bottles of wine and barrels, glazing the walls with frost.

On this wave of ice, she moves forward. Pulling from the cold of the earth, drawing from the winter around her, she levitates, her hair streaming around her head like a vast corona.

She does two things, noting that Nerissa's attacks have done nothing but break more bottles of expensive wine—why she had to go from that angle and get the most valuable vintages is beyond her. There are too many questions about Christabel Crane to let her be devoured outright.

The first attack is a simple ice shield. It is colder than naturally occurring ice and far less permeable. Up it juts between Christabel and the monster, creating a wave frozen in mid-crash, sharp spikes reaching up toward the curved ribs of the cellar ceiling.

This works long enough for Vivienne to slip down and grab Christabel by the waist, or at least in theory gives her enough time to do so. But the moment she touches the girl, she feels a wave of sickness. Revulsion. It is the sensation of something that she despises more than anything is the world: pure, unadulterated innocence.

Not the innocence of mind, but the innocence of soul. This girl is a virgin in every sense of the word. Practically an angel.

Or perhaps even worse.

Nerissa is glad to see Vivienne's shield wall in action; it has been decades since she was in the presence of such powerful and showy magic. She is able, at least, to gather herself more properly and think again about causing at least a fire, if not an explosion. Enough fire would help keep the creature confused, at least; but too much, and they would all expire. Especially Vivienne, always so vulnerable to the hot weather. It is one of the reasons London remains her favorite city; she flourishes in damp, dark, foggy places. Like a mold, but far lovelier.

Regular wine may not prove flammable enough, and Nerissa is

relieved to find a bay of spirits to her left. Focusing her already draining energy on healing her wounds, she slithers along the side of the cellar, watching in horror as the beast flickers a sickly yellow color and begins tearing through chunks of Vivienne's immense wall.

From above, Worth cries out, pouring out a stream of acidic fire down upon the beast with a rain of green and glittering sparks. For a brief moment, Nerissa is positive that his attacks are helping, but then the unthinkable happens.

One of the tendrils reaches up and grasps Worth with a silvery lasso and calls out his name. His true name.

Nerissa does not need any longer to puzzle this out.

These energies. They are residues of dead creatures, either killed or maligned, but unable to cross their energies to another realm. And they have collected! Some great mass of tortured souls.

Yvan. And countless others. Not Aberrants and Exigents as she had worried, but beasts…

Conjured.

How many of her people had been killed over the centuries here and beyond? The Circle of Iapetus claims they are the protectors of mortality, so perhaps their aim is to punish those who fed upon the living?

And that would mean Christabel had been set up by them, that they suspected she is something more than she appeared. Because the only creature strong enough to call energy of that sort, the only thing pure enough to gain that kind of precise attention is…

There is no time for thought. Worth is being pulled into the mass.

"Barqan! Your mistress commands you to protect the unicorn!" The words sound small in her mouth, just saying the name repulsive enough as it is. But Barqan does not hesitate.

The blue mass of the captured djinni swoops forward, elongating into a round ball of energy containing Christabel.

And Nerissa sees through the azure filter of the djinni's magic that she is indeed correct. While her form is still new—she's a bit fuzzy on the details of unicorns, owing to her general distaste for them and their scarcity—Nerissa can see a distinct horn protruding from the girl's forehead.

∾

The djinni obeys Nerissa, and it's enough stop Vivienne in her tracks. Her hands fall to her side like leaden gauntlets, and she searches across, desperately, for a sign of the lamia. But she has slunk out of view, no doubt ashamed to fess up to whatever nonsense has befallen them.

There is no time to hesitate, though. Worth is being dragged deeper into the filamented mass, the voices calling his names over and over again, his body twisting into a hundred different bodily variations, each smaller than the next.

She must attack with all she has left. She must go even deeper than the permafrost. She must drive herself into the heart of the beast.

Nerissa anticipates Vivienne's next move. It is a bold one, but she loves Worth. She always will. It is a desperate, unavoidable love, one that Nerissa herself knows all too well. It is a sweet thorn, a bloody kiss.

As Vivienne drives her power into the heart of the beast, the walls of the cellar shudder, plaster dust and bricks disintegrating with the cold, the hot, and the pressure of the place.

The sylph cuts into the heart of the beast, her body a sharp weapon, like a star falling from the heavens. The creature shivers, pulling back all its long arms at once, a great glowing anemone of souls, but then dims.

The voices slow.

Christabel fights against her restraints.

Nerissa glances from the unicorn—just thinking the word makes her skin crawl—to the pulsating mass containing her best friends who may, or may not, be alive.

"Barqan!"

Misstresssssss.

It is not his voice, and it is his truest voice.

"I need you to save them. Then I need you to destroy the creature."

I am not strong enough, missstressssss...

"I will free you when you deliver them to me."

Barqan shifts back to his more or less humanoid shape as Nerissa finally manages to make her way completely around the perimeter of the creature, now significantly smaller than it had been before. She puts herself between Christabel and the creature, drawing up to her full height, sprawling out her long tails and raising her hair, opening her mouth and eyes wide to show her black teeth and yellow irises. It once was enough to scare Medusa, a distant half-cousin sadly lacking in skills of concealment.

"Go, servant, and deliver me my friends," she says to the djinni.

Barqan changes, twisting into a high column of blue glass rotating at dizzying speed. A tornado, it seems. His magic is different, tastes and feels different than anything Nerissa has experienced. In all her travels, none had the acrid tang or lingering dryness she experiences now.

The tornado gathers remarkable speed, and at first it looks more like a pretty showpiece than anything, so much so that Nerissa calls out most unkindly.

But then the tendrils about the beast begin, one by one, to pull away from Worth and Vivienne. As if taken by the wind, they flutter and are consumed, joining the rest of Barqan in a dizzying dance. Again and again, and in spite of some remarkable resistance, screaming all the way, the lost souls—likely promised a great deal of redemption were they to regain Christabel—depart.

Christabel moans behind Nerissa, and she catches a backward glance to see she has fully transformed herself. So disappointing, unicorns. So small. Really not much larger than a healthy goat and nowhere near as elegant as a deer. The idea that one might ride one is not only preposterous but a literal impossibly. Still, that's part of their power. They do not look powerful. Little white faces with big black eyes, silvery mane of thistledown fur, just the barest of indication of spots about their backs. It has been a very long time since Nerissa has seen one and is reminded again of just how ugly they are.

For her part, the unicorn seems entirely unaware of what is going on, likely struggling to accept her new body. Pushing the revulsion aside, Nerissa plows forward, anchoring her tails to the flagstones to buffet the wind. It is getting most difficult.

At last the final tendril is cast aside, and Nerissa sees both Worth and Vivienne stumble—helping each other—to stand. Worth is a combination of a hart, a boar, a hawk, and something else that might be extinct. It's difficult to tell, but clearly his time among the filaments has left him a little befuddled. He has never been quite so out of context.

Vivienne looks resplendent, save for the look of fury and betrayal in her eyes. She is always most lovely when she is furious, and perhaps that's why Nerissa never goes out of her way to avoid it.

But this time…

Mistressssss… your promise.

"I'm sorry, Vivienne," Nerissa says. "I should have told you earlier."

Misstressss…

The spinning tornado will destroy all that is left in the place if left to its devices, and so Nerissa says the words she has avoided since the day Barqan was gifted to her.

"Djinni, your life is no longer mine. Do as you will."

She recalls the words written on the bottom of the box in which he was delivered, clear as day. Only Nerissa rid herself of the box, burned it, smothered it, buried it. She wanted the gift to be Vivienne's. Not hers. Not hers. Never hers.

The words change everything. Nerissa cannot ignore the call of her slave.

What was once blue flickers into bright magenta, a saturated, intense color befitting of the deepest sunsets. Then Barqan expands again, going wider, then flattens into the shape of a disc. Upon the ground, a pair of shackles drop, making an ugly metallic sound, but are then whipped up again into the roiling mess.

Then the room goes bright, so, so impossibly bright. It's a light that burns and breaks, a light of freedom and judgment and righteousness. All that prevents the rest of the house from going into flame and the people with it—though, Nerissa doesn't think, that would have been so much of a shame save for the irritating headlines—is Christabel. Somehow, she counters the djinni's magic, as well as the dissipating power of the filaments.

~

They stand at the feet of a giant for the briefest of moments. The djinni, in his full size, has skin like lit lava, a beard as smooth as obsidian, and eyes as radiant as ten thousand stars.

Now, the price.

Worth is wounded, his body whipped in a myriad of places by the filaments trying to claim him as their own. They burrowed into his skin like maggots to a corpse, and only his quick thinking and shifting smaller prevented complete penetration.

Vivienne is shivering. She never shivers.

It's the unicorn, of course.

Christabel.

Worth is never fond of feeling an idiot, but now…

Barqan.

Nerissa.

The price!

He sees the look of confusion on the lamia's face. She is at a loss.

But when Barqan swoops a long-fingered hand toward them and takes Vivienne, as effortless as a little girl taking a corncob doll, and pulls her through the floor itself, it makes sense.

He takes what is most valuable to the lamia in return for his long tenure as her servant—which, clearly, he is. Worth would have to get the full story from her soon enough, but now is not the time.

"Vivienne!" The lamia is screaming, scrabbling at the floor as if her digging will bring back the sylph.

Worth abruptly vomits, all four tongues experiencing the same acrid burn. Between knowing, feeling Yvan's pain and seeing Vivienne destroyed, he is rather beyond any emotion known to him. Purging seems the best choice, all said and done.

The unicorn has found her human form again, but she is most naked. He will have to show her how to pull a glamor, providing she can do the same as they.

"I didn't know it," Christabel says, touching her skin with her little fingers as if for the first time. "I didn't understand what it meant. The feelings I had. This… need that could never be sated."

"Christabel, are you well?" Worth asks, mostly because he knows Nerissa is not currently, nor will ever be, capable of asking such a question.

"I'm alive," she says softly, looking at her fingertips. "I don't think I was before."

"Well, we've figured out what's been haunting the Rockefellers, at least. As to whether or not…"

"How can you even mention them when Vivienne is gone!?"

This is, of course, our lamia, who has perhaps for the first time in her life, gone entirely hysterical.

"You loosed a djinni," Worth points out, "and I know you needed to. But, together, we can find her, we can save her."

"I doubt she needs saving," Christabel says, blinking into the spot where the sylph disappeared. "I suspect she is putting up a fight."

"Not if she's shackled," moans Nerissa. "They're worse than old iron, he said. Gods, what have I done?"

Worth looks down at his feet. There, the cover a little charred but mostly intact, is Vivienne's journal, annotated with Yvan's work. He takes it into his hands, the leather still warm, and cradles it to his chest. Someday soon he will have to look deeper, but tonight the pain is too deep.

GOODWIN, WALDEMAR, AND CRANE

E ven aside from the utter devastation of their wine cellar, the Rockefellers count the event as quite a failure. It goes down in the books as a rather boring event, for once everyone had returned to the house after the explosion, no one had the heart to dance.

You must understand that these people were not intentionally malicious, the Circle of Iapetus, only careless. They dabbled in magic far deeper than they ought have, and as a result, nearly killed some of the most wise, powerful, and entertaining creatures on earth. Had they known they had a unicorn in their presence, and not merely the great-great grandchild of Ichabod Crane, they never would have bothered with fake tinctures or going toe to toe with our Beasts of Tarrytown.

Christabel, Worth, and Nerissa eventually find their way back to Lyndhurst, and then on the road. The ride is not easy, as the Glatisant must sit between the two women constantly to prevent the lamia from continually gagging in the presence of the unicorn.

"We will find her," Christabel says when the silence has grown too great. "This is all because of me, and I feel terribly guilty. I really thought the Circle of Iapetus would help; I never stopped to think I might be attracting these creatures."

"We make mistakes," Worth says.

"Though generally they end in less despair and depression," adds Nerissa.

"Why couldn't you tell what I was?" asks Christabel.

"Unicorns are so pure they are invisible to us," Worth says. "It is a protective reflex, and wisely done. Not all the Fey react with revulsion; many would devour you or sell you to mortals so they could seek their immortality."

"And here we thought we would give Vivienne her wish," Nerissa says. "That this journal would be the key to..." She trails off. Since taking it from Worth, Nerissa has not let the ledger go.

Christabel frowns into her stole. "Where shall we go next?" She is glad they have promised, however reluctantly, to bring her into their work. Even Nerissa admitted that having a unicorn would speed up their chances of finding Vivienne, or avoid anything untidy along the way. Unicorns are almost as rare as Questing Beasts, and few have managed their study. It is a cold comfort amidst the loss.

"We have to meet with the sultan who gave the djinni to me, or else his descendants. And then we have to trace it to its home. My guess is that Barqan would take her to his cave, or castle, or wherever it is he lived. The djinni are most territorial. It may not even be on this plane, neither in Fae nor the Grey."

"How far away is that? Like New Jersey?" Christabel asks.

Worth chuckles. "Much, much farther than there. But perhaps a little less in the way of cow pies. New Jersey has always struck me as one big pasture. Difficult to get around without messing your boots."

"I will work hard," Christabel said. "I don't have family, and I owe a debt to Vivienne."

"I know you will," Worth says. "Goodwin, Waldemar, and Crane has a nice ring to it, don't you think, Nerissa?"

PART II
MASKS & MALEVOLENCE

BEASTS OF CAIRO

"There are only two tragedies in life: one is not getting what one wants, and the other is getting it."

— OSCAR WILDE

"The hunger of a dragon is slow to wake, but hard to sate."

— URSULA K. LEGUIN

SAND SNAKE

One of the most challenging issues facing a lamia is the weather. It is for this reason that Nerissa Waldemar has chosen, for the bulk of her life, to live in moist climates with consistent humidity and mild summers.

Her folk are, after all, made up of around ninety percent scales, and once the little armored bits lose their lubrication, the result is both itchy and pathetic in terms of appearance. Since they do not molt like more conventional lizards, lamias must keep their scales as hydrated as possible. She is very attractive for a lamia, but between her slimy lips, fangs, scales, and yellow eyes, her general appearance is less than acceptable to most human beings. It is made only worse without sufficient humidity and a poor diet.

But in the arid climes of Egypt, maintaining moisture is no simple task.

Inside the ramshackle automobile jolting through the streets of Cairo, Nerissa pulls at her collar again, where the clothing chafes against her skin. Though the glamour she wears is impressive, too much motion and irritation will make her scales visible, so it requires her utmost concentration.

At the moment, Nerissa appears as a rather plain woman, dull brown hair tucked up into a wide-brimmed hat, scarf about her neck, and glasses perched on her narrow nose. It is her favorite vestment, and is usually easy to sustain, and in this particular situation, she has chosen a riding dress and long linen coat. It is not quite the fashion of this new decade, which veers toward short hair, short dresses, and fringe, but it is sufficient in this weather.

"Nerissa, you must stop fretting," says the man across from her. He is dressed as an explorer, an adventuring hat on his head, a white linen shirt beneath a khaki jacket, and an array of pockets, most of which are there purely for show. "You'll draw attention."

"I'm not the one who looks like he walked out of the pages of a penny dreadful," hisses the lamia. "You are a walking sartorial cliché, Worth. The goggles are particularly offensive."

Worth Goodwin should be forgiven his eccentricities, considering his existence as a Glatisant, or Questing Beast, and like Nerissa, potentially one of the last of his kind. But his personal lack of style is legend. They both know he's a lost cause, and if their mutual friend—and mutual object of affection—Vivienne du Lac were around, she would mince words.

But the sad fact is that Lady du Lac is quite put out. Imprisoned, in fact, at the hands of a very powerful djinni named Barqan. Technically, Barqan was Nerissa's, but she had let Vivienne live under the perception that the djinni was hers to command. So Vivienne had gone about as Barqan's mistress for almost a hundred years while Nerissa orchestrated from the sidelines. When the lamia at last loosed the creature from his bonds, it was only to save Vivienne's life, and indeed half of Tarrytown, New York. But in recompense, the djinn took Vivienne, and the Rockefellers never forgave them the mess.

It is for this precise reason that Nerissa and Worth are bothering to work with one another once again. Half a century ago, they functioned as Waldemar and Goodwin, dedicated to finding and expunging Fae creatures gone mad, known as Aberrants and Exigents. Their partnership did not end well, but through the events in Tarrytown, not only did they re-instate their business, but added another partner: Christabel Crane.

"I *like* the goggles," Worth says, steadying them about the band of his hat. They are useless, Nerissa knows, since his eyesight is uncannily perfect, but he insisted they made him look professional. "Christabel said they gave me a dignified air."

"She's a *unicorn*. She wouldn't know dignified if it popped out of a pie at brunch."

And there is that, as well. Christabel is beautiful, intelligent, *and* a unicorn. Nerissa hates her as both a matter of principle and a deep, rooted disgust for anything with hooves that she can't eat.

"That isn't very nice," Worth admonishes.

"I don't have to be nice to her. The very fabric of my being is antithetical to hers. Besides, she's always so...*energetic.*"

"Her energy and knowledge are essential components in our success as Waldemar, Goodwin, and Crane. She is helping us tremendously."

"Is she? I had hoped we'd have seen more from her." Nerissa does not like admitting that the unicorn is any help. But she is essential. She's much better at blending in with humans, and since she grew up among them—not knowing her own provenance until the Tarrytown incident—she even likes them.

"You mean the incident with the poisonous goats," Worth says in that infuriatingly sarcastic way of his.

"An easy mistake. They looked perfectly edible to me." Nerissa is not about to give the Crane woman any acknowledgement. She adds: "From a distance."

"Yes, their chartreuse eyes and crimson spiked horns were practically invisible. What of the Stone-Tooth tiger? Her quick thinking got us out of that."

Nerissa snorts. "I would have been able to share the same incantation if my teeth weren't petrified at the time."

"They might still be if she hadn't intervened."

Nerissa groans, peering out the window into the dusty world beyond. All she sees are camels, bright colored caftans, and the glare of the noonday sun. Her stomach heaves with the fumes from the engine. "I wish you would stop trying to convince me to like her."

"She has taken very well to instruction in martial arts," he says. "You've got to admit that, at least. And she's a crack shot."

Nerissa sighs like a scolded child. Her scales are starting to ache again. "All this talk of goats has made me hungry. How far are we from the Abattoir?"

"Not far," Worth says. "We're slowing already." The car soon comes to a complete stop.

The local Abattoir—one of many such establishments in the Red Camellia Network, which deals specifically to the more eccentric tastes of the Fey—is a rather banal name for such a nefarious place. As is the case with most lamias, Nerissa must dine on blood to survive. And while settled in at home she usually makes due with animal blood, however grudgingly, it is rather impossible to travel with a herd of goats halfway across the globe. She's relied on these places to get her animal blood when she cannot find it herself.

At least the Abattoir in Cairo is easy to find. For their trip across the sea, they'd had to travel with two sheep, and Nerissa down in the manger with them. If seafaring wasn't bad enough as it was, only two sheep to feed off of meant rationing. By the time they arrived in London, she couldn't tell if she was sick from the constant bobbing of the ship or the lack of food. Since then, she's been fasting for long periods of time, eating only when she can get supplies from the Abattoir networks by delivery. But in Cairo, it's not a good long-term plan. She knew she's got to make a long-term contract.

"When was the last time you visited an Abattoir?" asks Worth as they disembark the car.

It is hotter and drier, somehow, than she'd dreaded. While there is wind, all it seems to do is swirl about and fan the flames of heat. Nerissa feels as if she's roasting from the inside, half expecting to see smoke rising from her glamour.

"London, I think," Nerissa says, trying to recall. "A short trip, but necessary. When we had that week-long stalemate with the ghoul in the tower who was in love with a gargoyle sconce." She looks up at the building, Arabic letters glittering with new paint, and lifts an eyebrow. "It certainly wasn't this impressive, though. More like an apothecary shop. The blood was not fresh, but...I can't be picky these days, unless I start stealing livestock or eating people again."

Vivienne would never forgive her. Ten years ago, she might have considered it, but now, without Vivienne in her life, she feels a stubborn need to follow the life the sylph worked so hard to give her. A life of helping humans, not eating them.

"Help, don't eat," Nerissa mutters.

"Curious," Worth says, double checking the address in his ledger. He snaps it shut in one motion, a soft clap following suit. "I was expecting a seedier part of town. Weren't you?"

That is the trouble with the building. It is *very* nice. Flanked by places of business booming with commerce: a tailor overflowing with imported silks, a bank, a haberdashery, and a garish jewelry store specializing in unusually placed Egyptian trinkets for the more daring set. Such decorations are, if the signs are to be believed, rather the rage these days.

An Abattoir should not present such a bold facade to the outside world; in London, Paris, France, or Milan, such a visible storefront would never pass muster, not with their stock.

While Cairo has always had its eccentricities, catering to weird and wild magics quite beyond Nerissa's own understanding, it is still nonetheless a far cry from the subtlety she's used to. In the decade since Vivienne's capture, she and Worth have seen all manner of cities, and when goat is not available, finding an Abattoir has never been easy. Always an alleyway or a sewer grate or a hidden doorway.

Here, though, the words upon the sign describe bloodletting and prostitution in detail. There is even a bronzed young man standing by the door, gold chains around his sunken chest, looking expectantly toward their car.

"I don't like the look of this," Nerissa says as Worth makes to leave. She puts a warning hand on his knee. "This is the sort of place I've only dreamed of—our world made visible."

"And because you like to ruin every dream of every creature, somehow you distrust it."

"I simply mean that it's very out in the open."

"Perhaps the Egyptians have a different view."

"Oh, they have different views on everything, to be sure. But I'm nonetheless doubtful that they would be prepared to put an Abattoir on display for all to see."

"Shall I check ahead, then?" Worth asks. "Ask a few questions? Do a bit of undercover work?"

"They can already see us," Nerissa points out, gesturing to the windblown opening in the carriage, and the waving figure of a young man beckoning them enthusiastically.

"In that case, I suppose we should develop a backup plan."

"Which is?" Nerissa asks.

Worth grins, flashing his teeth. "Run like demons are in our wake if things go sideways."

"That's your backup plan for everything."

"But it's so *effective.* It worked in Kiev."

Nerissa hesitates, looking back at Worth. She feels vulnerable, and she hates that. "Worth, do we have to do this?"

"It's either this or visit the vampires," Worth says with a shudder.

She nods. Anything is better than dealing with vampires.

Not wanting to think about Kiev, Nerissa rolls her eyes and gathers her rather impressively tailored skirts—meant to give her a significantly better range of motion—and, belly grumbling, slowly makes her way to the front door of the Abattoir. Worth falls into step behind her, and she tries her best to give the boy a warm smile. This is complicated by the fact that she is a lamia and more than half snake. Even her best smiles are no more than sophisticated glamours, and as such, the fellow deflates a little as she approaches.

"Good morning," she says to him in smooth Arabic.

"Hello and welcome to the Thousand Suns," he replies, bowing low and moving his gaze to Worth, eyes full of curiosity. "And you, as well, sir."

"We were curious as to your establishment's offerings," Nerissa says, trying not to take offense to the fact the young man is far more interested in Worth's business than her own. She should be used to such behavior, and yet it still stings. Would that she could avoid all the trappings of proper society and still find Vivienne. Or that she could simply cut herself off. People are drawn to Worth no matter what ridiculous outfit he wears.

"We don't speak of business in the sun," the young man says, narrowing his eyes at Nerissa as if she has just committed the greatest of sins.

She snorts. "We aren't aware of such habits," she says smoothly. "We are a *very* long way from home and looking for a bit of rest and refreshment."

Worth shifts uncomfortably. "For her," he says. "Not...ah, not for me. Not right now."

The young man tilts his head and looks appraisingly at Nerissa. "You're older than you look," he says, as if just coming into this knowledge. Then he shrugs. "But no matter. Follow me. Cook is always happy to entertain guests from far-off lands. We simply must introduce you properly first, and then make a match."

The inside of the Thousand Suns does not disappoint. The walls boast thick carpets and silks, woven in shades of purple, crimson, and gold, and the furniture is clean, well-made, and the scent of wax and sandalwood waft toward them. But there is an undercurrent odor, too. A pulsing, musky smell that Nerissa notices immediately despite the liberal application of incense. It's human blood. Fresh blood. Willing blood. It's enough to make her dizzy from it.

But there are no food stores in the room directly. It is a waiting room and no more. Three heavy doors, pointed and inlaid with filigree and cloisonné, lead elsewhere, but are, for the moment, impermeable to Nerissa's own powers of sight.

She is tired.

Nerissa feels Worth's hand on her shoulder, and she casts him a withering look, but the old bastard is looking at her with such pity, with such understanding, that she can't quite summon the visual daggers.

"We've got to figure out something more permanent," he says gently. "You know as well as I do that we can't find Vivian if we're weak. Perhaps they have access to camel blood. You haven't tried that yet."

Nerissa frowns, well aware of her limited capabilities. She's grown less reliable over the years. Her brain fuzzy. Her reflexes slow. This loss of abilities only fuels her irascible nature, which is already likely to sour milk. And while playing the simpering lady adhering to culture and societal niceties has never been high on her list of to-dos, she's quite aware that failing to do so could land them in some trouble.

The young boy excuses himself and goes through the middle door, a blue and green affair that reminds Nerissa of some of Vivienne's favorite kind of pottery. Why must everything come back to Vivienne? It shouldn't still hurt this much.

Worth and Nerissa do not sit, but rather remain a comfortable distance from one another, each observing the parlor. In the ten years that they've been on Vivienne's trail, Worth has learned to avoid filling every silence with words. He offers what he can and leaves Nerissa to her stewing, which is a much-needed reprieve after almost a century of open hostility. She would almost admit to liking him if it wouldn't compromise her reputation so much.

Shortly, a man appears in the doorway of the third door—the red and orange one—and emerges, rearranging a caftan over a set of jacquard pantaloons. He is red in the face, as if from copulating or exertion or both, and wipes a hand over his almost bald head before offering a graveyard smile.

Nerissa tries not to stare at the fellow, but there is something sticking out of his head at a rather curious angle. It's unlike any protrusion she's seen before. From where she's standing, it looks as if there is a pipe shoved into the center of his forehead, cracked and hollow and rather unsettling. She is immediately bothered and can't stop thinking about the grating noise it would make should wind move across it.

117

In fact, when the odd man starts coming toward them, she wants to beg him to slow down just to prevent any kind of misfiring.

"Are you the cook?" Worth asks, and Nerissa is glad that one of them is paying attention enough to attend to the task at hand. She must be hungrier than she thought.

"It's what they call me," the fellow says, wiping a hand down his slick cheeks and trying again with a smile. He smells of stale wine, and rancidity besides. "Cook is fine enough."

"We don't mean to impose," Worth says, but is immediately interrupted.

"Of *course* you mean to impose. That's what the Thousand Suns is for. *Imposition*. We survive on it. If people didn't impose on us, we wouldn't be in business," Cook says with a light shrug. He coughs and then sucks a good deal of phlegm back into his sinuses, and then swallows. Nerissa orders her face still lest she display a grimace of such disapproval they would be ushered away. "I was just doing my morning sparring."

"Is that what we're calling it now?" Nerissa asks, almost too quiet to hear.

Cook doesn't rise to her bait but continues to address Worth. "Al says that you're not from here and looking for some refreshment. For the *gorgon*, I imagine."

"I am not a gorgon," Nerissa says, willing her voice even. "I am a *lamia*."

"A snake is a snake is a snake is a sssssssnake," Cook says, raising an unconcerned eyebrow. "So my dear mother always said."

"And what was your mother?" Nerissa narrows her eyes, squares her gait. She was hoping to avoid bloodshed so early in the day. "An expert on the serpentine?"

"A peri, actually," Cook says. "Some half-demon, half-angel." He looks askance at Worth, and his grin widens. "A rather curious creature, like our fellow here. And yes. She had a passing interest in gorgons. I'd never seen one until you."

Worth clears his throat. "This is Nerissa Waldemar, my business partner. She's a decent lamia."

When Worth makes no retort, she says coldly to Cook, "And this is Worth Goodwin, an *indecent* Glatisant."

"A Glatisant?" Cook asks. "And here I had thought them extinct."

"Clearly not," Nerissa says. "But we were talking about you, sir. Weren't we?"

Cook makes a sad smile at the two of them, then says, "I'm not what I was, it's true, and I suppose I don't blame you for the suspicion. My business isn't a pure one, but my life has not been pure either. Let's just say someone found out what I was and took it into their own hands to remind me they had a considerable say in how I was to live the rest of my days." He points to the protrusion on his head. "I used to be able to make music with this."

For once in her life, Nerissa truly wishes Christabel was with her. There's something she should remember about creatures like him. A name, a warning. She wracks her brain for it, but all she can think of is that dissonant music going through his horn, and she feels nauseated again.

She could taste him and find out.

Worth gives her a warning look, eyes bulging, before he continues.

"So now you're the fine proprietor of the Thousand Suns." Worth attempts to keep the conversation away from such melancholic themes. "It could be worse."

"I sell creatures to settle debts to bigger fish than me," Cook says, as if his business would bring him to sainthood. "They bleed, they rut, they kill to grasp what shards of their soul still exist. But I suppose you're right. Most of them live. Though the jury's out as to whether or not that's the good side of things."

Nerissa can't find any words that will make sense in this situation, and for once cannot summon an ounce of sarcasm or vitriol. So she does what she's learned to do in the last decade: she stares fiercely at Worth in hopes that he does something significantly more tactful than she can manage.

Worth's nostrils flare, a sure sign that she's angered him, and he sighs. "Now that you've thoroughly made us feel loathsome, I still must ask you for business. My traveling companion here…"

"You've got good Persian," says Cook. "But I know you're not used to such brazen visibility among the mortals." He smiles a little sadly, then shrugs. "I honestly don't know what you are, or why I'm so keen on telling you." He looks a bit embarrassed, flushing a shade of puce.

"I'm of no particular interest, I assure you," Worth says. "Simply a lone beast in a world of monsters."

"You remind me of someone," Cook says, half to himself. "I'll figure it out in a moment. But in the meantime, my friends, I believe I have just the loaner for you, if that's what you're looking for. She's been begging for a bit of an adventure, and I can tell by the look of you two that sitting still isn't what you're thinking of doing."

Before either of them can argue to the contrary, Cook is back through one of the doors again, and Nerissa and Worth are left staring at one another. There wafts a distinct scent of pistachios, and Worth's stomach gurgles audibly. For once Nerissa isn't the only one famished.

"We're always looking after *your* food," he says, self-consciously.

"You're the one with four tongues, and you're a vegetarian," she says with what spite she can manage. "I only have to feed once every few days."

"I hear the dates in the market are quite delicious," he says longingly.

"What did he mean by 'loaner'?" Nerissa asks. "I just want access to a blood supply."

There is no time to answer. The yellow door opens again, revealing Cook flanked by a young woman. She has what can only be described as luminous eyes, catlike and clever. They are like nighttime pools of twilight. She has jet black hair, straight as silk, and wearing kimono of sorts, though cut from fabric of Egypt—Vivienne, if she were around and not imprisoned by a mad djinni, would be able to cite the exact pattern, but Nerissa cannot summon it. The young woman's skin is lightly freckled, especially about the eyes.

Still, she is very small. Even for a monster. Perhaps she knows the way to the blood supply.

"This is Kit," Cook says, waving a dramatic hand her way. "She comes to us from quite far, having run afoul of Heqet a few years ago. A bit of a mischief-maker but should do the trick."

Nerissa understands this situation slowly, the pieces falling together. "She is a… not a mortal."

"Of course she isn't a mortal," Cook says with a laugh. "What kind of place do you think this is? We don't deal in mortal bodies."

"I just need food," Nerissa says, trying hard to keep the growl from her voice while ignoring the look of sheer amusement in Kit's eyes. "I don't want…a…a person."

"I can catch you food," the young woman says. "Or serve as your meal. It doesn't bother me either way."

"It *should*," Worth intones, clearly discomfited by the whole business.

"It bothers *me*," Nerissa says, which is not entirely true. "I wanted access to a blood network."

"The vampires deal in blood, and they've got quite the stranglehold. I deal in a bit of a loophole," Cook says. He ponders for a second, then says, "You said you wanted food, not fun, unless I'm mistaken."

"Food," Worth and Nerissa say at once.

"Good, well, I won't lie to you—she's trouble in her way. But she won't run away, and bleeding doesn't bother her," says Cook, as if this is a selling point. "But she should be able to run food errands for you whenever you need. Tireless little thing."

Worth blinks eight times in succession, perhaps twice for each pair of eyes beneath his glamour, and he shudders. "I honestly don't know what to make of this."

"They come from a far away, our guests," Cook says to Kit. "They have to live in secret, hiding in dark corridors, fighting one another just to keep alive. I know they've come a very long way, and they've run out of warm bodies. They do not mean to be insulting."

"That's not our aim," Worth tries.

Kit grins, leaning forward on the balls of her feet. "I'm a very skilled person," she says. "In ways you can't imagine."

"Skilled enough that you landed yourself *here*," Worth says.

Kit tilts her head one way, then another, as if trying to size Worth up. "For someone with so many brains, you are a very concrete thinker."

"I like her," Nerissa says, and then hears a dissonant chorus of music lift around her, and she decides that having a person like this isn't such a bad idea after all.

KITH AND KIN

orth can't say how the transaction went about, but now they are in possession of a *kitsune*, a trickster creature of Japanese origin, and are standing outside of the Thousand Suns with a contract for her servitude.

What would Vivienne say to this? She would be appalled. Worth shrinks back from the thought, as if his old paramour stood by him now, judging him with her starry eyes. He is well aware that they have suffered some enchantment at the hands of the creature named Cook.

Vivienne would never have let them set foot in the Thousand Suns. But she is, for all intents and purposes, gone from their lives. They have looked for her every step of the way, finding their own set of adventures and helping round up more Aberrants and Exigents—monsters gone wild for one reason or another and threatening both mortals and the Fae—but the clues of her disappearance are few and far between. Barqan is older and wiser than any living creature they've hunted and has evaded most of their attempts at finding clues. And now they're both quite certain that the old djinni is simply playing them for fools, planting false evidence, and laughing behind the doors of some ancient fortress as he watches them from a distance.

Travel is slow because Nerissa has refused human blood at every turn, but their work has slowed, as well. They both know they can't risk forgetting things. Ten years has gone by far too fast, and while Vivienne is long-lived, she is not impervious to pain or to madness. Every day she is imprisoned makes finding her and freeing her even harder.

The strange thing is, macabre feeding habits aside, Worth has grown to like Nerissa, even depend on her. While they were colleagues in years past, it was a strictly professional arrangement. Their bond was in destroying monsters with skill and panache, but once off the field of battle, they had little to talk about.

He could never call what he feels for Nerissa love because, on every level known to him, she is repulsive. But he has a deep, abiding respect for her. The way her mind works. The way she fights. Her strategy in approaching things. She is never of two minds on anything. In every way that Worth is tentative, shy, reserved, she is sure, forward, and clear.

Besides, she reminds him of Vivienne. And try as he might, he can never get the sylph out of his mind entirely. Not even with Christabel around. As fraught as the love between he and Vivienne—and despite the fact that Nerissa's hearts, however unrequited, would always be turned toward Vivienne—he cannot help but be fueled by it. Perhaps that is why he and Nerissa can communicate with scarcely a word between them at this point. They have Vivienne in common, and more specifically, that unreflecting love.

And knowing Nerissa so well is largely why he is so worried. In particular, how a creature named Cook enchanted them into taking Kit. That's his only explanation for what happened, and not for the first time he wishes he had insisted Christabel come along. Enchantments are not his strong suit.

"I haven't the faintest idea what I'm supposed to do with a…whatever she is," Nerissa says, shielding her eyes and shrinking back into her high-collared blouse.

They are awaiting Kit and her things. Al is helping her within. Worth has only a vague memory of agreeing to the transaction, but each signed a contract for the *kitsune* and provided payment: seven silver coins, a vial of each of their blood, and signatures. Kit is theirs for six weeks.

"She's a *slave*," Worth says, hating the taste of the word. Inwardly, he cringes, the bestial parts of him all too familiar with those who would claim him as their own. His whole life he's been treated as a prize, as chattel. He was told, very early on in his life, by the shadowy figure of the woman he presumed to be his mother, that he would be hunted all his life. And it has mostly proved true.

"She's…" Nerissa tries to find a word, but falters, pulling at the scarf tie over her hat. Too much sun makes her skin flake, and that breaks down her glamour. Like Worth, in order to walk among mortals, she must constantly construct a human appearance. But even those have limitations.

"I'm closer to being free, if that's of any help," comes Kit's voice from behind them both.

Nerissa and Worth swing around to see her standing with a small red suitcase on the other side of the street, coming into view as a carriage rattles by. She is otherwise a rather unremarkable thing, dressed a long dun-colored duster and a white shift, taken of the finery she wore to impress them inside the Thousand Suns. No sandals, though. Just bare feet, toes wiggling.

"And to be quite fair, you're not my first owners, and you probably won't be the last. My sentence is *very* long," Kit continues, hopping along toward them with the telltale gait of a fox. "I did get myself into this trouble in the first place. I can't help it. Though that doesn't get you off the hook."

"We didn't see you there," says Nerissa with clenched teeth.

"First, that's not surprising because I have a very important, very special, *extremely* rare kind of glamour that lets me hide from even your eyes. All of your eyes. You have so many eyes. Does it get overwhelming?" she asks Worth, tilting her head.

When Worth goes to explain, Kit just continues talking.

"It must get overwhelming."

"You can see through my glamour?" Worth feels panic rising in him.

"Of course. Well, that's not exactly true. I can sense your true being. All the eyes, the wings, the power. It's amazing that you can keep it all to yourself without screaming all the time. I'm surprised you're still sane," Kit says.

"Well, I hadn't—" Worth tries to say, but she continues on.

"I'm sorry. That was inappropriate. I have a hard time stopping my mouth when my brain gets going." Kit takes a deep breath and then tosses her little suitcase up and catches it again, as if it were made of feathers. She grins, and there are a lot of teeth for such a little woman.

"I'm starting to see why Cook was so eager to lend you out," Nerissa says drolly. "Do you have a silence mechanism I might flip?"

Kit makes a short barking noise. It's a laugh, Worth realizes. "I'm afraid I am an endless stream of thought," she says lightly. "But you get used to it after a while."

Worth realizes, in that moment, another reason he's learned to cherish Nerissa. She adores the quiet. They have long silences between them, many times a day, where neither is self-conscious or concerned. Comfortable silences full of the pleasure of merely existing in a space together, trusting one another.

That pleasure may be a long time in coming.

He is sweating and strangely aware of his glamour gland. He idly presses it with his fingers, as if reassuring himself that he is still whole. It *has* been aching a bit as of late, but he attributed it to the change in climate. Now he's not certain.

"I'm still confused as to why we agreed to this. I'm willing to walk back in there and contest."

Kit frowns, shaking her head. "Please don't. I've been in there a very long time, and Cook... well, he is an old creature, a *shadhavar*. Full of old magic. And his horns might be broken, but that doesn't mean they're not effective. When he's particularly desperate to make a sale, he uses them. You can hardly hear it, but the magic is there."

"He said you were indebted to a goddess. Heqet?" Nerissa asks. She swats at a fly. "Isn't she a spider goddess, or something like that?"

"*Frogs.* Not spiders. I'd welcome spiders! And if you don't mind," Kit says gently, her voice half the volume it was before, "I would prefer if we keep discussion of my debtor to a minimum. We are here, in the heart of her land, and while you might find her demesne rather laughable, I can assure you that she is easily angered and very much alive. I much prefer to be with you, able to breathe the air outside."

"How many times have you been...ah...lent?" he asks, tentative and as kindly as he can manage.

It takes a moment for Kit to remember. He can see her doing the mental calculations. The longer she waits, the more dread he feels inside.

Finally, the *kitsune* says, "One hundred and twelve. You're lucky one hundred and thirteen."

This does not make Worth feel better about the situation. Not in the least. But Nerissa seems unconcerned and, if he's honest, a little hungry. So, either they accept that they've been coerced rather unfairly by a *shadhavar* and his indentured servant, or they go back and try to find access to the vampire network.

But now he's seen Kit, and spoken with her, and damn if he doesn't feel sorry for her. He feels protective toward her, though he's quite certain she's a good deal older than he is. It's an asinine thought, and he wonders if it isn't some lingering magic from the *shadhavar*.

When none of them speaks, Kit asks, "Now, which way are we going? And what's our mission?"

"There isn't a mission," Nerissa says. "You don't have to know our business. You're here to find me food."

Kit bows. "Very well. But if you get into a fix, know that I'm better than simply providing sustenance."

"We have a room at the Semiramis," Worth says. "It's got a lovely view."

He doesn't know why he says such a thing, really. It's because he doesn't know what to think of this business, and he wants to make Kit feel comfortable. He knows the change of subject is terribly non-sequitur, and both Nerissa and Kit look at him questioningly.

"Why, I've never been there. But I've read all about it. Biggest hotel in all of Cairo, and such a view," Kit says at last. "Do you know when they called it when it was first built?"

"A hotel," Nerissa says.

"No, a *monster* hotel."

UNDER THUMB

She had a name, once. It was a nice name. But now she has forgotten it. If she has a moniker, it is simply, "Now." Or, sometimes when he is less angry, "Help."

There are bangles around her wrists, except no, they're not bangles. Bangles are a nice way of thinking of them. Part of her remembers that, before she wore them, she would have found them interesting. She understands that this is a coping mechanism, that her brain is fighting to keep sane, and imagining bangles is better than imagining shackles.

Her master is not a bad creature, not in the way she has known bad creatures—she remembers this, but no specifics—but he is full of rage and bitterness. He was not always free as he is now, and once was like her, and while she almost remembers how they knew each other once, she can never put her mind to it. It always slips away like a fish into a shadow.

She is contemplating the scrollwork on her bangle—not bangle, *shackle*—when the master calls her. "Now."

He will ask her to do terrible things or craft unspeakable spells. And even when she tries to refuse, she cannot. She is a string, and he the hand that plucks it.

ALACRITY

C hristabel has been the best hope in finding Vivienne, not just because she moves more easily among mortals, but because she has a mind for deduction rather than action, which cannot be said of either of her counterparts. In fact, the bulk of clues leading toward Vivienne in the last ten years have been at the hand of Christabel Crane.

To be fair, being a unicorn has a rather impressive set of advantages other monsters simply cannot comprehend. It is unbalanced, but a fact of life. Christabel is pure, of soul and of body, and so mortals trust her implicitly. It has led to more than her fair share of marriage requests, it's true, but it has also opened many doors and spurred many fascinating conversations.

Once the Cairo lead came through, well, Nerissa insisted they all travel together. And Christabel warned against it. A lamia without a food source is dangerous enough—a reformed lamia in the streets of Cairo is quite another story. Her primary concern is that now Nerissa is no longer feeding off goats that she will revert to her more predatory ways.

If she had it her way, Christabel would be far from such a hot, dry place as Cairo. She would be in a library in London or Paris, surrounded by books.

She can easily shift her form to reflect the beauty standards of the day, or her location. Now, she wears her hair cropped short to her ears, darker than when she was in Tarrytown, her clothing comfortable: a middy blouse, pleated skirt, and flowing cardigan in ivory. In ten years, the fashion has changed a great deal, but she is most certainly glad to be done with corsets.

What Vivienne would say about these clothes. She would be thrilled. The stab of sadness pierces her, fresh as it did the day Vivienne was taken. Vivienne was captured because of her. Because she hadn't figured out that she herself was the very source of a mad monster's hunt.

And that she loved Worth. Loves him, still. And a part of her, a very strange, uncomfortable part, is afraid that if they find Vivienne again, the sylph will take him away.

When there's a knock on the door, Christabel knows it's Worth, but rather than call him in, she does the proper thing and answers herself. No point in alarming the guests with shouting and breaks in decorum. They already make enough noise as it is.

"I'm still getting used to the way you look," he says when she opens the door. It wouldn't be appropriate to let him in, so she remains in the doorway.

"Getting used to the way I look?" she asks. "I can grow the hair out again. I just blend in better when I'm á la mode."

He grins, and she loves the way that his human face—tanned and freckled from his time in the sun—dimples just below the eyes. She doesn't tell him this because she's been *very clear* that she has *absolutely no romantic interests*. Except that's the problem with unicorns. To love him, to make love to him, or anyone, would be the end of her. At least, that's what she's gleaned from what research she's found.

Worth understands this. But it doesn't stop their long awkward pauses together. Like now.

"Are you alone?" Christabel asks.

"For the moment."

Christabel sighs, relieved. She doesn't hide her dislike of Nerissa in front of Worth.

"You could try and get to know her, you know. She isn't that bad once you get past...everything."

"There is no 'getting to know' Nerissa Waldemar. She is physically repulsed by my very existence."

"I suppose that's a legitimate hurdle. But once she isn't hungry all the time—"

"I take it you've found her a more portable meal source, then?"

Worth purses his lips, and Christabel knows a dozen things in that simple expression, the least of which is that she will be very unhappy with whatever has transpired. Venturing into this part of the city with little protection is dangerous enough. Heavens knows what they've gotten themselves into this time. But it is better than vampires, which is a small consolation. Still, the Abattoir network makes her cringe.

"It didn't go exactly as planned," Worth says, looking behind him as if expecting a specter to jump out at them both. He looks more like an embarrassed paramour than a great, impressive creature as he ought. That bothers Christabel considerably. *He is happier in his human state*, she thinks. Though he would never admit to it.

Christabel forces a smile. "I'm sure it's not as bad as that."

"Oh, it is. It is as bad as that. Worse."

"Worse?"

"You see...we may have ended up with... I think there was some magic involved, and before we knew what happened... We ended up with...."

"Me!"

This proclamation comes not from Worth, but from behind Christabel, in her own room, from a small woman with shiny black hair and dark eyes shaped like narrow leaves.

But that doesn't explain how she got into the room.

Or the enthusiasm behind her declaration of servitude.

"You could call me a slave, but this one doesn't like the way it sounds," she says.

"Stop using that word," Worth says, exasperated. "And stop going into rooms you're not supposed to be in!"

The woman grins, baring all her teeth. "You said we were visiting the unicorn. You didn't say I couldn't go into her room. I thought that visiting someone predicated upon actually *staying* with them, not lingering wistfully out their doors for half an hour before summoning up the courage to knock."

Worth tries to make words but struggles to form anything coherent. Christabel almost laughs. He is strikingly beautiful when he blushes like that.

"Does she always talk like this?" Christabel asks as she watches the curious guest make herself comfortable on one of the divans.

"Her name is Kit," Worth finally manages. "She's a *kitsune*."

"Ah, a wily fox," Christabel says. She has spent her life dedicated to understanding Fae creatures, categorizing them, and gleaning what can be found. Still, the *kitsune* is fairly rare, especially this far out of East Asia.

"I heard you," Kit says from the other room.

"She always does," Worth says with a sigh.

"What does she know?" Christabel asks.

"Almost everything," Worth says. "Details aside. She knows we're looking for Vivienne, but we've kept everything else rather vague."

"I'm still not sure how you found yourself with her. Contracted, is it?" Christabel asks.

Worth explains how he and Nerissa ended up with the *kitsune*, and Christabel immediately regrets not having gone with them.

But a *shadhavar*? This is why she had suggested to them that they ought to undergo more training to better deduce glamours and charms, but they are both stubborn and consider themselves experts already. It is hardest to teach a calcified mind, and neither are willing to admit that she, younger and far less experienced in the field, could ever offer more than cursory warnings or, at worst, paranoid ravings.

"What did I tell you about Cairo?" Christabel presses.

Worth rolls his eyes. "That the Fey is different here."

"Yes, and it's not even *called* the Fey. And as much as you're on a different continent, you're also on a different plane of existence. You are far from the powers that make you who you are, and therefore, you must look with more than your eyes. You need to feel your way through these situations. I suggest that you bring her back, explain to this *shadhavar*— who should be very ashamed of himself for such duplicitous behavior— and ask for an exchange."

"I can still hear you," Kit calls from the other room. Christabel is quite certain there was some kind of vermin scuttling around and that Kit has dispensed with it, but she is not keen on taking a look. "And I don't want to go back."

"Then you, too, should be ashamed," Christabel says. "We have no need of meddling *kitsune*."

Kit curls her fingers around the doorjamb and peeks in, her hair falling in a straight line away from her face. "Ah, but you do need a *guide*. Not even clever unicorns know all the alleyways of Cairo. Or even what they *call* the Fey in Cairo. Though she acts as if she does. *Duat* is the closest, but even that isn't quite right. Because Duat is many places." She cackles, then holds up a dead rat by the tail, asking Worth, "Do you think the gorgon will like this?"

"She's not a gorgon. She's a *lamia*," Worth insists, and Christabel can sense it's not the first time he's had to correct her. "And we don't meet with her soon, she's going to be so hungry she might eat both of us."

Christabel wonders, not for the last time, if they will ever find Vivienne du Lac, or if she will be stuck with these two—now three—utterly unfathomable creatures for the rest of her long life.

ACROSS THE NILE

Nerissa does not, in fact, like to feed off of rats. Especially dead ones. But once she arrives back in her room, she takes Kit's offering. She is very hungry, and there is little other choice within the city itself. After a few tries, she gets a handful of living rats and arranges them in a makeshift cage in her room.

"The blood needs to be *fresh*. From living creatures," Nerissa tells Kit that evening, realizing she must be more direct. "I told you, I used to have a whole flock of goats for the sole purpose of providing sustenance, and sipping from rats just doesn't quite do the trick."

Kit is hanging upside down over the back of the sofa, defying gravity in some strange way, her hair pooling on the thick carpet like black ink. Her eyes are closed, but she's been conversing like this for nearly a half hour and has managed to hold up her end of things. Nerissa is finding herself surprisingly unbothered by Kit's curious behavior.

"I am more than willing to provide sustenance myself," Kit says, swaying slightly. "I don't even need my blood. It's just one of those curious vestigial effects of being intertwined with humankind. I replenish my blood supply very quickly. You know the *kitsune* can even reproduce with human beings? It's quite common, actually."

"Fascinating," Nerissa says, which is not the case at all. The lamia wishes to know as little as possible about the *kitsune* so she can go on with her life after this creature's sentence is up with them. "But I told you, I'm not comfortable… I mean I don't know what you're used to, being part of the Thousand Suns, but I'd rather not feed *directly* for food."

Kit flips back up, hovering on the edge of the couch back for just a second before perching on the cushions with a wide grin. "Well, cultivating a whole mischief will be difficult."

"A what now?" Nerissa asks.

"A *mischief*. A group of rats is a *mischief*. Like a herd—or flock—of goats. Or a murder of crows. They're useful words to know in English. English is a very strange language. It sounds like chewing and groaning at the same time."

"You sound like a natural speaker," Nerissa says, going to the cabinet and searching for the maps she's carried with her since Tarrytown. They have been tracking rumors of Barqan since Vivienne's disappearance, and while much of it Nerissa had to do from a distance, now that she's closer to the last place he was seen, she's eager to start plotting their next excursion.

"I speak any language," Kit says, "with precision. Or else I won't speak it at all. You truly have no idea what I'm capable of, do you?"

"I'm afraid that's Christabel's business," Nerissa says. Ah yes, they were looking at an area just outside of…

"How many people like yourself do you know?" Kit asks. "Aside from Christabel and Worth et al."

"I'm not good at making friends," Nerissa says, which is more or less true but definitely evading the question.

Kit shakes her head. "I won't pry. I'm just here to get you food. However that may be. I'll simply say that, since you are trying to find someone, this Vivienne you keep muttering about, then you ought to know the world you're playing in. You need to know the *rules*. You've already been pressed into buying something against your will, and you can't always have the clever unicorn around."

"Are you implying I'm not clever?"

"All things in their own measure," Kit says with a yawn. Nerissa deserves that, she supposes. "I'm connected. I'm capable. If you need eyes and ears and an extra set of tails, I'm not encumbered by my need for sustenance. I can get into places most cannot. I can slip back and forth between the Fey, as you call it, and go impressive distances."

"You talk a lot about yourself for someone who's just here to deliver my food," Nerissa says, turning her back on the *kitsune* and smoothing out the maps on her table. She flicks on the light, turns it down a notch, and traces her fingers along their route across the Atlantic, to London, and then to Cairo.

Kit is there, casually looking at the maps, twirling her hair around her thumb. Nerissa tries to move them out of the way, but she realizes quite quickly that such an attempt is useless. Keeping Kit to the sidelines about this business is not going to be easy, especially with the way she keeps showing up at all hours with food tokens.

Nerissa straightens and looks over to the *kitsune*. "Well, how about this," says the lamia. "We think the person responsible for taking our friend Vivienne is using antique jewels as currency."

"That's quite curious," Kit says.

"It is. He is an unconventional person. And he wants to avoid metal. So, his payment is almost always in the form of lapis lazuli or sardonyx, or sometimes amber. Regardless, they're old. Old stones in strange cuts. The last auction sale we found record of was last month here in Cairo to a Swiss banker named Claude DeBos. His house isn't far from here, as he works at the Swiss consulate."

"You want me to bite him?" asks Kit, a little hopefully.

Nerissa would very much like that but has learned to refine her responses and outward appearance enough to gently decline.

"What would be helpful is if you could let me to my research while you visit Imbaba. Someone purchased six camels there two days ago and paid with some unconventional pieces. No ties to DeBos, though."

"That's very specific. And I know a few things about payment, so if—"

"Please, no more distractions," Nerissa says, interrupting with a flick of her hand. "I'm too tired to go myself right now, and you seem brimming with energy. I need you to ask questions, get some descriptions, and figure out if they know anything about the transaction. Providing you come back."

"I *have* to come back," Kit says, pulling aside her collar. There are two vials there, one filled with green gold liquid and another with a kind of silvery pink. Nerissa and Worth's blood. She had wondered where that had gone off to. Some minor charm, then. "If you need me more presently, just use this."

Kit rummages in her pocket and retrieves a small bamboo pen. "Use your spit. Or your blood if you want. Write my name. I'll show up."

"Does the magic require the use of this precise pen?"

"No, but it's a bit more civilized," Kit says. "Don't you think? Writing in blood with your fingertips is very messy."

"Very well," Nerissa says. "Go to Imbaba. Question the camel sellers. See if you spot anything unusual."

Kit clasps her hands together with unfettered joy. "I will. And if I can, I'll find you a better meal on the way back. If I get you the blood fresh enough, can you drink it?"

Nerissa considers this for a moment. She knows her brain is not working to full capacity. But some blood is better than no blood.

"If you can attain it by honest means, then yes. If it's kept warm. Once it cools, it's of no use to me, really, other than to make me less hungry. It gives me indigestion."

The *kitsune* nods twice and, with one smooth motion, slips outside the window swift as a shadow.

∼

K it decides very quickly that she doesn't like camels up close. First of all, they aren't very good conversationalists. It's not that they don't like to talk—they do, of course, as most pack animals descended from noble ancient creatures do—but they're very gossipy, and they wander from subject to subject. She realizes that it's somewhat hypocritical of her to note, but her wandering always has purpose. Theirs seems only to solidify ages-old rivalries between their clans rather than make any particular point.

Secondly, the camels are very unobservant, or else so tainted by their own opinions as to be no help at all. No matter how many she asks, and there are hundreds of them in Imbaba, none of them appear to know anything about the person who purchased six of their companions. Or if they do, they aren't saying. The Three-Foot clan asserts that if someone was dumb enough to get themselves sold to a bad owner, then it is their shame. The Last Fly clan camels claim to be utterly neutral in terms of buying and selling, believing such things to be part of a divine kind of justice for previous lives lived as asses.

After two hours, Kit has spoken to thirty different camels and her lips feel funny from having to use their language. All drool and spittle and chewing. Not that different from English, she supposes, but significantly moister.

She decides she's going to have to start looking for food now, and that gives her an idea. They have to bleed the camels they butcher. If she can somehow manage to talk to the right…

Ah, there it is. A child. Kit's relief is like rain on her skin. How she dreads speaking to adult humans. They can never follow her brain. They get fickle and angry and easily confused.

But little children have always liked her. And if she can't talk to animals, those who have speech, she'll have to talk to the more advanced human beings.

The child is, well, young. But it's hard to tell. They are small and clear of skin and body, which is a good sign. Black eyes. Curly hair pointed out in ten directions at once, like a lovely brown flower. Eating something sweet and sticky in one hand, leaning belly forward and watching the camels go by.

"These camels don't know much of anything," Kit says to the child as she comes up by their side.

There's a moment's hesitation, then the child nods in agreement. "They're stubborn. Get into too much trouble. Father has such a hard time with them, but he says he's been blessed to have this job, as his fore-fathers before him. And me, I guess."

"All this will be yours someday, then?" Kit asks.

It's not that much of inheritance, unless it's being measured in dung. Though it is a clean place as inheritances go, notwithstanding the necessi-ties of pack animals. The traffic is good, the stalls are clean, the ground well swept. But Kit cannot help but notice there is a sincere lack of clien-tele. She doesn't need to ask why. Motor cars might be a far grander investment in the long run, but their speed and curb appeal are hard to compare to horses and camels.

She hates when she can sense a change in the world, hates when those reverberations of premonition start to curve toward her.

"No, that's for my brother," the child says. "He's oldest. And a boy."

Kit thinks the little girl, then, might not have the odd end of the stick after all.

"I'm looking for someone who bought six camels a few days ago. I don't know what they look like, but they paid in strange coin. In jewels," Kit says, breaking off a bit of marshmallow off from the pack she lifted on her way across the river.

The marshmallow takes most of the little girl's attention, and she dismissively says, "Jewels?" Clearly there is a conflict there. But Kit just smiles, popping the spongy sweet delicacy into her mouth and moaning in pleasure.

"There are the best marshmallows I've ever had," Kit says dreamily.

The little girl takes the proffered bit and examines it from every angle. It doesn't take long for her to devour it, though. It never does.

Between chewing, the girl explains, "There was the fellow with the grey uniform and the long white beard. He was American, dressed in their style, I think. Papa said it was just another British soldier, but I think he's wrong. Didn't sound English. He doesn't have very good eyes, and he wanted to be paid. But I know what I saw. These are delicious!"

Fellow in a grey uniform. That's *actually* interesting. Kit is surprised, having banked the lamia's little errand would prove nothing of interest. But who wears grey uniforms?

"And you're sure he paid with jewels?" Kit presses.

"Well, afterward I heard father complaining about having to take them somewhere to get exchanged and that he wasn't sure he got a good rate. I followed him halfway to Mr. Ghali's before he saw me following and told me he'd whip me if I didn't get back home."

If Kit remembers correctly, and she almost always does, Mr. Ghali's shop is not far from Khan el-Khalili. Which means if she's going to follow this lead, she's going to have to be around tourists. She thinks about biting down into delicate flesh because she knows, without a doubt, that would make her feel better. Not the child's, never the child's.

"Thank you, little one," Kit says to the girl. "You have helped me, and a friend, a great deal."

"Do you have any more marshmallows?" asks the little girl.

"Do you have any more information?"

The little girl pouts, and Kit gives her the rest of the marshmallows, anyway. When she goes to thank Kit, the *kitsune* is already gone.

VOLUNTEERS

Worth awakes from a dream of Christabel and has to pour a good deal of cold water on his head to calm himself down. It's been a long time since he's known another that way, after losing Yvan to a terrible death and then Vivienne... But he shouldn't think about the unicorn in such manners. It's inappropriate. It's base. It feels wrong down to the fiber of his being.

His gland is itching again.

He looks in the mirror and sees his human face, then frowns. After all these centuries, he still doesn't like the look of this glamour. But it's become like a comfortable pair of shoes, in a way. It's always the first face he makes, and always the easiest to hold. Even easier than his beast form. Perhaps it's true, that he has enough human components in his body, and he's spent so long presenting as human that it feels natural. But he doesn't know any other Questing Beasts, and he was left with so little information.

Even though he's surrounded by his friends, Worth has never felt as lonely. He wants to find Vivienne. But he doesn't want to lose Christabel, either. And he just feels off-kilter. At first, he thought it was the sea journey, but nothing has settled since he landed in Cairo. It's like a constant sense of foreboding at the back of his mind, worry tinged with excitement. What on earth could that mean? He could ask Christabel, but she's told him there's next to no work on Questing Beasts, save some vague medieval texts.

Sulking, Worth makes his way to the lobby after he's dressed and picks up one of the papers. Someone famous is at the hotel, one of those moving picture stars, and he's glad for the attention being thrown elsewhere. Camera bulbs flashing, the air thick with the metallic stink, he settles in to read the paper while enjoying a good cup of tea. That, at least, they have going for themselves here in Cairo. Damned good tea. Which is far better than can be said for America. Whatever happens in transit there is a disservice to humanity.

The Egyptian Gazette is a relatively decent little paper, and reading the news has always been a bit of indulgence on Worth's part. While he is most certainly not human, nor considers himself so—though he is aware he affords many of the privileges of humanity—he's always enjoyed a gander through the tabloids. It gives him a glance into the everyday lives of mortals and helps him understand what he's fought for his whole life.

They've never understood him, mortal kind. They've never given him much but a headache. But at his hearts, Worth Goodwin is dedicated to the chivalric ideal—you can blame his mother, of whom he only has wisps of memory and remnant teachings—that mortals are worth protecting because they cannot protect themselves. They do not possess magic or glamours or psychic bonds. As beings of magic, his mother argued and Vivienne later reinforced, it is their duty to look out for those without.

He's got a soft spot for people in need. The poor. The infirm. The haunted. Reading about their day-to-day struggles with minor litigations and news anchor him a bit. He has always worked to keep peace, to allow people to enjoy the inane daily lives they inevitably complain about if given the chance. They don't realize how precious it is, to live boring lives. And as such, it's a comfort to hear that people are bickering.

He always makes himself read the obituaries, too. Death is uncommon among his kind, and never in such a way as described in obituaries. The short ones are always the most heartbreaking. Or the ones without names.

But his voyeuristic learning comes to an abrupt end when he sees the last entry. A child. Found dead in Imbaba. Choked on a frog. No, *frogs*. Multiple frogs. Seven frogs found in their...

He loses all his appetite for the tea.

~

140

When Worth finds Nerissa in her room, she is waving the same edition of the *Egyptian Gazette* around and shouting rather impressively at Kit who is, at the moment, perched on the edge of the chandelier. It doesn't make much sense until he's able to parse the words right: *Imbaba...child...death...camels...*

Kit, for her part, says nothing. She's got her legs pulled up under her chin, and the chandelier only barely swings with her weight. Her hair covers her eyes, and her shoulders are so slumped she looks slight as a beaten child.

"Nerissa," Worth says softly, then realizes this solves nothing. She doesn't react to sound the same way others might. To get her attention, he's going to have to touch her, which he tries to avoid at all costs. But when he says her name again and she doesn't budge, he steels himself. Well, he can try scent first, and then if all else fails, he'll touch her.

Taking a deep breath, Worth reaches into his jacket pocket and produces a rather ornate lighter. It's a pretty little thing that he picked up during his time in Tarrytown, a gift from Vivienne. She said it was probably made for a lady but that the bright silver flowers reminded her of him.

With a sigh, Worth plucks a hair from his head and lights the end of it. It sizzles quickly, sparking blue, and sends the stench of burned feathers into the room.

This stops Nerissa in her tracks, rendering her silent. But the look in her eyes, oh, Worth is very glad not to be on the receiving end of that. Well, not for the moment. Nerissa's glare is saved entirely for Kit.

"Nerissa," Worth says again. Then, "You are frightening the guests downstairs. And Kit."

"Did you read the paper?" she asks, waving the *Gazette* in front of his face.

"It's very sad," he says softly, taking the *Gazette* from her and placing it on an ornamental table as if it were a brandished weapon put aside for safekeeping.

"I sent her to Imbaba last evening," Nerissa says. She's very pale. Pale in her special, flaky, snaky way. Her skin glamour is slipping. "And *this* happened."

Worth processes the words slowly, then goes back 'round to the actual problem, the one he can deal with in the moment. "You sent her to

Imbaba. Nerissa, she's here to make you food, not to act as your personal clerk."

He glances up at Kit, who has still yet to show as much as an eyelash through her hair.

"I am getting desperate. And the lead in Imbaba was going to go cold if we didn't get there in time," Nerissa says sharply.

"You don't have proof that Kit was involved…do you?" Worth feels the dread of the last question.

Nerissa frowns. "Do I need to? She told me this very morning that she spoke to a child in town, meeting this child's description. They ate marshmallows. Who am I to say that she could have poisoned the child out of spite? Eating marshmallows is foul enough."

"Kit, please. I know that Ms. Waldemar is acting a bit rabid at the moment, but she has a rather soft spot when it comes to human children," Worth says, looking pointedly at Nerissa. It's not something they talk about often, but even though the lamia is bothered by children in general —they talk over much and have a habit of being sticky—she has seen one too many horrific scenes play out to remain neutral in such situations.

Kit shakes her head. A definitive no.

"There were frogs on site," Worth says, going to pick up the paper again and trying to spare the gory details. "That does not sound like something a *kitsune* would do. They are tricksters, so I have learned from Christabel, and they cause mischief among children. But I don't think they would ever go to these grotesque lengths. Although considering Kit's debtor, it is strange."

"Don't speak her name!" Kit squeaks, then retreats back into her balled-up position.

Nerissa wipes at her brow, her glamour shifting subtly as she calms herself. Relief floods Worth, and he takes a tentative step toward Nerissa.

"Besides," he continues, "if she had done something terrible to the child, why would she have told you? Or come back to you?"

"She's been enslaved a long time, and it might be that she doesn't realize how fast news travels here," Nerissa says.

Worth glances up at Kit again. "And did you give her a chance to defend herself?"

"No," Nerissa says shortly. "She just went up there. And I got angry."

"In that order?"

"Well, no."

"When was the last time you ate?"

"That's has nothing—"

"It has *everything* to do with this."

Her stomach growls so loudly that it borders on comic. Hungry though she may be, she's not quite ready to let go of her fury, but they have a point. She's been ousted by her very body.

"Get me some wine," she says to Worth.

He consents, finding a good vintage in a glass goblet. Once she's drained the glass, she looks a little more centered. She isn't going scaly or flaky around the edges, and her eyes are clearer.

"Does that feel better?" he asks her.

Nerissa speaks slowly, the words clearly causing her anguish. "You're right. I was brash. Kit, will you please come down?"

The *kitsune* does not move. The chandelier crystals tinkle just slightly, a rather gay sound after all the shouting.

"She was actually quite helpful," Nerissa says. "I suppose. She tracked the sale of six camels to a figure in a grey military uniform with long white beard and hair. And she knows the location of the shop the seller had to pawn the jewels."

"A grey military uniform? Like a Confederate soldier?"

"That's what it sounded like," Nerissa says. "Seen enough of those in my life to know, but Kit's not exactly the foremost historian on the American Civil War. And I can't imagine it would be a *real* soldier. He was old, she said, but not that old."

Worth feels himself prickle with excitement and apprehension. He can't get the idea of the frog murderer out of his head. There's something familiar about it, and he can't imagine why symbols of Heqet would bother him to this extent. Kit's the one indebted.

"If it's a lead, then we should go there. And by 'we,' I mean Christabel and myself. Nerissa, I think you ought to stay here until you have a steadier supply of food."

"I *found* her food," Kit says from above, peering out of her hair. Her eyes are red. Blood red. Flecked with yellow in the sclera. It sends a chill down Worth's back, but he tries not to show it. "I even arranged for them to deliver it warm. I've told them she's an experimental cook, but they don't seem to care as long as they're being paid."

Worth frowns at Nerissa. Were they alone, he would truly tell her what he thinks of her behavior. But he knows they have both been through a great deal. What frightens him now is that Kit is not afraid. She is furious. She is keeping her distance because she is bound not to harm her owners. But there is a simmering fury inside.

"I want you to remember what happened with Barqan," Worth says to Nerissa as he replaces his hat. "I want you to think long and hard about what you lost the last time you *owned* someone. And perhaps you might think twice about speaking to Kit that way again."

MR. GHALI'S JEWELRY SHOP

Christabel meets Worth far from the Khan el-Khalili at El Fishawy, her favorite coffee shop in the area. It's one thing she admires most about this city, the proliferation of coffee. And not just any coffee. The best coffee she's ever had. Worth is always going on about the tea, and she supposes that's fine. He is rather Continental in his ways. But it's coffee that makes her heart sing. It always feels a bit sinful. So dark, so bitter, and somehow so delicious when melded with just a touch of sugar.

She is almost upset at the interruption because her cup of coffee has just hit optimal temperature. But Worth looks troubled, and Nerissa isn't anywhere to be seen, which, thankfully, is a kindness. She isn't sure she's got the energy to deal with the lamia today. At least not until the coffee does its good work.

"I don't know how you can drink that stuff," Worth says, making a face at her.

"Not all of us think tea is ambrosia," Christabel replies, trying not to notice how handsome he is. "Besides, the proliferation of mint makes me sneeze."

"For such a refined creature, you have limited taste," Worth says.

"Nerissa is not well?" Christabel asks.

"She needs to rest," Worth says, and it's perfectly clear that is but part of the story. "But Kit helped us with a lead. You were right about the jewels, those carcerons?"

"Cabochons," Christabel annunciates clearly.

"Yes, those," Worth says. "Kit did some asking around and found a camel dealer who was paid in strange jewels…" He trails off and shakes his head as if gathering himself. "Well, we know that the seller prefers to pawn his wares all the way out here from Imbaba. At Mr. Ghali's. It's not far from here. I thought you and I could make some inquiries."

"Inquiries are my *favorite*," Christabel says, taking a long sip of her coffee only to find it has gone colder than she would like. She sighs. There are so few mortal indulgences she actually enjoys, and even those seem fickle in their presentation. Coffee hot, or nothing.

Worth sits down across from her, surveying the bustling crowd. Since Vivienne's disappearance, he's been visibly uncomfortable in busy places, claiming that the presence of too many people breathing at once makes his head spin. She knows he wasn't always like this, and she hasn't tried prying too much, but Nerissa agrees that his tendency to withdraw has only gotten worse in the last ten years.

Nearby, a mother and her children pass through, the children's faces bright with wonder as they look around the busy shop. The little boy begins to cry, and his mother scoops him up without as much as a thought, and he settles into her as if they were still connected.

"What do you remember most about your parents?" Worth asks.

"Don't we have more pressing things to speak of than my memories of my foster parents?" Christabel asks.

"You don't remember life before them."

"Not really. I don't know whether or not they knew what I was, but their deaths were at the hand of that monster we killed in Tarrytown a few years before, you know that. I had a rather unremarkable childhood, though I never lacked for anything. I was curious, perhaps, and struggled to keep friends patient enough for my long hours in the library."

He is watching her mouth when she talks, and that doesn't help anything.

As he seems to forget he's in the midst of a conversation, and rather than linger in the awkward silence, she asks, "Why so curious?"

"I've always believed that my mother was like me. From the moment my memories begin, I heard her voice. Never her face, though. I don't know what she looked like, even. Only her telling me what I am, who we are. That I would be hunted until the ends of the earth. But I don't remember a childhood. Isn't that strange?"

"It was a long time ago, Worth. Not even minds as deep and clever as yours could be expected to retain such things," Christabel says, but knows immediately it's the wrong thing to say, even though she's worried it sounded too much like a compliment.

Worth sighs, leaning forward. "I feel as if there's something I've forgotten. About Cairo. Isn't that the maddest thing? I've never been here before. But ever since we arrived, I'm unsettled. The longer we stay here, the more it gnaws on me."

"I can tell you're not sleeping well," Christabel says. "I think you should consider less tea in your diet."

The humor does nothing to lift his dark mood. He studies the grain of the table before him with particular care. It's easier not to look her straight in those eyes.

The silence breaks down her resolve; he can see it in the slump of her shoulders.

With a sigh, she reaches across the table and takes his hand. "Worth, I'll see if I can find any connection between Questing Beasts and Cairo, if that will help. I've got another delivery of books and scrolls coming to the hotel tomorrow. Maybe there's a correlation between Sir Palomides, one of the famed hunters of the beast, and..."

No, that wasn't how it was supposed to go. He lets go of her hand, not wanting to tread those dark alleyways in his mind. "No, I'm sorry, don't... not on my account. We have a task at hand, and I'm just sending us into misty memories of no substance. Have you had enough coffee? We've a jeweler to visit."

Mr. Ghali's store is rather straightforward as jewelry shops go. There is nothing particularly curious about the place; in fact, it could be a shop in almost any city in Europe, save that the lettering is different and the carpeting is better than usual. Christabel is set with a sudden longing for New York City as she enters the store, the bell tinkling her arrival. She's always loved baubles, though she never wears them unless necessary. A unicorn wearing jewelry is just beyond gauche.

But that doesn't stop her from looking. And by her initial appraisal,

Mr. Ghali's store is rather impressive from a wares perspective. There are more modern pieces toward the front, designed to pull in a Western eye looking for a bauble on the return visit. And this blends so well with the Egyptian aesthetic that one could almost miss the wares toward the back. Old stones. Older settings. Rough gold.

"That almost looks like a Questing Beast," says Worth, pointing to one of the filigreed creatures twisted into the ornamentation. It's more of a sphinx, perhaps, but there are some similarities.

"And you're sure you ever met another Glatisant?" Christabel asks.

"Never once."

"I ought to check my sources again. I recall some vague texts by a woman calling herself Morgan Frye in the sixteenth century," she says with a sigh. "But research can wait, as Nerissa is always reminding me."

At first, the store appears to be deserted, but within a moment, a balding man in his mid-fifties appears, wiping his brow with a red cloth. He does not look pleased to be interrupted, as if their mere presence is an inconvenience. But his expression changes when he takes in Christabel, softening around the edges as if her mere presence makes the interruption worthwhile.

Worth squirms, uncomfortable. She wishes she could do something more for him.

"Good morning, good morning," the man says. "What brings such a handsome couple into my shop? Perhaps you are looking for a ring of troth? Or a fancy delight to bring home, sir, to sway your lady's favor?"

Why is it that every time they enter a room, people assume they are a couple? Christabel doesn't even look as if she matches Worth in her current glamour.

Knowing it's best if Worth does the talking, however, Christabel follows suit with the man's half-devised story. Not because she's incapable of holding up this part of the conversation—to the contrary, she's far better with banter than Worth—but due to the fact that this shop, like many in Cairo she's visited already, takes its lead from the man's perspective. She doesn't hold it against these people. They are old fashioned. As much as has changed in Cairo, much still stays the same. It's better if she merely observes. She links her arm through Worth's and smiles prettily, and she's very good at doing that.

"Well, we'd like something to, um, remind us of our trip here," says Worth rather haltingly. Christabel laughs inwardly. Judging by the look in

Mr. Ghali's eyes, she's quite sure he believes them to be a couple having a torrid affair. Let him think it. She rather likes the little thrill that courses through her thinking about such implications with Worth. Her cheeks blush, convincingly, but that is no act.

"Of course, of course. Nothing speaks to the magic and the mystery of Cairo like a jewel or bauble," Mr. Ghali says. "Do you have any preference regarding materials? Makes? I have some lovely Lalique just in from France."

"No, no, nothing imported," Christabel says. "We'd like something authentic. Something old, perhaps. A cabochon or antique setting."

Mr. Ghali looks a little disappointed. No doubt he makes a pretty penny on those Laliques, which, Christabel thinks, are far from authentic. The ones she's seen sidelong look like impressive reproductions.

"Let me check," says Mr. Ghali, going down the long row of display cases and making a show of looking with struggle across his wares. As if he wasn't completely familiar with every single pin and chain. It was endearing, in a way.

"This? No, too garish. Perhaps this one? Oh, no, not with those eyes. My pardon, mademoiselle," Mr. Ghali said to Christabel. "But it is difficult to find something that will not conflict with such rare beauty."

Christabel smiles at him again, and while he continues suggesting various unimpressive and overpriced stones and settings, she starts to meander on her own a little, trying to pick up any clues that might not be obvious on a first glance. At first she is disappointed, finding the average collection of what one might expect. But then she notices something very unusual. It's a smell. And the smell leads her toward the back of the room.

How to describe the scent? It is an old scent, full of fire and flux. Not the sort of thing that would be needed for the current inventory. No, it's a smell that comes from a magic anvil made of Fey ironstone. And only one kind of person would use such a thing—and that kind of person would not be in plain view, in order not to frighten customers. She smelled such a scent during her travels in Ireland, and while she doubts any mortal would be able to detect the sharp smell over the incense, she can.

Worth does as well. He gives her a subtle clue, two fingers on his wrist, which indicates he smells something.

"Do you have anything truly authentic?" Christabel asks lightly, dragging a finger across one of the dustier glass cases. She wants to get particulate on her gloves for later observation.

Mr. Ghali frowns just slightly, aware of the affront. "What do you mean?"

"I mean one-of-a-kind. Something, I don't know, rustic and unusual. The kind of thing that might belong in a museum? That I could only find in this great city and nowhere else?" Christabel says.

"I did just get a few new things from the Levant... Let me go see if they are finished with their cleaning."

Mr. Ghali retreats into the back room, and Christabel grins at Worth.

"A dwarf," she says quietly.

"That's precisely what I thought."

"I'm quite sure of it. And I think we've stumbled into a considerable breach in the Treaty of 1919, and that means it involves..."

"The Circle of Iapetus," Worth finishes with a sigh and a very wrinkled nose. It is abominably adorable. "Well, rather, this becomes their jurisdiction...if we tell them."

The Circle of Iapetus are, for lack of a better phrase, close colleagues of Christabel before she realized she was, in fact, part of the Fey menagerie herself. They fancy themselves as experts in the arcane, but in all truth, they are no more than a cult of wishful thinking. They just happen to stumble upon actual creatures of power now and again, thanks in large part to Christabel's own family connections (the Cranes, after all, are nothing short of New England magical royalty) and her own abilities to sense and understand Fey creatures.

Though she retired from their membership shortly after discovering her innate abilities, all while losing Vivienne du Lac in the process, she still oversees a bit of their activities. Most importantly, working with people in power to prevent unsanctioned magic from falling into the wrong hands. The Treaty of 1919 strictly limited the enslavement of Fey creatures by mortals, and expressly forbade the creation of magical objects from the aforementioned. The last thing this world, which seems hellbent on destroying itself as the Great War reminded everyone, is dangerous magic intended to malign. Besides, such objects created under distress tend to be far from predictable. The outcomes are less than advertised. And it's just more of a headache.

As a compromise, Christabel set up trade centers around great cities, with the help of the Circle, to provide legal, helpful, tested magical objects in case of great need. It is widely believed that her intervention and organizational skills contributed to the armistice of 1918.

Still, Christabel prefers not to entangle herself with the Circle whenever possible. The integration of the force into what remains of the Pinkertons causes her a great deal of anxiety, to say nothing of their work across the continent in Siberia. She does not relish the idea of working with them, as now she stands on the other side of their work as a rather freakish creature with long life and preternatural abilities. She will have to write Ms. Sharpe.

"They won't know if we don't say anything, but if anyone asks, I never said such a thing. I just can't help but think that their intervention would overcomplicate matters," Christabel says. "For now, act natural."

Mr. Ghali comes in, but he looks a little sweaty and quite green about the gills. This does not bode well. He is distracted. Poisoned? A little drugged, perhaps? Either way, he's got to use the cases to steady himself as he tries, in vain, to regain his balance.

When he turns, Christabel understands why. There is a dart in his neck. Delicate and tufted with a white peacock feather, expertly fletched. His fingers cradle it thoughtfully, a faint trickle of blood seeping out between them in a slow, dark procession.

"It's a good thing we didn't bring Nerissa," Worth says, crouching, poised for action. "She's been very hungry; I can't imagine this ending well."

Christabel feels her insides squirm, the way they always do when danger is at the edges of her perception. If she knew another unicorn, she'd ask them if it was normal. What it is, she suspects, is a kind of magical revving, like she's seen people do with motorcars. Priming the system, getting things ready if danger rears its ugly head in the form of violence.

Oh, but she hates when there's too much blood.

W orth leads the charge, hopping over the display cases just as Mr. Ghali goes entirely unconscious. The poor man will have a mighty hangover if he doesn't die from the poison, but there isn't time to check. Someone screams, long and ending with a moan, back behind the curtain. Whether the old fellow alerted the dwarf to attack, or if it's something else altogether, Worth has no idea. But it's too late to consider the alternatives.

And he was honestly hoping to avoid having to get blood out of his jacket again.

Christabel is on his heels, and he can feel the heat emanating from her. In these situations, she's practically incandescent, so it's a good thing she's wearing relatively dark garments. The trousers are a particularly lovely touch, and while he hadn't thought much about women wearing them before he's certainly spent most of the day pondering Christabel's most magnificent form.

No, no. He mustn't think such things.

Unicorns. Purity. Banish such lecherous thoughts. Heavens know what would happen if she were to lose…

Worth anticipates a slight change of temperature and lighting when he bursts through the curtain toward the source of the noise, but what he encounters is so much more alarming and ghoulish than he anticipates that he almost loses his footing entirely.

He is quite proud of the advancements he's made in the few decades between Vivienne's most unfortunate kidnapping and now. He and Nerissa have been through a great regimen of training with a handful of most helpful Fae guides on this side of the world.

But that's the problem now, isn't it?

Worth beholds not just a dwarf—and a female one at that, judging by the patchy beard and steel blue eyes common in their sort—but one that is sitting, chained about her feet, in a chair overlooking what he supposes might be the Fey in this part of the world. It is both beautiful and terrible. And while he would love to spend some more time taking in the sights— the mountain peaks in the distance, the purple sunset, the sighing fields of reeds—he is distracted by the boil-riddled green demon stepping over the dwarf and wielding a mace made of twisted, petrified imps, stacked one on top of another, with an ancient spiked turtle as the head.

Thankfully Christabel has better reflexes than he. She is a whirl of iridescent ropes, a form of fighting she's designed for herself that somehow incorporates the very essence of her power. She pulls them out of her chest, which, he will admit, is disturbing to watch the first few times, and wraps her arms with the stuff. Then she can lash out from a distance without endangering herself right away.

Judging by the howl of pain coming from the demon as Christabel's ropes make contact with his corded, angry, pustule-filled arm, it's got quite the effect.

Worth narrows his own focus and puts his head down, shedding his human guise and plunging deeper into the room to protect the dwarf. Because while the demon is quite angry—and are his boils flashing odd colors? That might not be a good sign—it is most certainly focused on the dwarf. For the dwarf's part, she's in a bad way. One of her feet has been shackled to the ground of the workshop, and she cannot free herself from it. Worth sees the fury in her eyes, though, and is willing to bet that she would be quite helpful if she had a mace in her hand.

Ducking as the demon's attack goes wide, the air from it moving the fur on Worth's head, he goes for the full combination. As a Questing Beast, he has a considerable arsenal when it comes to transformation, and though he typically prefers things quick and venomous, this time he considers that he'll need a bit more brawn.

For his head, he chooses one of his favorites, the grizzly. The maw is a horror, the jaw pressure enough to crush human skulls like eggshells. He's going to need quite a bit of frontward grasping, and as such, he opts for the arms of a gorilla, tinged with silver and rippling with muscle. The hind quarters are a little more challenging because he needs strength and speed to support the rest of his rather top-heavy frame. Then, the legs of a white rhinoceros. Then, lastly, that extra bit. A yellow dragon tail. Mostly because it looks impressive and allows him to lean back and attack with all fours if needs be.

The change happens in an instant, like a strike of lightning, though internally he must concentrate intensely.

Once he is arrayed thusly, Worth bolts forward, a roar coming from his many throats like a freight train through a tunnel. He swipes at the demon with a calculated punch, just under where, presumably, it might have ribs. But while this jostles it, the impact does not have the intended effect. The demon, judging by the lack of give, is not entirely substantial. Likely due to the rift.

In his many years of tracking Exigents and Aberrants, he has never seen anything like this conflux of magic and creature, and it throws him off kilter. Waves of nausea travel down the length of him, clenching his stomachs after he's made contact. The boils, he imagines. They feel more substantial. Like grit on a ghost. They may be poisonous.

Christabel does not seem as impacted, as per usual, and Worth repositions himself as her whips come cracking by his head, twisting around the demon's body so tightly some of the boils burst, flecking his fur. Worth swallows back bile and charges forward, head down. With the demon's arm restrained, he's able to get a little more leverage, but not quite enough to get a good attack in.

That's when he notices the dwarf muttering words of power. He doesn't know the language—it's one of the few he isn't able to compre-hend inherently—but there is no doubt to the power of the speech. Except, every time she gets a few words in, blue sparks tumble out of her mouth and she starts coughing.

No help there.

He readies himself. Worth doesn't relish the idea of biting this pustule-ridden monster and has little hope that it will accomplish much other than a general distraction, not to mention a most unpleasant flavor. But things aren't going well. With every moment the demon lashes out, the rift behind it widens and widens, pieces of the back room and the store going with it.

Christabel redoubles her efforts, using her long tendrils as a base—a kind of glowing braid rooted into the ground—and spins around to strike the demon directly in his chest as it's focused directly on Worth. It hesi-tates just long enough for Worth to bull rush, changing at the last moment to a bison head instead of a grizzly.

The demon howls in a frequency most human ears cannot detect, but for Worth and Christabel—and presumably the dwarf, though the look of pain on her face makes no specific indication—it is as if a series of long notes are being scratched across their tympanums, perilously dissonant and redolent of twisting iron.

Worth recoils, shakes his head, trying very hard to dispel that noise. It's so horrid it makes his nose start to bleed, and he can taste its sweet-ness down the back of his throats. A glance at Christabel demonstrates a similar state, but her own silver blood flows down her lips. Her eyes bob pleadingly to Worth, but he is entirely overcome with the sound and rather incapacitated. What a marvelous team they make.

During some part of the fray, however, it appears that the dwarf managed to get one of her feet out of the shackles. No, that's not right. She's gone and entirely pulled her foot off.

Worth's head swims, putting together the pieces of what he sees, as the dwarf woman twists on her one good arm and shoves a stake of iron right into the heart of the demon. It's a right good aim, and he's quite certain that if the circumstances were different, he might consider inviting her along with the rest. But she's iron-touched, and that's not good for anyone.

As the iron makes contact with the demon, he abruptly ruptures in a fetid disk of jagged flesh and hot fluid. Like one enormous pustule, ripe for the bursting, not even long enough to make the appropriate noise. In some sad, strange way, Worth is almost sorry not to hear it.

And part of it, Worth realizes, is that the rift simultaneously popped the demon and sliced him in half.

The rift vanishes, leaving behind a thick mist, and the dwarf shakes her head, wiping the viscous remains of the demon from her eyes.

ALMA

Well, *now I'm going to need to grow another foot again.*

        Alma Stonefoot has spent the better part of the last year tied up in Mr. Ghali's shop against her will, shackles preventing her from spellcasting. She spent her last foot a few months in, and when she tried to escape last time, he found her. It takes her generally about six months to grow a good enough foot to shed, but probably due to malnutrition and the general piss-poor nature of her indenture, it was taking an even longer time.

But then, there was a demon this time.

That wasn't supposed to happen.

The timing of these two new creatures is tremendously suspicious. One is bleeding silver. The other is such a strange amalgam of animal and human that it makes her stomach turn watching him. Even when he shifts to a pale man-shaped thing with a three-piece suit and a pair of goggles on his head, she doesn't like looking too long at him. The pieces don't fit right. She wonders how he can even manage to look himself straight in the mirror without vomiting everywhere.

The woman-shaped thing looks at Alma, such a look of compassion on her face that it almost makes her cry. No one has looked at her like that in a dozen years, least of all woman-shaped creatures.

"Are you alright?" asks the woman-shaped creature. She's still wiping the demon shit from her face, and Alma doesn't have the heart to tell

156

them what it is exactly because they're clearly even more confused than she. "Your foot...it's...oh, heavens, I'm sorry. We didn't know what was going on... Damn it all! We should have gone on instinct instead of taking our time."

Alma isn't used to being apologized to. Nor is she used to being spoken to with any kind of politeness. How long has it been since she's seen her family? Spoken to her gran? Now that she's free of the shackles, she feels the truth of her absence around her like a stone cloak.

"Perhaps she's in shock," the man-shaped thing says. He looks around the room as if the demon might return at any time. Then to her, he says in his halting, hesitant tone, "If...dwarves can be shocked. Is that insensitive to say? I'm afraid I know next to nothing about dwarves."

"She's a Nith dwarf," the woman-shaped one says. "She's from very far away."

The name of home makes Alma startle. Is she in shock? It's quite possible. She looks down at her foot and sighs. She had to take more off than she would have liked, and it's starting to itch now.

"A Nith dwarf?" The man-shaped one frowns. "I've never heard of those before."

"You've never heard of a lot of things, Worth. That doesn't mean they aren't true."

"I'm not disagreeing with you. I'm simply making an observation."

"It's pronounced 'neeth,'" says Alma, to the woman-shaped one. "It's a common mistake. Most people have trouble with the First Tongue."

They both stare. It's quite comical. Long man-like creatures are always too tall and gangly, and everything they do is out of proportion anyway, but Alma has to remind herself that laughing at them is probably not a good idea. As with most of her people, she was taught at a very young age to stay away from such things—magic or no—because it would ultimately lead to death or dismemberment or both.

So far, she'd avoided the death part, at least in principle. Working for Ghali and his boss made her wish many a time she had the power to end her rather lackluster existence. If only she'd listened to Gran...

"You speak English," the man—Worth?—says with a look of relief flooding his features.

"Your foot," says the silvery one. "How...how are you... Are you in pain?"

"Don't know *that* much about Nith dwarves if you don't know about our feet," Alma says. She's not surprised, mind you. Her people have always gone to very great lengths to keep their talents guarded. That demon left her no choice, though. Something else from *over there* got Ghali, and she didn't want to leave a blood trail. Not yet, anyway.

"I only know that you're arctic," replies the woman-shaped one. "And that you are extremely proud, talented, and private. It's rare enough that you leave a trace let alone have a conversation with anyone other than yourselves. In fact, some scholars believe you're entirely made up by the Qoth dwarves, those famed self-absorbed minstrels."

Alma barks a laugh, and it feels good. "I'm Alma Stonefoot. Most of the Nith can shed their feet if need be—some can shed more than that. But the growing back's the hard part."

"I'm Christabel Crane," says the woman. "And I'm, well, a unicorn. And this is Worth Goodwin. He's…well, more complicated than that."

Alma doesn't know what that is but can tell Christabel feels it's a rather important thing. If the Nith don't know about it, it can't be that important.

Worth says, "I'm pleased to meet you, but why didn't you…ah…shed earlier?"

"I did once," says Alma. "But I got caught. So he put two chains around me after that, and in the fight one of them got free. Took me seven months to grow this one back and now I'm going to have to start over again. I was looking for an opportune moment, and your arrival seemed the best chance I'd had in a long time."

Christabel's eyes shimmer with wonder at every word Alma speaks. She feels both exhilarated to have such a captive audience and a bit embarrassed. The only man-shaped people she's met have wanted her to simply make magic for them. But these two aren't your regular sort.

"How did you end up here?" Christabel asks.

"I had to travel. Had a…" She searches for the dwarven word for it but can only come up with one that's halfway there. "I had a need. To move. My grandmother called it pebble feet. Never could stay in one place for long. So I got dispensation to leave. Then I pissed off a demon or two and got sold to Ghali's boss, and I've been here ever since."

"Then you decided it would be best if you summoned the demon?" Worth asks. He's still picking demon shit from his hair.

Alma tries not to feel offended. But these people certainly know absolutely nothing about dwarves to even contemplate such a thing.

"Ghali summoned the demon, since he thought you were going to rob him," Alma says. "I'm supposed to work, to make items only dwarves can make. I ran afoul of Ghali's boss, and well, here I am."

Worth blinks as if it might help his brain, and Alma has to stifle a laugh again. The man is rather insufferably strange. "I'm not sure I follow."

Alma sighs, hobbling across the room, looking for something she can use to wrap her stump up before it starts throbbing. "Mr. Ghali thought he could summon the demon. He's not supposed to do it without my help. But, well, he didn't listen, did he? Gate opens. Assassin guard shoots through the hole, then disappears. I start making noise, hoping I might get my foot loose, then the demon shows up late, and you both appear. Shortly, the demon explodes because I don't just know how to open rifts, I know how to close them."

Demon shit everywhere.

"You killed him with *iron*," Christabel says, wincing as she says the word.

"Oh, right. I forgot. You're fragile things when it comes to that," says Alma with a sigh. "But that's not my fault."

"I didn't say it was. We are just glad that you're safe, Ms. Stonefoot."

Alma goes to correct this unicorn person, but then thinks better of it. She's never been addressed so properly in her life, and she imagines she might get used to it, even.

"Did you come here...for me?" Alma at last asks, still far from convinced that's the case—her family would only resort to sending such creatures after her in the direst of situations—but something has to explain all this nonsense.

Worth looks uncomfortable again, and Alma wonders if it's just his natural face that does that. "We were looking for someone who might be using gems as currency," he says. "And we followed the trail here."

"Ah, well, you were right partially, then. That's Mr. Ghali's boss. He's a bit of a connoisseur of the old and ancient," Alma says. "I don't know his name. Or where he lives, though. Though I've heard him a few times, on the rare occasions he comes to the shop himself. Had a rather strange voice. Reminds me of rushing water."

"That's not terribly helpful..." Worth tries, looking around the truly demolished room.

"He's got offices on the inside and the outside," Alma says, pointing to where the rift was. "Spies, lots of them. Demons at his beck and call. Only thing he steers clear of is the Egyptian deities. They won't let him in."

"Were there records, then?" Worth asks.

"We don't have long before the authorities come," Christabel says. "We can't be seen here. Between the Pinkertons and the Circle..."

Alma points to a smoking, gaping hole in the wall, still dripping with demon shit. "If there's anything, it would be in there."

Christabel gives her a faint, sad smile. "Well, let's search the room quickly. Alma, I'd like to formally invite you to stay with us at the Semiramis hotel; we're on the second floor, rooms 102, 103, and 105."

This time Alma cannot stop herself from laughing. These beings and their jokes. Neither seems to understand the joke in the least, but when she's done, Alma politely declines. A dwarf going to a hotel! It's a rather thrilling prospect. She's always wanted to try a good canape.

"I've got some work to do in town," she says, pointing to her foot. "But I'm happy to help you, if help is what you need. If you're after Mr. Ghali's boss, well, I'm not past enacting a little revenge."

She reaches down and finds what remains of her petrified foot. With a sharp crack, she snaps off the big toe and takes a bite of it. That will help things along. The other beings do not appear to approve of her behavior, and instead gape at her in horror.

"I've got some ends to tie on my side," Alma says. "I've got to get these trinkets somewhere safe." She points to what's left of her workbench, the array of beautiful metalwork, emanating green and grey auras of magic.

Both man-shaped things are staring at her, and she finds a particular pleasure in examining the ground before her. Then she finds a good place where the tiles have separated and the earth is exposed. Just big enough for her to get under and go back underground. She just catches their stunned faces as she slips beneath the building and into the dark below.

"See you soon," she says, and means it.

DEMONS

Nerissa cannot quite put together what Worth and Christabel are trying to tell her, and truly, she's far more relieved that Kit has started speaking to her again than concerned about a footless dwarf. It's the demon part that has her worried. And not so much the demon itself, but the rift between this world and the next and this mysterious boss of Mr. Ghali's. Could it be Barqan?

And that's to say nothing of Duat. It isn't that she's a scholar in Egyptian lore, far from it. But she has spent the better part of her life *avoiding* going back to the Fey at all costs. There are thousands of reasons she and Vivienne and Worth no longer live there, too many to account in the small space of this particular tale, but it's mostly because Nerissa is afraid of who she *was*. It's the water, or the air, perhaps. Or maybe it's simply that the whole place reverberates with whatever passes for divine magic. But it makes judging right and wrong decidedly more difficult. She fears that were she to head into the Fey again she would likely spiral down into despair and deranged feeding.

She would be the way Vivienne found her.

Don't you want to use reason instead of impulse? Those were the words Vivienne had said. *We have been slaves too long to the rules of the Fey. And we do not have to stay there if we are strong enough to find our way in the world of man. As long as we keep our heads about us. We have a duty to protect, not to destroy.*

But where did that get Vivienne?

The memory of her face, that look of betrayal, when Barqan took her away, it almost makes Nerissa feel faint.

Or, that could be all the rat blood she's been drinking lately. Nothing she eats helps. Since Vivienne was taken, not even goat blood was helpful. It all tasted like ashes.

"We don't have much to go on," says Christabel. She is standing prettily by the window, nervously twirling her short hair around her finger, making a little curl at the end. It occurs to Nerissa that there is no single way the unicorn stands that does not look like a piece of art. Regardless of her particular flavor of glamor, she is always the picture of purity.

Worth is going through a pile of wet papers that smell like they came from a Fey latrine, but the writing is too smudged to make any sense. "This word almost looks like 'street' or 'straight,' but I can't tell."

"You are, as always, an immense beacon of deduction," Nerissa says.

Kit, after a few hours of talking and, oddly, singing, has now situated herself on the edge of the sofa, perched like a bird. Her ears are out, which was a new addition to the glamour, and they flick this way and that as each member of the group speaks, but as of yet, she has not said anything. At least she's not up in the chandelier any longer. The plaster was starting to crack. And the last thing Nerissa needs is to explain that kind of damage to the waitstaff.

"I still don't understand why the dwarf didn't just come back with us," Worth says, ignoring Nerissa's jab as usual. "We could have helped her."

"Dwarves are prideful creatures," Kit says, at first sounding as if she's talking to herself. When the rest turn to face her, she shrugs and continues. "And if she's a Nith like you say, then she's even more than what would be considered typical. Do you know how hard it is to keep a dwarf captive? They would need *eitr*, and that's not only expensive, but it attracts demons like you wouldn't believe. Plus, there's the whole hunger thing. If she's been chained for a long time, she's going to be so hungry she can hardly think straight. Dwarves don't get hungry like we go hungry—they can go for weeks without eating. But they eat rocks. It's a slow process, and intensely private."

"We saw the eating process," Christabel says evenly. "But I thought *eitr* was a myth."

"Says the unicorn," Nerissa says.

"It's just contradictory to some of what I've read," Christabel says. "*Eitr* is like iron. But worse. And largely considered a misreading of the Nordic texts."

"Sometimes you learn more in a brothel than you do in books," Kit replies languidly, raising her nose at the unicorn as if she might have the odor of academia about her still. "It's our business to know the needs of our guests. It's practical learning. And, yes, while it's very rare for dwarves to seek the company of those outside their own circles, it's not unheard of. She would first look to secure her hoard. I'm guessing that's what she did."

"Yes, she mentioned that. Did you entertain a dwarf, then?" Worth asks.

"Worth, that's rude," Nerissa says.

"We need *information!*" he says, waving the sodden papers in the air. "Christabel and I have been out risking life and limb trying to scour for clues about Vivienne, and all we've got is a dwarf that can sink through dirt and sheds her feet like a skink."

"She has a *name*," Christabel says, her cheeks flushed so prettily that Nerissa thinks of biting them immediately. The stress is not helping her. It isn't doing anything other than making her hungrier, and as she devolves into malnutrition, she knows she'll be no good at helping. She'll be more of a hindrance than she already is.

She should have never come to Cairo.

She should never have accepted Barqan.

She should never have hoped to go beyond her bestial nature.

"Enough!" Nerissa shouts.

It's been a very long time since she's used her monstrous voice, and it both surprises her and frightens her. There are layers within her speaking range both dark and destructive, and she has not had cause to use them since Vivienne was taken.

It works, though. All three of her friends—they are her friends, and she thinks of them this way, even if she can't stand them most of the time —look at her in attention.

"I believe we're missing some essential component here," she says, clenching her teeth. She looks at Kit because, so far, she's been the only one providing helpful action instead of making a bigger mess of things. "Who would have use for gems? We've got the description of the man in a soldier's uniform. A demon. A rift between here and the Fey. Now, we can't very well go into the Fey right now. And we can't question the demon, he's dead. And Alma is probably on her way back home by now. We've got to figure out more about this money and this soldier person."

Kit purses her lips and leans back on her haunches as she considers this. "Everyone comes through the brothel," she says. "If someone goes in and distracts Cook, I can take a look at some of the records."

"Of course. But it does seem rather tidy. Seems rather curious that you bring this up now, after we've been doused with demon slime," Christabel says, an acid tone slipping into her voice.

"It was probably demon *shit*," Kit says with a yawn. "I did try suggesting this method of questioning to the lamia yesterday, but she was very clear that I wasn't to distract her and I was to only follow the camel purchase, and that's what I did. It would have saved a lot of work doing it this way, but I was just following orders."

Worth squints back and forth from Nerissa and Kit, and the lamia has to agree. "I was a bit agitated," Nerissa says lamely. "I am beginning to think that Kit is far better served as an agent than a food source."

At this Kit's ears perk so far up they almost touch one another. She is beside herself with pride.

Christabel's face is a cloud of frustration.

"It's worth trying," Nerissa says. "But isn't a risk for you to go back there, Kit? Cook seemed most eager to be rid of you." Nerissa asks, surprised at the depth of worry in her voice and in her hearts. Why does she feel overwhelmingly protective of the *kitsune*?

Kit grins. "Firstly, Cook is an old, sad, tired creature. I exhaust him. I'm forever asking him questions and trying to puzzle out guests, and he'd rather not think about it. As to the Thousand Suns—well, it's not anywhere as terrifying as you think it is. I mean, of course some rooms are. But the place. The layout. The actual building. There are lots of ways in and out. I'm never terribly good at staying in one place. I learned a long time ago that if I'm where I need to be *when* I need to be there, that's all that matters."

"What do you need us to do?" Christabel asks. She looks tired but, as usual, she's first to put herself in bodily harm. Hero complex, Nerissa is quite sure. Or perhaps an overactive guilt complex. While Vivienne's kidnapping was Nerissa's fault on some levels, if Christabel had taken the time to actually look beyond her own pedantic nose, she might have known she was more than a run-of-the-mill mortal.

Precious unicorns. Nerissa would never eat her. Not really. It would probably kill her. And she'd be lying if she said she didn't enjoy Kit giving Christabel a run for the money in the brains department.

"I'll get you some food," Kit says, just as Nerissa's stomach growls. "Then, if you permit me, I can work with these two and figure out just what might be the best way to distract Cook. If he's distracted, he won't be making wind—ah, I mean, with his horns. And I'm willing to bet the unicorn won't be sensitive to his charms, but I can show her how to pretend to be."

The way Kit looks at Christabel fills Nerissa with a rather delicious sense of anticipation. A pristine unicorn on her way to a brothel. If only the storybooks told this kind of tale.

"Meanwhile," Nerissa says, before Christabel and Worth can argue one way or another, "I will continue to look into Mr. DeBos's transactions and remain here in case our erstwhile dwarf friend decides to come back with more information."

If Vivienne were here, she would ask Nerissa if it was a good idea and insist someone stays behind. But Christabel, Worth, and Kit are all afraid of her—they do not see the weaknesses she possesses, they are only intimidated by her bravado. She does not let on how weak she feels, how absolutely insubstantial, and how sad. And so, they agree with her, and once Nerissa has had her dinner, they retire to their own rooms to plan for an evening visit to the Thousand Suns.

And Nerissa cannot help but feel miserable in their absence. Oddly, even more than in their presence.

BENEVOLENCE

Kit does not relish the idea of going back to the brothel, but she's hoping that it will serve to mend some of the burned bridges between her and the team. She loves this idea of being an agent, of being part of this group of mysterious beings. Every day she comes across more creatures like her, living wild and free without the lash of Cook or the curses of the world between...

They are very slow, though. Slow in thinking and slow in speech. Even the unicorn, who thinks she is very smart—and perhaps is by measure of unicorns—ought to spend some time experiencing the world rather than reading about it. How can one taste a peach without putting it on one's tongue? A thousand words can bring it to mind, but only holding the soft flesh and breaking it with the teeth, feeling the sticky sweet juice run down the chin, makes it real. Makes it memorable. Else-wise, it is simply shadows and whispers of a real thing.

Kit doesn't like peaches, but the metaphor is apt. Perhaps she'll bring it up to Christabel if she'll permit her to speak. Not that she needs *permission*, but the unicorn's judging eyes bother Kit. Make her feel like there's worms all in her belly. Christabel would probably love peaches.

The Thousand Suns is much longer than one would guess from the outside. Kit has had plenty of time to explore it, but she finds it very amusing to observe it from without. It is partially shaded by glamours, so to most mortal eyes, it's a rather plain building with dusty chairs and cracked windows. It's an old kind of magic that bends wavelengths of light, adding a kind of refracted camouflage to the place.

It is twilight, her favorite time, and she can venture to use her claws a little more. Kit delights in the feeling as they slide from her nail beds, black-pointed and smooth. How many tricks she's played with them; what sweet music she's played. She almost remembers a song, and a someone, but then she catches herself. No time. No time. One mustn't go down those roads of weakness. She is *kitsune*.

Now, to climb. Beside the Thousand Suns is a squat series of buildings that were once part of an open-air market, but have, over the centuries, been reinforced and turned into stalls and, a little farther away, a mosque. The easy part is accessing the Thousand Suns by way of the unintentional passageways between these stalls; the difficult part is the only good access that won't get her noticed is through one of the topmost rooms which is, at most times, the laundry.

Kit hates the smell of lavender, and it's what Lulwa the washerwoman always uses. Lulwa and has never snitched on a guest or escort, but Kit does not assume for one moment the washerwoman is without her senses. On the contrary. Lulwa says too little to be uninformed.

Skittering between a sweet-smelling perfumery and another stall still coming down, Kit swings up to the second level, hooking her feet around a beam that's gone a bit too loose for her liking. The result is a rather death-defying loop-de-loop to the top awning of the fishmonger's stall. Kit just catches her balance and avoids going bottom first into a pile of guts and brine, the unaware assistant below mopping up the remnants of a good day's work.

Taking a moment to regain her breath, Kit wishes she had waited to volunteer a little longer after bleeding. The lamia will be very angry if she finds out she opened her own veins to feed her, but the rat blood was clearly making her sick, and Kit was getting bored hunting for them. Camel blood was too frothy, and even though Kit didn't live off blood— not if she didn't have to—she didn't like the smell.

Sweat beads at her forehead. That's unusual.

No, no. Focus.

Looking up, eyes clear now, Kit spies the possible routes up to Lulwa's window. There is a set of drainage pipes, ceramic and probably dating back to the last pharaoh. There are also a series of awnings that might get her high enough to make the last jump.

And she could also fly.

Well, *flying* is a bit of stretch. She doesn't exactly fly, but if she's hidden well enough, she can get a bit of lift with her tails—all five of them currently—and manage to propel herself that last little bit. It's a considerable distance, but she has no doubt she can make it. In her life before, she would never even have to consider the likelihood of failure.

But then she hadn't been bleeding herself, had she? And she certainly hadn't been working off a debt to demons and worse.

Stop stop stop stop.

She admonishes herself, and it seems to work. She gets a handhold and then a foothold, and before she's fully let herself drown in the despair of such foolish actions and her dwindling abilities, she's clinging to the narrow stone outcropping, her sharp nails digging in for dear life.

Her tails do not function as she hoped, but they still allow her to swing back and forth, still silent as a cat, until she's able to position herself up by the window by pure feat of strength. The lamia looks at her funny when she climbs and crawls on things, but she doesn't understand that it's a matter of keeping fit. It's important. If she sits still too long, she goes all wobbly in the muscles.

Lulwa's window casts a faint orange yellow light. It's open a crack, just enough for Kit to smell the all-familiar scent of lavender. She wrinkles her nose and tries to think of nicer things. Why anyone would want to smell like that foul stuff is quite beyond her. Shadows play along the pane, too. There are people inside. But far, judging by the light.

Kit takes a deep breath. She will just have to wait a little longer.

~

"So impressed you had to come back for more?" Cook asks, but Worth does not think he's convinced. He hates being duplicitous. He sweats enough for four when he's nervous, too. "I'd have thought Kit would have kept you busy enough."

"She's proven to be a most helpful assistant to our friend," Christabel is saying, and she doesn't even look concerned. Damn the unicorn, but she's never so much as kissed a man and yet she stands in front of a known flesh peddler without batting a single, perfectly curved eyelash. Smiling even. Making jokes. "But you understand, my needs are very *specific.*"

"And...ah," Cook asks, rubbing his bald, shiny head with one hand, deftly avoiding his broken horn. "What sort of thing would that be? I'm told we have something for every taste, but I'm not certain what yours might be."

"That is classified," Christabel says, "you understand."

As many before him, Cook is besotted with Christabel. He can't stop looking at her, can't stop watching her eyes, the play of her hands. But he doesn't quite know what she is. Worth knows the feeling all too well, and even though he's had time enough to get used to her presence, he's finding it more and more difficult to muddle through these days without falling into pits of despair and rather inappropriate daydreams.

He is just a man, after all. No, not a man. Not in most senses any mortal reader would understand. He is a creature of needs and wants, and he needs and wants Christabel very much. Nerissa has told him on countless occasions to keep his mouth and his mind clean, but the more he tries not to think about touching her, tasting her, knowing her, the more it comes back to him. Especially in his dreams.

"...but it's not for me, since I am quite sated in those terms," Christabel finishes saying.

Stars above, she's going off script again!

"It's for my colleague here, Mr. Goodwin," she says, gesturing to him. Her hands look so delicate in the lurid red light. It's horrifying to say it, but she's positively beautiful in the glow of the brothel. Maybe it's supposed to be that way, designed to make people look their best, but by the gods above and below, he isn't sure what to do with himself. If he doesn't get control of himself soon, he's going to be even more of an embarrassment than he already feels.

He's supposed to say something. They're both looking at him now.

"Right, Worth?" Christabel presses through slightly clenched teeth.

"Ah, yes," he says slowly. "For me. Yes. Absolutely. Definitely me. I would like all the joys of the flesh." It's not even a lie, but he makes it sound like he's never known another in all his life.

Christabel gives him the faintest of frowns, saving all the fury for the eyes.

"I, ah, well, it's been quite a long time," he confesses. "And my friend... here she...thought it might help things. Yes, you know, if I indulge a bit since we're here. Where we're from, there aren't places of this...caliber?" Worth knows immediately that he shouldn't have inflected at the end of that sentence, but he's absolutely certain he is being put quite unfairly in this position, so he forgives himself momentarily.

He's got that crawling feeling again. And his gland itches. He does anything he can to not think of scratching it, but then his eyes start watering.

"How long?" Cook asks, with all the thorough lack of concern one might when asking about the weather.

"How long is what?" Worth manages.

"I'm not asking for specific measurements unless you're offering, of course." Cook leers. "You said it's been a long time since you performed the act of love. Just how long since?" He makes a very rude gesture with his forefinger and opposite thumb and pointer.

Worth cannot bear to look at Christabel, but he says, through gritted teeth, "At least ten years."

"Well, that's not unheard of, though somewhat surprising. 'Specially for a man of the likes of you. Good and fit. Sturdy frame. Practically exudes the sort of thing they'd be lining up for given the circumstances. I could always use someone like you here. I have a feeling you've got quite the talent under all that nervousness. You need to channel it somehow. I can show you."

Cook is just stating facts as a businessman, but it's making Worth progressively more uncomfortable. Christabel looks altogether unbothered by the events and glances over at him expectantly.

"I'm not in need of *employment*," Worth says, all too familiar with that deep-seated pull of desire. People want him. To hunt him. To couple with him. To take him. To own him. It's what he is. It's perhaps why he enjoys being with Christabel so much. She somehow evades their notice, but she understands what happens when you are sought after. "Just…entertainment."

God above, he hates talking like this. He wishes they had come up with a better plan.

"If you change your mind, just let me know," Cook says with a nonchalant shrug. "Now, I just need to know your preferences."

This makes Worth panic even more. He is painfully aware that they are using this ruse to create a distraction. And he is woefully unprepared for the mental anguish the question arises in him.

What *does* he want? He doesn't often get asked. Of all his lovers, across all the years, he has almost always been sought. He never had much of a say. He fell in love with them for a variety of reasons, but they were always first attracted to him. And their types and talents were so far and wide that he can't even begin to create a type for himself.

Except with Christabel. He wants Christabel. But he doesn't suppose Cook has any other unicorns about.

"Nothing too exotic, I'm sure," Christabel says, coming to his rescue. "Perhaps an errant sylph or a half-demon?"

"Oh, we can arrange for something a little more exciting than *that*," says Cook. "You've seen Kit, so you know the quality of our wares. We pride ourselves in quality and rarity."

"Then show me what you have. Your very best," Worth says, squeezing each word out through a tight-lipped smile as Cook refers to Kit as just another piece of commerce. He can hardly stop himself from fleeing, but Christabel puts a calming hand on the small of his back, and he finds he simply can think of nothing else in the world than that slow pressure. His senses return to him, and he remembers: they are here for Vivienne. Even if he can't entirely understand what he feels about her, even if he's not sure he even *wants* her around again, since he could never say know to her wiles...

Cook nods. "Give me five minutes. And prepare to be dazzled."

As soon as Cook is out of the room, Worth goes to speak, but Christabel is already looking at him with pity and kindness, and all he can manage is a strangled gurgle of a noise that isn't from his human glamour at all. Likely some lily-livered lizard deep within him.

K it finally gets herself into the washing room, crouching tight against the wall and down toward the floor as soon as she enters, using a big gust of wind to cover her tracks. Lulwa is yelling at one of the maids, the usual diatribe, and her voice is loud enough that it's fairly easy to track her way across the lavender-stinking room toward the loose grates she'd worried open during her long years at the Thousand Suns.

The stones move aside with relatively little effort, making Kit pause to wonder if someone else—Yuya, perhaps—found this exit in her absence of the last few days.

Doesn't matter. She's got to keep moving. Find the books. Read the pages. That is her task now. To impress her masters because maybe then they would want her to be part of their company. She would be immensely helpful. It's the first thing she's hoped for in so long that she has to bite down on her tongue.

Taking a deep breath, Kit uses her abilities to shrink down into two foxes. It's a curious thing she can do and is dangerous to her form should they get separated, but now's the right time. She's got to move fast and silently, all while keeping track of her two sides is difficult. Her own consciousness splits, and through what is like an invisible filament, she can pass thoughts from one to the other.

Kit is now a white fox and a red fox. The white has a red-tipped tail, and the red has a white-tipped tail. She thinks in double, but not quite synced. There's always a bit of a delay between them, an overlapping of words and thoughts. And they are not always in her control.

Down through the grate through the gate down below. Below to the room below to the book where Cook where Cook writes the numbers writes the sums and sum and numbers.

Eat the beetle!

Crunch the beetle!

We fight the beetle and for the beetle and don't forget the books the sums and books where Cook where Cook...

Down they go, red and white, slipping through the inner ways of the Thousand Suns where Kit has been kind enough to make room for them. They are quite happy to be free and always try and think of ways to stay like this when Kit is not here. They love the freedom of not having to be in person form. Person form is tedious. And naked. Even with clothes on, barely any fur.

They make good time on the way down, their little paws getting sandy and dusty with the progress, but their sharp eyes in the dark keep them away from the bad room and the sad places and find a burst of joy in the rooms where people are loved and love loving and gambol and play. It is never one bad thing or another, as some people like to think. There is beauty even in the darker places, and not everyone works here because they have no choice.

But then they stop short. Red stops first, always the better listener.

They know where they are. Cook's office. But there's a light purple hue coming from it.

Purple hues mean bad things. Especially in Cairo. Especially in the Thousand Suns.

It means Itke is awake.

~

Christabel has rarely felt so uncomfortable. She is standing with Worth in a very small room, into which one of the servants has escorted them to await the prospects. Pillows and low chairs rise around them, a deep musk in the air so pervasive she can, in fact, taste it. The velvet wallpaper is mostly covered by draping silks and beads, but she still cringes inwardly at the thought of what these walls have seen.

She is not immune to Cook's suggestions, even though she tried very hard, and now she is face-to-face with Worth in a very cramped space.

Her heart throbs in her chest as she tries to say something, but the sounds of lovemaking in the rooms adjacent to them make it impossible. There's nothing she could say to get herself out of this predicament, and giggling is not an option. Even though her head swims and her eyes tickle with the desire to.

Worth is looking at her that way again, too. All eyes and eyelashes. His lips slightly parting, the very heart of him emanating toward her.

"It's taking a while," he says at last, moving just a bit closer toward her. The edges of his lips raise in a smirk. "Though the same can't be said for our neighbor over there." He gestures with a thumb toward the only recently quiet room.

"You..." she starts, then stops, taking a small step away. But there isn't anywhere to go. She wonders idly if this is the plan. If Cook wants them to...

"Yes?"

"I hope... I hope Kit isn't in any trouble," Christabel says, meaning to turn away from Worth but somehow finding herself a step closer. She fiddles with the edge of her sleeve, her fingers brushing the fabric, and takes a quivering breath.

"You're thinking about Kit right now?" he asks.

At first, Christabel thinks that she's offended him, but his eyes are sparkling.

"Worth..." she says, his name coming out deeper than she intended. She is glad for the red light in the room because she can feel the blush creeping up on her cheeks.

"I was about to make a fool of myself, blow this whole ruse," he says. "But then you reached out. You make me a better person, Christabel."

"I do no such thing. You are a good person."

"A good monster, perhaps. But that isn't saying much. It's just hard to connect. Do you know what I mean?"

She nods, breathless, as Worth reaches up and touches the side of her face, his fingers brushing against her skin whisper soft. His flesh is warm against hers, and she is immediately reminded of the first few times they met—the heat between them—before she understood what she was and where her power came from. She kept refusing him then, and she did not know why. Now, she avoids him even though with each passing year in his presence she desires him more.

"I cannot stop thinking about you," Worth says, seeking her eyes with his. "You must know that."

"It's the brothel," Christabel says, hoping it to come out scornful. Instead, her voice is low, almost husky.

"I don't know what to do. I know that you...that this is complicated. And I haven't felt myself lately, so perhaps I am just mad, and you should..."

There are a variety of words she'd like to share at the moment, many clever and intelligent ones, suffused with knowledge and warning. But he smells so delicious. Has he always smelled this good? She feels a deep pressure in her belly, a hunger to taste him, to know him, to press her very essence to him, to envelop him.

Enough.

When their lips meet, it is like fire. His breath is hotter than she remembered, the coolness of her own body meeting it like a thunderclap. She kisses him hard enough to feel his teeth, his human teeth, and then other teeth—sharper, fiercer—waiting for her. Wanting her. Promising to devour her and pleasure her and take her in the way only monsters can manage.

Worth's hands find their way, timidly at first, and then with more surety, to her shoulders, then down to her waist, pressing into the small of her back.

A kind of joy burbles up in her throat, coming to light as a raspy laugh when they pull away from each other. She runs her hands over his cheeks, feeling the bristle of his hair against her palm. She slides her fingers around his neck, the soft hairs there rising as she does so. He lets out a low moan as his hands find the buttons on her billowy blouse and—

Then she stops short because something black and oily is dripping on Worth's forehead. He goes to kiss her again, and she puts a hand to his chest, her own fingers trembling, to stop him.

Then they both look up.

A black figure stares down at them, roughly the shape of a large dog, if it also had long, sinewy tendrils reaching out from its appendages. It takes up the majority of the ceiling, and it is breathing heavily, a thousand eyes all across its dark body coming to life.

A dark fluid drips from its mouth, fresh blood. Worth wipes the filth from his brow.

Then the monster springs, and the walls around them pulse toward their bodies, hungrier than the void itself.

～

The red fox goes one way; the white fox goes the other. It takes a great deal of effort from Kit, and she's not been at her best to begin with. But if Itke is awake, then someone has to warn the unicorn. Itke will be drawn to her, will want to taste her pureness, if only because it sees her as a threat.

Scurrying down the pipe toward the receiving rooms, the white fox goes toward Cook's room. They each shrink in size considerably, preserving energy to keep this way, not to mention they lose a good deal of their quickness. Kit knows, on her strange third consciousness, that she cannot keep it up for long.

The red fox can feel the unicorn easily enough. It's a nasty, strange feeling the creature emits, even when she's trying to keep it at bay. The right, or the wrong, monster will know exactly what she is, or at least have enough curiosity piqued they won't be able to resist.

This was not a good idea, the red fox thinks, and decides to have a word with Kit when the opportunity presents itself.

But Itke is already there when the red fox arrives, even though Worth and Christabel don't notice. How can they miss that glow? The red fox hisses under her breath and waits until she can help. For now, she just listens to the inane prattling on of the two creatures within trying to prove to one another they don't love each other as they ought to.

Now the white fox has to move fast, struggling as the red tells her of the mounting threat. They're going to need Kit soon.

The white fox shrinks down again, now the size of a mouse, and makes her way toward Cook's room. There are a great many locks and wards on his door, but they're unlocked because he's standing just a few feet away.

"I won't have Itke *kill* them," he is saying to someone too shadowed for the white fox to see. "Just get them out. I am tired of catering to their whims, especially when I can see so fully through their guise."

The white fox creeps up against the edge of the wall, listening. She can see the light from within his office. If she just sprints...

"Frightening them might not be enough," says another voice, heavily accented. It sounds like Arabic with a European accent. French, perhaps? Kit would know, but the white fox is only part of Kit right now. She files it away to remember later.

"I know your employer has specific rules not to kill them," says Cook. "Or has that changed?"

The second figure shuffles. The white fox feels sick to her stomach, as if the ground is moving beneath her feet.

"Get them off the trail, and there will be no need," says the figure.

The white fox looks closer, straining her eyes in the dark. She sees the outline of an old-fashioned soldier's uniform with big bold shoulders and a wide hat.

Below, she feels the pulsating power of Itke wake up. No, no, no, no. Not good. Not good. Itke is a beast of both worlds. If Itke takes them, gets rid of them, throws them to the Other Side...

"Once Itke's done with them, I'll have them returned to the Semiramis alive. Providing the payment earns out."

"The payment always does."

"I'm just concerned about Heqet's enemy. If they show up, it might cause problems. You know her history."

"Heqet's debts are her own. You know we cannot comply. But she will only take what is hers. There is never a guarantee, you know that."

Cook sighs, shakes his head. "It's better than nothing, I suppose. Just don't expect me to take the fall if the boss is upset."

"The boss will be compensated," the Frenchman says, and it occurs to the fox that perhaps he's not talking out of his mouth. Which is a rather curious thought, but one that makes perfect sense. He is a puppet, strung along by magic she doesn't understand.

Then comes the sound of stones clicking one upon the other, like soft pebbles worn smooth by the rushing waters. It reminds the white fox of her home, that faraway place she was born before she was Kit. When her twin spirit was free...

But that is enough.

The fox slinks back just in time to see the face of the stranger come to light. He is taller than she would have thought. And also, well, alive. But there he is, no mistaking. She doesn't remember much about Western history, but there are a few people you can't avoid running across. Napoleon Bonaparte is one of them.

~

The kiss is worth a great deal, but perhaps not this horror. One moment before, he was quite sure he was going to spend a good part of his evening delightfully tangled in Christabel's hair and legs, tasting her skin and tracing the lines of her face with his fingers. But now he is most inconveniently delayed by an immense monster with innumerable eyes and somewhere about six mouths, all gaping at him and drooling black slime.

Part of him is relieved, a sliver of cool amidst the hot currents of fear. Fantasies aside, it wouldn't have ended well, and he was going to embarrass himself even more with her if they had not been interrupted. Granted, he would prefer a little less blood, drool, and impending death, but...

The mouths on the beast above them all open at once and, in addition to dripping down even more blood, start to emit a high-pitched sound that Worth feels right down to the core of him. Namely, to the crystal-like organ at his chest that's responsible for his glamour. One moment, he is quite comfortable as Worth the man, and then, the next, he is lying prostrate on the ground, incapable of moving, a ringing in his ears so loud he's convinced his eardrums are going to burst.

Christabel does not appear to be affected this same way, and the way she looks up at the creature on the ceiling makes Worth love her even more. She lowers her chin and rears backward, her arms and legs lengthening until they reform. Her fair face stretches, the nose turning brown, while the rest of her thickens and turns white—Worth has never seen her as a unicorn here, but he can already tell her shape is different, though no less fair.

When she is done, Christabel shakes her head, the one, single, silver horn rising unfathomably high from her forehead. Worth knows what the animal is, only because Christabel insisted that he learned what kind of animals were native to Egypt before they visited. An oryx.

A scimitar oryx, to be exact. Like her previous incarnation, her shape holds none of the romance of the unicorn of yore. She is stocky and strong, made of muscle and fat and power. And full of fury and protective rage.

Before Worth can admire too much longer, the tendriled creature on the ceiling whips out toward Christabel, twisting neatly around her middle like an American cowboy. But one twist of her head, the long horn —twice the height it was the last time he saw it—easily slices through the black material. As the two make contact, Worth notices a stream of purple smoke pouring from the assailant above.

For his part, he is still most useless. The sound slicing and whining through his brain is slowly killing him, he's certain. It's hit such a pitch now that Worth begins to lose track of his thoughts, his present, his future, and anything that has happened to him in his long life. He feels he must end. Because life with this feeling, this pain, this dizziness, is not worth the living.

At least he'll see Christabel one more time before he gives up. Even if it is her derriere, and she is mostly a goat.

UGLY UNICORN & SCRAGGLY FOX

The thing on the ceiling is making Christabel very angry. She was quite enjoying that kiss, even if that is far from appropriate. While her lips were pressed against Worth's, she felt more alive than she has in ages, and she wants it again, desperately. Of course, proper women shouldn't gamble with their purity so much, even if Worth's lips tasted like September rain and she was desperately curious just how much of him was under his glamor. But she's willing to second guess propriety if it means more kissing.

It's just a shame that this growing, spreading, oily mass with mouths is interrupting her romantic interlude.

Now she's being toyed with. Attacked. And for reasons unknown to her, Worth is completely incapable of helping her. In fact, he's worse than useless. He's dying.

It's been ages since Christabel felt this way, and though her body moves a little differently, it is relatively the same. The powerful legs, the long nose, the towering horn. This time it's towering even more, higher and thinner, drawing power from the animals of the land.

That thing on the ceiling is laughing at her. How she understands that is quite beyond her, and truth be told, she is a little unnerved by it. Why would a unicorn understand the mad ravings of a creature with six mouths, two dozen tendrils, and a thin cover of slick black fur? It doesn't even make sense to look at it, let alone have a conversation.

Not that monsters have to make *sense*. But Christabel has spent years researching creatures, and this does not fall into her ken. It isn't even remotely Persian or Egyptian, which given the—

A slash of the beast's long hair protrusions slaps the thoughts right out of her. Winded, Christabel rears back, pulling the sinewy black assailant's tendril with her and snapping it in a burst of purple light. It hurts, though. Everywhere it touches her is like ice, freezing through her fur and cutting into her skin. And reminding her of reedy fields and rolling mountains.

"They knew we were coming back," she says with gritted teeth, even though Worth can't comment on her. "We rose to the bait, whether or not Kit was aware."

It's hungry. And angry. Never a good combination in her experience.

But there's more a unicorn can do than stomp and stab, and for that she's grateful.

"But we can't exactly talk to her about it right now!" Christabel rears her head back and lets out a high whinny that's more like a bleat, but for the sake of romance, we'll say it's a sweet sound (though some might hold argument with that statement).

Then, stomping her front hoof, the room quakes in response, little flecks of plaster crumbling in the corners. Some of it lands on Worth, and when Christabel spares a glance at him, she sees that he's clutching at something on his chest and there is blood coming from his nose. Writhing in pain, gagging on air...

She must focus. She must protect him.

But it's very difficult to do so when the creature above her is not responding to her attack. In fact, it's now bigger and more of a void than it was before. And it's sprouted a few more mouths.

More tendrils come down, faster and with more precision. Christabel feels her head hit the ground, and then sparks fly before her eyes as she's pulled up, up toward the ceiling, every inch an agony.

From the corner of her eyes, each second her vision darkening as more sinewy fibers wrap themselves around her, she sees Worth being pulled up in the same manner.

And then they both fall up into the ceiling and into darkness.

〜

Nerissa is sleeping when she feels, rather than sees, that things have gone amiss. Out of a dark dream, which she rarely has, the pressure inside her ears shifts and alerts her to an intruder.

Then two.

Coming up through the ground, somehow. Hearts pounding, she hisses and slinks back toward the shadows of her room in the Semiramis, claws and teeth at the ready, preparing herself. She breathes in and out, stilling herself.

Then the top of a dwarf emerges from the ground, carrying what looks like a dead red fox in her hands. The dwarf looks rather confused, and a little bit irritated, and then surprised when she sees Nerissa in her full glory.

"I can't be poisoned, so keep your spit to yourself," the dwarf says, holding up her free hand in a peaceful salute. "I'm Alma Stonefoot. Your friends Worth and Christabel freed me from the jeweler's shop."

"What are you doing here?" Nerissa chokes out, her teeth and claws far from retracting. She has never been the kind of monster to do as she's told, and it would be beyond her to show submission to this dwarven woman.

Alma holds out the red fox. "Someone ripped a hole to the Niðavellir. Or maybe even to Niflheimr. Not sure which one, given I'm still on this side. I'm attuned to such things, and they shouldn't be happening—especially not this far south, since the realms are a little trickier this way."

"You just said words that make absolutely no sense. And I have no need of a dead animal..."

But Nerissa's words trail off as she makes sense of what is happening. She's been so incensed that she hasn't been paying attention to what is right in front of her.

"Where are Christabel and Worth?" Nerissa says. Demands.

"That's what I'm trying to tell you, slithering one," says Alma. "My business is *portals*. Gates between this and there. I know when something goes wrong. I was trying to finish up some business when I felt the earth shift, felt the immense presence of...shaking, trembling energies toward the Thousand Suns. When I got there, half the building was caved in, and I found this half-dead fox limping away. She smelled of unicorns and lamias, and I remembered where Christabel said you were staying."

"Kit?" Nerissa asks.

"I suppose so. She is a *kitsune*. Well, half of one, anyway."

Kit. Half of Kit. Nerissa's head is pounding, the blood whooshing in time with her heartbeats, sending a painful ache down her forehead and into her jaw. "I told the bellhop...we are supposed to be kept free of visitors."

Alma gives her a dubious look. "I can rise through stone and wood and metal. There's no keeping me from anywhere."

"I can't...I can't *leave*..." Nerissa stutters. She presses her hand to her chest, feeling the gnaw of hunger at her already.

"Do you care about your friends? About the *kitsune*? We may be her only hope." Alma is surprisingly level-headed and logical about this.

Nerissa doesn't say anything, just makes a wheezing noise as she looks down at the red fox. She's missing patches of fur. Nerissa thinks of Kit hanging from the ceiling, of the bright, clever look in her eyes. Whatever happened, she put her life at risk. Even if the Thousand Suns turned into a trap for Christabel and Worth.

"I have limited mobility," Nerissa says slowly.

"Oh, that's *right*. You've got to have good blood." Alma does not keep the disgust from her voice.

"A snake is a *snake*," Nerissa says. "And I'm afraid without food, I'm quite useless."

"Well, then we'll have to make time. And since the Thousand Suns appears to have been just a terrible trap for your friends, we're going to have to call in a favor elsewhere."

Nerissa nods, numbly, then stops herself as she rearranges her glamor. She glares down at the dwarf. "Why are you helping me?"

"I got bored," Alma says. "And I have some special interests in maintaining the balance between this world and the other ones. Your friends woke something up, and I'm curious as to why."

"Boredom is a good a reason for adventure as any I've heard," says Nerissa, appreciating the dwarf's candor. She's never met one before, not from Nith, at least. Even though her face is maggot white and her eyes far too pale, there's a sincerity in Alma that Nerissa likes.

"I'm not much for embellishment," Alma says, looking down at the fox with a particularly mothering look. "But I'd hate to see this creature perish. And if she's what I think she is, we don't have much time to spare."

～

K it is broken. Shattered. She sees the world through six eyes. One set is darkened. Another is all brightness. Her own is shrouded in mist. Caressing hands, familiar voices. But everything is going cold around her, her consciousness like a shroud around her shoulders.

She tried to save them. But she waited too long. As the white fox, she just didn't have enough energy. All that was left when the Thousand Suns turned inside out on itself was the red fox, hit so hard in the head she couldn't remember herself.

It won't be long, now.

And perhaps…perhaps that's for the best.

She was never going to pay her debts, anyway. She was going to be a slave forever. And the shame is enough to keep her from hope.

C hristabel feels as if her body is being flayed wide open, her skin separating from her muscles with the deft flicking of a thousand cruel knives. It sears and burns, her nerves ricocheting messages across her body in fevered filigree. She cannot take this any longer. If Worth is dead, if that creature killed him…

Her rage is so sharp and clear it blocks all pain. Christabel feels her whole framework, the bits and pieces of magic and flesh exploding out from her in every direction until…

Calm.

Sweet, utter calm.

She is standing in a wood, now. No longer in her unicorn form, but human in shape. She glances down at her hair and sees it has gone a rather pale red, shot with golden streaks. Reaching out her arm, she sees it's dappled with freckles as if from tree shadows. And, indeed, more shadows play on her skin.

Her legs are shaky, but she is whole, though her heart still beats in her throat. It takes a moment for her to realize, so focused she is on the cool moss on her toes, that she is not alone.

There is a white fox on the ground, unconscious. And Worth nearby, completely naked.

She startles and looks down at her body, but she is very much clothed. The material is springtime green, studded with yellow daisies and sewn with spider silk. She isn't sure how she knows these things, but she has the sense she has worn this dress before, in this place, in another time.

The fox breathes slowly, too slowly. But Worth does, too, though quicker and punctuated by wincing. He is as she first met him, save for the terrific show of impropriety. Still, she cannot help but marvel at his form as she approaches, and not just the human trappings. It is another power that moves within him, a kind of shifting...

Broken.

The moment her hand touches his shoulder, she understands. Worth is naked because his magic is broken. He is stuck this way, as a human, while his insides roil around. He can't even fashion himself a simple pair of clothes. And his ribs are bruised, to say nothing of the scratches and lash marks down his legs. And on his back, she notices two sets of silvery scars, parallel to one another. The scars are strange in that they look like lace, or sewing, rather intentional. She goes to touch them and then he stirs.

Worth flips over, eyes flutter open, and Christabel almost falls over in surprise. His pupils are an electric green, an otherworldly color that in a normal circumstance would seem almost garish. Absinthe is the only thing she can compare it to, that liquid, translucent eldritch hue of her least favorite alcoholic beverage.

"Christabel," he says softly, reaching up to touch her cheek.

Then his eyes close again, and he goes back to softly snoring.

Taking the fox in her arms, Christabel stands slowly and takes better stock of where she is. The furry animal breathes a little irregularly, but it cuddles against her for warmth, and she can't help but feel as if, maybe, she is helping it. Going from the chaos of what happened at the Thousand Suns, she's willing to take a moment of calm if she can.

The wood is dense, here, everything limned in lavender fog. In the distance, past the tree line, Christabel can see fields of some sort. Reeds, perhaps, like the sort she saw at Mr. Ghali's rift what felt like ages ago. There is no doubt where she is, then. Everything about the place is upside down, warped, twisted, like reflections of reflections. Some may call it home—indeed, she realizes she should—but nothing about the Fae feels right to her. Everything is alive. Even the air.

She feels fresh, though. And while she was certain she'd taken a beating from that many-mouthed creature, there's no sign of damage on her body. Whatever it did to Worth, she was spared.

The little fox begins to twitch, and Christabel goes stiff. She senses a shift, too. An ever so subtle shift of the light, a stirring in the wind, though the leaves do not move.

Christabel kneels on the ground, her body between her wounded friends and whatever comes for her. If it must end now, and it is likely, she will not go without a fight.

A sound like a scythe through wheat resonates through the whole wood, and then the trees part. Christabel almost rubs her eyes to be sure she's not seeing things, since the trees don't move out of the way, exactly. They split like a curtain, making way for the creature on the other side to come through. A creature of indeterminate shape and smaller, strangely formed footmen.

The woman, for she must be called that by her form and presentation, is twice the size of an average human being. Her skin is like burnished copper, too smooth to be skin and yet too alive to be wood or metal. Her long hair falls in tight braids down to her narrow waist, the proportions just off enough to set Christabel's heart going. There is a wrongness —or a rightness, depending on how you look at it —to the waspy waist and the broad, broad shoulders. Power and fragility. The gait of a monster. Her eyes are black through and through, though dotted with stars. On top of her head she wears a great crown, a scorpion poised to strike.

Then Christabel realizes it is not a crown. It is a real scorpion, twice the size of the little fox she's holding.

Christabel ought to have the right words to say, ought to explain herself. But this tangible presence goes far beyond its visual qualities. The very world around her seems thickened, like great sheets of velvet pressing against her, promising sleep and sweet repose.

Who comes to Serket and wakes her children from their slumber?

The voice does not come from the woman, nor does it come from the wood. Instead, it comes from a mouth that somehow exists below the front carapace of the scorpion.

Yes. There she is. Serket. Scorpion goddess.

Nerissa is sweating and exhausted by the time that Alma finally stops walking. The confounded dwarf manages to slide and walk at the same time, with no impediment over stone, brick, mud, or tile. It is far less easy for the lamia, who is not only exhausted, but also far from peak physical condition. It's been months since she had her own flock, tending the fields of her goats in her spare time. All this living inside, shying away until her next meal, has left her rather doughy and breathless. Vivienne would scold her.

Alma, meanwhile, might as well be made of wet clay the way she moves. At least Nerissa isn't in charge of the dying little fox. Kit. The...no. She can't think about it. She shouldn't care for this creature. She was a *transaction*. She was a way to get food more reliably. But even Nerissa isn't fooled by her own mental protestations. She feels a fondness for Kit, and she cannot help it.

"We're here," Alma says, gesturing to a narrow alley.

Nerissa has entirely lost track of where they were going in the first place, and the dry sand and ceaseless sun have left her even more discombobulated than usual.

"Here," however, does not seem to be any particular place other than a smelly, rat-infested alleyway. No doors. No windows. Nothing. Just walls of pale brick rising to the skies.

"What do you mean, *here?*" Nerissa asks.

Nerissa is smart enough to know that there are magics more complex and difficult to see with the naked eye, but her eyes are most keen and attuned to magical seals, portends, and...

"You're standing on it," Alma says, pointing to Nerissa's feet. "Well, the welcoming mat, as it were."

There is a grate below her, Nerissa notes, worn smooth by sand and time. And it is indeed covered with strange runes, although she doesn't know the language.

Instead of acting surprised, Nerissa just gently steps aside and makes a broad gesture for Alma to take the lead.

Alma looks at her as if she's sprouted two extra heads.

"I can't go in *there*," Alma says. "Do you know what they'll do to a Nith dwarf? No, no. We never meet on *their* turf. You'll have to go alone. With the fox thing. I'll wait out here. Keep guard."

"Who are we meeting?"

Alma sighs. "Who else provides blood at need?"

"I don't get along with vampires."

"No one gets along with vampires. So don't go thinking you're special."

"I don't know." Nerissa is actually afraid. She hasn't had any good dealings with vampires, the few she's had have been Aberrants or

Exigents, driven mad or choosing to destroy humans. A bloody, awful mess.

Alma continues. "There's an entrance a few feet from the back. Look for the limestone with pentagram on it. Just press it and they'll be alerted to your presence. If they aren't already, that is."

"A pentagram? How terribly cliché."

"We can't all be clever, *snake*. And vampires have quite the sense of irony."

"Thanks for the reminder, *dwarf*."

Alma does not appear bothered by the tone of Nerissa's voice and merely gestures again and wags her hairless eyebrows.

Taking a deep breath, Nerissa cradles the little fox and immediately feels a sorrow like she's only felt a few times. This tiny, dying creature is heavier than it should be, and its breath comes so infrequently that tears spring to her eyes.

No, no. She mustn't show weakness. Not in front of the dwarf, and absolutely not in front of the vampires.

Vampires.

With each step down the alley, Nerissa recounts her own memories, remembering the last time she worked with vampires, all the sordid details. They make her scales itch with their brazen debauchery, their endless orgies, and their constant and mind-numbing chatter. Really, she could overlook all their other faults if they just shut up every now and again. Tea with a vampire was like an unexpected tea with a distant, gossipy great-aunt who's remarkably well-preserved. One who's lived centuries and amassed enough knowledge to actually pose a threat. They are so social it makes her feel nauseated.

The fox twitching in her arms settles Nerissa's resolve, though. She thinks of Vivienne in that moment, the way she always approached vampires with her own silky smoothness and wit. Nerissa could never be as adaptable, even if she could change her countenance any way she wished. Vivienne always liked vampires, she said, since they were some of the only creatures she had no desire to eat.

Nerissa presses on the small limestone square chiseled with a very recent pentagram and tries not to roll her eyes. Their lack of creativity is appalling. Of all the thousands of ancient symbols, they choose…

The door slides open with a soft grinding noise and reveals a tall vampire leaning against the doorjamb as if he had been there the entire time listening to Nerissa's thoughts. The unfortunate reality is that some vampires are telepaths, and this causes Nerissa to recoil slightly.

"Hello, darling," the vampire coos. He's got straw-colored hair in absurd ringlets, one side tied back with a blue bow. The rest of him is a mess of a silk suit cut so tight on him it might burst, made complete with a garish chartreuse scarf. "We heard rumors you might be coming along."

His eyes are brimming with a curious, cold light. As a dead creature with no pulse, he presents some challenges to the lamia. She cannot read his body temperature or his emotions. She must watch his expressions very closely.

"The fox is dying," she says. "And I need—"

"Say no more," the vampire says. "Michaux will help you and slake your thirst."

The vampire is named Michaux. He is sickly sweet, calls her "darling," and is dressed like a grandmother's tea table. She follows him down a narrow passageway hung with thick velvet drapery, a sweet incense smell deepening with every step and making her nose tingle.

Michaux talks about himself in the third person. And though he has a French sounding name, he has an English cadence to his words with but a hint of another tongue, likely his mother tongue. Michaux is most probably not his name. Vampires are ever fond of offensively foppish names, and repeating it endlessly does nothing to add to its credence.

"The fox needs food. Her *own* food. We do have a small store of a potion or two that might work. Michaux is no alchemist, but thankfully Betiko has worked the majority of her long, terribly boring life, steeped in the chemical arts. We are a haven for outsiders with curious...tastes..." Michaux grins at Nerissa, showing, for the first time, rows of sharp teeth. Two rows on top, like a shark.

"I'll see to her first," Nerissa says, though she can already smell blood on willing victims, their bodies warm behind walls and silks, ready to eat. Her stomach lurches, and the bites down on her tongue to keep from saying anything else.

"Yes, she does look like she's a few sneezes from death." He pauses, then appears to remember himself. "Michaux apologizes. You have a fondness for the creature."

"She is a friend," Nerissa says, finding the words thick in her throat.

"Beti!" Michaux shouts, rather than continuing the conversation, stopping abruptly and knocking on an absurdly ornate door. The carved wooden panels demonstrate about two dozen ways to drain blood out of a person during intercourse. Nerissa cannot help but look at it, spies arrangements she can only hope are illustrative, then immediately regrets it.

A few faces appear through long silken drapes now as Michaux continues to bellow for Beti. They encompass every race imaginable. A pastiche of vampires stemming from dozens of cultures. More than half are in some state of undress, or clearly mid-feeding—there is blood running down their mouths, still dripping in some cases.

Nerissa is caught between staring at them and fighting her hunger, or else continue to focus on the lurid orgy on the door before her. She chooses the latter and braces herself for yet another awkward vampire encounter, but is surprised to see a rather round, quite diminutive vampire standing there, pink smoke billowing out behind her and a thin dust of sparkles in her puffy curls. She is African by her look, but she is dressed like a Victorian mourner. Her eyes are clear and dark, her face smudged with ash.

"Michaux, I told you— Oh," Beti says. She looks not at Nerissa but at the fox and puts a hand to her mouth. "Is that..."

"Shh!" Michaux says, shoving his guests inside and shutting the door behind them. "Michaux does not wish to raise the alarm."

"The Circle tipped you off to them, then," Beti says, rolling her eyes.

Nerissa freezes. "The Circle of Iapetus?"

"Of course. You met with Alma, didn't you?"

"Yes, how did you—"

"She's been working with them for years. She's one of those foolhardy few who believes in the common cause. Fat lot of good that did her, though. Trapped in a jeweler's shop. We did everything we could to try and free her, but we are limited in our reach, and your friends did the trick," Beti says. She has a way about her, reminding Nerissa of some of the old witches she used to know. Not the bitter, dangerous kind, but the slightly mad, terribly over-informed sort.

"I..." Nerissa starts.

"Here, hold this," says Beti, taking the fox and putting a flask in Nerissa's hand. The lamia is shocked enough that she doesn't realize the fox is gone until she's staring blankly at the stoppered fluid in her hands. As soon as she feels the glass warm, the contents begin glowing a deep purple flecked with blue.

Beti's room is incredibly small. Calling it a glorified closet would be a compliment. There's barely enough room for all three of them to stand

and turn around because the room's walls are shelved from floor to ceiling with hundreds of implements, herbs, tinctures, and badly labeled bottles. Nerissa wonders what would happen if she sneezed in such a place as this. Not a good idea. Not at all. It would likely go up in flames.

"What's in here?" Nerissa asks of the flask.

"Lunch," Beti says, distractedly, waving a hand at the lamia.

Nerissa sighs and tries again. "What can you do for the *kitsune?*"

Beti pokes the fox and sniffs the air. Then she stares at Nerissa as if seeing her for the very first time.

"She's *yours?*" Beti asks.

"After a matter of speaking," Nerissa says. "It's rather embarrassing how it happened, but there was this shadhavar."

"Cook. What a piece of wretched garbage," Michaux says. "Michaux is so sorry that you had dealings with him."

"I had to eat," Nerissa said. "I misunderstood the purpose of the Thousand Suns."

"But you signed in blood?" Beti asks. She gently turns the fox around, and there is a shape there, a patch of white fur among the brilliant red, and if you look at it right, it looks like two hearts.

"Lamias have two hearts, don't they?" Beti asks, half to herself.

Nerissa nods slowly.

"Sometimes a *kitsune* can half herself. This is generally done in close quarters, when the risk is high but the need for stealth is even greater. Since the other half is not near, I can only surmise it went somewhere else."

"Hopefully with Worth," Nerissa says quietly.

"Who's Worth? Sounds delicious," says Michaux.

"He's a friend. And Kit's other...keeper," Nerissa replies, not wanting the taste of the word "slave" on her lips again, let alone "master."

"You're her *owner,*" Beti says, and Nerissa has to hold back a hiss. While she may not look like a vampire or act like one, Beti still has that ability to slide in and out of fact and insult as if they were but twin tributaries in a stream. "She's your indentured servant, if not your slave. But that's your problem to fix. I think it is her bond to you that is keeping her alive, which won't be without consequence. If she is with her other master," Nerissa bites back on her tongue as Beti continues, "then there is a chance she is still alive."

"But where is Worth?" Nerissa asks. "Alma said half of the building collapsed around a rift."

Michaux laughs, and Beti shakes her head.

Nerissa presses her free hand to her forehead while the bubbling liquid in her other continues its multicolored shifting.

"You look like you're going to faint. Why don't you eat?" Beti says, not looking up from the fox, but clearly addressing the lamia.

"I...don't have anything to..."

Michaux giggles his most elaborate and high-toned laugh yet. "It's in your hand, silly."

Nerissa looks down at the vial in her hand and cringes, both at her stupidity and at the contents. "What is it?" she asks as quietly as she can manage.

"We heard you're rather squeamish about eating from the source," Michaux says, not in a whisper. "If you'd have come here first instead of the Thousand Suns, you might not be in all that trouble."

"Michaux, the task at hand," Beti scolds.

Michaux pouts pathetically. "It's blood of a common imp. You're a Fey creature, born in the very bowels of that famed land. Unlike vampires who are made here. We can add a little imp blood to our cocktails if we like—makes our teeth glow blue in the dark. But it won't sustain us."

"Lamias who came up from the Fae learned to drink human blood as a replacement for imp blood," says Beti. "You'll feel a lot better drinking this, though."

"How...did you get it?" Nerissa asks, taking out the stopper and smelling it. It smells like the seaside, briny and salty and full of minerals.

"We collect it in buckets," Michaux says cheerily. "The bastards make so much of it."

"I mean, are they *willing*?" asks Nerissa.

Michaux rolls his eyes at her as if she is the most pathetic excuse for a monster in the entire world. She probably is. But she also remembers what it was like having to learn not to drink human blood, how everything else tasted like ash in her mouth, how Vivienne sat with her, night after night after night...

"They are *imps*," says Michaux. "Do you not remember anything from your time in the Fae?"

"I was only there a short time," Nerissa says, willing her thoughts of the place away. She doesn't like to think about what happened. She's more willing to face her life as a monster, stalking the moors for human lives than she is to think about what she was born into. "I don't remember much."

Michaux gives an impatient sigh as Beti coaxes the fox to drink a little milky fluid. "Imps cry blood. They sweat blood. Thankfully, they don't piss blood, but you get Michaux's point. You don't have to hurt an imp to harvest it. And plenty are willing to collect their tears for you—it gets a pretty penny."

"You want me to drink imp sweat," Nerissa says.

"Imp *blood*. Chemically it is no different from their sweat, but whatever you want to call it is fine with me. As long as you drink it, and soon. You look like you're starting to molt. My guess is the *kitsune* blood has worn off," Beti says, offhandedly as she smooths the red fox's face.

"I didn't drink her blood," says Nerissa.

Michaux and Beti look at her and both laugh. The blond vampire is the one to speak, though. "My serpentine darling. You smell of *kitsune*. Whether or not you know it, you drank her blood."

Nerissa tries to go back, to remember. The blood had been left for her, but Kit was *always* leaving blood for her. She just assumed it was rat, or fresher—camel, perhaps—but then... It did taste oddly floral. Hints of moss and just a smattering of berries and plums.

She drinks the imp blood in a long, thirsty gulp, trying to hold back her own tears.

SCORPION AND SERPENT

S erket's voice comes both from the scorpion and the very ground
they stand upon. Christabel flinches with the noise, feeling reverberations ripple through her ribcage, up her throat. It is a most
unpleasant sensation, and she would throw up if she had anything to give
it shape.

"We escaped a creature… It was a giant mouth, gaping…" Christabel's
voice is faint, and she realizes that her ears are ringing so loudly it's hard
to gauge the volume. She puts her hand to her lips and tries again, but
Serket has heard her. "It brought us here."

*You came from the mortal lands and you reek of death and itke and
dying.*

Christabel has never considered just how disturbing watching a scorpion speak with a mouth under its thorax could be, especially since the
mouth has human teeth and purple mottled lips, but she is quite certain
she has no desire to ever see it again. Every word it speaks feels like
worms in her stomach.

"We were attacked," Christabel says. "By a creature that dragged us
here by magical means. I could not fight it. My friends are mortally
wounded." She gestures to Worth and the fox, unsure of how to explain.

The two figures on each side of Serket are dog-headed things, but they
each have long tails like a scorpion. They flit back and forth, curious in
their timing. They are never in sync and yet move at the same cadence.

193

It's dizzying to watch, but significantly less stomach-churning than watching Serket.

Then do you suppose yourself their heroine, monokeros?

Christabel hadn't heard anyone outside of a book speak that particular title before. It was what the Greeks called her kind, back when there were more than one or two unicorns upon the face of the Earth. She supposes it makes sense that an Egyptian goddess might know her by such a name, considering their relatively close quarters with the Greeks from time to time in antiquity.

"I suppose myself nothing," Christabel says, straightening up. This place, this reedy plain, makes her feel strong. The longer she looks at Serket, the less frightening she appears. She is flaking, for one, along her carapace. Her body is withered, the skin like that of an old mummy. One of her hands shakes. The dog-headed creatures beside her seem more obsequious than concerning, now. "I only want to help my friends and to find one who has been lost."

I care not for your wayward companions.

Taking a deep breath, Christabel tries to assess the situation, painstakingly separating her logical mind and her emotional responses. She knows there is a scientific explanation for what is happening, or else a rationale that is beyond simple fear. Even if it is beyond her own ability to understand at the moment. There are rules, laws by which they must all abide. If only she can understand them in this part of the Fae.

It occurs to her that Serket may be more like her than she imagines at first. Most beings, monsters in from the Fae, have distinct defense mechanisms. But if she remembers correctly, while Serket embodies many aspects of the scorpion, she is also a healer.

Flattery gets you everywhere, even with insectile goddesses. And Christabel is a unicorn, after all. Flattery is like breathing.

She feels the soft earth beneath her feet, closing her eyes for just a moment, anchoring herself deep like the roots of a tree.

"Majestic Serket," she says at last, bowing her head and raising her eyes. "I am lost in your realm, taken here against my will, in a search of a child of the Fae who was stolen. I seek revenge and understanding. My sorrow is as deep as the asp's bite, and I beg for your help and blessing in this. I beseech you and believe our paths have crossed for this very reason."

Christabel pushes out her emotion like a shield before her. It's been quite some time since she's expelled her powers in such a way, but it feels easier here, which she supposes isn't much of a surprise. Though she has no memory of the Fae, it is her home. Even if it's not called the Fae, it's connected. From the same source.

It starts as a tingle on her forehead, a subtle pressure like a drop of unexpected water. That is where her horn resides, even if she is able to hide it.

At first Christabel is certain that Serket is going to rear on her, but then the goddess simply sits down all at once in a puff of dried grass, letting out a sigh like the bellows. Her dog-headed servants curl up on her immediately, as if she's made some inaudible command. She bows her head and her shoulders shake as if she weeps, her hands trailing lines across her dog servants' fur.

Serket's voice shifts when she speaks, going softer and full of whispers. "No one ever asks me for a blessing," she says. "They only seek me when they want me to smite their enemies or heal family members who have fallen prey to venom. They do not understand who I am."

Relief floods over Christabel like a silken shroud, and she watches Serket continue to sink, her head bowing deeper. The goddess lifts up her scorpion head to reveal a shriveled old face, wrinkled with deep caverns of sorrow. So many lines of wear. So tired. Christabel feels the weight of twenty thousand years.

"My friends are dying," Christabel says. "But I need your guidance. Your healing touch."

Serket directs her dogs with the point of a trembling finger, and they pad over to the unconscious fox and Worth. Christabel swallows down fear as Serket stares deeply toward the unicorn. This new face is strange.

Christabel realizes with a jolt that Serket has no eyes, only sockets where two fireflies dance.

"Goddess?" Christabel asks.

"You belong here," Serket says. "I realize you want to leave now. But the time will come when you will stay, little monoceros, and I will teach you. That is the bargain we will strike."

Christabel nods. It makes sense. In a strange way, more sense than anything has made. She does need a teacher. And Serket feels...akin to her. She realizes Serket is not bothering to request this boon. The deal was already struck when they locked eyes. Or whatever you call those bugs in her face.

"The beast is shattered, and my magic cannot heal his wounds. But I can take the poison from him. He needs more than I can offer," Serket says, raising a hand as Worth's body glows with a thousand brilliant threads. "But he will live."

"We need to get back above. How do we leave?" Christabel asks.

"The fox will lead you to her other half, and you can start from there."

~

W orth opens his eyes and immediately feels as if he's suffocating. His whole body is surrounded in pressure, his skin pressed to the point of bruising, his chest heaving in breath in huge, gasping rattles. Pinpricks of light appear at the edges of his vision and then form to make a familiar face.

Christabel. Her hair is down over her shoulders, no longer the dark brown that it was in Cairo but now a pale russet. On any other woman it might look odd, but it perfectly matches her eyes and her dappled skin. There is dirt smudged across her cheek and down across her lips, little pieces of soil barely hanging on, tear tracks through the filth.

And he is being licked by a warm, small tongue, somewhere on the vicinity of his feet. But that is a small detail in contrast to the beauty of Christabel's face. While his entire body spasms in pain, it is nothing compared to watching her.

Then there is another face, abruptly wretched and shocking to behold. It looks like a peeled, shrunken apple topped with a carapace of some kind. And the eyes are nothing but empty caverns with no seeming end, and worms and flies crawling around inside. One of them might be a firefly, or maybe he's just gone mad and he's dead.

He tries to move, but he's immediately nauseated, completely discombobulated in his form. Worth at first thinks that he's restrained, since his body has curious limitations it's never had before. But he's moving arms and legs, human arms and legs, it's just that everything else he is has ceased to be accessible.

"Worth." Christabel's voice drifts to him, calm and firm. "You need to stop thrashing. You're going to hurt yourself or...me." She's grunting in between her words, and he understands that he's kicking out against her, against the firefly eyes, but he's drowning, in a panic.

He cannot access his true forms. That strange, liquid part of him always beneath the surface.

He is trapped.

"Worth!" Christabel admonishes, and then her face swims up into his vision again. He's given her a bloody nose. But she's a unicorn, and her blood glows light blue as it courses from her nose and across her hand.

"Your blood will not save him, child," says the hideous old crone, firefly eyes dancing lazily in the skeleton sockets.

"Bloody fool kicked me in the face," Christabel says, and to Worth it sounds as if she is very far, and he thinks that a bloody nose is the least of their problems.

He cannot be a Glatisant if he is stuck in his human form. There is nothing redeeming about him in such mortal, fickle flesh. He will age and die and fall out of use, and all his friends will live long, strange lives, and he will become a mere footnote in their wild, storied tale. He will never see Vivienne again. He will never kiss Christabel again, he will never...

Something stings him hard, and he goes to cry out but finds he has no breath to give it life, no strength in his throat.

As the thrashing goes on, it is the crone who acts, moving toward him with unexpected quickness, and he feels something press hard into the center of him. Then, the crone is standing away from him, tilting her abnormally large head. Rigid with horror, Worth stills himself and looks down where his glamour gland used to be. It is cracked. And in the spectacular fissure now sits a gold-green scorpion, its tail firmly embedded in the rocky organ.

∾

Worth dreams of Christabel. And yet he is also dreaming of Vivienne. They are intertwined in a single figure, languid and queenly, draped across a throne, head tilted, watching him. The face is all Christabel's, gentle and full of curves and smooth lines. But the mannerism, the body, is all Vivienne, long and lean and confident in her power and sexuality.

He is in a hallway carved with Egyptian hieroglyphics, but they move as he looks at them, always slipping away from comprehension. And the closer he gets to the Vivienne/Christabel hybrid, the more distant she gets, and the more aroused he becomes.

∾

W orth wakes from his dream and smells fur. Damp fur. And while he is painfully aware of his broken state, he does not shriek or thrash because the poison from the scorpion has subdued him. It's a bit pleasant, though it still stings. Quite like a very good, or very bad, drink.

Christabel is across from him, brushing her long hair behind her ear as he slowly sits up, eyes full of sadness and hope. The white fox at his side pops open a silver eye and rising, stretches luxuriously, its little tongue curling at the end like a punctuation mark.

"Finally," Christabel says, a little shyly, as if there is something embarrassing between them.

Worth looks down at his naked body and is painfully aware.

"That's…" Worth tries, taking the fox and positioning it strategically before him. The fox, on its part, does little to dissuade him. She seems rather fond of him, and quite resigned to manipulation. "Christabel. I…"

"You were injured, coming through the gate," she says softly, trying to avert her eyes, but to little avail. Worth is entirely naked. Vivienne would be aghast and titillated. "Your glamour is broken," she says, somewhat unhelpfully.

"I'm *aware*," Worth says, rubbing at his raw throat. He must have screamed for hours. There is only a hint of his other forms, drifting somewhere inaccessible and strange. He feels oddly one-dimensional. The world is too quiet. There was something else.

Fireflies.

"She's gone," Christabel answers as he frantically looks about. She gestures to his chest. "That was her gift."

"What was she?" he asks, not wanting to know the answer, though he feels it in his chest before Christabel says her name.

"Serket," the unicorn replies, standing elegantly. Her hair is long enough that it falls to her thighs, and while it is entwined with twigs and moss and detritus, it is no less lovely. All of her is like spun moonlight dappled through the trees, and he wants to take her in his arms so badly it aches. If only he weren't exhausted to his marrow.

The sting of the scorpion reminds him that he is broken.

"A goddess," he marvels. "This is as strange a place as I have ever seen."

"It's an extension of the Fae. *Duat.* A crossroads, as far as I can tell. A place between what we know and where Serket resides. The beast we fought tried to take us to a darker realm, but Serket said our own magic confused it."

She takes a step toward him and holds a pile of cloth out to him. It is black as the night sky itself but wound with bits of shinier floss.

"I wove it from spider silk and some of the moss that grows on these trees," Christabel says. "It isn't much for fashion, but it should fit."

The material is soft as a cloud, and once over his skin still gives the impression of being naked from within yet is perfectly opaque on the outside. It soothes his skin, most of which feels fit to bursting and raw.

"Thank you, Christabel," he says, wanting to take her hand but too afraid to find out what would happen should he touch her. He folds his arms across his chest. "I'm forever in your debt."

"Nonsense," she says with a flick of her hand. "We've got another fox to find. Serket went on ahead of us, and she's clearing the path. But you know as well as I do that there's danger in staying here."

"They're always looking for you," Worth said.

Christabel nods slowly. "Even here, in my home, I am not safe. It's why my parents took me from the Fae. It's why they kept my true being a secret. I had intended on returning at some point, but…"

The little fox at his feet starts running circles, hopping toward a barely distinguishable path. Upon closer inspection, Worth realize that the path is lit with thousands of tiny mushrooms, just barely rising from the ground, lighting their way.

"We'll do what we can," Worth says, willing his voice to sound firm, but not truly believing himself. He thinks of Kit at the Thousand Suns. And Cook. And all the creatures in his service. What happened to them? Surely, the blast was beyond anything even a strong Fey could survive.

And he is mortified. Just a few steps and he's as weak as a kitten, unused to the constraints of a truly human form. When Christabel reaches out a hand to steady him, though, even he's surprised at the flare up of pride as he bats her away.

He's going to need to figure this whole business out. If his healing is dependent on Vivienne, he may be waiting a very long time.

MEANWHILE BACK

"The *kitsune* will naturally seek out her other half," Beti says, stroking the little red fox who has taken up residence in her arms. It ate a little bit, mostly some crushed up beetles and crackers, and then fell asleep contentedly in the arms of a vampire. *Curious things*, Nerissa thinks, not for the last time.

The imp blood has done a great deal of good for her. True to the vampires' insistence, it warms her and fills her with a sharp clarity she has not felt in some time. She's loath to admit it, but it's a good deal better than even human blood. All this time she has dined on the equivalent of sugar cubes, decent for quick energy but not good in the long run. The imp blood is like a fine meal of flesh, sitting comfortably in her stomach without making her drowsy.

They are now sitting in Beti's parlor, a much more pleasant room deeper in the coven halls. Though there are no windows to speak of, it is nonetheless kept rather bright with candles and gas lamps, the yellow walls made of velvet jacquard.

"So, my spies tell me that Itke reared its ugly head at the Thousand Suns. It is a beast, but more properly, it is a beast that works as a kind of sucking void from one plane to another. You must have really gotten Cook angry," says Beti, holding open a small book on her lap, which she's been consulting for the better part of the last hour. Somehow, she has managed both the book and the fox, and her powers of deduction. "It was probably an attempt to kill the *kitsune,* or else kill your friends. Or lure you there. Either way, you'll be off the trail now whether or not you like it."

"I should have been there," Nerissa says.

"You would have suffered the same fate. But do not lose all hope, my dear. Your friends, and the other half of this creature, must still be alive in the Underworld. Or at least the other half of the fox and her other master. She must be a strong *kitsune* to manage the distance. But she won't last long."

"How do I know where to look?" asks Nerissa.

"Like I said, you let the fox lead you to the right place."

"I don't take trust lightly. It appears that I'm having to put a lot of faith in vampires, which generally doesn't end well."

"I didn't poison you. I nourished you. I took you into my home and gave you succor," Beti says, straightening up. There is something behind her eyes that speaks of an ancient, powerful hunger, and a threat. "I could have killed you ten thousand ways, child, and I did not. What more proof do you need?"

Nerissa frowns, looking down at her hands. They are softer and smoother than they have been in ages. The veins barely visible under her skin. She feels almost giddy with health and vitality.

"So I go to the Underworld," Nerissa says.

Beti gives Nerissa a pitying look, the threat dissolving like frost on a window, and there is a surprising amount of genuine warmth in it. "Here they call it *Duat,* and it is likely inhabited by the folk of this pantheon. I am astonished that this information is new to you. I thought every Fey child learned the basic geography of the Fae. I have had to cobble together my knowledge from the outside and apparently am far more knowledgable than you."

"It's...never been my area of study," Nerissa says, trying not to take offense, but unable to quell the rising shame.

"You know so little about yourself it almost breaks my heart. Well, if it were still beating," Beti says, correcting herself. "While you are not of our kin, I cannot help but think of you as a kind of lost cousin, and as such, I am beset with the need to help you. It's quite unsettling, as even though you're a friend to Alma, I cannot help but feel as if you are in need of instruction yourself."

"I'm fine right now, thank you very much," Nerissa says.

"Well, don't hesitate to seek out our covens, wherever you may rest.

And I have tickets you can use for trading in imp blood, as well. I can do you that service."

"Thank you. But to the matter at hand. If I need to get to the Underworld, can you take me there?"

"To *Duat?*" Beti asks, raising an eyebrow at the lamia. "You want to know if a vampire can take you to Duat?"

"I…like you said," Nerissa tries, diplomatically—or as diplomatic as a snake can be. "I don't know much about the realm."

"Clearly. Duat is not just one place. It is many places. It is a whole realm, and the Fae is, shall we say, an adjacent realm to it. There are pathways to and fro. But for a vampire to go into Duat," Beti says, shaking her head and looking down at the fox, "that would be a true death. We are *already* undead. And I'm afraid we would not fare well."

Nerissa is about to contribute more to the conversation but decides it prudent to shut her mouth. Perhaps imp blood is good for her mood, as well.

Beti grins, sharp teeth showing, as if Nerissa is her star student.

"I will, however, give you access to one of our crypts, and within it is a gateway to Duat. Alma will be a good guide, and besides, the fox knows where to go. The only way I imagine she is still alive is because her other half is there, as well. They will find one another or else perish."

"I don't know what to say," Nerissa says.

Beti raises one finger. "Don't thank me yet. I do have a price."

"Of course," Nerissa says, trying to keep calm. But her hearts are pounding and she's ready to go running in the direction of the crypts.

"You have been searching for Vivienne du Lac, have you not?"

The sound of Vivienne's name is so sharp and unexpected that Nerissa physically jolts in surprise, like someone has put a fish hook through her and tugged.

Beti shakes her head sadly. "You don't need to answer that. You've all made enough noise to rouse the Circle and the vampire network, to say nothing of Cook's nefarious employer. We've been following the Crane woman quite closely for some time."

"We cannot be threatened," says Nerissa.

"I'm not threatening you; I'm just gathering information. We protect our own."

"What do you want?"

"I'm giving you a price. I will provide you with everything you need for your journey to rescue your friends. Weapons, clothing, passwords, and plenty of food. On one single condition. You leave Cairo as soon as you find them."

Nerissa wouldn't have argued a few days ago. Cairo was everything she hated. Dust and sand and busy streets, strange magic and the constant press of people. Sun! Heavens, she hated the sun. To get back to comfort, and moisture, and familiarity would be remarkable. The thought of the English countryside almost makes her cry out with longing.

But if Beti was telling her to leave...that must mean they are closer to finding Vivienne. Mr. Ghali's employer. They must all be connected somehow. And Vivienne is everything.

Isn't she?

That dark, sad place in her mind thinks that if Vivienne wanted to, she would have sent word. She would have done more than wait for them. Vivienne's powers are so wide and deep, so well-honed. Perhaps she doesn't miss them at all. Perhaps she's given up hope. Perhaps, after Nerissa told her the truth of her affections, she wants to start again...

No. She cannot think that way. Vivienne saved her. Lover or not, she owes her more than she can ever repay.

"I don't expect you to give up looking for the sylph, of course. And I am happy to connect you to covens outside of Cairo. As I said, they are a wealth of information and sustenance. But you are interfering with the work we need to do here, and people are asking questions. You must understand that the protection of my coven is of utmost importance. We have lived, uninterrupted, for hundreds of years in this city and do not wish to be put at risk."

They must be close. And Worth and Christabel will never forgive her if she promises to leave Cairo when they're on the right trail. But then, she'll never be able to find Vivienne without them.

"What do you say, Ms. Waldemar? Fancy a deal?"

~

They walk when Worth is capable. Time feels slowed, strange, so Christabel has no idea how long they wait for him to stand, nor how long it takes to steady him. But, at last, they begin.

Christabel sees Serket in the distance, a hunched shadow against the darker mountains. The presence of the goddess fills her with a sense of calm.

Worth is too miserable to notice. He is pale and clammy, his dark hair stuck around his brow in little curls. His eyes are wide and fearful, but even worse, full of pain. When he speaks, it is with barely more than a whisper. And he shivers all the time. But at least he speaks, and responds, and, albeit with agonizing intensity and torture, look at her with love.

The fox mostly sleeps on Christabel's shoulder, having decided it was an optimal place to rest.

And the world around them...

Duat is a mystery to the unicorn. Neither time nor distance obey the same rules as they do in the mortal world. It is a land of always twilight, the firmament strange and shifting above them but the sun never rising. Water flows away to the east, she can hear the rushing of it wherever they go, but they never cross it. There are animals in the distance, too, but they keep a good space between them. Insects are aplenty—mostly flying beetles and worms in the soft ground—but they do not interact with the travelers in any way. Not even the midges bite.

"How did you get those scars on your back?" Christabel asks Worth. The white fox perches on her shoulder, tilting its head in a mimicry of attention to the question.

"I have scars?" Worth says, turning to her, his eyes hollow. He pauses to reach back, encounters the dark shift Christabel had made him, and then stops. "I have never noticed scars."

"It looks like you were run through, except there aren't any on the other side. Like four swords," she says, stealing another look at him. She wants to cry, seeing him so broken like this.

And yet, to heal him means finding Vivienne. And she doesn't know if she can bear it. How are they so close to her and yet so far away? She hasn't wanted anything other than to find Vivienne for years, striving only to make up for her mistakes, to apologize for what was done. And now, faced with the opportunity to get even closer to the sylph—for they must be close, now, if Cook went to these lengths to get rid of them—she does not want to.

"I don't remember," Worth says, and he sounds utterly defeated. His usually crisp, kind voice, is rough with wear from all the screaming.

"Worth," Christabel says, reaching out to take his hand.

"No," he says, looking away from her. "I am broken in this body..."

"This is still you," she says, trying to be helpful, but knowing her words only make light of the situation. "Isn't it?" She adds the last bit hoping to soften the blow.

Worth frowns and takes a step sideways from her, her hand dropping back by her side. Her heart feels raw, bruised. She truly does love him, and it feels like she's got glass in her stomach.

"I don't remember," Worth says, grasping at the place on his chest where the scorpion lies. "I'm no longer shattering but…it's like an open wound. And everything inside of me is on fire."

She knows that feeling all too well, but only now is she willing to admit it to herself. Christabel chokes back a sob and looks toward the horizon.

"I'm sorry," she says. "Worth…"

I love you. I love you. I want to help you.

"Yes?"

"I'll help you. I promise. I'll get you out of here."

They walk onward, until their feet hurt. The little fox knows where to go, indeed, and always Serket is in the distance until, inexplicably, she vanishes.

Christabel takes a deep breath as the mists rise before them.

Two great mountains emerge, with a triangle structure between them, coming down from the sky. No, not just any triangle. A pyramid. Inverted. It is so incongruous and yet so perfectly suited to the environment that it takes a good half mile—perhaps, as the distance has never been clear—for Christabel to understand exactly what it might represent.

"I think we're almost there."

It looks like one of the pyramids of Giza. Khafra's, to be precise, because it was capped with residual limestone at the peak. Unlike her companions, Christabel had taken time to learn the pyramids from one another and had even taken a few day trips to the dig sites. She had the opportunity speak to some of the excavators and learn what history they knew of the place. Much was circumspect, as the date of the pyramids was almost beyond fathom, even for creatures of the Fae.

The wind picks up, trailing sand through the reeds and sighing with longing.

"I'm tired," Worth says, half to the wind, as they come to a stop. "I'm cold."

"He'll be tired until he gets used to the poison," Serket says.

Christabel startles but does not see the goddess. Then she notices a small scorpion by her foot, copper in color.

"Serket," she whispers.

"Tell him he's through the worst of it," the goddess says.

"What?" Worth asks.

It's then that Christabel realizes Worth cannot hear or see Serket at all, even as a scorpion. He's staring right through her and into the grass.

Christabel says gently to Worth, "I think we're through the worst of it," but he does not look convinced. He just shivers.

"I cannot go farther," Serket says, with no particular inflection. Just a simple observation.

"But how will I know where to go?" Christabel asks.

"Follow the alabaster path," Serket says, gesturing to the ground before them.

Instead of a faint impression in the reeds, there is now a paved path of alabaster before them, clearly cut and moving outward between the mountains and toward the pyramid.

As Christabel narrows her eyes, she sees that the path rises toward the peak of the pyramid, almost touching it at its pinnacle.

It is a very long walk. And she is so, so tired.

"Serket, how can I thank you?" Christabel asks.

Serket shakes her shoulders, and little puffs of dust rise about her.

"You made things grow in my wood, you fashioned them into beautiful things, you give me hope," she says. "It is a gift enough. Perhaps you will come back some time."

"Christabel?" Worth asks. "Are you well?"

"He is not of here," Serket says as she turns away from Christabel.

"What does that mean?" Christabel says. "I know he's not of Duat."

"Duat is a cousin of the Fae, where you were born. He was not born in the beneath of places. He smells of…" She pauses, her carapace dimming for a moment. "If he permits you, speak to the sphinx before you return."

"Christabel?" asks Worth again, now touching her shoulder. His eyes are piercing, clear and lucid for the first time since they arrived. "I'm sorry I haven't been myself, but you seem to be speaking to thin air."

When Christabel turns back to Serket, all that is left is a pair of fireflies dancing in the reeds that swirl and extinguish.

"I'm fine. But we have a long way to walk," she says to Worth, purposely avoiding that gaze. "Are you up to it?"

"Christabel," he says softly. He squeezes her shoulder gently, and she feels her heart soar and ache at the same time.

"Later," she says. "We're losing time. We've got to save Kit."

"If I remember, you didn't much like her," Worth says.

"That's not the point. As usual, I'm making up for your mistakes. And

Nerissa's, too, wherever she's gotten herself to. I can't walk around knowing I didn't help Kit, and let her die, when she was trying to help us."

The little fox nuzzles at Christabel's neck as if in reply.

Worth nods, then squints toward the endless stairway. "I'll do what I can." He presses his hand to his chest, wincing. "Just promise me... promise me that if I don't..."

"Worth, you'll be fine," Christabel says, though she doesn't think that's the case at all.

His eyes are that strange absinthe green again.

"Just don't forget," he says, his voice fading into whispers.

"Don't forget what?"

Worth sighs. "I don't remember."

~

"You made a deal with the vampires?" Alma asks Nerissa when they meet in the alleyway. The lamia is laden with good weapons, new clothes, and maps. Not to mention a disproportionate sunniness to her attitude.

Alma is losing her patience with the snake person. First of all, she looks beautiful. She looks refreshed. She isn't wearing her spectacles, and her skin is practically glowing. There is a power in her that wasn't there before, and Alma doesn't trust it. Because vampires shouldn't be trusted. Unless they're being trusted to kill someone. Or feeding someone. That, they're very good at.

"It's none of your concern," Nerissa says, looking down the length of the alleyway and adjusting the leather straps at her waist.

The new clothes are expensive, too; not that Alma takes notice of such things. Dwarves don't even need clothes because their skin is perfect the way it is, diamond hard and practically impervious to heat and cold. But fleshy creatures always insist that walking around au naturel is somehow scandalous, and they tend to get offended by flawless dwarven bodies.

That said, Alma has learned to take notice when fleshier creatures make abrupt changes. They can say a great deal with fabric and lace that they don't with words. Things like stature and wealth, all woven into the lines of their petticoats.

"Why are you dressed like that?" Alma asks.

"Dressed like what?" Nerissa asks, reaching up to straighten the hat on her head, a wide-brimmed affair with a scarf tied about it to keep it on and to keep dust out.

"You look like you belong on one of those horrible expeditions by the pyramids," Alma says, almost off-handedly.

Nerissa stops in her stride, turning to look the dwarf in the eye. "Well, that's… Beti said that you would take me. That you're the best guide they have, and that the Circle would be glad to know of your service."

Alma curses in her own language, and it causes some of the plaster nearby to crackle and send out puffs of dust.

Nerissa, to her credit, hardly flinches.

"I don't like pyramids," says Alma. "Why you'd ever build caverns above ground when there are plenty below ground makes no sense."

"But you were chased by a demon. And you know about portals. And the vampires have granted me access to their crypts," Nerissa says, holding out a set of black metal keys. They bear the insignia of Barker House, the most preeminent coven in Cairo.

The crypts.

Alma has to hold back a moan. It is rumored that within those crypts are unfathomable stones and craftwork long ago lost to her kind. She would never venture to take them, of course, but even a slight look would give her a wealth of information in terms of her own handiwork. And now that she's not beholden to Mr. Ghali…

"We'll go through the crypts and into Khafra's pyramid," Nerissa says, as smoothly as if talking about the newest fashion.

"And?"

"And what?" Nerissa plays the fool very badly.

"There's always more."

"And then to Duat."

Oh, Duat. That's all. Alma takes a deep breath, holding it longer than most creatures can manage, because it helps her think. She does not like the idea of any of this. But she can't go home, not until she's whole and can make sense of her adventures. She can't go to the Circle because they'll scorn her for turning away Nerissa, one of the creatures they swore to help after the business in Tarrytown. She can't go with the vampires for obvious reasons.

"Alma?" Nerissa asks, almost poking the dwarf. "Are you in there?"

Alma forgot that her stone state is a bit unsettling to flesh creatures. She shakes her head and resumes her more or less acceptable appearance, and shrugs.

"I don't suppose I've much of a choice," she says. "But we're going to need more artillery than what you've got."

~

Alma is reluctant to bring Nerissa into her apartment, since she's never done such a thing in her life for anyone. But she has this snake person and her friends to thank, more or less, for her freedom; besides, there is only so much standing outside and waiting one can do before it's past decorum even for a Nith dwarf.

"You lived here?" asks Nerissa.

It's true, from the view of an Upsider, it isn't much. It looks like a blank, limestone cave, which is not an unfair assessment.

But that's where the fun comes in.

"Of course," Alma says, and gestures to the wall. She draws a rune on it, and after a decisive click, the wall slides open, a hidden drawer now in plain view. "I've got to keep my things safe, you know."

Nerissa puts an exploratory hand on one of the walls, but it does nothing, of course. Alma almost laughs.

"You look different," Alma says, finding her pike and giving it a loving pat. It's not impressive upon first glance, but it's wound with a most precious metal, mostly unknown on this part of the plane. Iridium. Just feeling it on her skin makes Alma shiver a little. "Brighter."

Nerissa looks down at her hands, and her eyes widen. In the darkness of the cave, her fingernails glow. To the Nith dwarf, it's quite bright, but for the snake, it's probably just a subtle effect, but even untrained eyes would meet it.

"The vampires fed me," Nerissa says, turning over her fingers. "They gave me what they claim lamias eat in the wild. I confess I didn't think much of it then, but now I feel...well, clearer than I have in a very long time. As if a fog has lifted from my mind. I am strangely calm."

"Well, it looks good on you, I suppose," Alma says. "Let's just hope it helps you keep your wits about you. Where we're going, the world goes a little topsy-turvy."

"You think I should trust the vampires about the food?" Nerissa says, watching carefully as Alma ties on her belt and pulls out her shield from another drawer, along with some foodstuffs—no doubt looking like common limestone to the snake—and re-plaits her hair in the warrior fashion.

Alma sighs. "They take their food very seriously. If Beti gave you something and told you it was best for you, she's right. It's not in her nature to nourish wrong. No, no, don't tell me what it is. I get sick enough thinking about what you people eat *without* knowing."

Nerissa grins at Alma, and for the first time, the dwarf realizes just how sharp her teeth are. Were they always so pointed? "Well, you look the part, now."

"I'll take that as a compliment," Alma says, though she isn't sure that's what's intended.

"Alma," Nerissa says.

"No, please, no overflow of emotion and gratitude. That's not how the Nith work. We say thank you with our strength. We break the stone and hold our oaths. I'm trusting you with my life, and I'll protect yours. But when this is over and your friends are safe, I'm leaving."

"Fair enough," Nerissa says. "I would expect no less."

But even Alma knows she can't hold to that promise. She feels needed for the first time in a very long time, and if they get through this alive, or else die in the throes of battle as is befitting a Nith, it will have been worth it.

THE CLIMB

"Christabel," Worth says. Then with more concern, "Christabel, please. Stop a moment."

He is lucid again. She's starting to dread those moments.

They have been climbing the alabaster stair for so long that Christabel had fallen into a kind of trance. She thinks of it as the alabaster stair, even though there aren't any stairs, because it sounds good in her head and gives her the sense of accomplishment. But it's more of a continual rise up the side of a great mountain. A mountain that has no peak or purpose and only serves to bring them around and around in a corkscrew toward the pinnacle of the great upside-down pyramid protruding from the sky.

Worth has oscillated between sulky and silent and fearful and questioning.

"I can't help you right now, Worth, I told you," she says to him.

"You're...you're not in your human form," he says. "Did you always look like this?"

This brings her up short. She looks down to see that she has transformed against her own will, or at least without thinking about it. The white fox has taken up residence on her back like a little rider. What she can see of her body is pale and shimmering.

"What am I?" she asks, unable to see.

"Not like I've seen you before," Worth says, coming up to her and looking her in the eyes. So she's taller, then. She has been an oryx, and she has been a goat-like creature, but never as tall as this.

She begins to cry because everything hurts, and she misses Serket, and she's quite afraid that they will never stop climbing. She's afraid that Worth is irreparably broken, and she will never be able to love him the way he deserves. She is afraid of knowing what she is and what she is truly capable of. It's always there, burning inside, waiting to come out. A beautiful monster.

"Am I terrible?" she asks as Worth smooths the tears from her snout.

"You are a wonder," he says, and all the weariness is gone from his voice. She can almost see herself in his luminous eyes. "You are tall and fine, white on your nose and back, but going to a silvery charcoal by your flanks and hooves. You've got the most beautiful black hair, cascading down almost like a mane. Though your tail is more like a lion's..." He trails off, shaking his head. "And your eyes..."

Don't look at me like that. Don't look at me like that, Worth!

"Well, at least I look like a proper unicorn, then," she says, tossing her head.

"It's better than I can do," Worth says with a sigh. He reaches up to touch her soft nose and rests his cheek there for a moment, breathing softly. "You are a wonder, Christabel. I just want to say, before I go away again, that..."

The ground trembles, drowning out the rest of Worth's words. Christabel shudders with the reverberations, now making their way up her hooves, cursing under her breath. How had she not noticed? What kind of sorry fool lets herself go this far without control? She is one breath from utter annihilation but too besotted with Worth to notice!

The fox digs its little claws into Christabel's back and then hops off, skittering across the white stone a moment before finding balance. Its ears twitch this way and that, and it takes an almost defensive stance. Amusing, considering its size.

"I felt a pressure in the air the first time I saw you," Worth says, drawing closer to Christabel, winding his fingers into her mane and stroking her side to calm her. But really, his voice is the most calming sound in the world, low and resonant and full of music. "And I felt a shifting inside of me, a settling, of years of pain and confusion. When I saw you, it was as if I was reminded of something I'd forgotten a long time ago. A song or a memory. And you were part of it. I know that sounds utterly daft, Christabel, and..."

"Worth, that is quite beautiful, but we have company," Christabel says, turning her head toward the shape in the middle of the path.

Neither of them need be explained what it is. Serket warned of the sphinx, but Christabel did not imagine that the sphinx on this side of the plane would be so small.

He is not much bigger than a large dog and is sitting directly in the middle of the alabaster stair, the little fox making its way toward him carefully. Then, with a happy little bark, the fox starts running circles around the creature, filling the air with swirls of fog from its snout.

His head is that of a man, his body that of a lion. His wings spread out on either side of him and are not, as Christabel had once imagined, bat-like or frightening in any way. Rather, they are the wings of a swan, soft and downy and spotless. The sphinx's face holds an ancient wisdom in those lines, a wide nose and thick lips with a broad brow. He reminds Christabel of the men of the Sudan, dark and fearsome and striking.

"Welcome," says the sphinx. "You are almost back where you'd like to go."

He smiles pleasantly at them, and Christabel is struck dumb. Oddly, it's Worth that steps in.

"You're a bit smaller than I expected," Worth says, kneeling down to get a better look at the sphinx.

"I'm much larger up there, so they say, where they have chiseled me into a still, strange statue," the sphinx replies, taking one paw and gesturing upward toward the pinnacle of Khafra's pyramid. "It's an ugly thing, but we've had to make peace with it."

The sphinx looks over at Christabel, and she says, "We've been sent by Serket; we're hoping to get home."

"You are home, *monoceros*," says the sphinx.

"You can call me Christabel," she says, uncomfortable with the moniker yet again. "Christabel Crane."

"Ah, human names by human brains. Pitifully limited. What kind of name is that for one such as you? Did they ever tell you where you came from? How they found you? What you were doing? I should think you'd be pursuing those answers instead of following this fellow," says the sphinx.

Worth frowns at this, drawing his clothing tighter around him. There is a distinct chill in the air, but Christabel can only feel it in her snout.

"That isn't why I'm here," she says, tossing her head. Those questions cut right through to the heart of her. They are all things she has wondered about—of course she has. But since discovering her true nature, it's been so easy to concentrate, instead, on finding Vivienne du Lac, the woman who was whisked away on account of Christabel. And Nerissa. And probably Worth.

She stomps her hooves. "That's not the point."

"There are infinite points. And infinite paths. This is just a particularly scenic one," the sphinx says, rolling his eyes up again toward the pinnacle. It's like an enormous stalactite, descending from the clouds. "I am but the gatekeeper."

"I suppose you'll ask us questions, then," Worth says. "At least that's how the stories go."

"The stories are, by and large, Greek fabrications of a large scale," the sphinx replies, his tone again sharp where Worth is concerned. What is the trouble? "The Greeks simply came later to the game, as most civilizations did. Here, in Duat, we pride ourselves on having carved some of the oldest, most sophisticated roads between the worlds. But I don't quiz the travelers coming through."

"Then what do you do?" asks Christabel. "You certainly posed a great many questions to me."

He looks fondly at her, his face changing from irritation at Worth to a kind of beatific calm. "Because I've never seen you before, nor one of your kind. And I have been around a very, very long time. You are so comfortable in your human skin that you're practically shivering to get out of this one. But up here, on the peak, it's hard to hold any kind of glamour, so I'm not surprised," the sphinx says, adding a yawn. Once he's recovered, he folds his paws one over the other and lays his chin upon them like a dog by the fire. "I'm just here to do what I do best. Consider you worthy. And you are. I'm just not sure about your friends."

"We need to get back," Christabel says, her thoughts feeling distinctly muddied once again. The sphinx is just too full of information to allow for focus. "We're just trying to get above and help our friends find our other missing friend who was taken by a very powerful djinni."

"I am not surprised, given your general company, that you would soil yourself with mad djinn," the sphinx says, turning his nose at Worth.

"You aren't fond of me. I can tell that much," Worth says, putting a gentle hand on Christabel's flank. His hands are cold, and she fights back concern for him to stare down the sphinx. "I would have thought you welcomed a kinsman."

Now the sphinx begins to laugh. It's a barking, strange noise, and it sets the fox at ill ease. Until this point, she has been sitting and examining the curious creature at a distance.

"I don't understand what's so humorous," Worth says, looking desperately at Christabel.

"Serket says this isn't your home," she says to Worth, trying to remember what it was the goddess had indicated. It was getting harder and harder to remember, not the least of which was because the air was getting thinner. "Perhaps that's part of it. Maybe Glatisants come from elsewhere. Maybe they are antithetical to sphinxes."

The sphinx continues laughing until Worth says, "I am the son of the Questing Beast. A Glatisant. I was under the impression you were of a similar ilk, considering our makeup."

Finally, the sphinx stops laughing, leaning back on his haunches, and sighs. "It is a dreadful thing being able to see so many ways at once," he says, shaking his head. "You are both orphans; perhaps that is some of the trouble."

"My gland is broken," Worth says, pointing at the lump on his chest where the scorpion is. "Once I am healed, I'll show you."

Christabel frowns, looking up toward the pinnacle again. The skies are getting darker; at first, she thought she was imagining things, and considering how long it's been since she's had a decent meal, it's no surprise. But now she's quite certain.

The air is shifting, too.

"I will let you pass, but it won't be easy," the sphinx says. "Just know what I said. You are both orphans. And your...*gland*..." He tries not to laugh when he says it again. "It is merely a bit of powerful magic. I suppose you will figure things out soon enough."

The sphinx is about to say something more when he raises his hand and frowns. "Wait," he says.

Christabel was going to ask a question. She needed to know more about how to help Worth. Perhaps if she asked the sphinx, he would provide some clues.

She feels wrong. She feels pinched. Uncomfortable. And she keeps looking at the pinnacle of that pyramid, wondering how in the world she's supposed to get upside down. Or right-side up. Or...

They all turn their heads up at the same time, moved by some invisible power, to see a small figure falling out of a round hole in the side of the pyramid—which was not there moments before—at roughly the rate of a boulder off the side of a cliff. There is something vaguely familiar about the size and shape, even at this distance, and it takes a moment for Christabel to realize who it is. But she has unicorn sight, and before long, she understands.

It's the dwarf, Alma, propelling downward with impressive speed, but lacking the resistance one might expect of someone unwillingly tumbling toward the ground of the underworld.

She's got her arms crossed over her chest, and Christabel is just about to call out Alma's name when the dwarf picks up speed, improbably and yet observably, and makes a heavy enough impact to shake the tiles at their feet.

The sphinx sighs with all the weariness of an old schoolteacher and says, "People used to fear me. Used to respect me. This borders on farcical. Is that your dwarf?"

"I'm not in the habit of owning people," Christabel snaps before she starts moving toward Alma's prostrate body, a puff of white dust still rising around her body.

"He is," mutters the sphinx, gesturing with his paw toward Worth. "Well, half of a person, anyway."

By the time Christabel reaches Alma, the dwarf is sitting up. She is half stone, the unicorn observes, and while the impact has caused some subtle crazing along her left side, she looks more or less no worse for wear. Thankfully, she's not missing any appendages this time, which is a considerable improvement upon the first time they met.

The dwarf shudders and then coughs out a mouthful of mica before opening her hands and producing a small red fox with white patches.

The other half of Kit.

But it is barely breathing. Whether the trouble came from the fall or before, it is difficult to say, and Alma is still choking up mica, so Christabel simply leans back and lets the white fox slide off her neck.

The white fox pads over to her other half and sniffs at the red fox, then lets out a high, tremulous whine. It's a sorry sound, and it makes Christabel think about her dead parents—though they were not hers by birth, they were still quite important to her—and she has to choke back a moan of sorrow herself. She's glad to catch herself, though, and calm her own nerves because the sound a unicorn makes when they are in distress is both disturbing and humorous. It ends in a long belch and begins like the call of a rutting walrus. There is no accounting for evolution in the world of the Fae.

～

The white fox is quite certain that this dry sandy place with the broken sky is going to be where she dies. But then there is red fox. And white fox is falling to bits, inside and out and hasn't had any good beetles to eat.

Nothing place and the sky, the sky with the broken ceiling, if we don't get out before time is over, we'll never find never find the beetles and deliciousness and the end of our own time.

She isn't thinking about anything other than the sadness she feels when she considers her sister, but still she is pulled inexorably toward the stone creature and the white fox. And it's been so long and yet it has also been and instant.

One breath in, one breath out. Beetles between her teeth, and then...

～

Kit feels like she's been pummeled right through when she reforms again. And hungover. And seasick. She's never been divided that long before, nor for such a distance. Across to the underworld, to Duat, this long extension of *Ashihara no Nakatsukun*, the place on the way to Yomi. But now that she is here and looking with her *kitsune* eyes, she sees that it is more like the river in Yomi. It is a between place.

Taking stock, she notices she has fallen through the top of the pyramid. She half remembers how she got there, but that side of her is bruised and tired. Looking down at herself, she realizes she is in her full *kitsune* form, and not the one she usually wears to keep humans from screaming.

In a way, that's good, though. It means she's not entirely naked. Instead, whorls of red and white fur swirl about her body like eddies in a pool; her four tails spread out behind her almost like a peacock, and she yawns widely, showing all the sharp teeth in her snout. That hurts, though, and she lets out an involuntary whimper.

She's also bleeding freely from her side and down her leg.

"Kit?"

It's one of her owners. Except he's broken, and she almost doesn't recognize him. He is off.

"Hello," she says to him. "I'm sorry, but I'm a bit worse for wear."

Alma, the dwarf, is still coughing up billows of glittering mica and seems altogether incapable of replying.

Kit frowns, trying to remember what it was she was supposed to say to the unicorn woman.

"Kit, are you well?" Worth asks her, taking a tentative step forward. He's moving all wrong, like the pieces of his body don't align right, and it's very distracting.

Kit is most certainly not well, not in a thousand ways. She didn't make it in time to warn them about Itke, and now she feels like she swallowed a gallon of broken glass.

And she can't remember what she was supposed to say!

"Alma," Worth says, limping over to the dwarf, who thwarts any attempt at help. "Alma, where's Nerissa?" He looks to the sky as if he were expecting the snake woman to fall down like a meteor. When nothing happens, he touches Alma softly on the shoulder, and Kit is fairly certain that if Alma weren't still incapable of speaking, she might have bit his fingers off.

"You are the most frustrating group of beings I've ever encountered," says the small, cobbled together creature sitting in the middle of the road. He doesn't seem very friendly, but Kit senses that he's deeply connected to this place and might not be the best person to cross. He's the only one that feels rooted.

Rooted.

Nerissa.

"The snake is in the brambles!" Kit shouts, and everyone looks at her as if she's said something inappropriate. Which, at second thought, is a fair assumption.

"Beg your pardon?" Worth asks her.

She sighs and tries again, trying to untangle her memories. The two halves of her are trying to reassemble themselves into a more cohesive whole, but it's far from smooth. The two narratives diverged so much that there's a constant roiling conversation happening in her head. Besides, the white fox is so badly wounded that it's a wonder she's even standing now.

"Nerissa. The snake," she says slowly, forcing out English when all she wants to do is shout in Japanese. "She's...been captured. In the crypts..."

"Nerissa has been taken by the grey soldier and the Napoleon!" Alma finally says, her voice raspy. She shakes her head as if to dispel the last of the dust. "We tried to fight him off, but she pushed us through the portal and now we're here, and she's there, and if anyone has a better idea of how to get back up there rather than to float, I'd like to hear it about now. This place makes my teeth rattle."

THE CREEPS

Nerissa should have known it was going to be a trap. But as she and Alma enter the crypts with the diminishing red fox in hand, she feels elated and quite a bit proud of herself. That's not a feeling she's used to having about, and she can only attribute it to the imp blood, of which she has had plenty. Before they entered the crypts under the cover of darkness, her favorite kind of cover, she drank a little more. Again, she felt the flush of health course through her veins, and a clear-headedness she had no recollection of ever feeling in her life.

It makes her think of meeting Vivienne. It makes her think of how she saw the world once Vivienne explained things to her. How kind she was. How much good she saw in human beings, and how noble her cause to help them. While her life before had been satisfying from a comestible standpoint, it had not been a happy one. Every time she tried to live among the humans, they would find a way to oust her and chase her and try to kill her. No glamour lasted forever.

But Vivienne helped her understand. Showed her that hating the humans was far more heartbreak than protecting them.

And that she wasn't alone.

Except, as Nerissa walks down the narrow stairs to the crypt, she feels both as close to Vivienne as she has in ten years but also the farthest. Ten years isn't much in the grand scheme of creatures such as she, where decades and centuries slide one into the other. But it's not the same without Vivienne in them. Each day feels like a decade. Every little thing she took for granted—most specifically their friendship—plays back in her head like it never had before.

Is that the imp blood, then?

"You're awfully quiet," Alma says, pausing to look back over her shoulder at the lamia.

"I'm contemplative," Nerissa says, straightening the tie at her throat. "I've been looking for my friend Vivienne for a very long time, and all of this—the trip to Cairo, our involvement with the Circle and the vampires—it's all because of that. Worth and Christabel wouldn't be in this trouble if I hadn't gotten Vivienne into this mess in the first place."

Alma gives the lamia that same, maddening, expressionless look, where her face practically turns to stone. Nerissa knows there must be some nuance she's missing. It's the face Alma makes whenever she's been approached with emotion.

"How's the fox?" Nerissa asks when Alma doesn't response. "And, ah, your foot?"

Alma shrugs. "The fox is still alive. But not by much. The foot is sturdy with my alterations."

Her alterations included a cement and pebble contraption that was strapped on with a variety of buckles and leather pieces to ensure the feet were lined up well enough. While it is growing back, as Alma had assured it would, it is still a bit on the wobbly side.

"Shh," Alma says when Nerissa is about to make some other kind of useless small talk. The lamia can tell that the dwarf is keen to stay in silence and likely regretting her pleasantries earlier.

Michaux and Beti had given them a very clear map, plenty of supplies, and better clothing for their trip. They had also arranged for safe passage through some of the sewers in order to arrive undetected.

"I know we're being followed," Nerissa says. "It's been a while now."

"And you haven't mentioned it."

"I figured you could feel resonances or something," Nerissa says dismissively.

"I'm a dwarf, not a portend. It's awfully insulting to assume that just because I'm a dwarf I can feel all manner of reverberations. It's one of the reasons we like to keep away from you lot."

"I'm probably the only lamia left in existence," Nerissa says, "because we were mistaken for vampires a few hundred years ago and killed systematically." Then she softens. "But you'll forgive my lack of knowledge in the realm of Nith dwarfs. I will try to do better."

Alma doesn't say anything in reply, and they both keep walking as the air thickens around them, the dust becoming pervasive. Nerissa's been aware of their guests for the better part of the last hour, but seeing as they have not been attacked or even hailed, she has decided it best to keep walking.

There are not many ways in which they could be found out. One is the fox. There is a chance the fox is still connected to the Thousand Suns, whatever is left of it, and Cook is coming for them. However, Cook smelled strongly of sandalwood and smoke, and she hasn't sensed any of that at all. Plus, she doubts that Cook would be in any position to follow them, considering the massacre at the brothel.

The other option, and the far more likely scenario, is that whatever killed the little girl, whoever was lurking behind the scenes at almost every turn, has finally found them.

The grey soldier.

She will not act afraid, not even as they get closer to her. She will keep moving forward.

Nerissa waits until she is at the door to the crypt, the key in her hand, before turning around. It is a direct conduit from here to Duat and will only take a good turn and a few uttered words of power. She puts the key into the lock and then deftly moves between Alma and their pursuers.

"Greetings, lamia," says the grey soldier. "We've been waiting for you for quite a while."

Voices in the dark, the shadow of a grey uniform. Gold glinting.

Nerissa knows two things in the moment. One is that if Kit isn't reunited with her other half soon, she will die. And considering everything that's happened in the last ten years, and her undeniable affection for the ridiculous creature, Nerissa just can't allow such a thing to happen. The second understanding is that Alma is the better Duat visitor. She has experience with traveling across portals and has a significantly better grasp on the magic involved.

And, well, technically there is a third thing. Hovering under her skin like a boil waiting to burst. They're the closest to Vivienne she's been in ten years.

"Go, go!" Nerissa hisses in Alma's ear. Her skin is cold to the touch, rough like sand. Expected, she supposes, but still unsettling.

Just as the other man gets close enough for Nerissa to see his face in the light of her lantern, she twists the key in the lock and shoves Alma back into it, throwing the key with her.

The door, as she was instructed, swings shut as soon as Alma is through, the muffled yelp coming from her and the fox dissipating quicker than Nerissa could have imagined. Then follows a slurping, squelching noise, a rise of pressure, and a slow boom.

The portal. The rift.

Nerissa sighs. And it's also at that moment she realizes she's looking into the face of Napoleon Bonaparte.

She has never been much of a historian, herself, but there are some faces one cannot help but know. And the visage of Napoleon is one such.

But that's not entirely right. He is garbed as the man, but its similarities to the human form are tremulous once the eye strays from the face. Toward the guns.

The grey soldier is no simple grey soldier, either. He is a man in his fifties, with a snow white beard and the insignia of the Confederacy. Another figure out of history that no American can avoid. Robert E. Lee.

"You'll excuse me," Nerissa says, backing up against the cold crypt doorway. The stone is very solid, helping to remind her that she has most certainly sealed herself up in an underground tunnel far from the ears of anyone who could help, no matter how loud she screamed. "But I wasn't expecting such renowned guests at this hour."

Lee sniffs the air. It smells strangely aquatic in the room.

"Your friend is gone," says Napoleon Bonaparte, with a decidedly French accent, but one affected rather than earned. "You should not have thrown her out so fast. We would have liked a little pleasant discussion."

"Wherever you are there tends to be death," Nerissa says as Lee slowly lowers his bayonet, bringing it just within a breath of her hearts. "I was trying to protect her."

Napoleon's arm darts out, the cold skin of his hands encircling Nerissa's neck. Not hard enough to choke her, but enough to slide the glamor off of her like a second skin. It's a little-known fact that lamias cannot keep their glamour when their necks are encircled tightly. It's one of the reasons you'll rarely see them wearing chokers.

"There she is," says Napoleon, dropping the accent. "I wouldn't have believed it if I couldn't see it with my own eyes."

"I have a name," says Nerissa.

"Of course you do. What shall we go with?" Lee asks. His breath is tinged with a sour alcoholic scent, that off hint of metabolized ethylene. It makes Nerissa's stomach churn. She hasn't had a thing to drink since she lost Vivienne.

Vivienne.

"Slimy?" Napoleon asks, tilting his head. "How about Snakey?"

"I've clearly found my way to the most brilliant henchmen in the history of all crime," Nerissa says, bearing her teeth.

Their glamour—for that's certainly what it must be—cannot hide their lack of intelligence.

Lee tightens his grasp around her neck so hard that she sees little sparkles in the edges of her vision, swimming around like tadpoles with glittering tails.

"She's not slimy," says Lee, measuredly, fingers tightening experimentally around her neck again.

Lee is ungodly strong, but she could still outmatch him if she wanted. If Nerissa didn't need information from them, she'd be putting up more of a fight. But she's come too far to simply tear them to shreds.

And yet, even as she thinks of it, she feels somehow diminished in their presence. As if she cannot summon up her full power in front of them. As if they see every chink in her armor. As if they have all the information on her, laid bare.

Her tails swish side to side, feeling for the edges of the wall. There is nothing there, no indication that Alma is behind. Without her glamour, she is a marvelous creature, likely the most beautiful of her kind ever to grace the earth. But unfortunately, such features as slick, mucousy lips, blood red eyes, and black teeth, coupled with mottled scales and ridges do little else than frighten humanity.

"Ugly works well enough for me, then," says Napoleon, taking the saber at his hip and rattling it at her.

It shouldn't hurt. That word. But ugly stings.

"Then I was right. You're working for Barqan," Nerissa says, gritting her teeth. It's getting harder to breathe, to think. She needs to twist her way out of this, and yet she wonders if it should end this way. "Tell me where Vivienne is."

"She's right here," Lee says, and holds up a mirror to Nerissa's face, still keeping her pinned to the wall with his side and hand. "And she's got a message."

∾

The trouble with falling down into Duat is that falling back up is very difficult.

Christabel trots around the top of the hill closest to the pinnacle of Khafra's upside-down pyramid and can see no method of getting in. The hole from which Alma and Kit fell is no longer visible.

And the rest of her company is not terribly helpful. Alma is still coughing up dust and mica every now and again and limping even more than usual; Worth is frightened and keeps pawing at his broken gland in a most disturbing manner. If only she were an alicorn, she might be more useful, but as it is, Christabel has no knowledge of what it would take to sprout wings.

"There aren't any ways I can see to construct a ladder that would be strong enough to support our weight up there, and that's supposing we could get something with enough propulsion and grip to make some kind of dent in the limestone," Christabel says, thinking aloud to herself.

"Christabel," says Kit, from behind her.

Christabel shakes her head at the *kitsune*. "Shh, give me a moment. I feel like we have the solution right in front of us, I just have to assemble the components."

"But Christabel," Kit says, and Christabel can feel the *kitsune* behind her, crouching, likely rather ineffectually. "Please. The sphinx is gone and..."

Good riddance to the sphinx. He probably went to go whine alone somewhere.

"Kit, I need you to be silent so I can concentrate..."

"Please..." There is a note of pleading in Kit's voice, pitiful and frightened enough that the unicorn does, at last, take notice.

"What is it?" Christabel asks.

"I shouldn't be here," Kit whispers. "I'm not... I'm not supposed to be here..."

"Heavens," Worth says from behind Christabel. "What is that?"

"That," Kit says, "is Heqet."

Then she sees exactly what Kit is trying to show her. Floating about seven feet above the ground across the slope is a tall, robed figure, materializing out of the dim atmosphere.

Heqet blends into the horizon and the sky. She is too tall to be human, too narrow to support the framework of muscles one would associate with man. Her hair streams out in black ribbons behind her, twisting in the wind and flapping loud enough that Christabel can feel the vibration in her chest. She is wrapped in the tradition of those who have been mummified, but the wrappings are the color of blood. Lightning crackles around her perimeter, tiny sparks blossoming like deadly flowers.

And her *face*.

They call her the frog goddess, and Christabel sees why, though the features are not altogether amphibian. Her mouth is five times larger than the proportion of a human, her eyes wide-set and limned with glittering jewels that do nothing but accentuate her truly alien proportions. There is no nose to speak of, and no ears. But lots of wrinkled, folded skin, mottled like lichen. When she opens her mouth, words flow, though the lips do not form the sounds.

I am Heqet. This is my city. And you bring an enemy into my midst. Bow before me. Hide your filthy form.

Christabel feels fury rising in her, feels her body shifting to its human form, feels herself losing hold on everything. Diminishing. It's terrifying, like being forced down into a crouch when all you want to do is stand.

Just being in the presence of Heqet is discombobulating. Not like with Serket. That goddess felt akin, familiar. Strange, but not incongruous. Heqet feels like older, beyond ancient, like the bones of the earth rising.

"We do not intend to stay here," Christabel says, wiping wet hair from her eyes, her limbs shaking from the forced glamour. "The *kitsune* is our friend. Our thrall. And we only seek to return to the land of the living."

It is nearly impossible to tell what Heqet is thinking. If she is angry or sad. She just *is*. And her being is everywhere, oppressing and powerful. Not a quiet, strange power like Serket's.

Christabel has never seen such an inscrutable, incongruous face. The goddess crackles, and Christabel puts herself more squarely in the way, even though she can no longer hold on to her unicorn state. She feels her stomach churning as if she's been hooked with an invisible string.

You were judged, but not all may pass. The enemy may not pass.

What follows is like thunder from down below, crackling like a great spine getting ready to rise. The sound ricochets through Christabel's body, and by the way Kit is grabbing onto her arm, the feeling is mutual. A quick glance at Alma shows the dwarf is gritting her teeth, but otherwise immovable.

Worth is glowing blue.

Worth is...

Hand over the enemy, monoceros!

Christabel cringes at the name. "Kit came here because we made her. She almost died. We will not hand her over."

I do not care for the fox. She is not a friend, but she is no enemy. Simple trickster child.

Give me the angel.

~

Worth cannot quite pinpoint just when everything fell apart, but it was somewhere between being pummeled nearly to death by an embodiment of the void with razor sharp teeth and being pulled into the Egyptian underworld. There was a lovely moment in between all that when he saw Christabel's face so close to his that he could almost taste her.

Now he feels ill, though. Ill through and through. He hasn't been ill many times in his life, as is often the case with creatures such as he, so he isn't sure how to manage the nausea and chills. It seems to be coming, radiating out, from the broken gland in his chest. He keeps worrying his fingers around it, hoping to get some kind of grasp on it, but it keeps bleeding, skin flaking off in a hideous manner.

He glances down at the gland, roughly the size of the last two segments of his thumb, the little scorpion affixed to it as if welded in copper. The jewel was once a faceted, a lovely thing, but now it's riddled with occlusions. He's always thought of it as a part of him, and yet now as he looks upon it, he cannot help but think ridding himself of it would be the best course of action.

It feels as if he's being *poisoned* by it.

Have you ever met another Questing Beast? He can hear Christabel's voice in his head. *You know, no matter how much research I've done, I simply can't come across anything definitive. Just some vague texts by a woman calling herself Morgan Frye.*

Every detail he knows about himself is engrained. And all his life he never questioned those details. He remembers his mother's voice, telling him, her words written…

He presses on the gland.

It isn't a gland, though, is it? It's more of a stone. Why has he never considered this before? And why can he not remember the face of his mother?

The nausea rolls over him again, and he sees Christabel shouting toward the frog goddess before them, challenging her with raised fists. Sees the goddess reaching her tendrils toward Christabel. Remembers fragments of another time. Another life.

"Worth?"

Someone is calling his name. The fox creature.

The goddess is getting closer.

She knows.

She sees.

Worth knows instinctively that the broken stone in his chest means death. It's killing him. It's...*suppressing* him. It's been confusing him for too long.

He stands up on wobbly feet, Alma reaching out to grab him, but he rebukes her. Then Worth grits his teeth and digs, hard, getting his nails around the stone. He pushes back a memory of his once lover, the vampire Yvan, who pulled his own heart out in agony and at the bidding of black magic. He pushes back the thought of Vivienne's hands on his chest, tracing the lines of his body and marveling at the facets on the stone. He pushes back the memory of the voice of his mother:

This is your shield. Your glamour. This is how you can change, how you can move, how you can be all things at once.

Worth rips the stone from his chest. It does not come loose all at once, and not without a tremendous searing pain that goes right through him, as if he's been speared in both lungs. Tendrils of glistening silver follow as he pulls, drawing blood and sinew forward, a good foot out from his body, before he throws it on the ground and screams.

Then he is flying.

Vivienne's face is limned in frost in the mirror. The reflection is not a good one, not clear like a photograph, but Nerissa would know the shape of her eyes across a thousand miles. The lamia has to stop herself from touching the glass, from hoping to make contact with her friend and the object of her affection for over a hundred years.

She looks pale, tired. Nerissa can tell that Vivienne has put a lot of makeup on, relying on that instead of a glamour. She does not look well.

"Vivienne..." she whispers.

In the mirror the sylph looks so sad, looking over her shoulder and then at Nerissa.

"Nerissa, please. Stop looking for me."

"No, Vivienne, I..."

The clutch at her throat gets stronger, and she coughs out the last bit. What was she going to say anyway? *I love you.* That hadn't worked before.

"It is too dangerous," Vivienne says. "He told me you were getting closer, and he agreed to let me see you one last time, to discourage you. We are leaving Cairo. We will not return. I want you to go home, to tend to the goats. Let me go, Nerissa. Live happy and free."

"Vivienne...you're...you're...everything," Nerissa gasps out, tears burning down the sides of her cheeks. Hearing Vivienne's voice is like knives in her hearts, cutting her one by one.

The image of Vivienne wavers and turns away, speaking to someone behind her. There is a subtle shift of green and yellow, like a sickly shadow, and then Vivienne stares at her again. Her dark hair has been cut short, something she never would have allowed. And her cheeks are sallow, as if she's been drained. Frost rises at the corners of the mirror.

Then Vivienne touches the side of her own face, a sweet tender motion that Nerissa might mistake for flirtation, except that the sylph's eyes are on fire. With fury. With pain. With knowledge.

A signal.

Lee drops the mirror, the glass smashing on the ground before Nerissa can cry out.

But enough is enough.

They clearly have no idea what she's capable of, and Nerissa is tired of playing weak. Now that she's fully anchored on the wall with her tails, and quickly losing all sense of her own motives, save the one to find Vivienne again, she makes ready.

Except Napoleon moves forward quicker than she ever would have imagined and slides a cold, painful blade into her side. Not enough to kill —oh, Nerissa is far too hard to kill for a blade—but with the singing pain comes an ache she knows too well.

Old iron.

As Nerissa slumps against the wall she realizes that being killed by the ghosts of Robert E. Lee and Napoleon Bonaparte was not her first choice of death, but it will have to do. If anyone ever finds out what happened, that is. They'll probably hack her to bits and sell her parts to the black market for trinkets and minor artifacts, and she'll be the last living lamia in all of existence.

And she thinks of Keats' words, written on the page.

"When from this wreathed tomb shall I awake!
When move in a sweet body fit for life,
And love, and pleasure, and the ruddy strife
Of hearts and lips! Ah, miserable me!"

∼

C hristabel rushes forward because she's all they have. Although she's spent the better part of the last decade with her nose in books, she has not avoided the health of her body. She and Nerissa sparred regularly, since sparring with Worth was too much agitation, and while she is not terribly thrilled at the prospect of losing her life to this angry goddess, she is willing to do so for her friends. Even without her horn.

Before she was part of Waldemar, Goodwin, and Crane, she fell in with the Circle of Iapetus. She tries not to think of that time, which she now knows is wasted, but she did at least learn that even the best of intentions can lead a person astray. What the Circle would think of this event is quite beyond her own understanding. They stalk the world looking for signs of the Fae, but that they could descend here into Duat, while reeds rushed and sands flew and the firmament twisted and turned above them like diamonds in coffee, the pyramid becoming more and more obscured with fog and dust…they would never have understood.

It was a good run, she decides. Even if she loves Worth and can't tell him and will likely find herself skewered by the goddess of frogs. It's not a good end. And she does wish, to her surprise, that Nerissa was here. Because they are friends, even if they can't get along most days. And it seems quite unfair that she doesn't get a chance to say goodbye.

Thinking of her friends, she feels a grasp on her power again. Heqet is focusing elsewhere, and Christabel channels her fear into fury and then into magic. Her body expands, twists, elongates. It is as a star being born into the heavens, so beautiful the metamorphosis. Her coat is dark as coal, shimmering with a silver light. Her mane and tail are golden, each strand suffused with the power of the sun. And her horn, proud and spiraled, iridescent as mother of pearl.

The goddess notices.

She rears back, tears tracking down her soft cheeks, just as Heqet's tendrils reach her. They sizzle against her, singeing the fur and tossing up a horrid stench to the skies.

Dying is going to hurt. She was hoping to avoid that.

But then there is wind on her face, a shadow across her vision, and her tears dry as she looks up.

"Stand down, Heqet," Worth says from up above. "Let us pass."

Christabel only knows it's Worth because he *feels* like Worth, except amplified, perfected. Purified. He looks nothing like the shape she once knew, that of a handsome young man able to transform his body in a thousand ways, a latticework of animal power just beyond his frame. He is holy. Divine. Transcendent.

She first notices the two sets of wings, one feathered with pure white and the other with jet black, each one outlined in the world of Duat with the precision of a silver ink pen. That must have been what those scars were for. His body is difficult to absorb all at once. He is human, or at least part of him remains that. His face is neither male nor female, of indecipherable race, and so fine and beautiful that she feels she must kneel in order to understand it all.

But that is not all. No, behind the human head, its hair in soft brown waves, rest three more faces: a lion, an eagle, and a bull. They are not substantial in the way the human form is, but they look as if they are painted on the surface of a crystal pool, shimmering and shifting. They are as much a part of him as his human form, and complete.

Christabel can barely keep her eyes off of him. The longer she looks, the more she sees. There is more behind him. Unfathomable wings and eyes and faces, all turned toward Heqet. All prepared to fight with a power that had been dormant for too long.

The word is on her tongue before she can stop from saying it aloud: *cherubim.*

Where the crystal gland once lay now rests a swiftly healing hole, just in the center of him. It must have been concealing him somehow. And given the reaction from Heqet, with good reason. But how? And why?

And, gods and demons above and below, she loves him. She loves him more now that she sees him like this. It's as if her heart will die on her just by watching him, watching as he moves closer to Heqet, brushing aside the smoky tendrils as they close in on him.

How did he fall to the earth? How was he bound? Who is he?

It doesn't matter, now. The ground rumbles beneath her hooves, and with what feels like a great tearing in her chest, she looks away from Worth and toward the earth before her.

At first she thinks the ground is boiling. Little bubbles appear everywhere on the surface, giving the impression of mud or thick chocolate.

But then the spheres take shape, blink open, as long arms and legs protrude, webbed and flecked and mottled in a dozen shades of brown and green.

Frogs the size of men. Men in the shape of frogs. Six of them, with a host of smaller frogs at their feet. They have the same gaping mouth, full of horror and pestilence, croaking forward as their goddess takes aim at the angel above.

~

Worth is burning away. What had bound him is gone, turned to ash. His mind reels with a thousand memories and sensations, rushing him in a tidal wave. It would overwhelm him if it wasn't for the enemy before him, if he didn't still possess a spark of the bound creature he was before.

The innocent are below him. Innocent, at least, of any great sin. They still smell of the corrupted power that brought them here, against their own will. Inadvertently bringing him along with them.

Heqet. She is difficult to forget, and yet why exactly she hates him has not yet surfaced. No matter. As the unicorn—Christabel, her name is *Christabel*—readies herself to charge, it is time.

Ophaniel.

That is the right name. Not Worth. Ophaniel.

His own name is on his lips, and he shouts it in four voices, harmony and epiphany ringing to the skies.

And then Ophaniel remembers another name. Khonsu. And love. And the moon. Together they rose, together they fell, and Khonsu...

Heqet loved Khonsu. But Khonsu fell in love with a cherub while he visited the moon. And...

Ophaniel sees a woman's face. Mother, but not mother. Teacher, perhaps. Savior. Remembers a small cottage, deft fingers, the pressing, aching pain as words are muttered...

No time. No time!

Arms at the ready, mouths and wings at the ready, Ophaniel flies forward, hearts pounding and throat rasping with the cries of battle.

~

K it is pretty sure that this is much, much more than she signed up for. First she risks everything to try and help her new owners. Then they end up taking her to the very place the asked them not to. And finally Worth…well…

He's not Worth anymore, is he?

It's hard to look directly at him, which isn't saying much. It's hard to look at Heqet, too, but Kit is used to that kind of feeling. Looking at Heqet is looking into the jaws of life and death, the gaping hole that we come from and return to, that unknowable question. Kit stole from Heqet a long time ago, and only through the good graces of Ame-no-Uzume-no-mikoto, they were able to agree to a lesser punishment. One that stated, very clearly, Kit was never to step foot in Duat again. And then Ame-no-Uzume-no-mikoto personally escorted her to the Thousand Suns.

Kit can't help but feel a little conflicted, however, as part of her enjoyed being the focal point of the goddess's ire.

There's no time for more contemplation, however, as she's soon face-to-face with a frog-man creature, his wild eyes rolling in his head and his sticky tongue lolling in an almost comical mimicry of a dog. He smells of rot and wet wood.

Deflecting his first blow with her forearm, Kit shudders when his skin makes contact with hers. It stings at first, and then as she pulls back to a more defensive stance, she realizes it's vibrating.

Poison. Of course, they're poison frogs.

OF SWORDS AND ANGELS

Nerissa is trying to breathe, but the pain is so intense it's almost as if she's forgotten how. The knife is lodged in her, and through her, and into the wall behind her. Impaled, incapacitated.

The assailants relax immediately, laughing to one another.

"She's harder to kill than that, though," Lee says, looking down the length of the crypt passage. He bends to pick up his lantern and squints at the writing on the walls, shaking his head.

"Still, that's what we were told. Take care of them," says Napoleon, shifting uncomfortably. It reminds Nerissa of what a child does when wearing itchy clothing, incapable of standing still.

Strange.

If only she weren't bleeding everywhere. She's paralyzed with it, the old iron slowly making its way into her bloodstream, poisoning her. If only she could get her hands—

Lee sees what she's doing and slaps her hand hard enough that one of her nails goes flying off and tinkles against the limestone.

"You might as well get it over with," Nerissa says. "There's no point in dragging it out."

Lee gives her a dubious look—and for a moment his beard looks darker than it should before going white again—and shakes his head.

"You're hiding the rest. Orders were to get all of you. Now show us where the dwarf got through the door."

"I can't," Nerissa says. "She was my way through. I have..."

Lee wiggles the knife, and Nerissa gasps as pain ricochets down her side and into her tails. She can feel the warm blood from her ripped nails dripping down her scales, too. Red blossoms of light limn her vision, beckoning to that final slide down.

It's frustrating on many levels, not the least of which is that Nerissa won't have a chance to bite off their heads, and she was hoping that she'd be able to. It was worth the descent into drinking human blood for the looks on their faces.

But they knew her weaknesses. Old iron and Vivienne du Lac.

Ten years is not a terribly long time for a lamia, yet without Vivienne in her life, it has felt like an eternity. And she supposes, dimly and a little gratefully, that her suffering will come to an end. She won't have to miss Vivienne so much anymore. She won't have to live rethinking that conversation they had when Nerissa finally confessed her love, and Vivienne did not.

The wall behind her shudders, limestone falling down around her and getting into her eyes, down into her collar.

"What's that?" Napoleon asks, looking not at the wall but at the dark hallway behind him.

"Nothing. Now hush. I think something's coming through the wall."

"What?" Napoleon asks.

But he doesn't say anything more because a sword has somehow made it through the front of his face, glistening with blood and glowing with a silvery green light. And as the sword cuts through bone and veins and muscle, it takes with it another layer. A *mask*, Nerissa realizes, balancing on the edge of the blade.

Whoever wields the sword has, at least, helped her thus far, though she can see nothing other than swirls of dark material.

With Lee still shocked at the sudden and grotesque death of his companion, Nerissa springs, tearing her side as she uses what strength she has left in her to tear at his face. As soon as she touches it, her nails raking mercilessly, she shudders with familiarity. It's Vivienne's magic, cold and perfect and deadly. Her nails take flesh along with the mask, and the face behind the mask is young and terrified.

Nerissa is just about to go for his neck as he crumbles to the ground when she is interrupted by the figure who killed Napoleon. She puts a calming hand on Nerissa's shoulder and turns her to look her in the face.

She is a woman. Stunning. Black hair curling in waves across her face, skin pale and splashed with freckles, eyes like ice framed in thick lashes. Her lips are incongruously red in this dark world, and magic practically roils off of her. She is all roundness, plump as an apple left in the sun, strong and soft at once.

But she is no beast, no creature of the Fae.

"Nerissa Waldemar," the woman says, her voice low and resonant. She wipes the bloody sword on her cloak without even looking at it, as practiced and nonchalant as a lady rearranging her hat. "Stand down before you die, please. I know this has been taxing on you and yours, but we need this man alive if we're to get to the bottom of this."

~

Alma wishes that she'd been able to grow her foot back, though she's got to admit, her little engineering feat is holding up pretty well. There is plenty of sand around, rocks and the like, and while she's not technically supposed to show her *bjarg-vald* to anyone that's not a Nith dwarf, she's quite certain that if she doesn't do something helpful soon, she's going to end up on the very bad side of those frog people.

Amphibians have always bothered Alma. She finds them not only hideous but offensive from a moral sense. That anything should start out as a fish and then grow legs is as disturbing as the way human beings procreate.

She's not sure what to make of Worth, other than he's clearly not Worth any longer, and Heqet is intent on destroying him. Christabel could be a help, and Kit, too. But someone's got to work on these damned amphibians.

Bjarg-vald is an entirely different practice than the *dyrr-vald* she practiced to open gateways, or the *málmr-vald* in the forge. *Bjarg-vald* is the power of commanding stone, rock, and clay. It's not often seen outside of the Nith, but given the circumstances, she's willing to give it a go. As she is made up of stone herself, it requires understanding the landscape around her before making an attack, and this is done the usual way: mastication.

So while Kit takes on one of the frog men, Alma leans down to take a handful of sand. She's about to put it into her mouth when she realizes with nothing short of abject horror, that it is riddled with black and red tadpoles.

And they are all whispering her name.

~

S kewering the first frog man is delightfully satisfying. Christabel snorts and grunts as her horn parts his skin and pops into his viscera, then tosses her head and watches him fly off out of the pathway before them. Some of his goo gets into her eyes, and though it stings, it doesn't appear to be poisonous to her, as she was worried it might be. Given the shouting from behind her, she's guessing that wasn't the case for Kit.

"Let me to the frogmen!" Christabel shouts over her flank, just in time to see Alma fall to her knees, shuddering as a black shadow of tadpoles creeps up her arms and legs, making for her mouth and eyes and ears.

Above, the sky crackles with energy as Heqet and Worth—Ophaniel? —crash together. Somehow, he now has a sword, long and deadly but translucent, shot through with sparkling silver threads. And while he's at an equal altitude to Heqet, he's still struggling to get close enough to make any kind of impact.

Meanwhile, the frogman that Christabel skewered a moment ago is getting up, a long tendril of smoke snaking down from the goddess giving him enough power to somehow revive him.

Backing up, desperately making her way toward Kit—who is now throwing up on the ground and convulsing—Christabel meets another frogman, as the ground beneath her feet shifts with more tadpoles.

The frogman, this one with a purple patch on his back, goes straight for her, arms and legs splayed, wrapping his appendages around her neck before she can get a good swipe in. He smells of a bog, wet and dying decay, and gurgles like a contended swine.

Christabel rears, once, twice, and finally the third time she manages to get the assailant to the ground, where she tramples him and runs him through twice for good measure, once between the eyes. He trembles beneath her, the little tadpoles sinking back into the ground around him like black bugs, and then he is still.

"I am not endeared of these things!" Christabel shouts, turning to make her way to Kit. "But we've got to hope Worth can hold out against Heqet because they're—" one of the frogmen rams into her side, winding her a moment before she slices him across the middle, withdrawing her horn dripping with frog viscera, "—they're coming back to life quicker than I can kill them."

~

Ophaniel remembers there is a name for this feeling, but the best he can come up with is *battle joy*, which he's certain he knows from his time as Worth, and not his time as an angel. For most minds, this would be disturbing and frustrating, but he finds it rather comforting. Worth is still a part of him, a dimmed version of himself. And those memories are still inside.

He knows, above all, that he must protect his friends, and he must get them up to that pinnacle and out of Duat. But what is an angel to do? The sword is a very nice touch, of course. He can't complain. He hasn't quite remembered the name of it, but he's confident it's a damned good name.

Heqet is somewhat distracted by the fray below them. She keeps having to resurrect her frog emissaries and is not capable of having more than six out at a time. The tadpoles are an especially horrific little addition to the mix, and as much as they bother him, Ophaniel can't help but be a little impressed.

He hasn't had a good brawl like this in a long time.

Now that his wings are warmed up, he's feeling a bit better about this whole clash with a goddess business. As Heqet extends two long tentacles of smoke down to the dead and dying frogmen, he takes the opportunity to fly up, and then down behind her, slashing through the cloth strips flapping around her.

She screams immediately, twisting to meet him face-to-face, as a parade of black half-formed tadpoles rush to meet him in a geyser of amphibian flesh. They don't get close enough to bother Ophaniel, merely sizzling and burning up once they come close to him, but it is an impressive attempt nonetheless.

"Heqet," he says to her, grabbing one of the long scraps of cloth streaming from her body as it passes his hand. It smokes in his touch but does not hurt. "Enough."

Ophaniel. Your name is a scourge. Your face is an open wound.

"I want only to leave this place," Ophaniel says, and his voice is like the mountains, like a thousand trumpets, like the deepest thrumming of the seas. But he knows his visage is still exceptionally handsome, so he takes no particular offense to Heqet's insult. This coming from a goddess with a face like a puckered snail... "You want me gone. But you keep trying to kill my friends, and that is making it much more difficult."

They are worthless children. Not like you and me. Nothing but bits of smoke, where we are flame. What care do you have for them now that you are freed from your body?

Ophaniel is having a very difficult time remembering just why he was imprisoned, but the part of him that is still Worth presses: he understands that the people below him, his friends, are priceless, even if they do grate on his nerves, sometimes. Especially the snake one, who is not on this side of the plane. And he knows, even as Ophaniel, that friendship has been hard won through all his existence.

"They fight for me because they love me, and I the same. I don't need disfigured demon creatures to do my bidding, enslaved and twisted with anger," Ophaniel says. He pulls tight on the long cloth, pulling Heqet closer, just enough to get her attention. "I'd rather not have to hurt you."

Every slash against my children is like a needle to my heart. You will pay for all you have done.

"Don't you think I've paid well enough? Four hundred years, trapped. Suppressed. Confused. And now, I am telling you that I want to leave and all you—"

But Ophaniel doesn't finish because Heqet rams a spear through his side, and he's completely out of breath from the pain.

◌

They're just tadpoles. Just regular tadpoles. That happen to be whispering her name.

Alma presses through her fear and finds a part of the sand she can swallow without getting the wriggling horrors in her mouth. As soon as she tastes the earth, she gets a jolt of recognition, the complex composition as obvious to her as an experienced sommelier.

Her grandmother used to tell her that all stone is the same. Oh, of course there's sedimentary and igneous and metamorphic rock, but with enough pressure and knowledge, even the chalkiest dirt can be fortified, the hardest stones shattered. Every rock has a crack somewhere, even if it's not obvious.

It begins quiet enough that it's like the rumble of distant thunder, mingling with the already turbid, angry skies above. She presses her feet into the soil, spreading out the vibrations she knows as *bjarg-vald*, and closes her eyes.

It's not easy, here. The ground is replete with other things, magic things, and she tries to work with or around them as the continues to chew on the sand and identify the best course of action. The angel isn't going to last if he can't get Heqet to stop resurrecting those damned frogmen.

Kaolinite, smectite, and dolomite. Quartz, of course. A good portion of oxygen there, too, almost as if the sands themselves are lungs, breathing in the ages.

She's not undertaken *bjarg-vald* of this magnitude in a very long time, and certainly never in a place like this. But though there are variances in the soil, there are more familiarities.

Alma keeps in mind that her friends—well, there's a new word—won't be able to scale sandy hills like she can, just drifting through. Therefore, she decides she'll go an easier route.

~

The tadpoles vanish suddenly as the ground vibrates, and Kit takes a deep breath, trying to stop throwing up. She's never had a problem killing people, let alone frog people trying to get their mucous on her. But when it touched her, it also gave her the sense that...

No, now she's forgetting again.

Where was she?

At least the tadpoles are gone.

At least she...

A blur of dark silver rushes across her vision, and Christabel is standing almost on top of her. Kit knows that she's supposed to see Christabel as the unicorn different as Christabel the human, but she honestly has a difficult time doing that. Yes, the horn should be a dead giveaway but...

"Kit, listen to me," Christabel says, throwing off another assailant with a sound between a growl and a whinny. "Kit, stay awake. I'm almost positive that this is going to work, but you have to stay calm."

Kit is thinking about the moon. Every time she looks up at the angel, she thinks about the moon. And that makes her want to sleep.

"Kit!"

Alma is nearby, and the ground is shaking like a volcano is nearby.

"Oh, damn it," Christabel says.

Before Kit can say anything, the unicorn rears up and then aims her horn directly at Kit's heart. With considerably little show, she then presses it into Kit's chest with what should be a good deal of pressure, and somehow isn't.

Even in Kit's poisoned state, she's expecting pain. But it isn't pain. On one level, she is quite certain she's being impaled. Her body tenses, her muscles taut, her spin arching. But she feels...minty. Full of light. Cool like the moon. It spreads through her whole body, the sensation whirling through her nerves and structures, banishing corruption from her body.

Just long enough before Christabel is overtaken by three of the frog creatures, all resurrected and showing the gaping wounds of their previous deaths.

Kit is ready now, though. While she isn't likely to go through that whole unicorn horn purge again if she doesn't have to, she has the strength at last to pull herself together wholly. The two halves of her have never felt so complete. Her wounds heal. Her body shivers, comes together, fur thickening and glistening.

Christabel is going to need some help getting out of this.

Kit wheels around, making for the closest of the frogmen, a sorry-looking creature with a gap in his stomach big enough to fit a squirrel in. She can actually see through it, and it almost makes her laugh in its absurdity.

Except they all startle and turn because somehow a stair has risen behind them, up toward the pyramid's pinnacle.

Kit laughs, then, letting the sound ripple through her. It startles the frogmen enough much that they cover their ears and back away. And Kit laughs even harder as she pushes at Christabel and starts making her way up the stairs, Alma behind them, her pike in hand.

~

"Forgive me if I dispense with the pleasantries," Nerissa says, sliding back down the wall leaving, no doubt, a most impressive green bloody streak behind. Even if she wants to eat Lee's head, she doesn't have the strength. "I'm a little...dying...right now."

Lee makes a half-hearted attempt to go after the woman, but she counters him almost without thought. Then she hits him on the head with the butt of her sword three times until he's completely unconscious.

"It usually takes more than one blow," the woman says with a wry grin. "Dime-store novels make it sound much easier."

When Nerissa can do nothing more than gurgle, the woman tilts her head as if remembering something and approaches.

"I've got just the thing," she says, rummaging in a rucksack at her side. It smells of rosemary and mint, and Nerissa winces. She hates those smells.

Thankfully the woman doesn't retrieve any of those herbs, but rather a thin sheet of leather. When she brings it up into the light, Nerissa sees the delicate latticework, a scale pattern. Snakeskin.

"Mindfully harvested," the woman says, indicating that Nerissa should show her the wound.

With shaking hands, and no attempt to cover her natural form, Nerissa pulls away what's left of her blouse to reveal the ragged bleeding mass of her wound. It's pulsing with her breath, the edges a sickly rust color.

The woman shakes her head. "Any longer and you'd be dead. But this won't be the end of you. Here, keep the pressure while I prepare the dressing. Like this."

With no concern for the blood, the woman presses her own hands to Nerissa's wound and then goes about slathering a thick paste from a small metal box on the dressing, then sprinkling it with what looks like salt.

Nerissa does as she's told, and finally manages, "Who are you?"

"I thought you'd never ask," the woman says with that wry grin again. She brushes away the wisps of her hair at her forehead. "I'm Dr. Morgan Frye. More or less."

"How did you find me?" Nerissa asks.

"Just a moment," Dr. Frye says.

Nerissa makes a sharp intake of breath as Dr. Frye presses the dressing to the lamia's side. It stings like the dickens, pain zigzagging up Nerissa's spine and down her arms. Just when she's ready to slash the woman upside the head, the pain abates, and the dressing tightens like a second skin.

It feels much better.

"I wasn't looking for you," Dr. Frye says. "I was actually looking for someone else. And I knew he'd be here."

"I'm alone," Nerissa says, shaking her head. "My friends are all gone. And all I've got is dead Napoleon and sleeping Robert E. Lee, and none of it makes any sense."

Dr. Frye gives Nerissa a sad, knowing glance. "Well, I'm afraid it's not going to get any easier. But once my guest arrives, we'll be able to answer some of these questions together."

Nerissa is too tired to respond to this woman, who is most clearly out of her mind. Still, being in her company is better than being killed by Napoleon Bonaparte.

⁓

F ending off the frogmen, Christabel begins to make the ascent up the stairs, slowly and thoughtfully as one can manage in such a situation and with hooves. She wishes that Alma had thought to construct railings, but seeing as this is their only hope of reaching the pinnacle, she is going to count her blessings instead.

Kit is doing some remarkable fighting of her own, bounding up and down the stairs and confusing the daylights out of the frogmen. Halfway up the stairs and there are only two frogmen, the others falling so far down that to reach them again will take too much time.

Alma is at the head, reinforcing the steps and muttering words of power in some derivation of Old Norse. She can't be sure, but she's fairly certain a good deal of it is cussing.

Of course, there is still the matter of Heqet, who is twisted up with the angel that was Worth Goodwin.

Christabel pushes aside her grief. Swallows it whole. It's bitter as her tears. She always knew he was special, that there was a magnetic, powerful magic in him. But this is quite beyond her reckoning. She wonders as she tears through yet another frogman and tosses him over the side, if she shouldn't have spent more time studying Judeo-Christian mythology instead of every other branch in the world. She knows next to nothing about angels.

And who's to say he'll stay around now?

Her fears are focused again, however, when she hears Kit shouting.

"They're tearing the stairs! Quicker, my friends. We must go quicker up the stairs!"

Alma is straining. Christabel notices that the dwarf's whole body is streaked darker, and then she realizes it must be perspiration. Alma is, more or less, completely made of rock at the moment. She moves slowly, deliberately, but the stairs are not going to hold forever. Even now they tremble.

243

"Go ahead of me!" Kit shouts at Christabel. "I can fend them off a little longer. We've got to make more altitude."

The expanse before them is close to hundred feet, perhaps more. And scrabbling on hooves simply isn't going to do it. Christabel shivers and sheds her unicorn form, coming instead to the very one she had when she first met Worth: small, pale, and dressed in a more practical version of the peacock gown she wore to the ball. It's a sentimental, silly thing to do, but she feels as if it's the right choice.

It's much easier to climb the stairs now, but Christabel is exhausted. Every step feels heavier than the last, her head spinning with fatigue and confusion.

Alma meets her at the top of the stair, and the whole structure shudders again. Below, the three remaining frogmen are making quick work of the sandy stairs, their bodies barely staying together while their rabid destruction continues.

The heat of the fight above them is hot on Christabel's face, and she turns her head up to see Ophaniel twisting in Heqet's embrace. One of his lower wings is bent at an unnatural angle, and his other visages have vanished, the light in him dissipating.

But then she notices, high up above her, the pinnacle of the pyramid— there is a door. It's not open all the way, but certainly enough to get through if they need. Alma didn't even have to open a gate. It's right there!

"Alma, you need to get Kit to safety," Christabel says, putting her hand on the dwarf's shoulder. "Do whatever you have to do. If I don't make it… tell Nerissa that I'm sorry. And help her find Vivienne if you can."

Alma stares at the unicorn with that blank, unknowable gaze. But, bless her, she doesn't argue. She nods solemnly.

"I never thought I'd say this to anyone, but thank you for being a friend," Alma says. "And a fellow soldier."

If Christabel didn't know any better, she'd say the dwarf was crying. But with all the sand flinging, it was difficult to tell.

"Can you give me a lift?" Christabel asks. "I've got an idea."

⁓

"Here, this might help," Dr. Frye says, walking past Nerissa and pressing on a small indentation in the limestone wall. "They should be here shortly."

Without a key. Without a word uttered. The door simply caves to Dr. Frye's command.

It slides open, a whoosh of salty, dry air coming in with a rush of heat. It's the very weather that Nerissa hates the most, and her scales tighten in the anticipation of molting.

The dressing is helping. Whatever is in it, some sort of analgesic she's guessing, has stopped a good deal of the pain. It hasn't strengthened her, not really, but it's given her hope that she won't die here in this accursed land.

"And...right on time," Dr. Frye says, consulting a silver pocket watch before standing aside from the doorway.

"What is on time?" Nerissa asks, but the answer is immediately apparent.

The forms of Alma Stonefoot and Kit tumble into the chamber, a grinding, furry, dusty mess. They look absolutely terrible but bring with them the distinct tang of the Fae. Kit is in a full fox form, whorls of white and red fur all across her body, tails fanned out behind her almost like a peacock. Alma crashes in to the side of the crypt walls, cursing in a language that sounds like chewing rocks. And Kit is laughing. Raucous, beautiful, marvelous laughter that peals through the dull, dark crypt like much needed rainfall.

"Guard the...the door..." Alma says at last, heaving breath in between words. "They might have...followed us..."

"Where is Christabel?" Nerissa asks. "Where is Worth?"

"You've lost a whole lot of blood," Kit says, suddenly sober, looking at Nerissa.

"And you're alive," Nerissa says, surprising even herself.

"Oh, and hello, Dr. Frye," Kit says, waving at the woman with a familiar ease. "Good to see you again."

"You *know* each other?" Nerissa asks, momentarily distracted by the problems at hand.

"Of course," Dr. Frye says, unfazed by the new guests. She squints down the hallway through the door, frowning slightly. "They should be back by now."

Nerissa fights the urge to fall asleep, her lids heavier than lead. No one has told her where Christabel and Worth are, and that can't be good. But she's exhausted. Wrung out. And she doesn't have much fight left in her.

~

The plan was to jump, take unicorn form, and stab the goddess as hard as possible. A distraction. Unicorns, she knows, are perilously difficult to kill. Maybe one of the most difficult creatures to get rid of in all the realms.

But it doesn't go as planned. Once she enters the gravitational pull of the two beings—that's the only analogy she can make that has any sense to her whatsoever—she is pulled toward the goddess, swathed in dirty, dry rags, and then held up, dangling like a doll. She's unable to shift, her body throbbing with magic but strangled.

Is this your little savior?

"She means nothing to me," Ophaniel says.

Christabel gasps back fury and despair, closing her eyes to focus instead on a memory. Her physical pain will pass; if she dies, or is cast out, she is not afraid.

Then—

"But she means everything to Worth," the angel says, snatching back his arm from the goddess. She cannot hold onto both of them at once and flails after him, hissing like the shifting of ten thousand cockroaches at once.

SISTERRRRRRRRR... YOU HAVE GONE TOO FAR. HE HAS PAID THE PRICE.

Serket.

Christabel bursts forward, out of the goddess's clutch, tongues of fire leaping from her fingers and feet, blazing from her eyes. The goddess hisses and shouts, losing altitude and taking Christabel down with her. The drop makes the unicorn's stomach flip and her vision darken.

Go away.

SISTER. IT HAS BEEN SO LONG, FORGIVE AND REST.

Feathers fill Christabel's vision, another fire mingling with her own. And she is blissfully, perfectly happy as she takes flight and is borne upward, toward freedom.

ENDS AND BEGINNINGS

The sun is just rising over Cairo when Christabel Crane stumbles out of the dark crypt to meet her friends. Her clothes have burned off, even those made by glamour. Her hair is a snarl from her forehead to her waist. Every inch of her is red and raw and burning, especially on her face and under her eyes.

"Christabel!"

It's Nerissa who greets her, embracing her. The emotion is so surprising and so out of character that Christabel chokes back an inappropriate laugh. But taking stock of the crypt, she realizes they are not alone.

Nerissa looks worse for wear, having suffered a series of wounds in a fight with the most curious figures. A woman stands by the crypt opening, frowning, her lovely face a mask of worry.

"He should be here by now," she mutters.

"I lost him," Christabel says, untangling herself from Nerissa. "I was burning, on fire, and he flew me up, setting me at the mouth of the gate, and I just...I slid down here. Or up here. I can't tell."

"It is a confusing trip," Kit says, bringing Christabel an ornate early nineteenth-century jacket befitting Napoleon Bonaparte and wrapping it around her shoulders.

And then she sees a mask on the ground beside a dead man, his face caved in.

"It's Vivienne's magic," Nerissa says, shaking her head. "I don't understand how it works, but—"

"Death masks," Kit says, simply. She's reverted to the familiar shape they first found her in, and she's paring her nails while leaning nonchalantly against the limestone wall. "I couldn't see it then, but now it's clear. You find a good death mask, and with the right magic, you can embody some of their strengths. I didn't recognize who these people were, but now it makes sense. I saw the Frenchman at the Thousand Suns before everything happened."

"Napoleon Bonaparte and Robert E. Lee," Nerissa says weakly.

Christabel looks at her, puzzled, then tries to piece it together. "Many people commission death masks. If Vivienne is providing the spells to imbue the masks, she must be combining it with some other magic. So, we *were* close."

"Yes," Nerissa says. "Close enough but terribly wrong, still."

"Should we be talking about this in front of..." Christabel gestures to Dr. Frye, but then stops.

The woman's face is illuminated, and her smile along with it. She puts the silver pocket watch away and smooths the front of her shirt as if preparing to meet a suitor. She seems a little beyond the age of marriage, but then... Christabel can't quite pinpoint her age. She is an earthy, strong woman, but her magic, her power, is of a different wavelength than she's familiar. She feels mortal, but she...

Worth stumbles out of the crypt, still wrapped in the spider silk shift Christabel knit for him. He is pale, pale like the moon, with deep shadows under his eyes.

Her heart leaps when she sees his face, and she makes to run to his arms, but he stops when he notices Dr. Frye.

Then he says one word: "Mother."

WHAT WAS AND WHAT WILL
NEVER BE

T hey gather one last time at the Semiramis before they take off. Bandaged, exhausted, frightened. Christabel is trying to listen to Dr. Frye, but the words keep churning in her head, twisting around rather than making any sense.

"I found Worth a long time ago," Dr. Morgan Frye is saying. She has dressed and assisted all the members of the Waldemar, Goodwin, Crane et al, and is now sipping a glass of wine while they gather around to listen. "I hid him, it is true. Locking his true nature away."

"I never was a Glatisant," Worth says. But it is not Worth. It is a shadow of him, a sort of dormant state he goes into when his wings go away.

Dr. Frye sighs, looking sad for the first time. "You fell. I heard you dying. I protected you until that time that Heqet might forget her scorn."

"Judging by your exit, I suppose that wasn't quite the case," Nerissa says to Worth.

"I expect Heqet is wounded. Or else she has decided to give up. Or someone has petitioned on your behalf," Dr. Frye says.

"You used Dwarven magic," Alma says to Dr. Frye. She hasn't spoken much since they came back, mostly just eyeing their new addition suspiciously.

"A keen eye. Yes, it is a synthesis of Dwarven magic and my own healing arts. It both gave Worth the power to change at will, and to protect him from Heqet's gaze," Dr. Frye says.

Christabel is trying to keep her face from erupting into rage or tears and can't tell which one will win. She wants to hate Dr. Frye, but the woman is so kind, so honest, so open. Not pure, not by any means. She has machinations going on behind her eyes. But Christabel suspects she would be forthcoming about those, too. She is old, very old. Not of the Fae, exactly, but something else.

The Questing Beast. Christabel distracts herself by thinking back. That name is familiar. She wrote about Questing Beasts nearly six hundred years ago. And if there were Questing Beasts, then all of King Arthur…

"Morgan Frye," Christabel says softly. "Morgan le Fey."

"Ah, yes," Dr. Frye says, giving Christabel a bright smile. "That is one of my monikers."

"What are you?" Christabel asks.

"We would call her *Toyotama-hime*," Kit says, her eyes gleaming as she looks upon Dr. Frye. "She is a dragon."

To the shocked responses, Dr. Frye waves a hand. "It is an old word, and nothing to be afraid of. But yes. I was called Morgan le Fey. I am descended of queens older than the mountains. And Worth is quite lucky I found him. Not much happens in Monmouth, but he fell like a star from the sky one evening while I was out gathering herbs. A fortuitous fall."

Worth has that same, faraway look he's had since they returned. "You nursed me back to health. But Heqet came looking for me, ransacked the town; people died. So we worked together to…" He swallows and puts his hand to his chest where the jewel used to be.

"We concealed you, taught you how to live as a man among the world of mortals, taught you the basic rules of how to survive, but left you with only a barest impression of me. It was best you didn't remember me. I would draw attention. I didn't want you in harm's way," Dr. Frye says softly.

Christabel feels a cold dread rising in her. It doesn't take her long to realize what it is: grief. She has felt it many times before. But now it is worse. Now she sees the ghost of Worth, and his eyes do not know her like they used to.

"Thank you," Nerissa says to Dr. Frye. "Worth and I worked together a long time. He was a good companion."

"He's still here," Worth says, but not even his voice is the same though he may look the part. "More or less."

～

They all agree that London is the best place for the team, now. Kit promises to visit, but with her newfound freedom arranges to visit Japan and reunite with her friends and family, those who still live. Heqet's curse is off of her, and she is practically shimmering with the possibilities. She has promised to track the jade cabochons they found on the dead men in the crypt to see if she can help in their search for Vivienne.

Christabel arranges to meet them in London separately, choosing to travel with Alma through Turkey and do a bit of research on the other cabochons, as well as track down a lead knowledgeable in Persian history and religion Morgan has suggested, a Professor Palomydes. The work will distract her. Nerissa looks at her with pity in her eyes, a new expression since she's found a better source for her food, because she understands without having to say anything. They are both mourning a loss of love.

Every day that passes, Worth fades more into Ophaniel. Dr. Frye explains that, in time, it is likely that Worth will be nothing but a memory. A whisper. Yet, Christabel reflects, it is astonishing how much pain a simple whisper can exact on a person.

"I'll meet you all in London," Christabel says at the door of the car getting ready to take her to the ship. Alma will find her way through Nith tunnels and arrive in Istanbul on her own.

Nerissa nods. "Are you sure you don't want to say goodbye to Worth?"

Christabel shakes her head a little too fervently. "I need some time," she says. "I am..."

"I know," Nerissa says, and brings the unicorn into an embrace. "Be careful out there."

～

London: A Month Later

Dear Vivienne,

I have started writing you letters because I don't know what else to do with myself. I know you told me not to seek you out, but I'm incapable of following directions when it comes to you, my dearest and dearest friend.

We discovered your masks, and their magic, but as you know, you've long ago left Cairo. After speaking with Mr. Cuddy, the man who was dressed as Robert E. Lee, we learned that the mask network is rather vast, and those left behind in Cairo were intended to distract us elsewhere. Where Barqan has taken you now, or what he wants with this elaborate plan, I have no idea. That you are being used to this nefarious purpose makes me so angry I could vomit. I know you must be in great distress. But we will find you.

Christabel is doing well considering what she's gone through. I have to admit, she's one of the toughest people I have ever met. Her work in Duat and her continued research are what has led us to you thus far. And, oddly enough, it is she who has cemented relations with the vampires, and they are the ones helping us with spies. It turns out they did not mean us harm, and they are, in fact, happy to help us. Their imp blood is significantly better than going through the Abattoir network.

As I wrote last time, Worth is...not himself. During the day he is a quieter, more reserved version of the man we know, but with memories like Swiss cheese. He doesn't seem to miss Christabel particularly, but has asked for her a few times. In the evenings, he is wholly Ophaniel. His foster mother, this Dr. Frye I told you of, has observed that it is simply the effects of his transformation. I don't know how much of that to believe, but I know that we are losing him, regardless. And I have seen his angelic form myself.

In time there will be no more Worth. Only Ophaniel.

Vivienne, I hope we do find you before that.

Vivienne, I am tired. The old iron scars ache when it's cold, and here in London it's cold all the time. I miss making fun of your stupid hats. I miss arguing with you over teatime. I even miss you not loving me.

For my part, I am enjoying the company of Dr. Frye at our Notting Hill townhome. We are healing, but we will move soon. Christabel and Alma plan to meet us in two weeks' time with news.

We will find you.

Nerissa signs her name on the paper and sighs, running a hand across her scaly face. Since returning to London, she only uses a glamour when she leaves the house. She is getting used to the crags and valleys of her body. She is learning not to hate them. Dr. Frye calls her a wonder.

The masks lay on Nerissa's writing table, and she goes to them, not for the first time, and examines them. The magic is somewhat dissipated, but she still feels the same shiver of power that she did when first touching them. It feels like Vivienne.

Just as she's about to put down the Napoleon mask, its shriveled lips turned downward in a frown, she notices an impression in the metal mold. She had taken it for a mistake of forging, when metals do not cool smoothly, but now she sees it is tiny handwriting. She takes it over to the light.

"To his nephew Mercury. On the cold hill's side. Asphodel."

Her heart leaps. She'll have to write Christabel immediately. It makes no sense. Nephew Mercury? Her mind spins but comes up with nothing but visions of Vivienne's face.

She is calling out.

She wants help.

A soft knock on the door, and Nerissa startles. She takes a deep breath and puts the mask on her table.

It is Worth, holding a candle, shivering and wrapped in a thick blanket Christabel knitted for him and had sent.

"Hello, Nerissa," he says. Some days he forgets her name. Especially toward the end of the day. But now he is lucid, his eyes shining.

"Is it time?" Nerissa asks.

"If you don't mind. I don't like being alone," Worth says, childlike.

"Of course," Nerissa says. "Give me just a moment."

Nerissa goes to her desk, picks up the letter, looks at it a moment, and throws it into the fire. She pauses just a moment to watch the edges curl, kindle, and burn.

"Now, I'm ready," she says softly.

Together, they go up to the rooftop balcony to await the coming of Ophaniel and the rising of the moon.

EPILOGUE

I n the dark, Vivienne startles awake. Her heart aches, and while that is nothing new, it is a raw, nasty feeling. Like a part of her is missing. She rubs at her chest and frowns, kindling the small lantern next to her bed as the shackles clink dully against one another. She's gone and frosted the whole room again, and the lamp dims and rises, dims and rises.

She thinks of Worth. She thinks of the scars down his back. Thinks of the curve of his spine when he is in pleasure. Of the strange outfits he always cobbles together trying to impress her.

"Mistress Vivienne," a voice at the barred door says.

It is Nadine, the ifrit in charge of her transportation and work. "It's time."

Vivienne wipes the tears from her face and rises, smoothing the sad excuse for a dress they make her wear. Honestly, she's seen burlap bags with more style.

"Just a moment," Vivienne says.

She goes to her barred window and looks out, the ship bobbing up and down with each step. The pale moon rises, full and resplendent. And for one split second, she thinks she sees wings flying across the face of the moon, dark and brilliant and beautiful.

And she feels, for a sliver of a moment, a bit of hope.

"Mistress Vivienne," Nadine says again, her blue limned head visible beyond the grate.

"Yes, I'm coming," Vivienne says. "Beauty can't be rushed, you know. And he does hate it when I'm in a state."

PART III
TIME & TEMPER

BEASTS OF LONDON

LANDLEGS

We begin again. This time, not with the lamia known as Nerissa Waldemar, nor with the unicorn known as Christabel Crane, but with a sylph who calls herself Vivienne du Lac. You will recall her adventures came to a rather abrupt halt some twenty years ago when she was taken, quite unfairly in her opinion, and sold in bondage. The previous volume, *Masks & Malevolence,* features her sparingly on account of her life falling into the sad, monotonous patterns of servitude she would prefer left untold.

But now, things begin to change. And with change, sometimes, comes hope. At least, we sincerely wish that is the case for Vivienne. She has been out of the picture a bit too long, and nothing perturbs her more than being overlooked.

So, Vivienne finds herself in Spain, of all places, and in Andalusia more specifically. She has arrived by boat and is quite vexed at the state of the villa once they reach it. She has no right to be—unlike in years past, she has no claim to the arrangement—but this is still considerably worse than her master's usual fare. Even with her magical capabilities sincerely dampened, she has not lost her knack for seeing details and quality. Though her master is many things, he is not typically one to skimp on luxury. So, she deduces that something must be amiss.

A few years ago, that fact might have kindled a bright glimmer of hope in her, finding a weakness in her bondage, but now she feels only a low, distant memory of optimism. How strange it is to grow accustomed to enslavement after so many centuries of freedom. Millennia, even. She has rather lost track. And though she has only been in bondage for twenty years, Vivienne feels the weight of that time more than any other in recent memory. Though if she digs deep enough…

As if in acknowledgement of her mere thoughts, the thin bangles on her wrists pulse with a hot current of magic, a searing counterpoint to hope. There is no doubt now. Her master is near.

Vivienne has been waiting, sitting on a large, moth-eaten suitcase, in the central garden of the villa. She knows the routine by now. She is to wait for her master. And even though her arcane power surges beneath her shackles, she is helpless to do anything other than wait. And Vivienne du Lac has never liked waiting. Not that it matters any longer.

The servants scurry as the master's footfalls echo across the terracotta tiles, boot heels reverberating with every step, crunching against the detritus of so many years upon the floor. Leaves skitter away from his presence as if they, too, were aware of his general poisonousness.

When Vivienne sees him, she feels the uncanny pulse of her shackles again, incapable of suppressing the sense of awe whenever in his presence. Which she resents. Woe to her for being such a helpless aesthete.

She likes to think there was an air of regret in Barqan's demeanor when he sold her to her new master. But she can only recall the djinni's final words to her: "Behold, a terror you do not know. May you drink deeply from that dark well, as I did."

She was busy at the time, rather preoccupied with the strange new circumstance of being bound in djinn-forged iron, and never asked the right questions. She honestly thought she would be able to escape.

Whatever happened to the djinni after that point, she does not know. It has been almost twenty years since her capture, and Barqan's affairs took him elsewhere. If not for the ultimate betrayal, she might almost miss him. If not for his droll company, or his treacle, which, when he was living as her servant, was second to none.

In the dim evening light—a strange, lingering light this close to the equator—her master's face is shadowed a moment under the balustrades and tree limbs stretching out overhead. Vivienne can tell he is wearing his good riding suit by the cut of his narrow shoulders. Maybe the navy one today. Or the tweed. She can make complaints about a thousand difficulties of being a thrall, but she must admit his taste in fashion rivals hers.

Nadine, the master's ifrit, greets him first, fussing over him and taking his coat and scarf. The ever-present blue light around her head illuminates his face just long enough for Vivienne to catch her breath. Like Vivienne, Nadine wears a chain; for her, though, the iron is about her neck.

Ah, yes, and there he is—her master. A chiseled face shaved clean as marble. There is not much mammalian about him other than the color and composition of his skin in its current glamor. He wears dark, round glasses to obscure his yellow eyes, but she rarely pays attention to them, anyway. It's his lips she likes, prone to smile and dip down in line with the widow's peak atop his head. A perfect V. A flawless specimen.

It's only when he talks that Vivienne notices the sharp teeth, the forked tongue, and she remembers what he is. She did live with a snake for centuries, after all, though not one full of such venom.

Her master, a man who goes only by a single name, is no lamia. Bastille, Lord of the Grey Moor, is a basilisk.

THE CELESTIAL TENANT

No snake has ever loved London so much as Nerissa Waldemar, of that she is confident. After far too long in the realms of sand and sun, she is now happily ensconced in a basement apartment in Shoreditch, reveling in the constant wet of the world, the chill tendrils of cool currents moving through the city, and the ever-present whisper of the Thames. Though she is a snake, she is a lamia, and as such prefers the wet to the dry, more like a salamander. She's never taken the time to ask why she is different from her other reptilian cousins; knowing certainly would not make life any easier, so she declines the research, even though Christabel would likely have hordes of research, and theories, on the subject.

In the three years since arriving in London, she has managed quite the setup for herself. She has a residence, for one thing, which she has taken the time to decorate to her tastes. Her tastes, such as they are, might be considered "bog chic" if there were such a thing, as she tends toward verdant hues and draping netting as decor, to better mirror the landscape of her nascent years. Granted, there was a great deal more bloodshed during that time, but she comforts herself knowing that, for the last seven years, she hasn't had to drink a drop of blood.

Her food source comes courtesy of the vampire network, an ancient and revered group of creatures living on the fringes of society. Though she does not claim kinship to them, two of them in Cairo, Beti and

Micheaux, took her under their wing and provided a new way to feed: imp sweat. It is a silvery sweet stuff, a bit more expensive than she would like, but she only requires a small amount to keep her moving. Gone are the days when she had to fight tooth and nail to keep herself sated, breeding animals and pushing down her bestial needs to rend arteries and suck at bleeding flesh.

She doesn't even miss it. No, Nerissa is fully cured of her bloodthirst. If she finds herself panicking a little now and then if she doesn't get enough implet, as she calls it — a play on "gimlet"—she doesn't worry. This life is a better life. She is clearer of mind. She is sounder of body. She has time to decorate.

All but one corner of the apartment, that is. Behind a wooden screen, her companion Kit takes up residence, usually perched or dangling from the shelf she's installed for such use. Kit is a *kitsune*, a kind of fox spirit, who began her days as an unintentional slave, but now considers herself an official part of Nerissa's work chasing down monsters gone mad. Once, it was Goodwin and Waldemar. Then it was Goodwin, Waldemar, and Crane. Then things got complicated when Goodwin became an angel, which he'd always been, apparently, and Crane decided she needed an extended vacation. Now it's Waldemar and Kamiyama. And they make a very, very good team. Even if the name doesn't have quite the ring to it that she'd like.

So, it's been up to Nerissa and Kit to keep London safe from Exigents and Aberrants, the monsters who either are driven to madness or else embrace it, for the last few years. In between her work, Nerissa has done all in her power to track down the kidnapper of her once (very unrequited) love, the sylph Vivienne du Lac. It has been twenty years since Vivienne, the one person who gave Nerissa a chance after she'd nearly gone Aberrant herself, was abducted, and they have little go to on concerning her whereabouts. They know a few things: her magic is most certainly dampened, because no one—not even the most sophisticated seers or birch benders—can locate her specific arcane imprint, which Christabel long ago derived during a holiday in Budapest.

Sometimes, Nerissa pretends that Vivienne is dead, because honestly to know she has quit the world and is at peace is better than thinking she is still in thrall to some genuinely abhorrent creature. But Nerissa, while scorned from a romantic sense, is sure that if Vivienne were to die, she would know. Their bond, while not of love in the sapphic sense, exists on another level of consciousness. The old snake may not be particularly religious—even among her closest friends, no particular pantheon makes sense, and so she relegates them all to the "geographical and cultural arcane"—but she does believe in the bond between people who share common experiences.

Which is also why she cannot ever quite do away with Christabel Crane or the angel. Or the dwarf. At this point, they have endured mad monsters hell-bent on destroying all other beasts, Egyptian goddesses with blood feuds, and the very tragic love story of a cherub who never seemed to get things quite right. And in between all that, dozens of arrests, imprisonments, and, thankfully, rehabilitations to her credit.

To some, Nerissa supposes, she is considered a traitor to her kind. But she genuinely appreciates humanity for what it is, which she has Vivienne to thank for, and does not think that they deserve to be considered food on a daily basis. They are, except for precious few, incapable of magic. Though their technology is disturbingly improving with every century, they are mostly powerless when it comes to defending themselves against the supernatural and arcane. Humans have a few redeeming qualities, she supposes. And also domesticated cats. She quite likes cats.

Life would be good—and it is, in moments—if Nerissa didn't consider herself a complete and utter failure. Despite her success in London, her friendship with Kit, and the fact she no longer must hunt for her food, she has nothing to show for the last twenty years of her life. Every year lived without Vivienne du Lac. What Vivienne would say about the décor of her Shoreditch apartment, she can only imagine.

And it isn't just Vivienne's absence, that constant gnawing shame of failure. Now, Nerissa must also check in on the angel every night, especially around the full moon when he is at his most melancholic and dramatic. That has gotten rather tiring as of late. He is so dull when he's in his divine form.

She misses Worth Goodwin, the insufferable newspaper-reading foppish monster the angel was before he was freed, even if he was a lie. And she knows Christabel misses him more. To say nothing of Vivienne, if she ever finds out.

Nerissa is just finishing her afternoon nap when someone raps on the door with light knuckles. A lovely side-effect of the implet is enhanced hearing. She discerns the precise hollow sound of more fragile fingers versus the hard pulse of meatier ones. As such, she knows it is Micheaux before the door is even opened. That, and the vampire wears so much cologne he's practically able to generate a personal miasma. The odor of *Quelleque Fleures* knows no limits when it comes to Micheaux.

As she opens the door, Nerissa takes in the garish figure of the French vampire. No matter how many times she sees him there's no less shock. He wears his hair in blond ringlets, tied with a different colored satin ribbon every day. Today it is shades of periwinkle blue that match his silk kimono and weskit below, emphasizing the bluish tone to his undead skin. But for the splash of blush at his cheeks and the gentle wrinkle of his forehead he would be otherwise indistinguishable from a corpse; a handsome, overwhelmingly floral corpse, but a corpse, nonetheless.

"My dear Ms. Waldemar!" Micheaux opens his arms wide in expectation of an embrace, or one of his cloyingly sweet kisses to the cheek, but Nerissa has learned how to evade him. "Micheaux has so very much missed you."

The lamia steps out of Micheaux's way and gestures inside the room. "Come, Micheaux. You are welcome."

Micheaux is delivering Nerissa's weekly store of implet, which he does not have to do and yet finds every reason to do so. Nerissa would wonder at his motives except she long ago realized the vampire was simply dim. If the fact that he always refers to himself in the third person isn't enough of a giveaway, his fashion sense would undoubtedly raise enough red flags. Silk, in October?

The phials in Micheaux's briefcase clink together and Nerissa feels a welling of anticipation rise in her. Food, glorious food. Nourishment. Not just sustenance. It is truly one of the most marvelous days of the week when the delivery comes, even if she must endure Micheaux.

Kit, who has been sleeping off her last adventure, stirs in her corner and Nerissa vaguely wonders if she's going to make herself known. Her dislike of the vampires is one of the most intense reactions Nerissa has ever seen, though Kit does seem to tolerate Micheaux when necessary.

"I hope you are enjoying the season," Nerissa says when Micheaux takes a seat on one of the less moth-eaten divans.

The vampire stretches out his long legs, looking down at them as if for the first time, tilting his head to the side and gazing quizzically. Nerissa is just about to ask him if he's quite alright when he holds up a finger.

"Oh, Micheaux had a note to deliver, along with the food. Which is why Micheaux spent his time coming to this...unusual corner of London. It is so...quaint," he says with a smile in his voice. "Micheaux sees the angel is not around. That is good. Good."

The angel, Ophaniel, once Worth Goodwin, lives on the highest apartment in the building, sleeping most of the time and complaining away the rest.

"Ophaniel will likely require my attention later this evening," Nerissa says, doublechecking her watch. It conveniently displays the phases of the moon. A few years ago, she would have shunned such a piece of technology, but being the guardian of an angel means she has to work within her limitations. "But you still have time."

"He has the strangest eyes," Micheaux says, encircling his own with long, bony fingers. "Micheaux gets the feeling the angel is looking through him when he comes into view. Like a window and not a being."

"You likely don't have a soul," says Nerissa. "It's probably confusing for him."

"Micheaux likes to think he is enticing to the angel. But that is probably hoping for too much."

"Yes. The utter absurdity of such a match is beyond even my ability to imagine," Nerissa replies, glancing—but not meaning to—at Kit as she stretches and stirs a little more, pulling back the long, black curtain of her hair to reveal her eyes. Such behavior—sleeping upside down—used to bother Nerissa to no end. Now, she finds she quite appreciates the *kitsune's* eccentricities. "Would you like some tea?"

Micheaux shakes his golden head, and Nerissa notes for the first time that the vampire is wearing a wig. She hadn't realized that. Curious. And the veins on his face stand out a little starker than they used to. He doesn't look particularly well. It is difficult to measure illness in one who is already undead.

"Are you alright, Micheaux?" Nerissa tries not to adjust her glasses too obviously.

Micheaux smiles a wan smile. "Ah, well, there has been a good deal of drama within the coven. But when is there not? Micheaux does not like to get involved but finding rest has not been easy with all the yelling."

"I'm sorry," she says softly. "I know how essential sleep is for you."

"Perhaps one of these visits Micheaux will sleep right here for a few hours?"

"Yes, yes. Of course. But not today."

"Of course," whispers Micheaux. "But there is not much time today. Micheaux is due back soon." He starts staring at his legs again.

"The letter?" asks Nerissa.

"Oh, yes, yes. You really ought to read the letter. It's quite important, I think," Micheaux says.

Kit's voice drifts over from her corner. "You better not have read it, scoundrel." Scoundrel is one of Kit's favorite new words. For all her complaints about the English language, which she relates to the sound dogs make when they're chewing tough meat, she is always finding a new word or turn of phrase to master.

"Ah, fox woman," Micheaux says, all the delight of a child in his eyes. "Micheaux had hoped you might be here. Come into the light so Micheaux can see you."

"That would require me having to look at you, and such an arrangement would make my stomach turn," Kit says from the corner.

"Now, this letter," Nerissa presses before Micheaux can process the insult.

Micheaux makes a grand show of opening the long blue kimono and withdrawing a blood-red envelope from the interior pocket of his weskit. With every movement comes the unmistakable scent of *Quelleque Fleures*, along with that lingering, sickly sweet stench of death that all vampires emit. Like lilies at a funeral.

Nerissa takes the letter in her hand, curiously cold, and breaks the seal. It is from Beti, Micheaux's coven queen. She is a rather unassuming woman for a vampire, uncomplicated and homely for her sort, preferring the arts of herbalism and potions-making to hunting and devouring as most vampires do, which is a refreshing change. Now living in Paris, Beti is the eyes and ears of the underground monster community faction known as the Vampire Network, a growing group of supernatural beings who wish no harm to humankind, or so they claim. Nerissa and Kit have a tenuous alliance with them, if only because they supply enough implet for the lamia to keep healthy and hale.

Beti's handwriting is archaic and beautiful, spidery and flowery at the same time. She writes letters as surely as if they were letter pressed, and at first Nerissa is so enchanted by the script that she doesn't quite grasp the contents of the letter. So, she must read it again.

Dear Miss Waldemar,

It has been some time since our paths crossed, but I believe I have located your missing friend, or at least I know of her last whereabouts and the ship she came in on. It is now docked in the Thames, and I will be making a special trip to examine the stores there. Let us meet and then go onward to Spain, where Vivienne resided the last time I heard.

You are welcome to bring Mr. Goodwin/Ophaniel. But I would not suggest bringing the kitsune. And if Miss Crane is anywhere to be found, she may find it of some use as well.

Most sincerely,

Beti

Nerissa feels her jaw jump before she realizes just how hard she is biting down on her teeth. She can't say what feeling arises in her, but it is hope mingled with a strange kind of jealousy. How did the vampires come by such information? And so suddenly?

"This is remarkable," says Nerissa, turning the letter over in her hands as if in the hope that it might be a joke, or contain some note of clarification. But there is nothing. "Beti sent this to you?"

Micheaux looks taken aback. "Of course, she sent it to Micheaux. How else would Micheaux find it? We saw her ship a few hours ago, on our way here at twilight, and a little runner vampire brought this to Micheaux's attention."

Not for the first time, Nerissa wishes Christabel were here. It is abundantly clear that the situation is off. Micheaux looks sick, even for a vampire. The letter does not read in Beti's voice at all.

And the information is too good to be true.

"I apologize, Micheaux," the lamia says at last, folding up the letter. "It's only that we've been searching so long and so hard, with so many instances where we thought we had turned the final corner to see Vivienne that...well, I don't know what to say."

Kit takes the note, appearing in a swirl of color. She reads so fast that Nerissa startles when she says, "Well, I believe the proper phrase, in this case, would be 'thank you.'"

OF SELKIES AND SULKING

When you do not age or grow old, ten years can feel like the space of a few days. But when you're still mourning the loss of your would-be lover who turned out to be an angel and isn't exactly dead, but also isn't exactly alive, each day can feel like an eternity.

Such is the case for Christabel Crane. She has tried to bury herself in work, primarily research pertaining to creature spells, traveling through Ireland and Greece and India with Dr. Morgan Frye. Together they have proven a most impressive duo, doing more than twice the work Dr. Frye had managed in her many centuries alone.

While not an immortal per se, as Christabel is by way of being a unicorn, Dr. Frye is an unclassifiable being. She is as old as the earth. From her conversations, Christabel has deduced that the woman has always been present on the planet in one way or another, but most usually in her present state. Born and reborn, she retains all the memories of the time before her and collects that experience into a wickedly sharp mind and curious presence.

Christabel supposes that one might call Dr. Frye a goddess. But the eccentric woman probably wouldn't like that. She's not one for formal titles or formalities of any sort, really. Dr. Frye is the kind of woman who wore trousers decades before they were fashionable. She refused corsets even in the height of the wasp waist, so when the twenties came roaring in, she was already ahead of the curve. Her hair is never to fashion, her language always a bit archaic, yet she never sounds out of date. And Dr. Frye is, always and forever, completely resistant to critique or general concern. Dr. Frye navigates the world with utter confidence and no need for affirmation. For Christabel's purposes, she has decided to think of Dr. Frye as a dragon.

They sit now among the rocks of the Outer Hebrides speaking to a young selkie named Jenn. Jenn's entire name is much longer, of a proto-Celtic derivation, and Christabel, to her surprise, rather likes the selkie. Christabel has never much cared for the sea nor the creatures in it. But as a selkie, currently in a seal state, Jenn is lovely. Her pelt is smooth as a pebble, reflecting the shining winter sun, silver and dark grey. Her eyes are like pools of dark water. And her voice is soft, lulling.

"Of course, when it comes to the frequency of selkie calls, well, it's entirely different than native speakers," Jenn is saying. Not only is she chief among her selkie sisters, but she is also an accomplished singer.

Christabel is trying to pay attention, but the moon is rising full over the bay of their little island, and she is thinking about Worth Goodwin again. Or, rather, Ophaniel, the angel he always was.

Dr. Frye leans forward, absorbing every word the selkie has to say. According to the doctor, such company is considered a great boon indeed, as selkies rarely share their secrets, let alone with strangers not from their islands. The only reason Jenn would speak to them at all was because Worth had contacted them a decade ago and had gained their trust by helping drain and dredge part of the bay so the selkies might better approach the island free from predators. Always generous, Worth Goodwin, even when he was supposed to be searching for Aberrants and Exigents with Nerissa and Vivienne.

"Fascinating," Dr. Frye says. "So, it is not simply a matter of wave-lengths, as I had thought before." She is furiously scratching in her book, fingers ink-stained, eyes bright. How someone could be so old and yet still so in awe of the world is quite beyond Christabel. She's already beginning to tire of it, and she's scarcely forty.

"Yes, our throats are different," says Jenn, raising her head slightly to display the speckled area there. Hers looks like a little map. "Every selkie has a neck brand, as we call them. We name them, rather than ourselves. So, among my sisters I am called 'heather flower'—you see how my brand looks like a sprig of fresh heather?"

Christabel notes it looks almost like a sprig of heather. Or a side of bacon. Or a newt phallus. But she keeps those opinions safely to herself. As mentioned previously, she rather likes Jenn. And unlike her sometimes companion Nerissa Waldemar, Christabel can keep her thoughts inside her head.

"Our throats must be different," says Jenn, "for the change to occur. We are born of seals but possess the magic of women, so parts of each must be present in the other. But not entirely."

"Then your ears much be capable of receiving unique wavelengths as well," Dr. Frye continues.

"Oh, yes. We can even hear the stars," Jenn says with a glimmer in her dark brown eyes. "Though I have noticed that the swan constellation is a bit quiet as of late. We've been listening to her now and again..."

On a regular day, this would be fascinating for Christabel, but she simply cannot abide by it any longer. She starts to stand and finds the selkie has sidled up next to her, looking up with sorrow in her eyes.

"It's the moon that concerns me," says Christabel. "It always makes me think of him."

Dr. Frye stops her furious writing and glances over her glasses at Christabel. "I've told you a thousand times, you don't have to be here with me. I can do the research on my own; though I can't argue that your help has been immense. Still, if I'm keeping you from him..."

"No, no, of course not, Dr. Frye," Christabel says. "I was lost in a moment of melancholy. It's been ten years, now. A quarter of my own, short, strange life. You would think I would have learned by now to accept that Worth Goodwin was nothing more than the phantasm—a costume—worn by Ophaniel to protect him."

Dr. Frye had a hand in the whole transfiguration of Ophaniel, and she so obviously feels guilty about it. "I was keeping him safe. I didn't think the persona would take so heartily. It is all a most unfortunate situation. How could I have anticipated a unicorn would fall in love with him?"

"I only thought I knew who he was—what he was," Christabel says.

"I didn't know what Worth was either if that's a consolation," Jenn says softly. "It wasn't easy to determine. Perhaps Dr. Frye's work was too good."

"You flatter me," says Dr. Frye. "It was old, strong magic. And I do wish the old fellow would stop being angry at me. Ah, well. I suppose I will incur Ophaniel's wrath to know he is alive, and that I kept him alive, despite the fury of a half dozen Egyptian deities."

Dr. Frye gives Christabel a sad smile.

"He's lucky to have you," says Christabel. "He just hasn't figured it out yet."

"There are a great many things Ophaniel hasn't figured out yet," says Dr. Frye with a snort. "I am very low on that list. Eventually, I hope, he will stop sulking and leave that tenement in Shoreditch, and we can have a proper discussion. But as it is, I have all the time in the world. And so does he. So, if it takes another ten centuries, so be it. I have waited before, and I will wait again."

Christabel wants to tell Dr. Frye that she feels the same way, that she will wait for Ophaniel. That she will hold out hope that Worth is there, somewhere. But she cannot. So, she falls silent and asks Jenn to sing a few more bars before the moon fully rises.

~

Over dinner that night in the cottage, Dr. Frye is frank with Christabel in a manner she has never been before. At first, Christabel is unsure what to do with such directness, but it doesn't take her long to feel a kind of relief in speaking freely about Worth. And Ophaniel.

"I cannot help but think this transformation is more difficult on you because of your very nature. Unicorns and angels falling in love...I would never have considered the ramifications in a thousand years." Dr. Frye never eats anything other than meat and mushrooms, with a sprinkling of vegetation now and then. Christabel prefers fruit and grains and always has to avert her eyes from the other woman's plate. Tonight, it is puffin breasts served rare, and it turns Christabel's stomach.

"It isn't angel and unicorns in love," Christabel corrects Dr. Frye. "We were not in love. We were not lovers."

"Ah, but your souls are connected."

"Even if that was the truth, Worth isn't *Worth*. He is gone."

Dr. Frye gives Christabel a pitying look that speaks volumes. "I have told you this a few times before and I will tell you again, my dear. Nothing of Worth exists without Ophaniel. Worth was a refraction, a distillation of a facet of Ophaniel. You cannot make or destroy matter. I could not shape Worth from nothing."

"Ophaniel is nothing like Worth. He is a stuck up, narcissistic, self-centered prig."

"Well, you didn't give him much of a chance."

Christabel tries to argue, but it's true. When Ophaniel looked upon her and didn't know her, the fury and sorrow were so great she fled. For months, while Nerissa and Kit kept guard, Christabel traveled, only returning to London when absolutely necessary, sending money to support, and occasionally research on celestials, but remaining almost entirely out of the picture. Even now they are in London, not far considering Christabel's far-ranging adventures, arranging their lives to best fit around Ophaniel's, and she has no plans on meeting with them, in spite of Nerissa's pleading letters. The guilt rises and Christabel washes down the berry compote from her toast with a sip of weak wine.

"I didn't know what to do, Dr. Frye. Twenty years ago, I thought I was a clever young woman uncovering the truth about the supernatural. I had a purpose. I had a calling. I was headstrong and likely full of myself, but I was confident in many things. Worth was the one that made me question my place in the world, but to also seek my own truth. But then he also was the biggest threat to what I am," Christabel says in a rush of words and air. "He made me want *more* knowledge. He made me want...many things."

Dr. Frye chuckles into her glass of wine. Stronger. Redder. Older. The same words could apply to the doctor in contrast to the unicorn. "I do not think that making love will destroy you, if that's what worries you. An immortal life without a good bedding now and again is a sobering thought."

Saying it out loud makes Christabel cringe. "Everything I've read speaks to the purity of unicorns as a source of power. Of magic. What if it meant I would die?"

"Sex is very nice," Dr. Frye says matter-of-factly. "I'd say some would be willing to take that risk."

While Christabel gapes, Dr. Frye continues. "All I'm saying is that there's a striking lack of information about you and your kind. And while I do believe some of it has to do with the sheer rarity of unicorns as a whole, that doesn't stop me from suspecting there may be other forces at play. You may hold on to your purity and insist that you have no future with Ophaniel, or anyone else for that matter, but it is rather myopic, don't you think? The world is changing. What makes you think that we monsters don't change along with it? There is no point in making your-self miserable without the facts. We are close to having more information; I can feel it."

"But you have spent your whole life searching for evidence on the rarest of creatures. What makes you think that it will be different now?"

Dr. Frye gives Christabel a kind smile. "Because I found a unicorn after all, didn't I? It only took a few thousand years, but here you are. And if there's anyone who knows more about unicorns in the whole world, it's you. Though, to be honest, I hadn't expected you would have a fully human form. But that probably explains why unicorns are so difficult to track in the first place. You had to come from somewhere. Unicorns don't just appear fully fleshed from the earth. Even the worst among monsters have mothers."

"I was adopted," Christabel says. "I found that out during the trials."

Ah, yes, that was Christabel's other work. The Prague Agreements. She took two years in the late 20s to work side-by-side with two factions within the community of the arcane: gods and monsters. It is a long story and one deserving of an extended telling, but the short of it is that she worked to broker an alliance between the two sides. She helped determine, in a court of law no less, that monsters and deities are truly no different from one another. In fact, many stem from the same source entirely. Plenty of monsters are children of deities—and indeed, some gods are the progeny of monsters. This alliance has been somewhat tenuous but gained her renown. It also brought to light the confirmation of her adoption.

"Regardless, even orphans don't metamorphose from thin air," Dr. Frye says. "You can argue all you want, dear, but you are both woman and monster. You are a rare instance—and that, I'm quite certain, is how you won over the factions in Prague."

"I rather prefer the monsters," Christabel says quietly.

"I won't tell Hermes you said that."

Yes, that. Well. Christabel is trying to think of a clever retort when there comes a knock on the front door of the little cottage, and she is delighted. She did have something of a dalliance with Hermes, the Greek messenger god. He was charming and mysterious, and they had a lot to say...and do. But ultimately the god had no interest in being steadfast or exclusive, to say nothing of tiring of Christabel's hesitance in terms of romantic relations.

Still, she does miss him.

The women exchange looks at the sound of the door, and Dr. Frye immediately goes for her longsword, which never seems far from her hands. Christabel stands slowly, taking deep breaths. She knows that keeping calm increases her ability to fight tenfold. Though it's been ages since she's managed to transmute into her unicorn form, she must be prepared.

When Dr. Frye opens the door, however, it's just a delivery man. He is very young and wears a wispy red mustache with great pride. He looks terrified at the sight of Dr. Frye, as most men are. She towers above him, muscle and curves and smooth, sun-kissed skin. Her hair tumbles in dark waves, and her eyes pierce as sharply as her sword.

"Good evening," Dr. Frye says to the delivery boy.

He is practically shaking in his boots, but hands over the letter, anyway. He does not ask for a tip, and Dr. Frye unceremoniously shuts the door and looks calmly at Christabel.

"It's for you," she says. "It's from Nerissa."

Christabel takes the letter, immediately curious. Nerissa has done very little in terms of reaching out since the whole business with Worth and the Egyptian underworld; the lamia is not known for her transparency, and no matter how much they'd worked together in the past, Christabel senses Nerissa doesn't like her much. They have kept a courteous correspondence over the last few years, sharing notes and providing any useful clues about Vivienne du Lac. But Christabel now thinks is an unsolvable case, too difficult to crack, now almost twenty years after the sylph's abduction. The trail has run cold. Du Lac must be dead, or worse…

But the letter would not have her believe so.

"It says they know where Vivienne is," Christabel says. Dr. Frye does not know the entire business, but enough to be surprised.

"I'll be," Dr. Frye replies. "I had begun to think this sylph of yours was a collective hallucination. It's not unheard of…"

Christabel rereads the letter, looking for any code or sign it might be in jest. Even though she's quite aware of Nerissa's general lack of humor in any capacity, Christabel still finds it difficult to believe there is any kind of validity to the missive.

But it is written in Nerissa's same steady hand.

We do not know yet of the exact location, but we know it is in Spain. Not far from Gibraltar. One of the servants at the facility somehow got word to the Vampire Network, and here we are.

The Vampire Network. Christabel has never liked them and wishes that it had been anyone but them involved. But then, she supposes it stands to reason that they would know. It's their business to know everything. Their currency is information.

"I suppose it's difficult for anyone to stay hidden for twenty years," Christabel says. "Even Vivienne du Lac."

"What a strange name," Dr. Frye muses. "It can't possibly be her real name. I knew the *real* Vivienne du Lac, and she was by no means a frivolous nymph."

"She's a sylph," corrects Christabel.

"Is she?"

"Yes," Christabel says. "And while she is vain and a bit conceited, she still does not deserve what has happened to her. All we know is that she is in pain, in trouble, and likely has been suffering for some time."

Dr. Frye raises an arched brow, pursing her lips. She looks almost childlike when she does that, the dimples in her cheeks deepening. "And you think it's likely that after two decades her captors simply decided it's not worth the effort to keep her concealed?"

"When you say it like that, no."

"I'm just saying that you should proceed with caution."

"I understand. And I'm sorry. It's just that we've been at this so long, and to have it conclude so abruptly. My intuition tells me that this is not as good as it appears. That there is something else at work here. But I worry for Nerissa."

"To say nothing of our angel."

Christabel hates it when Dr. Frye refers to Ophaniel that way. Yes, it's true his transformation is due in large part to Dr. Frye, protecting him for centuries before he could hold the bond no longer. But Christabel hates the idea of owning anyone, let alone an angel.

"I suppose this means I have to go to London," Christabel says with a sigh. "And our work here must wait."

Dr. Frye does not argue. "Well, I will be here, transposing selkie songs, if you need me. I look forward to your return. I think it will be good of you to get some closure if nothing else."

"Dr. Frye..."

"Do say hello to Ophaniel when you see him."

A HIDEOUS PROMONTORY

The memories are the hardest part to endure. They occurred so frequently at first that he wasn't entirely sure he was waking or dreaming. Now, even Ophaniel has trouble keeping them straight from his present, ridiculous, depressing, and altogether *human* existence. So is the difficulty of living eternally. Unlike many angels thrown down from heaven, Ophaniel had the misfortune of falling in love with an Egyptian deity and engendering the wrath of a goddess. And, by extension, his LORD.

Left alone. Shattered. If it hadn't been for that witch finding him centuries ago, he would have died an earthly death.

She—a woman who calls herself Dr. Morgan Frye, who is most certainly not a doctor or a woman—helped him avoid the eye of his enemies long enough that the blood feud dissipated somewhat. He lived for five centuries as a man who transformed into beasts, a Glatisant. It was the rarest of creatures, perhaps rarer than the unicorn. But then he met an actual unicorn and found himself in the Egyptian underground, and before he knew it, he was no longer Worth Goodwin, the Glatisant, but Ophaniel once again.

But now, unlike his years as Worth, when he had friends and lovers, he is utterly alone.

These days, Ophaniel spends a good deal of time in his high apartment, drawing the face of the unicorn. Her name is Christabel, and he has the feeling that he is supposed to love her. That he does love her. That just because he is no longer Worth Goodwin doesn't mean he can simply ignore the feelings he once had. But she comes to see him so rarely. And he doesn't know what to say to her because her eyes are so full of pain that he fears he might weep to watch her any longer. And crying makes him look peaked. And peaked is not a good look on him.

The snake isn't much help, though she at least is consistent. Although Ophaniel appreciates that the snake—Nerissa, her name is Nerissa—has taken him in and allows him space in their building, she does not give him much hope that his life will be anything other than misery, pining, and confusion. Nerissa is a creature of doubt, of cynicism, so it's not surprising that she's of no help. Still, the snake has a companion: the *kitsune*. Ophaniel quite likes Kit, and they have long conversations together since neither of them require much in the way of sleep.

And Kit comes to comfort him during the full moon, when his memories of his dead lover are the worst. Nerissa avoids him then, doubtless because she has lost someone, too. She claims that the bare, silver moon makes her ill. It makes Ophaniel weak, losing his tenuous connection to the celestial realm. But then anger and weakness aren't so different, really. So perhaps they understand each other more fully, would they each open themselves up and allow themselves to be truly vulnerable to one another.

But that is ridiculous.

So, he wallows. And sketches. And complains to himself that he'll be lost forever in this stinking apartment and never again see the face of his LORD.

"I can never get back," he mutters to himself, pacing the sparse room on the top floor of their house on Old Street. "But I should want to go back. Do I want to go back? Some days I don't think I do."

I can't imagine heaven is that good. I mean, they kicked us out and we found our way here and had quite a few adventures. Well, what I mean is that it's been a while. Centuries. No one's come looking. Surely if we're that missed then someone ought to be looking.

It's Worth. The one that Ophaniel was during his imprisonment by the witch's spell. Somehow, even though it's been a decade—which is just a mortal blink, but well enough time to recover for a celestial—he has not been able to shake the creature he once was. Worth exists, not always, but now and again, as a kind of resonance in Ophaniel's head.

And lately, Worth has become more insistent.

Ophaniel sighs, even though he's almost glad that Worth is there. It has been a very lonely time in this grey world since he awoke again. And when the moon is out, it's even worse. But speaking to oneself is perhaps not the ideal method of conversation; still, Ophaniel feels it's better than nothing.

"I'm tired of living on this hideous promontory," Ophaniel says.

It's not a promontory. It's a building. Not even an impressive building. Old Street does have some charms, I've always thought, if you can dig through the dirt. Did you know the poet Keats was born not far from here?

Ophaniel hates it when Worth goes on like this. As if such chatter could ever be interesting to him. What good would knowing the poetry of mortals be, seeing that he has heard the music of Yaweh himself? This Worth, whatever part of him he might be, seems annoyingly connected to such romantic notions.

"Whatever it's called, I don't like it."

The penthouse, if it was even worthy of such a name, is mostly comprised of ugly angles and narrow windows. Ophaniel has done the best he can to keep it clean, which means removing all the unnecessary furniture and retaining only the most essential pieces: a mattress, a chair, and a table. As well as a shelf which Ophaniel does not use for books but rather as a perch (perching being another habit he shares with the *kitsune*.). He doesn't know why, but when he's tired, he very much enjoys sitting up there and looking out across the city. What parts of it he can see, that is. This London place is rather horrible in terms of views. The ever-present fog is like a film before his eyes. But then, there are glimmers when even he, the skeptic of the stars, feels as if perhaps the grime and detritus of the city conceals a power just outside his field of vision; so he keeps trying to steal a glimpse.

You've said that every day for ten years. You'd think that you'd have figured a way out. I'm starting to believe you like these people. They are very kind to you, you know. They have been through a great deal, and the last thing they need in their lives is a whiny, melancholic cherub with a touch of narcissism.

"I'm not narcissistic if I'm genuinely superior to all of those around me."

Case in point. I still hold they're kinder to you than you deserve.

"I'm fairly certain it's because they think you're in me somewhere," Ophaniel mutters, rolling his eyes at his invisible conversant. "Just waiting to be let free. So Ophaniel can die, and everyone else can live happily ever after."

Well, we're talking, aren't we? Doesn't that presuppose that I exist in one form or another?

"That's beside the point."

You never tell them about me. So, they're kind because they're good people.

"They are many things, but good people is not one of them."

Depends on your perspective, I say.

Ophaniel sighs dramatically, batting the air at an invisible foe. "I just keep hoping that you go away."

You're worried that I'm why you can't fly. I told you I can help with that.

Ophaniel is about to growl at the voice in his head, but the floorboards at the top of the stairs are creaking, and that means he's got a visitor. There isn't time to argue with the unwelcome guest in his brain, so he does what is expected and opens the door.

Well, not entirely expected. Ophaniel can open doors—and only doors—telepathically. He must twist his finger just so, and the mechanism obeys and swings open. He doesn't find it odd in the least, but he doesn't remember how or why he should do it; his neighbors find it quite curious.

Flying would be a great deal more impressive. But in the ensuing years, he's lost the ability.

If you let me, I can help you.

It is the snake woman, Nerissa. As she enters the room, she has the same bewildered expression she always has. Except today Ophaniel thinks she might be paler than usual. Her glamour is slipping, and there are scales peeping through at her neck and shadows of her extra limbs if he looks just right. She doesn't make an attractive woman, but he thinks she might be an attractive lamia. He won't tell her this, of course, because he's worried it might go to her head.

"Ophaniel, hello," Nerissa says. It's a polite thing to say, but there is nothing polite about this creature. Ophaniel wishes she wouldn't come to visit him, and the fact she's here in the evening at a time when she's never arrived before is deeply unsettling to him. He is a logical, practical being, and schedules please him greatly. The snake woman is the embodiment of chaos, but until this point, she's been somewhat predictable. "I'm sorry to bother you."

She isn't. She never is.

"Nerissa," Ophaniel says, rolling the r. It sounds better that way, even if no one else pronounces it in such a manner. "Good evening."

"Am I interrupting you?"

It's a stupid question to ask, but Ophaniel bares his teeth in a close approximation of a mortal grin and says, "No. I was merely contemplating the meaning of existence and my place as a fallen celestial unable to commune with their deity. I assure you, whatever concern you have is more pressing than such petty musings."

Nerissa is trying to keep from getting frustrated, and it's one of Ophaniel's favorite states to goad her into. She really does work so hard to keep herself calm, and under the glamour her whole body is roiling with the effort of maintaining her composure. It's rather adorable.

"We've had some news," she says at last. "You see..." There's a letter in her hand, and she fiddles with the edges of it. "We've had a letter. From Beti. Do you remember her? Micheaux delivered it."

Micheaux. Ophaniel shudders inwardly at the name of that walking, perfumed corpse. The day does not appear to be going the direction he'd like it to go. Speaking to Worth was a significant improvement to impending problems. It's been ten years without impending problems. Or at least, any requiring his opinion.

"He's downstairs, isn't he?" Ophaniel sniffs the air.

"Yes, he is. I've told him he may stay the night. But you see...well, no, you wouldn't see. At the beginning there were glimpses, but now..."

The snake woman is making a sour face, and Ophaniel almost asks if she's got a stomach ailment when he realizes she's crying. All that roiling angst, all that pent-up energy, wasn't fury. It was despair.

He is unprepared for this outpouring of emotion. Nothing makes the angel more uncomfortable than such outward displays of feeling.

"Would you like some tea?" is what he asks. But he does not have tea, does not like tea, and has no actual intention of giving Nerissa tea.

When Nerissa speaks, her voice is hoarse. "You see, it's Vivienne. They've found her."

The name makes a searing sound in his head, and Ophaniel has to stop because Worth starts battering against the edges of his brain, yapping like an insistent shih tzu.

Listen, you fool. It's Vivienne. Listen! This is important!

"She's... she's the one you've been looking for?" Ophaniel hates how his voice sounds. Almost tentative. With none of the holy timbre it ought to have.

Nerissa nods her head slowly, taking a shaky step closer to Ophaniel. She is still far enough away not to offend him too much, but if she gets much closer, he may have more objections.

"I'm going to go to Andalusia. With Micheaux and Kit and Alma. I wanted to know…it's silly to ask, of course, but considering what she meant to Worth." She pauses. "It's going to be dangerous. We've all been looking for her for decades now, and nothing has come up. Leave it to the vampires to find her after all this."

Nerissa lets her words dangle in the air and Ophaniel can do nothing but keep his face still lest he offend her. The snake woman has been good to him; kept him from losing his mind in the beginning, fed him, found answers when Ophaniel had none.

You should go. We should go. Vivienne deserves to know.

"What about the other one?" Ophaniel finally asks. He tries to sound casual but fails miserably. "The odd one. With the funny accent. Is she attending the expedition as well?"

"You mean Christabel?"

"Yes. That one."

"It's not a funny accent. It's an American accent."

"The last time I was walking among mortals, there was no America," he points out.

Christabel won't be there. This is too hard for her. Certainly, you can understand that. She's not like Vivienne, who has seen and loved a thousand times. Christabel is…

"It's doubtful. I did write to her," Nerissa says. "Sent her a telegram yesterday when I got the delivery from Micheaux. But she's deep into her work with Dr. Frye, and I doubt she'll find the time to make the trip."

Ophaniel considers this.

After he takes a little longer than is customary, he proclaims, "I will stay here. I will ensure that no demons come to our doors. Should you need me, you need only call my name."

"Ophaniel. I will be in Andalusia. It's a good deal away from here. It's not like I'll be just downstairs."

"You have saved my life, Nerissa, inasmuch as it is worth. The God of All decreed my name," he explains. "It is written on the lips of the most holy on high. There is power in it for those to whom I grant it."

Nerissa does not seem impressed and gives him a flat expression, her eyes half-lidded, her lips pressed together. "Fine. You stay here. I won't beg this time. We meet at St. Katherine's Docks tomorrow night."

"Why are you telling me that?"

Nerissa sighs. "You know. Just in case you are overcome by a compunction to bless us with your celestial effluvium."

The cherub doesn't have anything more to say and isn't surprised when Nerissa turns sharply on her heel and leaves. It's true that he has nothing better to do, but he doesn't like to look desperate to the non-celestials. How could they possibly understand what it feels like to be someone like him?

You're making a poor choice, Ophaniel. In many ways. These people are the only key to you ever getting your wings. The world has changed so much since you fell...and I won't help you if you don't help them.

SWAN SONG

V ivienne never was afraid of darkness. As a night creature, a sylph with centuries of experience mulling about dimly lit forests and haunted ruins, the dark was a symbol of comfort and strength. She used to think that she could see better in the dark, discern the true from the false more clearly. After the tragic turns of her youth, darkness became a refuge, a balm to her soul.

Vivienne understands there is something worse than darkness.

Bastille is a creature of the void. Not of darkness. Vivienne laughed when he told her this the first time, thinking it some strange joke. In her mind, there were two primary poles in the world of supernatural beings: creatures of the day and creatures of the night. Some become good; some become evil. Others are never really left to their own choices. But one's affinity for sunlight has little to do with it.

But the void is a category unto itself, reserved for beings who have gone far beyond "good" and "bad" and straight into delusion. Except in that delusion is power.

Bastille is a *basilisk*, but that is the least of his unfortunate qualities. He possesses many of the charms of his kind: the ability to transform from man to creature, the presence of poisonous fangs, the capacity to turn people and objects to stone. These do not put him above and beyond the monsters of the world.

As Vivienne has learned these twenty years, Bastille is a priest of the void. She has discovered this not by asking after for such knowledge, but rather because he tells her frequently. Once she figured out he had no desire for her body and he just wanted to soliloquize, the captivity was at least a bit less stressful. But no less boring.

"I am one among few remaining who adhere to an old, old faith known to spring from the oldest of sources," he has said on many an occasion. "There was not only light and dark in the beginning. There was the *absence*—a chaotic vacuum of a void where great power awaited. Perhaps I am not the highest priest, but I am the most loyal. So many have fallen by the wayside, but I have remained Cygna's most trustworthy ally. Her Chosen."

Cygna.

Vivienne has never seen Cygna, but Nadine has. Nadine, the ifrit—and truly Vivienne's only friend—similarly fell afoul of Barqan ages ago.

"The Circle of Iapetus was our idea, of course," Bastille has told her repeatedly. "We didn't expect it to actually work. We were feeding them information. We needed the energy collected by that creature in New York to work as a kind of guide-star for our work. And lo and behold, under the rock came skittering you and your ridiculous friends. Barqan got his freedom, and we got so much more than we bargained for."

Except Christabel. They have still not managed to locate the unicorn, and not for lack of trying.

So, now it has been twenty years, and still Vivienne has not seen Cygna, but has heard her name thousands of times in Bastille's long monologues on his importance. Which of course means that he's rather unimportant in the grand scheme, and that makes Vivienne even a bit more bitter; she is held captive by a moron.

She has tried to learn more about this Cygna, but other than speaking her name as one does a goddess, Bastille gives nothing away. Sometimes Vivienne doesn't believe she exists at all. For who could? She does not seem to be monstrous in any measure, or at least Nadine says time and again that there is nothing particularly notable about the woman that she can remember. No extra legs. No powers. Not so much as a pair of mismatched eyes. But then Nadine has a difficult time telling the difference between most humanoids. She claims that those without fire in their veins look dull to her.

And now they are in Andalusia. Vivienne knows she has been here before, but in one of her other lives. It's how she makes sense of her long existence. She was not always as she is now; she's had to reinvent herself.

But she has been Vivienne du Lac the longest, and as she stands, she is the closest to herself as she can be.

Or she was once. Now, Vivienne lives without her magic. The metal about her wrists dampens her powers to the point that summoning even a single snowflake would be near impossible.

So, Vivienne seems to spend most of her time tidying things, and while at first that was a rather mortifying experience she has since found a kind of solace in the hard work. Since she cannot use any of her abilities, she has had to rely on the cleverness of her hands. She cleans, she mends, and from time to time, she creates. Though it is much more difficult sewing by hand, she has found pride in the clothing she has designed for Bastille and the other inhabitants of his ever-moving house.

And now the villa looks somewhat presentable. Far be it from her to welcome Cygna, but if she is coming, Vivienne at least does not want to be responsible for a slovenly abode.

"What do you suppose she wants with the master?" Nadine asks, combing her long fingers through her hair. Her skin is still kindled, but she cannot strike out in defense. Bastille is always frustrated that he hasn't yet deduced a method to dim her entirely, and he has gone through at least six collars trying to do so.

"I wouldn't know," Vivienne says through the needle between her teeth. She is giving Nadine her last fitting in the presentation dress she'll have for Cygna's arrival. Unlike Vivienne, Nadine is considered essential staff.

Outfitting the ifrit is no simple task. The first two dresses ended up singed beyond recognition, and Vivienne had to start from scratch. Nadine emits constant heat, a blue flame. It does marvelous things for her hair and eyes, providing a kind of blazing ripple about her skin and features. In fact, Vivienne finds that any clothing is superfluous on the ifrit, but that is not her decision.

So Nadine must wear an elegant dress made of intricately sewn metallic hoops, put together with silver floss, hardened leather, and wax-coated muslin. She does not burn hot enough to concern Vivienne with this combination of materials, but earlier in the process, she lost a great deal of work to spontaneous combustion.

"You look lovely," Vivienne says, walking the ifrit in front of the mirror. It takes a moment for Nadine's body to appear in the reflection, some strange delay she always has, but the result is rather breathtaking. The long, narrow dress falls to the ifrit's bare feet, deeply cut in the front and back. This ingenious material, so Vivienne is proud enough to admit, looks almost like silk from a distance, adding a sumptuous, liquid presentation.

Nadine smiles, each tooth flecked with dancing flame. "You are far too kind, considering everything."

"It is my duty," Vivienne says, holding up her hands in silent resign. "But, for what it's worth, I did find the process rather enjoyable, if not frustrating at times."

Nadine closes her eyes a moment, in a motion that Vivienne has learned to interpret as a blush. When did this flirtation begin? Vivienne can't remember. She tells herself it is merely a coping mechanism in this difficult place, and that perhaps she's just getting desperate. But Vivienne finds every flicker and tongue of fire on Nadine perfect.

If only she could see her in her full glory.

Vivienne has had many lovers over her long life, but very few women. Given Nerissa's constant mooning over her, she had honestly considered it just not part of her own personal spectrum. Until Nadine, and her fire skin, and her voice like hushed velvet, and her nearly unquenchable fire.

Nadine has a story; Vivienne is sure of it. Bastille made mention more than a few times that though Barqan is a king of the djinn, Nadine once held significantly more power. That is why she has two collars and two pairs of bangles at her wrists and legs. That is why she is not entirely dampened.

But Vivienne has not asked more. At first because of their strained relationship, but now the sylph is afraid to risk whatever they have by making Nadine uncomfortable.

For Vivienne's part, she wears what is expected and no more. A long pale grey veil pinned back on her slick black hair; her body draped in soft layers of tulle. In the old days, she would have woven it from spider silk. Now, and without time to spend on her own presentation, she must make do with local silk. A simple hammered silver belt adorns her waist. She has never needed much in the way of ornamentation. But without access to her charms, she is somewhat diminished. The layers of silk help mask her emaciated form, her sinewy arms. She is fed but not nourished here.

"Vivienne," Nadine says.

Vivienne looks up from her sewing kit, double-checking that she has accounted for all the pieces. Once she lost a pair of scissors, and she was made to pay the price by being cut down the inside of her leg with Bastille's claws. The infection and fever didn't kill her, but they did serve as a reminder not to lose track of the gifts he'd given her—if they could be called so.

"Yes, Nadine?"

"Thank you," says the ifrit in her soft, hushed voice. "I know this is not where either of us imagined we'd be. And with Cygna coming I...I don't know what will happen."

"Oh, it's nothing. In this dreadful place, I take what joy I can. And making you look the royalty you are is no challenge."

"It's only that I wanted to say..."

"Alas, my molars are aching, and that means I'm late for the master," Vivienne says, skirting by the ifrit toward the door.

Nadine takes just a moment to brush her fingers across Vivienne's face as she exits, the touch like a hot wind. Vivienne shudders against it, the full power of her desire still muted. She grits her teeth.

"I will see you this evening," Vivienne says, and makes her way out, averting her eyes. She can feel Nadine's own gaze upon her as she leaves, questioning and full of fire.

Cygna is set to arrive at seven, and so Vivienne makes the slow progression toward Bastille's wing of the house a little past six. He is quite precise about presentation and timing, the definitions of which seem to change with whatever suits him.

Bastille is sitting outside on the terrace, the shadows of vines falling across his angular face, waiting for her. As usual, Vivienne marvels at his beauty, his ageless features masterfully drawn. But then he turns his face to observe her, and the coldness in his eyes feels like iron on her skin.

Standing slowly, Bastille folds his arms across his chest, tilting his head just so to appraise his possession. Vivienne has to remind herself that he has never done anything untoward with her outside of corporal punishment, though he's had many the opportunity. She cannot recall a single time that he even put a hand on her, or even threatened ravishment. And yet the way he looks at her always feels a violation.

"Are you eating enough, sylph?"

The words are sharp, disapproving.

"Yes, Lord Bastille. I am eating what is given," Vivienne says.

"Can you not put some rouge on your cheeks?" Bastille draws a little closer to Vivienne, examining her face. "You look mottled. Like a corpse. Are you a corpse? I confess I don't know what a 'sylph' really is. Just a general term, isn't it?"

Vivienne replies, "I am a sylph. Perhaps there was another word long ago for what I am, but I have forgotten it." Which is not exactly true, but not exactly false either. "And with the rouge—I have tried. But something about my skin absorbs any attempt. I think it's likely, well, you know. I am a cold-natured thing."

"A shame," Bastille says. "Cygna certainly expects more than...well, whatever it is you are. But then, she may be too concerned with important matters to notice. Still, keep your face veiled, will you? I will not have my servants looking like half-dead mortals."

"Yes, Lord," Vivienne says. She feels the sting of his words while simultaneously scolding herself for such an emotion. For most of her long, long life, Vivienne has gone through her daily adventures with a keen understanding that she is the loveliest person in any given room. But since her imprisonment, she has diminished greatly.

What Nerissa would think of her now.

Nerissa.

There is not a day that goes by that Vivienne regrets how she dealt with her oldest and best friend. That Nerissa fell in love with her was unfortunate. But Vivienne knows she should have seen it coming, knows she should have expected it. Still, if she had paid more attention to Nerissa and not to her own reflection, she might have figured out the whole business with Barqan earlier. This entire mess is her doing, brought to pass by her pride.

At least the lamia has stopped looking for her. Vivienne risked everything to reach out to Nerissa through the masks she'd been making for Bastille during their time in Cairo, gathering elements needed for his grand plan. Ever since, she's been relegated to more prosaic tasks—none of them leaving the walls of the facility. But it was worth it. Even with the flaying. Her body healed, as it always did. Just not as fast as it used to.

Vivienne manages to keep going because she knows her friends— Worth and Nerissa and even that annoying young unicorn Christabel— are safe.

A half-hour later and the entire house staff is standing at attention in the center courtyard. They are a ragtag bunch, mostly cuffed and dampened, a mismatched mélange of dwarves, nymphs, satyrs, a *kappa*, and two vampires. There is a table set with lavish food; one of the nymphs plays a soft panpipe in the background. Nadine looks resplendent, her gown quite literally outshining the rest.

Vivienne is just starting to get uncomfortable with the waiting when she hears Bastille's clear voice.

"Ah, here she is."

Bastille is looking toward the center of the room, but Vivienne can't see anything of note. There are a few hushed murmurs from the staff.

"Welcome, Cygna. We, your devoted servants, are honored by your presence."

It may be the veil, or more likely her shackles, but for a moment it does appear as if Bastille is speaking into a void of nothingness.

But that is it, isn't it?

Out of nothing, and Vivienne cannot understand exactly how she knows it's *nothing* since it is not dark and it is not visible, a woman unfolds. She is not winged, not even caped, but coming through this slice of nothing in the world of *not nothing*, Cygna unfurls. The pieces of her body rearrange themselves: a head, broad shoulders, a compact frame. Her hair is short and curled, the color of a grey sky, the hue matching her eyes.

The rest of Cygna is, how can Vivienne comprehend such a strange thing, unapologetically un-magical. She wears mortal clothes, cut in the current Western fashion. She carries a briefcase. She wears Oxfords with a Spanish heel. Her hat has a white feather in it, and even Vivienne can tell her tailor is Parisian.

"Bastille," Cygna says. "At last. It's been too long."

Nadine pulls on Vivienne's sleeve and widens her eyes, hissing, "Kneel."

Every nerve in Vivienne's body recoils at the thought. Kneel to this woman? Kneel to anyone? Twenty years ago, Vivienne would have given the woman a long telling to. But now Vivienne is acutely aware of something she never had to worry about in her previous life: pain. The pain has changed her, rearranged her bones, taken hope and power from her very center.

And so she bows, watching out of the corner of her eye as Bastille does the same.

"Well, it's good to see people know their places around here," Cygna says, her voice smooth as honey and tinged with just a little roughness. It's a lovely voice. But it brings a chill.

When no one makes an answer, Cygna says, "Now, which one do we flay first?"

THE BLEAKNESSES

The mere idea of sailing on the open sea is enough to slow Nerissa considerably on her path toward St. Katherine's docks. That, and she is worried she hasn't packed enough implet. She's checked three times already, but now she's second-guessing her math.

Regardless of her food supplies, Alma will be waiting for her at the docks, and that is somewhat comforting. And Beti, the vampire and Micheaux's matron has promised to speak with them as well. But that does nothing to alleviate the dread of an inevitable sea voyage. The last ten years have given Nerissa a reprieve from travel, and nothing is worse than a ship out in the open. Except perhaps an airplane. But she refuses even to consider that option.

It is difficult to fall too far behind, however, because Kit is brimming with excitement so fully and inappropriately that she's beginning to garner attention from passers-by. So, Nerissa quickens her pace while cursing her companion under her breath. The last thing she wants is Kit running amok in London again. There are too many distractions and shiny objects, to say nothing of the unsavory underbits which so preternaturally draw Kit. The last time she went on a London journey, it took Nerissa six washes to get the stink out of Kit's tail.

Nerissa once hoped that a time of quiet and ritual might do well to temper the *kitsune*, but on the contrary, Kit is more ebullient than ever. Pent up, even. While Kit may have more hobbies—including knitting, archery, and occult arts—she is nonetheless a magnet for adventure. Though the old snake would be lying to herself if she said she didn't enjoy having Kit around, at least a little. Especially the flush of her cheeks when she is in a genuinely mischievous mood. And the light on her eyes when the moon is full. And the curve of her tails when she...

The docks bustle with the evening crowd, a constant din of human calls and cries flitting around them as incessantly as the gulls. It smells of fish guts and sweaty man bodies, and Nerissa has to take a discreet sip of her implet to give her resolve. It is not often she gets the desire to rip relentlessly into human bodies, sating herself on their moist, salty blood; but something about the combination of commerce and testosterone tends to put her in the mood.

Nerissa is nervous, doing her best to avoid the complicated emotions regarding Vivienne—the sylph who spurned her twenty years ago and then abruptly got herself kidnapped—and she doesn't quite notice the little figure beckoning her until she's almost trampled it underfoot.

It's a child. But it is also a corpse. A vampire child. It has limpid green eyes in a smudged face, eerily long fingernails, and a pair of crooked spectacles that look as if they do nothing more than make a strange fashion statement.

"This way," says the vampire child. "Mistress is waiting for you."

Miraculously, Kit has doubled back and slides up to Nerissa with practiced ease. The *kitsune* links her arm through Nerissa's with such familiarity that Nerissa is no longer nervous about Vivienne-related emotions and briefly can concentrate only on the pressure between them.

"What a strange little creature," Kit says as they take a winding route through the dwindling crowd. "It's rather lopsided for a vampire, don't you think?"

Kit is not good at whispering, and the little vampire turns around with a sly grin but says nothing more.

"Oh, Kit. Not every vampire is symmetrical. It's rude to point out their inequities. They already are so low on the rung of monsters," Nerissa says.

"The office is this way," the vampire says, pointing to a gap between two buildings. "Mistress is waiting for you."

"Oh good," Nerissa says, taking in the view. Kit has still not removed her arm from Nerissa's, and the lamia is having a tough time keeping her emotional armor up. Not that Kit has never shown affection or recognition, only that this time it feels different. Protective. Fond. "Curious that all our contacts never seem to have proper addresses."

The little vampire gurgles something incomprehensible, then beckons them forward. They limp as if they've been struck, and now that Nerissa thinks about it, perhaps Kit is right.

"Is this vampire familiar to you?" Nerissa asks.

"No, why?" Kit tilts her head toward Nerissa, her nose wrinkling just a second. "It smells like all vampires smell. Dead. This one is just a crooked dead."

As she's been in many similar situations before, parading head-first into nefarious and highly suspicious locations, Nerissa is not surprised by the narrow door that opens with a click from the little vampire. Nor is she taken aback when they have to wind their way down a long, twisting corridors. She also doesn't stop to question the musty smell, the guttering light from the torches, or the general medieval look and feel of the place.

But the ghost.

The ghost is surprising.

Though human lore is full of ghost sightings, Nerissa has found that they are either far rarer than believed or simply adverse to interaction with supernatural creatures like herself. In the hundreds of years since her birth, she has never encountered a ghost, and so she startles at the sight before her.

The ghost presents as a woman of middling years, not transparent exactly, but limned in purplish-grey light. The apparition is very keenly dressed, and Nerissa gets the sense her finery isn't an illusion. She is actually wearing clothes, but they have somehow avoided deterioration for the better part of a…what, half millennia? If Vivienne were here, she would know precisely the century to which this woman belongs, what with her wimple and her long, thick gown. She'd probably recognize the handiwork down to the specific artisan. But fashion blurs together in Nerissa's long memory so she cannot decipher Tudor from Regency.

The ghost smiles.

"Is she here?" the little vampire asks. It sounds afraid.

Kit's eyes fill with the light of refracted stars as she stares, her mouth parted slightly. "I see a miracle," the *kitsune* says softly. "Or, more properly, a vision I can only ascribe to miracles. It is a walking ancestor, unfettered by the chains of the world. Oh, glorious. She's glorious!"

"You see it, too, then?" Nerissa holds Kit's arm tighter.

"I can't see," the little vampire sighs, slicking back its long, pale hair. "But I know how to get through. Mistress told me."

The specter smiles placidly at Nerissa and then at Kit. Then she speaks in a voice that seems to come from all corners of the room. No, from the very stones themselves. "You may address me as Her Royal Highness, Queen Phillippa of England," says the ghost without a trace of irony. "Welcome to St. Katharine's Hospital."

Nerissa knows enough of general London history to remember that St. Katharine's Hospital is long gone, along with the abbey that was once here. She visited the place, long ago, and enjoyed a most satisfying meal of plump monks out gathering herbs by the Thames. They tasted of malt. And watercress. A lovely combination. That was another life, though, and she ought to be repentant about it. And she is. Mostly.

"Your Royal Highness," Kit says immediately, though she does not bow. She, as ever, remains unmoved by the doings of men. "You are a lovely being, and we are so fortunate to see you."

Queen Phillippa does not smile at this, but she nods slightly, looking at Nerissa narrowly. "Have I seen you before?"

"I doubt it," Nerissa says, though that is a possibility. "We are simply seeking passage through your...ah, hospital?" She immediately regrets the rise in her voice at the end. Ghosts, she has heard, are easily confused.

"You have very sharp teeth," Phillippa says, frowning down into her high collar, looking even more deeply at Nerissa. "But you won't be able to bite your way through. I guard this passage, and I decide who gets to go through."

Nerissa examines the walls. Yes, she can sense a bit of Geist magic interlaced among the stones. Even though the hospital is gone, it's clear Philippa has managed to weave her own power into the passageway. And indeed, when Nerissa tries to take a step forward, she's met by a solid resistance though there's nothing but air.

"You see?" The Queen gives them a sweet grin. "I am ancient, and you must placate me." Then she giggles. "I do like sounding so fearsome."

The little vampire pulls on Nerissa's jacket. "Give it this. Mistress says it likes books."

Nerissa feels a little book in her hand and pulls it dimly to her face. She does not have her spectacles on, but she can tell it's a precious creation. An illuminated manuscript, a book of hours, if she's right on her history. Christabel would know more details. Where would a vampire get it? And, moreover, how could a vampire even hold it?

She frowns a little. Perhaps this vampire is too young to concern themselves with religious artifacts...but still.

Glancing at Kit, Nerissa makes a desperate expression. This is the way to Vivienne; what other choice have they? If Beti is within, either she managed another entrance or had another book.

Nerissa feels tired, worried. But the *implet* is leaving her systems and, along with it, her senses; regardless of Kit's progressively concerned appearance, Nerissa agrees.

"I have a book," Nerissa says. "For our passage beyond."

"Yes, I will trade you," says Phillippa, her voice bright and musical. She holds up her hands and the book she was holding moments ago now rises with her motions, drifting across the space between them.

Nerissa tries the same, but her book fails to catch the magical tide, and so Kit picks up the book and hands it gently to Queen Phillippa as Nerissa opens the book for trade.

It is a small thing, this tome, and heavy for its size. Christabel will know what to do with it. It's a bestiary of some sort. As soon as Nerissa runs her fingers over the cover, though, Phillippa disappears into the walls surrounding them. The whole stonework around them shimmers that same purplish hue that so recently emanated from the Queen.

Nerissa is not surprised when the little vampire tries to grab the book from her, and even less surprised when Kit pins the creature up against the wall.

"I don't like being used," Nerissa says, quickly storing the book in her pocket, and feeling for her *implet* at the same time. The cold glass under her fingertips is calming and reassuring—a counterpoint to the fury rising in her.

Never trust vampires.

"I'm sorry. Mistress said—" the little vampire gurgles under Kit's clutches. The *kitsune*'s nails are out, her slick black hair rising around her as her power manifests.

"Apologies are dust," Kit says, pressing her face closer to the vampire. "Explain yourself, little wriggling creature of death and decay."

Nerissa stifles a smile. Kit always has the most endearing name for monsters even when she's interrogating them.

"We can't...we can't see ghosts..." gasps the vampire.

"Yes? And?" Nerissa walks a little closer, examining the passageway before and behind them. She can smell salt air. So at least the vampire was leading her in the right direction.

"She wanted the book," the vampire says. "Mistress wanted the book."

"Well, she'll have to ask nicely," says Nerissa. "Now, tiny vampire. Show us the way to Beti. Hopefully, Micheaux will meet us there, and we can chalk it all up to a misunderstanding. I have quite a lot to say about Beti's surprisingly bad taste in messengers."

"Nerissa..." Kit is about to say something long-winded and detailed, but Nerissa is having none of it at the moment.

"We don't have time to waste, Kit," replies the lamia. "We'll handle whatever comes our way. We always do."

~

Beti is there waiting for them in an immense cavern, cut out of the side of what must have been the hospital's foundation. There is a sandy beach, a little pier, and then, around the corner, a boat.

These are all good details, but Nerissa can see that Beti is not well. It has been nearly a decade since the last time Nerissa saw Beti, the rather humble-looking coven queen of Cairo, but the vampire looks wan and withered. And that's saying something for a vampire who, in Nerissa's experience, rarely look better than a barely cold corpse. She has a greedy, desperate look in her eyes when Nerissa and Kit emerge into the cave, but her features do not betray her emotions.

"Beti," Nerissa says, not letting go of the small vampire. "We found your emissary. We expected a peaceful transition, but I'm a bit confused with your lack of care. Bartering with a ghost? Stealing?"

Beti does not smile but shakes her head sadly. "So, you see the state of our affairs," she says. "Murmur. I told you to be careful."

The vampire shudders under Nerissa's hand. "I was tired. I was hungry. They would not give me the book."

"Did you bring us here under false pretenses, Beti?" Nerissa takes a step forward, tossing Murmur forward. The vampire staggers and almost falls, but rights itself before tumbling. "We've had a long peace between us. We've welcomed Micheaux into our home countless times. We've relied on you."

What she's really thinking is that if she severs her relationship with the vampires, how is she going to get her *implet*? That anger tinges her voice more than any general concern.

The cavern is eerily quiet save their voices. Nerissa notices how her speech reverberates across the water, sending echoes, like answering whispers, around the small enclosure. The Thames is just beyond. Their ticket to Vivienne...

"I am a desperate creature," Beti says, holding out her hands as if it explains everything. Her voice, though. It isn't right?

"Where is Micheaux?" Kit asks.

Beti shakes her head as if dispelling a bad dream. "I have sent him away. I do not think he is impartial enough any longer to remain in my employ. But nor are you impartial. I believe that celestial has corrupted your mind. You are not seeing clearly. I was merely asking a favor of you, not trying to steal. It was simply good timing, especially considering the information I so freely gave on the subject of Vivienne du Lac."

Nerissa knows this is not the way Beti speaks. It may be her body, but there is another force behind her eyes.

Best not to let her know yet, though. Not with her entire food supply at risk.

"As I asked a favor of you ten years ago," Nerissa says, taking a step closer toward Beti, watching to see the vampire's reaction. She does not flinch. "Did you think I had forgotten? That I would not give you something you sought if you had asked? But duplicitousness does not become you. I have always been open with you and gave my home to Micheaux when he needed it."

Murmur is acting curiously now as Beti speaks. Twitching. Eyes moving strangely.

"It is not a matter...not a matter of..." Beti, who Nerissa no longer truly believes is Beti at all, shivers. "Not a matter of...ugh, demons, he's here."

There is a curious light about the place. For such a dank cavern, Nerissa finds that she can suddenly see much better. And she smells a familiar scent, like hot rocks after a rain.

Ophaniel. Nerissa turns to look at him, and realizes her mistake too late.

Beti, or the creature she has become, is on Nerissa quicker than she can quite comprehend. The lamia reaches up to meet a blow from Beti, rending the vampire's hand with her claws as it comes down.

The flesh parts like paper.

Slowly, the being within, a creature of darkness and ash, emerges from the shell of Beti's body. It is not dark so much as it is *empty*, a void within the darkness of the cavern, like a hole punched through the heart of the universe. But very, very much alive.

"Drink the void," says the voice. "Before it drinks you."

MISSED EXITS

Kit knows the *ten no tsukai* is on the way before Nerissa does, but that's not unusual. It's one of the reasons Kit stays along with the snake woman. She likes her. She values her. She protects her. Kit does not want bad things to happen to her, even if Nerissa is far too reliant on that glittering imp ichor she drinks and has the habit of sulking all the time.

It feels like love sometimes. But then Kit thinks, no. It feels like the need to protect. Not that Nerissa is incapable of taking care of herself. She is a creature built from violence, even though she has learned to temper it.

It's only...

Kit wouldn't be able to forgive herself if anything terrible happens to Nerissa. The thought is like ice in her veins.

And she doesn't trust the *ten no tsukai* that was once her friend named Worth. Not that Ophaniel is an evil creature; no, Kit has learned in her many long years of life that good and evil are not so easily distinguished on first glance. Or indeed after successive glances. She just feels as if the *ten no tsukai* is hiding secrets and knowledge. Important knowledge that would help bring Nerissa's lost friend Vivienne to them. Or at least that he could perhaps be more helpful than sitting and complaining about everything all day long.

But it's good that Ophaniel appears and Kit cannot help but be a little glad. He is a glimmering form of feathers and skin the color and texture of marble—really not so glamorous as one might think—and as soon as he shouts, the void creatures that were once the vampires begin to vibrate.

Kit has never liked vampires, but she should have been more aware when the little one started acting funny. It was hard to smell it, what with all the saltwater and fish and the refuse from the day's trading. And the fact they were wrapped in corpse skin. Vampires smell like corpses. She just hadn't checked deeper. Nerissa's behavior was bothering her; she was becoming addicted to the *implet*. But every time Kit tried to broach the subject...

In the conversations she's had with him, Kit has learned that Ophaniel can no longer fly, but he can extend his wings. As a celestial, he is able to bend light to his will. It's not that he emanates light exactly, but he can manipulate light in any circumstance. Even in a dim cavern. He pulses one, two, three times, and the void monsters shiver again against the illumination. They don't like it, and that's good.

Kit must step around the discarded vampire skins, wincing as she slips in one of them, as she positions herself against the smaller shape. She doesn't hesitate. This is when the joy comes in, when her absolute appreciation of her being courses through her.

But it is much more difficult when one can't quite see their prey. The emptiness that is—or was—the little vampire called Murmur appears to appear and disappear around her, defying even the physics of monster magic. Kit's only aid is Ophaniel's light-bending. Where the light hits the emptiness, it turns an off-white that reminds her of dusty mold from mushrooms.

The longer they fight, the less human-shaped the once-vampires become. Nonetheless, Ophaniel's light helps, and for now, they outnumber the void monsters, so it's time for fun.

Kit lets loose her shriek, which is both very like a woman screaming and much worse, or so she has been told. The cry reverberates in the close quarters, and as the sound waves return to her she shivers and extends her tails. She now has five. She's very proud of the fifth one, but she isn't quite used to the balance, and she hesitates.

Pain lashes her, right across the back. That second of lost balance and the little shit of a once-vampire hits her so hard she sees stars. It feels like she's propelling forward into nothing for a heart-wrenching second, time and space melding about her, but then she is standing, winded, sweating, clammy. Kit has never felt *clammy* in her entire life.

Shaking her head to get her bearings, Kit tries to flank the creature with Nerissa, who has now gone full snake. Normally, Kit likes to admire Nerissa when she's like that—her glossy scales, the yellow flash of her eyes, the color of her blood-red lips, and those glorious, muscled arms—but there is no time for beautiful distractions, even if she aches for it. Even if she...

Kick. Bite. Rend. It is so hard to make any of these basic attacks when the assailants have no physical form that she can determine. In fact, Kit feels a subtle pull from them as they get closer, some strange gravitational current. What madness? She doesn't want to go closer to them, and yet her body seems to have other plans.

"Kit, you holding up?" Nerissa is breathless. Tired. She tried encircling the once-vampire with her tail, but that didn't work.

"I'm here," Kit says.

The *ten no tsukai* is not helping much, aside from his general light-bending which, while useful, doesn't do much to *stop* the violent creatures. Even when Kit is hitting them, her attacks aren't doing much in the way of damage.

It is not going well.

Kit catches Nerissa's eyes, her brilliant golden eyes, and she sees the same fear that beats in her own heart. It does not seem fair that they would perish here, not with such an unnamable darkness, not so far from everything. Not so close to Vivienne... if that's what Nerissa truly wants...

The bleakness—yes, that is what she will call them—smothers Kit, both pressing down on her and pulling her deeper into its emptiness. It was so small before, and now it seems like an endless expanse, an ever-growing nothing.

She hits the stone floor of the cavern hard, so hard that she gags on her tongue. Her teeth seek blood, contact, anything, but it is like fighting the wind, a vaguely sucking wind.

Kit's strength begins to wane. She has never felt a sensation so strange in her life, and she has been licked by a goat on her...

Who was she, again? She forgets her name.

What was she thinking? She will never need to remember again.

Yes, the bleakness. A soft, cold velveteen dissolution into...

Just when Kit is about to turn herself over to the bleakness, she becomes acutely aware of Nerissa standing between her and her quarry. The lamia is alternating between yelling and hissing, her scales dappled in the dim light, but oh so beautiful.

Kit is positive Nerissa is fighting, but she still can't quite shake the existential dread.

Until a sickly, snapping noise rouses her, that is, and the lamia lets out a scream so deafening the cavern itself trembles. Kit feels it in her teeth.

Kit slowly wipes dirt and a sticky substance from her eyes, burning and blurring her vision. What in the world is happening? Is the earth shaking?

No, it's Alma. The dwarf with the maggot white skin and the clear eyes. The one that can grow back her limbs—albeit slowly—like a skink. She's come up through the ground as she is wont to do, and while the smaller of the bleaknesses is gone, the larger one is no longer attacking Ophaniel because the dwarf is filling its maw with as many rocks as possible. Bricks, pebbles, boulders, they all come to the ground as easily as if they were rising through water.

"Yes, almost there!" Ophaniel is laughing, grinning, clapping his hands. Blood has splattered his face—who is bleeding?—and he looks livelier than Kit has ever seen him. "Keep the onslaught of rocks on, dwarf woman!"

Kit slips before she stands, just in time to hear a crack like nearby thunder and watch the larger bleakness vanish. Or, rather, simply leave. For how can a being already possessed of negative matter cease to be? Relief floods her body, and she shivers as if with new life.

She is almost ready to celebrate when she notices Nerissa. The lamia is on her knees, breathing heavy, cradling her right arm, ragged words tumbling from her with no coherence. She is in her human glamour, mostly. Which is strange.

Taking a few steps forward, her legs still far from compliant, the picture comes into view. It's Nerissa's right side. Or what remains of it from outside the glamour. From the elbow down it is...nothing.

Doing some mental calculation, Kit realizes that if she'd lost one arm of her glamoured self, then that would make two of her true body...

"Shit and limestone." That is from Alma. "I'm going to check the perimeter!"

"Nerissa!"

Kit shouts Nerissa's name a thousand times louder than she should have. Enough that both the *ten no tsukai* and the dwarf look at her sharply.

Before she considers the propriety of it, Kit has Nerissa in her arms, kissing her forehead. The lamia is in pain beyond measure and Kit can feel it through her skin. It is colder than she had thought, but not unlovely.

"Oh, oh, I need to help," Kit hears herself saying, her voice distant. "Does the *ten no tsukai*, I mean, Ophaniel..."

"I am fine; I am..." The *ten no tsukai* does not offer anything else. He, too, stares at Nerissa.

Nerissa is not fine. Nothing is fine. It will never be fine ever again. With a shudder, the lamia lets go of her glamor completely, utterly, casting aside what hints of humanity she has carried with her so long. Kit notices the subtle shifting of color on Nerissa's scales, the varying size and pattern down her neck, the way even swirls and lines cover her lips . Nerissa's hair is black and sleek, silky soft beneath Kit's fingers. She wants to kiss every strand. She wants to apologize for sometimes being annoying and demanding, for sulking and not saying what she should have said and instead filling up every bit of air with useless words.

And for failing to protect her.

She should have protected Nerissa. She should have fought off the bleaknesses. Kit's tears fall on Nerissa's face, the water filling the gaps between her scales and then vanishing.

But it is not magic.

The bleaknesses took two of Nerissa's arms. Snapped them off like the claws of a crab.

"She's dying..." Kit whispers. "Her body is shaking. She's lost a great deal of blood, and though her blood is not the only part of her keeping her alive, as she has a most complex limbic system that works as a kind of secondary circulatory track..."

Then there is a face before her, grabbing her by the chin, stopping her blubbering.

Ophaniel materializes before her through a haze of tears and Kit startles. Yet, when she looks up into his face, she doesn't see the alien lines, those cold marks she has noted on so many occasions. No, it is a familiar face. Mostly. Also, still the *ten no tsukai*.

Worth Goodwin.

"Worth?" Nerissa whispers.

"I'm going to check the exits," Alma says, sinking back down into the ground like a burrowing worm. Normally, the dwarf's strange method of moving through soil and rock bothers Kit, but at the moment she is too engulfed with the overwhelming dread that she might lose Nerissa.

"Hush, friend," Worth says, though he is somehow speaking through the *ten no tsukai*. Ophaniel/Worth—Kit is as confused as anyone—is most assuredly winged and naked, among other improprieties, but the voice is familiar. "Take a deep breath."

Worth leans down and puts a long-fingered hand on Nerissa's chest, just below her collar bone. A low blue light emanates from his fingertips, then soaks into the lamia's body like Kit's tears.

Nerissa shudders.

"I appear to be...missing my arm... arms...?" Nerissa makes a barking noise that might be a laugh, but Kit thinks she's just trying not to cry. "I'm sorry. I knew...something was... wrong..."

Talking is clearly laborious, and Kit tries to tell Nerissa to be quiet, but she's also afraid that if she makes herself more obvious, the lamia will notice Kit holding her and stroking her long, silky hair. And she does not want to stop doing that.

"We've got you, Nerissa Waldemar," Worth says. "Now take a deep breath. I'm going to apply some pressure, and it'll feel a lot better. Kit, get me that vile stuff she's been drinking. I'd normally not advise using it— she already uses it too often—but in this case, we need her alert."

"I can hear you," Nerissa hisses. "I'm not...dead yet..."

Kit doesn't know why she's crying more; because Nerissa is in pain or because she's hearing Worth's voice again. Either way, she steels herself. She must. This isn't going to be pretty.

"An astute observation, as expected," Worth says.

"We're going to miss the boat," Nerissa mutters, craning her head to look in the direction they were going. She gasps in pain as Worth, or a close approximation of him, peels off some of the material at the elbow. He whispers his apologies.

"You're not being metaphorical, are you?" Worth gives a shy glance at Kit. "She's not. There is an actual boat. I...almost remember."

Kit wants to ask him a thousand questions—how is he here again? Where has he been? Where is Ophaniel?—but she's incapable of speaking at the moment. She and Nerissa have faced down their fair share of strange creatures, but never has Nerissa been beaten so swiftly and so completely.

But sitting silent is not going to help matters.

"There was a boat," Kit says slowly, shaking off the numbness of seeing

Nerissa in so much pain, but also realizing what this will mean. "It came here from Andalusia. We think Vivienne was on it, or at least someone might have been on it who could show us the way. But now it's unlikely we'll make the boat at all, let alone find this Vivienne."

Both Nerissa and Worth look at Kit sharply.

"I mean your Vivienne?" Kit tries again.

Alma has returned now, in that strange silent way of hers. One moment she was gone, the next she's risen through the rock. It comes in handy and yet Kit has never quite gotten used to it, even if she is the one who gets chastised for sneaking into places.

"Oh, Alma, we were wondering where you were," Kit says, even though that's not true.

"Why is nothing ever straightforward with you people?" Alma kneels and studies Nerissa with her marble-like eyes. She whistles lowly, but it is full of sand. "That doesn't look good. You're going to need someone who knows how to put snakes back together."

"I'm fine," Nerissa says, trying to raise her head. She hasn't yet taken issue with Kit's stroking and supporting.

"Not fine," says Worth. "You'll die if we're not careful."

"I have made some outstanding efforts in that respect," Nerissa says, rasping even more than usual, "and I believe I may be incapable of death..." There is something in her tone Kit doesn't like, a note of sadness. She is babbling, yes, but Kit doubts that Nerissa is lying.

"I'll go to the boat. Quickly. I can go very quickly," Kit says, gently extricating herself from Nerissa and almost falling back a step again once she regains her feet. Why is this happening? Since when is she anything other than fleet-footed? Her whole body feels as if it is cast in lead. "Someone should send word to Micheaux about Beti and whoever that was. And... Oph—Worth?"

"For now," says Worth.

"Can you stay with Nerissa?" Kit doesn't like where this is going. "It's only that I'm not sure what will happen..."

"If Ophaniel comes back?" Worth finishes her sentence. "I'm not sure, either. But while we don't see eye to eye on everything, we agreed to come here. And I can think of no better guardian for a wounded lamia than a creature of the heavens and a stout dwarf of Nith. We can't move her yet, anyway, I don't think."

"We'll send word to Dr. Plover," says Alma. "I know how to get a message to him. And he's the best in the business."

"Good," says Kit, nodding her head because it sounds like a good idea. But she doesn't know who Dr. Plover is.

Leaning down, Kit whispers in Nerissa's ear. "I'll be back before you know it."

She isn't sure if she imagines it, but Kit believes she sees a glimmer in Nerissa's eye reminiscent of affection before pulling away. Or it could just be the incandescent pain generally experienced during separation of one's body and their appendages.

ALWAYS A HITCH

The coast of Andalusia is rocky and brown when Christabel arrives, nothing near the vast, verdant hills she imagined. She supposes that's a silly notion, that Spain would be green, and yet she cannot help but be a bit disappointed in the barren rockiness.

The airport is small, the airplane even smaller, and she has a touch of green about the gills as she walks across the tarmac, squinting through her sunglasses in an attempt to find her contact, a long-time correspondent of Dr. Frye. Dr. Frye has remained behind in Scotland, which is just as well, but Christabel finds herself missing the batty witch. During their work together she complained many a time in her journals at night, but now that she's on her own her thoughts are too loud, and she could do with some of the doctor's constant babbling.

She does not expect to see Nerissa and Kit right away, of course; that would be absurd. They will be coming by boat, as they always do, and wouldn't be at an airport. Christabel does, however, silently curse herself when she looks for Worth's face in the crowd.

Ten years. Not long compared to the other immortals around her, but long enough for her to feel it. And nowhere not long enough to forget him; or, worse even, to give up hope altogether.

Her contact in the region is planning to pick her up by motorcar, so she was informed. She's had a long correspondence with this local supernatural individual—a term she prefers over "creature" or "monster" regardless of what Nerissa thinks—named Kalum Angelos. Judging by his archaic writing style and penmanship, she had him figured as an elderly, judgmental, scholarly fellow.

But the man leaning against the bright blue Wolseley Hornet does not suggest any of those descriptions. He is tall, lean, and effortless, with no hint of glamour about him. She has heard this is the case with many of the Greek-descended supernaturals, but she did not think he would be so...beautiful. His hair is the color of black walnut, his cheeks molded at precise angles to accentuate his full lips and curving smile. He wears dark glasses, wire-rimmed, and now she is looking at his hair again. It brings to mind a summer night, shod with just the most delicate wisps of silver.

"You've overdressed for the season," the man says. He looks at Christabel, not hungrily or lustily, but with a precision to which she is unaccustomed. He sees her. Deeply.

"Yes, well, I came straight from Scotland," she says. She does not falter, though her heart beats strong, and his voice makes her want to close her eyes and listen. "There are fewer climates more contrary than the Hebrides and the Andalusian coastline. I did not have time to make a stop for better clothing. And I presume you are Mr. Angelos?"

"Call me Kalum," he says, tipping his head forward as if he were wearing a hat. Which is he not, as coarse as it may seem. But Christabel is glad of it, because it would obscure that glorious hair. His English is accented with vowels of Kent. She does recall him mentioning he studied at Canterbury.

"Kalum, then. I am Christabel Crane, as you have likely deduced. It is good to finally make your acquaintance," she says, holding out her hand.

Kalum takes her hand and turns it one way then another before shaking it gently. "You're so very American. And smaller than I thought you'd be."

"They always say such things about my sort. I suppose it's due to the general scarcity," she says. "Myths have a way of growing over the years."

"Your presence is immense in prose," he says.

"Well, I thought you'd be older."

"I am older," he says. "I just don't look it, I suppose."

"No, no, you don't."

"Thank you, I think." He lowers his voice, taking off his glasses for just a moment. His eyes are deep hazel green, amber in the middle, fringed with dark, glorious eyelashes. "You have the most complete glamour of any supernatural individual I've ever met. It's…" he replaces his glasses, "it's almost foolproof."

"Almost?" She hands him her luggage.

"It's in the eyes. The only place where the real you shines through. Like moonlight bursting through the clouds. Do you suppose you have two complete states?"

They both stand a moment, staring at each other. The wind whips Christabel's hair across her face, but she cannot find the strength to move it out of the way.

"If I do, it's one of the only recorded cases of it known to our history," she says, somewhat shyly. Studying herself is both a necessary and almost embarrassing line of work. "But as I have no one to compare myself to, it makes it rather difficult. Most supernatural individuals rely on glamours, glands, or telepathic ability to convince the onlooker that what they see is indeed human. And others, like yourself, appear human almost entirely."

"Ah, you don't know me yet to make that judgment," Kalum says with a laugh like honey, deep and rich.

Christabel presses at the bridge of her nose. The jet lag must be getting to her already. Such long travel does make her feel giddy, and Kalum is not helping matters at all.

Noting her state, Kalum gestures to the car. "Well, we best get going. Mother is waiting for us at the cottage, and she doesn't like to be left alone for long."

Mother? Ah, well. There's always something.

~

They drive southward down the coast toward a little town named Marbella. The quaint stucco houses and narrow roads break up the landscape, but Christabel can't help but almost enjoy herself. The sun is warm on her skin, the breeze a gentle counterpoint as she sits beside Kalum.

Yes, Kalum is very handsome. She steals furtive glances now and again, to make sure he really is at attractive as she recalls. The moment she looks away, she half forgets his face and must reassure herself that her memory was correct. So, she takes yet another look. Covert. Until he catches her and gives her a grin.

"I was surprised you came down where you did on the whole 'gods versus monsters' debacle," Kalum says casually. "Your correspondence on the matter was a bit spotty at the time, and I knew you were busy. But if it weren't for you, there might have been all-out war."

Ah, yes. *That*. While Nerissa and Kit kept Ophaniel, the angel that was once her boyfriend, in their London flat, Christabel worked closely with Dr. Frye not only on cataloguing the dwindling beast population but working as an emissary between gods—truly just monsters with natural human forms—and monsters for the better part of the last decade. It ended in court, a body she helped create with the help of the mostly reformed Circle of Iapetus, a human league dedicated to keeping the peace between monsters and humans.

"You know, I didn't think it would turn out so well, the Prague Accords," Christabel says. "You helped me quite a great deal with your research and notes. I never asked because I know it is impolite to do so, but I could tell you had considerable experience in similar circumstances."

"Gods and monsters have been fighting since the beginning of time," Kalum says, his voice softening, his gaze straying to the horizon. "Gods and their offspring are just lucky to pass in mixed company without raising eyebrows. Though it isn't that easy for us. I've been here in Marbella for the better part of the last two thousand years and I still feel like a stranger."

"Your name sounds local enough," she says.

Kalum laughs, shaking his head. "It's bastardized Latin, by way of Greece. Like Mother. Like Grandfather. Diluted, certainly, from the source. We're all a bit diminished these days. But certain... ah...circumstances still keep us here. Aside from my studies, I've not left Spain at all. So, I'm glad that the work I did was helpful. Precedence is necessary in these matters."

"It was very kind of you."

"Hardly. Your letters have always brought a challenge to my mind and a song to my heart. There are so few who are truly interested in the history of gods and monsters, to say nothing of the lesser beings."

"I always have been. Even when I was, as you say, 'passing' among the Circle of Iapetus. Though, twenty years ago they were hardly the league they are now."

"You're absolutely angelic to put up with them," Kalum says with another golden laugh. "I can't stand them."

"They grow on you after a while," she says with a chuckle. "Though finding you through Dr. Frye was a remarkable stroke of fate and certainly helped me bring the Circle, and myself, I suppose, to a position of more prominence. While Dr. Frye is primarily interested in the environmental ramifications of supernatural power, she grows tired of my questions. I know I'm young, but I like to think that it serves me well, my curious nature. So you were an essential conduit for my incessant lines of query."

"As I said, it was my pleasure. You've had the unique experience of living as a human for the first few years of your life," he says. "Most of us never have such a thing. My grandfather raised me for a time, and that was anything but typical. I had to work backward to connect to my humanity, and I'm still having to do that. So I valued your opinion and viewpoint. And look at you, the great peacemaker. Overall, relations between the god and monster factions have been good."

"I suppose I just feel as if I'm neither beast nor god," Christabel says softly. She wants to pour out her soul to Kalum, but she resists. Painfully. "I'm sorry, that doesn't make any sense; I'm exhausted."

"I think it makes sense if it's how you feel. I, however, would firmly categorize you as a goddess, given your glamour capabilities. You are entirely human most of the time, are you not?"

She nods slowly. "I seem only to shift when I'm...well, it's not very predictable, I should say. But yes. I am most comfortable when I am like this. It seems to be my natural state. And when I am in bestial form, it is not consistent. So perhaps that is why I relate better than my companions who have to work so hard to maintain their glamours to have even the barest of human experiences."

"Currently I teach at the University of Granada now and then. Classics, mostly, to ground myself in human experiences. It keeps me humble, I suppose. But I don't get out nearly as much as I should. I can never leave for long, not with Mother..." he trails off and brings the car to a stop.

They are at the foot of the mountains, now. There's a small winding path leading up and away to a square stone and stucco cottage, nestled so close to the hill it looks as if it's growing from the rock itself, like a strange square mineral. It is enclosed in so much rosemary that Christabel can smell it from the car, clean and bright and rich.

Christabel allows Kalum to open the door for her, and she has to shade her eyes from the bright light to see better. No sign of the aforementioned mother.

"You haven't spoken much about your mother before," Christabel says as diplomatically as possible. "I should have brought her a gift. I admit I feel a bit unprepared."

Kalum is looking back and forth between Christabel and the house. "You don't need to bring anything. She'll love to meet you. It's only that she's old. Very old. And she's often confused. And truly, one can never really prepare for Mother."

"You are a kind son to stay with her," Christabel says. There are many features she sees in Kalum, but kindness is not the first characteristic that comes to mind.

Kalum frowns slightly, then shakes his head. "For another time. For now, let us join and have some good wine. Do you drink? I hope you do."

~

Her name, Christabel quickly learns, is Makaria, and the wine is a comfort in the wake of her chaos. Makaria looks nothing like an old woman, and despite Kalum's protests to the contrary, she appears most ordinary, all things considered. Yes, she is about a foot taller than an average human woman. Yes, her hair is dark as pitch and light as smoke, and it forms a kind of moving art piece as she walks about, as if she is underwater. Yes, she dresses in black linen, and her arms are scarified rather intensely. But that is nothing compared to the kind of things Christabel has seen, having walked the Underworld more than once.

Makaria is so delighted at Christabel's arrival that she immediately pours three large glasses of dark purple wine and has a toast in her honor but forgets what she's doing halfway through.

"To a most magnificent creature," Makaria says. "To Christabel, who has come all the way from America to find...what is it you're looking for?"

"It's a bit of a missing person case," Christabel says. It is not the first time she has had to clarify. Makaria initially thought Christabel was asking to marry Kalum, which was momentarily confusing but not out of the realm of behavior for a woman of her means and bearing. "A sylph, to be precise. An unusual sylph."

"People go missing all the time, so I've learned, to say nothing of sylphs," Makaria says gravely. She's pouring more wine, and up until now Christabel has been very courteous about it, but she doesn't usually drink so much. It will not end well if she's not careful. Being drunk is not her preferred state.

"Mother, she doesn't mean it that way," Kalum says. "It's a friend of hers. And she's been missing for twenty years."

"Well, that's hardly a cause for concern," says Makaria. "I once lost a husband for thirty years, and I barely missed him."

Christabel tries not to laugh because she's certain Makaria does not mean it in jest. Once she's composed herself, she clarifies, "Vivienne du Lac was abducted. By a djinni."

"Was she now?" Makaria is half-replying, and Christabel is painfully aware she's not getting very far.

"Yes, and it's—a bit—well, my fault. At least, I didn't help in the matter at all. I've solved dozens of cases in the last twenty years, helped forge alliances in the arcane community, read enough books to fill up this entire house, and all I had on Vivienne's whereabouts was dust. Until now. We have evidence she's been tied up in some rather underground groups."

"I like it underground," Makaria says wistfully.

Kalum sighs, shaking his head, and gives Christabel an apologetic look. "Not everyone does, Mother," he says. "And besides, that's not what Christabel means. She means that someone has taken her friend against her will, and no matter what they've done, they haven't found any indication of where she might be. But now they have, and it's brought them here."

Christabel notices a shift in Kalum's tone. Slight. But just enough. The word "here." It's not the way one would say, "Here, at home." It is more like, "Here, of all places." Which, it does not seem, is terribly welcome.

"Then she must not be looking hard enough," Makaria says to her flagon of wine. She sloshes it around, dips a finger in, and removes a fat cricket.

"But we've got reason to think that she may be in Andalusia," Christabel says. "Which I why I wrote Kalum in hopes that he could show me around a bit and see if there are any lingering clues."

Makaria frowns suddenly, her once rather confused and placid state evaporating before Christabel's eyes. "Oh, that won't do at all."

"Your pardon?" Christabel asks.

"Kalum, why do you bring such people to me? Why do you involve me so?" Makaria stands and throws her glass, wine and all, shattering into the fire. "As if you and I don't have enough business to attend. As if the family legacy can sustain another interloper."

Christabel has never felt so out of place in her life. She chokes back her protest, and puts down her glass of wine, sending her gaze to the door. Kalum catches her, though, and shakes his head. "Not yet" he mouths.

Kalum continues, his voice so gentle it's like silk across satin. "Hush, Mother. Please, we are not asking anything of you. No one wants to use you to their benefit. I promise. This is simply between Christabel and me."

"But what *is* she?" Makaria peers over. Her eyes are dark, judging.

"Just someone looking for answers," Christabel says.

"You stink of *celestials*." Makaria sighs, and this is not a benediction, nor is it acceptance. But she appears a little calmer now.

"I have a friend who is an angel, mostly," Christabel says. "Though the word friend is perhaps a little generous. It's been some time since I've seen them, though, so I can't imagine that's it."

She tells herself that she doesn't miss Ophaniel. That she's gotten over Worth. That she doesn't ache when she thinks about the way he used to look at her, the feeling of his fingers intertwined with hers...

She tells herself a lot of other lies, too.

"You aren't *using* it," Makaria says, holding up her hands as if to protect herself. "You aren't using it. You aren't."

"I didn't say I was," Kalum says. "I didn't ask to use it. We don't even have to talk about it, Mother. I just want to help Christabel."

Christabel wonders why she always falls for the broken, strange ones. Why couldn't she fall for a nice eunuch? Or a boring satyr? She is beginning to piece together Kalum and Makaria's demesnes. The way the darkness gathers about them, how the shadows leak from their eyes when she looks away and has them on the periphery. It does not frighten her; she's seen chthonics before, and they had giant scorpions on their heads. Considerably more frightening than some shadowy eyeliner.

Still, Christabel has the sense that Makaria has been betrayed before and Kalum is merely looking out for her.

"I'm sorry others have deceived you," Christabel tries lightly. "I mean no harm. I only want a local guide."

"Everyone wants the Pit of Hades," Makaria says, her tone punctuated, vicious. "How dare you claim you are free from its call. Haven't you heard it since the moment you set foot here? It calls *everyone*, child." She glances at her son, and then back to Christabel, knowing.

Christabel makes to stand, but Kalum holds up a hand, beckoning her to stay a moment longer. She can't say why, but she sighs and nods her assent. This is as close as she's managed to Vivienne in twenty years. And though she's a bit worried that she hasn't gotten word from Nerissa or Kit yet, she settles back, trying to pull her most innocent, charming, and lovely face.

"I will explain to her, Mother, if you'll permit me," Kalum says.

Makaria's eyes flicker back and forth between the others in the room, much longer than one might consider adequate for such judgment. Then she sighs and shakes her head, her long hair twisting about her in an invisible current.

"Very well," Makaria says. "But if she hurts us, I will call down vengeance."

"I have no doubt," Kalum says, warmly.

Then he turns to Christabel. "It all begins with my grandfather, a god named Hades…"

NO NATURAL-BORN MONSTER

Kissing Nadine was a bit strange at first, but now, most evenings, Vivienne has come to anticipate it. She can't remember exactly when it began, perhaps around their journey from Tunisia to Sicily when they ran into that tempest, but she isn't sure. All she knows is that being with Nadine, tasting her skin, is both physically warm—she embodies fire—and numb at the same time. And she is quite certain she would not be alive if she did not have such a connection to the ifrit.

Vivienne's chains prevent her from using her own power in such an endeavor, as she used to. A hundred years ago she would have risen up, taken the breath from a creature such as Nadine, and inhaled her, body and soul, fueling her desire, the passion a form of ethereal nourishment. It would be great pleasure for both of them, but even more for Vivienne. She used to feed on that power, sate her body with sex and lust and possession.

But now, not so. She must make do the way mortals must, and it isn't so terrible.

"Your skin," Nadine says, running her fingers across Vivienne's belly, tracing the hollow of her stomach, trailing tongues of blue fire. Vivienne used to have a little rise there, a healthy glow, but now she is little more than a wraith. Still, the ifrit finds her beautiful. "It is like moonlight on snow. How is it so white without being transparent?"

"You forget that I'm a *monster*," Vivienne replies. Once she would have responded with power in her voice, that sturdy assuredness she once possessed. Now it is spoken softly.

"Tell me about how you were," Nadine says. "Please? Haven't I earned at least a glimpse by now?"

Vivienne reflects a moment inwardly and yes, were she to catalogue the indulgences in Nadine's favor, she would owe her a great deal on passion alone, to say nothing of friendship.

Until this moment, Vivienne has refused to answer the question. Trust came slowly between them, but then there it was, a full-fledged presence in their midst. And she is weary and a little drunk, and her lips are still warm from where Nadine kissed her moments before.

"I used to say that we monsters are all orphans, but that's not entirely true, is it?" Vivienne closes her eyes and tries to remember before she was Vivienne du Lac. Before she was *la belle dame sans merci*. Before she found her way to England, slinking through the fens like some hobbled creature. "I am no natural-born monster."

Nadine leans on her arm, tilting the angles of her face so beautifully that Vivienne smiles, resisting the urge to kiss her again. There is a child-like delight in Nadine, especially when Vivienne tells her tales. But until now she had not mentioned this life to anyone. Not even to Nerissa, at least not in full.

So she decides to tell a mostly truth.

"Oh, what a delight!" Nadine practically squeals with excitement.

"My mother was a nymph," Vivienne says. "And she was a sworn virgin of the Huntress, of Artemis."

At the name of the goddess, Vivienne swears she sees a flicker of surprise in Nadine's eyes. But the flame quenches as quickly as it came, and Vivienne's tongue is loosened with wine now. So much wine. Perhaps Nadine finds it ironic that Vivienne's mother was a virgin.

But Vivienne has enough presence of mind to obscure some of the facts. She cannot be entirely vulnerable. Even if all else is lost, she must keep some secrets, some power, to herself.

"My mother was named Aura. She was prideful, so they say. She dared compare herself to Artemis's beauty. Having overheard Artemis complain of Aura's treachery, Dionysus, who was in his usual drunken stupor and angry over a falling-out with Zeus, tracked Aura down," Vivienne explains. The story comes easier because it has been told so many times, just not by her. She feels the common line of the tale, the words forming before she even has time to consider them in full. "He saw Aura bathing in a stream, her long hair like a silver waterfall, and in his lust, he raped her, in hopes of claiming her beauty and possessing. I have read stories that claim Eros's arrow pierced his heart, or that Artemis put him up to it. But I do not believe it. What little my mother passed to me..."

Vivienne sits up and takes a long drink from the bottle of wine beside her, welcoming the hot sting of it on her lips. Her chains clink against the glass, and she sighs.

Nadine's fingers slip down Vivienne's pale back.

"They call the land Turkey, now, where I walked," Vivienne says. "But when I was a child, we called it Phrygia. My mother became pregnant by Dionysus and tried to drown the twins she birthed one night. In punishment for her crimes, she was turned into a fountain by Zeus, but not before her last labor pains."

Vivienne gestures to herself. "I had two brothers, and I do not remember them now, for they were raised among the new gods. I, born later, was given to my grandmother, Cybele, and raised deep within the mountain. They named me Apsinthos. Wormwood."

Nadine is silent, watching Vivienne's expression. "You remember all of this?"

"I was born with my mother's memories. They lived inside of me somehow, this dark fury and rage that I could not release," Vivienne says, holding up her fingers. "I was rebellious. Furious. I scorned my grandmother, I fled. My strange skin sought warmth but was never warm. I did not age. Men and gods fell before me and I became monstrous. I drank the blood of a thousand men, and I was still not satisfied."

"How ever did you stop?"

"I fell in love with a mortal," Vivienne replies, taking her once lustrous hair between her hands. "And I began to see the joy of humanity, as short-lived as it was. My beloved hated me in return, and though I knew I could woo him to my bed, I refused to use my power, and he left me. Desperate for love, I cried out to Artemis in the dark of night and heard only the whisper of the wind in the trees. I decided I would change myself. And I would seek out others like me who had been ill-made."

"I don't think you are ill-made," Nadine says, tracing Vivienne's cheek with her palm. "I think you are precisely what I was hoping."

"I am no goddess," Vivienne says.

"You are descended from goddesses. For isn't that what a nymph is? A child of Titans, or goddesses..."

"I have no desire to count myself as a goddess. Merely one of their malformed progenies, wandering the earth for too long, and now chained."

Nadine frowns. "I wish we could be rid of these."

Vivienne is done talking about the lives she once led and is ready for another kind of escape. She draws the ifrit close for another kiss. As ever, Nadine does not resist. She is unquenchable, even under Vivienne's icy touch. Vivienne presses herself insistently over the length of Nadine's body, feeling every curve and variation in heat. Nadine's kisses are fire on her lips, filling her lungs with painful, lusty joy. Like breathing into a funeral pyre. Release and relinquish.

When Nadine's kisses reach her navel, Vivienne loses herself in the old dance, hips moving and hands clasping, tongue reaching and tasting. But she weeps, and her cries of joy mingle with those of sorrow.

⁓

Nadine falls asleep, and Vivienne does not. Her body grows cold as soon her lover leaves for the land of dreaming, and Vivienne shivers. She rises and goes to the high window above her bed, watching the moonlight shimmer across the pale stone walls, wishing she had the gift of sleep.

A little Spanish moon moth, the *Graesllsia isabellae*, flutters across the pane, waiting a moment on the edge of the window. Bereft of her powers, Vivienne sees the little creature differently than she might have before. Its lines are clearer, the small eyes on its wings stranger. The world is all hard angles and outlines, shifts in temperature and consistency and composition. But the moon moth is not afraid of her.

It alights on her hand, so gentle it almost tickles. The wings fold, and it rests quietly. Vivienne dares not breathe. And she feels she should know this creature as if it is part of another, long-dead story where she once belonged. But her memories grow more sluggish the longer she is kept from her power.

Worth. Nerissa. Christabel. Aura.

Telling Aura's story was not been easy. She almost regrets it except she can't. She's had her guard up for so very long, so very, very long, that the expression of her former self feels a kind of release. She has lived so many lives over the thousands of years of her existence that she often forgets the details. Inevitably they return, though.

Another moon moth. Curious. Christabel would know the exact details, but Vivienne is fairly certain that they are on their way to extinction. She is about to reach out for the second when a third comes in through the window and lands on her shoulder, fair and light and luminescent.

The three moths then join in a circular gambol, twisting in and around one another, winding this way and that, until they start to flutter their way to the door behind her, leading out to the rest of the villa.

Vivienne stares at the barred door. It is not nearly as fortified as it has been during her incarceration; only so much to do in this old, remote villa. She may have dampened magic, but she can still be silent. The moths wait at the door, turning again and again, as she softly pads her way toward them.

Nadine is snoring. Her drinking is predictable; her sleep uninterrupted when it comes, which is not often. It would be best not to bother her.

As Vivienne runs her fingers over the lock, she is surprised to find how cold it is, as if she had been exerting her powers on it. Those long-lost powers once so easily possessed, to turn anything to ice, to draw heat from it and make frost. To feast on the warmth.

But it is not her magic. She breathes shallowly, casting a glance over her shoulder to see if Nadine still sleeps.

The moths twirl around her again and again, and Vivienne gently unlocks the door, the mechanism falling away under slight pressure. It makes her old heart, which pumps so much more slowly than a mortal's, quicken and rise to her throat. Is that joy she feels? Power? Hope?

The hallways are dark, and the tiles cool on her bare feet. Bastille's quarters are not far, but she cannot hear him or feel him at all. His presence is the only one she can attune to, some cruel fate of her incarceration. But helpful in a case like this.

Vivienne's moth companions flutter right and then left, then toward the cellars. *Come, come!* They seem to say. The entire house is utterly silent. No sign of Cygna. No sign of Bastille. She can smell the distant burn of petrol, hear the sighing of the sea in the distance.

But her moth friends do not lead her to freedom. No, they lead her elsewhere.

There are two entrances to the cellars: the one nearest her and the one via the kitchens. This one, by the living quarters, was likely intended to be the more impressive of the two, but a long-ago collapse has obscured the way and it is too much trouble to clear in such a short time. The moths linger there, patient, twirling.

But Vivienne is slight. Very slight. Even with her shackles, she is so silent, so tenuous, that one could almost mistake her for a shadow.

Ten steps down, however, and the stairway becomes treacherous. Gravel litters every step, the overhang so close to Vivienne's head she can touch it in places. Vines grow in, too. Honeysuckle and vetch, curling like the arms of an octopus down the wall. She does not want to look at them too long, for they seem to move, to threaten her, to spell out words.

She should have stayed in bed.

She almost turns around to find the comfort of Nadine's warm, drunk body, but then she catches the scent of an aroma so old and familiar she almost cries out in recognition. It is the thick, honey scent of asphodel.

Vivienne tries to rein in her excitement, mingled though it may be with much fear. A light glows dimly at the bottom, buttery yellow against the red clay walls. No one has seen her. No one will know. She must go just a little further.

She is about to reach the bottom step and turn to see what lies beyond, even though the hope in her breast tells her that she knows already, when a cold hand clasps around the back of her neck. Her shackles crackle in response, sending her to her knees.

A quick yank of her long hair and Vivienne is looking up into Bastille's face. Now that she is this close—or perhaps it is through the clarity of pain—she notes familiar lines. He is shockingly beautiful. Beautiful as the moon itself. But cold. So cold.

"Here, behold," Bastille says, grabbing Vivienne by the collar with tremendous strength. He flings the night sylph to one side, so she is staring at a small cell carved into the very earth. Vivienne knows the stone—of course she does—and she turns the thought in her head. Alabaster? Why alabaster?

There is a figure inside the cell. The source of the asphodel scent. She is somehow half-sunken into the stones; they crawl up her body like lichen.

"You see? My gift to my lady Cygna. Bowed and bent and in her rightful place," Bastille says.

"Artemis," whispers Vivienne.

Artemis is just as tremendous as Vivienne remembers, a massive woman of corded muscle and power. Her square face is punctuated by thick lips and dark-lashed eyes, eyes as white as alabaster themselves. She was never a wispy beauty, but one of earthy power and absolute presence. Even now, trapped as she is, Vivienne feels that power, diminishing though it may be. Artemis nods slowly, Bastille barking a laugh.

"I didn't expect to see you here, Aura," Artemis says.

NITWITS

Ophaniel comes back to himself, and there is a wounded snake woman at his feet bleeding all over the place. He vaguely remembers coming here, deciding at last that staying in his tower forever might not be the best course of action—and because of Worth's incessant pushing—but now he's quite confused as to where he's been the last bit of time.

Sorry about that, old chap. Didn't meant to take the helm. But you weren't doing much to help, and I was afraid we weren't going to make it.

"We were attacked," Ophaniel says out loud, forgetting that the snake woman can hear.

"Of course, we were attacked, you nitwit," Nerissa growls. "Do you think I just chewed off my arms because I was hungry? Now give me a piece of cloth and help me bandage this."

She is breathing in and out very fast, and Ophaniel first wonders why she doesn't grow another limb, then realizes, of course, that she is not a celestial, and while she is supernatural, she cannot regenerate so easily.

Ophaniel has little in the way of clothing, but long strips of linen wrap his legs, more out of propriety than a sense of fashion. He has tried walking around naked, his preferred state, but has not been able to do so in his present company. So he is more than glad to oblige.

The creature's blood is green, but it dries blue on his hand. Ophaniel is

322

not familiar with bodies that ooze and seep and so he has to look away numerous times.

"Angels don't bleed," he says. It doesn't sound apologetic the way he says it, but he means it as such. "We can be redistributed, but we cannot die from loss of blood or organs. We are creatures of pure energy, so we require no such barbaric structures beneath our skin."

"Aren't you just the luckiest?" Nerissa's form is unchanged, her glamour flickering through her pain. Ophaniel has not had occasion to look at her that way, and he finds she is not as strange as he imagined. Well, no, that isn't right. She is hideous, but there is a rhyme and reason to her form. Her mottled skin and yellow eyes, the long waves of her hair, the scales at her cheeks and neck. He can at least recognize that she is well-made, even if she is a horror to gaze upon. Even if the two bloody stumps at her side make him feel as if he is looking into the very Void itself.

"I thought we had a boat to catch," Ophaniel says, trying—hoping—to make pleasant conversation.

Nerissa closes her eyes tight, her jaw clenching. "Ophaniel, could you oblige me with silence while I writhe in pain? I may be no angel, but I have some capacity for healing. Though…" She grunts, agony seizing her features again for a moment. "If you do not keep quiet with your angel prattling, I may let myself die just to avoid having to listen to you any longer."

Ophaniel realizes that this is a jest, but it doesn't make him laugh. He doesn't understand Nerissa's humor. There is nothing prattling about him.

He's just lonely.

Or would be, if Worth would leave him alone.

Let her have some air. Keep an eye out for that dwarf.

Nerissa leans back and then reaches into her satchel to retrieve the disgusting imp ichor she's become increasingly dependent upon. If he cared about her, he'd tell her that it wasn't healthy for her, that there were better options, or at least less-addictive ones, and that she shouldn't listen to vampires. Look where she ended up!

But he doesn't say anything.

Once she has a drink of the stuff, her lids get heavy a moment and then, with a barely perceptible shimmer, she slides back into her mostly human guise, minus the arm. There's only so much one can do with magic, after all.

323

Rather than say anything inappropriate, Ophaniel just goes motionless and waits, listening.

"Was I imagining things, or was Worth talking through you earlier?" Nerissa's voice is a little less strained now.

Ophaniel doesn't like the question. He doesn't quite know the answer, himself, but he's aware that Nerissa is fond of Worth and, in the measure of non-angels, it must have been a traumatic experience.

"It's possible," Ophaniel says.

Nerissa gives him a strange, measuring look. Her eyes are still yellow. So the glamour isn't *that* strong. "How long has he been chattering in your head?"

Ophaniel just stares at her. He thinks he's very coy and clever about the whole thing, but the conversation quickly disintegrates.

"You've been talking with him this whole time," Nerissa says, struggling to get to her feet. She's wobbly. And if it weren't for the fact that Ophaniel felt the dwarf person returning, he would grab Nerissa to steady her. "For ten years you've been talking with him and you failed to make mention."

"I don't much like you," Ophaniel says in his candid way. "I didn't think it was an important detail."

Ophaniel is afraid of her for just the barest of seconds, given the look of poisonous fury in her eyes. But the dwarf shows up first. And on deeper consideration, Ophaniel thinks that Alma makes a much better recliner for a woozy lamia than he does. Touching her skin makes him want to retch, and he doesn't want to talk about Worth, because admitting it makes it real. And angels aren't supposed to have competing personalities.

"If I had all my appendages I would strangle you with all of them right now," Nerissa says between gritted teeth.

"Whoa, now, whoa," Alma says, reaching up to take Nerissa around the waist.

"Where's Kit?" Nerissa asks, gathering her breath.

"You were supposed to *help* her," Alma says, accusingly, to Ophaniel. "Not deposit her like a sack of oats."

The angel shrugs. "I don't bleed. Angels heal by singing. But cherubim songs would make her eyes explode, to say nothing of the long-term hearing damage. What do you expect of me?"

This, finally, stops the lamia from her excessive whining and whimpering, while the dwarf tends to her. Ophaniel enjoys the quiet of the cave, and he wonders about its provenance. London isn't particularly old by the measure of angels. But it's old enough that he can't remember its precise beginning or end. There were humans here a very long time ago, and of course, since there were humans, there were also monsters. And gods and angels and all manner of creatures in between.

Nerissa feels familiar to the place, though, in a way that Kit certainly doesn't. He doesn't remember Vivienne, this once paramour of Worth's, but he has a sense that she doesn't fit in quite so well. Nerissa is not a salt-water creature; she is an earthy creature, reminiscent of deep wells and cold springs in the mountains.

"Can you please stop staring," Nerissa finally says. She has shrugged off most of the pain, it seems, and is now walking around in a circle, more or less humanoid to the naked eye.

"I was just wondering about your provenance," Ophaniel says.

They walk a few steps toward the shoreline, the eerie moonlight casting glittering streaks across the water.

"My what?"

"Provenance," Ophaniel says. "I mean—"

"I know what you mean," Nerissa replies. "But I'm not a piece of furniture. I don't have *provenance.*"

Ophaniel knows she's not a piece of furniture. But to an angel, the differences between furniture and non-angelic beings is very subtle. Armchair. Lamia. Divan. Sylph. Ottoman. Dwarf.

Subtle.

"Very well, then," he assents. "Your place of origin, to be more specific. Every monster has a beginning."

"I'm from here, of course," Nerissa says as if it's the most obvious thing in the world.

"I surmised as much," Ophaniel replies. "But specifically. This region?"

"Nearly, yes," Nerissa's teeth clatter together. She's cold. At least colder than she should be.

"Malham Tarn is the first place I remember," Nerissa says, half to the water. "The fens there, they're alkaline. Vivienne...when she found me, she said she thought that was one of the reasons I was so vicious, so wild. Something in the composition reacted badly with my already difficult tendencies."

Alma is looking sideways at the lamia, though. "I don't know. You have some features that I would consider consistent with this area, but I sense you're from a little further afield."

"What do you mean?" Nerissa's voice takes on a sharp tinge. Irritation.

"Only that I am an expert in soil. And minerals. And we creatures, or monsters, are imbued with imprints from where we were made. You remind me of…well, the Mediterranean. Or deeper?"

"Deeper? That's not a location."

"I could take a sample and find out," Alma offers.

For some reason, Nerissa finds this extremely offensive, judging by the size of her eyes in response. But thankfully, there is no time to resort to fisticuffs or anything, because Kit returns.

The furry one—she is not furry right now, but on occasion sprouts any number of tails and ears—is breathing hard and not smiling, and Ophaniel has learned from experience that this likely indicates she is upset. Given the last half hour's events, this seems an expected reaction.

"The boat…is on…fire," Kit says between breaths. And indeed, she smells like smoke, and there are smudges on her face. "Someone knew we were coming."

"So I lost two arms for nothing?" Nerissa is joking. Perhaps. She looks like she might faint, and Ophaniel does not think that's a good thing. Even though he would appreciate the quiet.

"Fire doesn't bother me," Ophaniel suggests, more to get out of this awkward situation with his companions. Nerissa has been kind to him, he understands this, but she also grates on him. And he feels uncomfortable when the furry one looks at the lamia too long, and vice versa. "I can go look."

Flying is complicated but running is not. And since cherubim aren't tied to time in the same way most creatures are, Ophaniel can blink forward toward the right destination so long as he can see the next location. It's a trick of light, and not complicated, but challenging to teach to those convinced that their mortal bodies are so inflexible.

That isn't quite right. He forgets. Someone told him once that even immortal non-celestials would turn into pasta should they travel by such means. There was a specific pasta. Rigatoni? No, cavatappi.

There is a chance that the others would try and prevent him from going, but he is already too far away to hear their startled cries.

~

The boat is easy to find because it is indeed a great conflagration. It's been a long time since Ophaniel has seen such a display, and for a moment he considers just watching it. He's always liked the way that flames rise and fall, how the colors indicate the temperature and the fuel, how the smells and the sounds become so intermingled.

It appears as if some of the local mortals have given up on trying to save the boat. There is enough smoke that most of them are doubled over, coughing into their sleeves, or just sitting on metal buckets and shaking their heads.

If Vivienne were here, it would be fairly obvious.

Worth is there again, and Ophaniel bats at him internally. But that never works.

"Why won't you go away?"

Trust me; I would if I could. I'm starting to think I've always been part of you. I would like rest, but it appears I won't get it. I can help you in this instance. As I said, Vivienne always leaves an impression. She is, by nature, incredibly cold. She is also a restless soul who can never keep her hands still. She would have left her handiwork somewhere.

"It's burning too fast."

No, it isn't. Not for you. For us. It looks like they started the fire in the fore-castle. But I doubt anyone would have kept Vivienne that far away, knowing her capabilities. A sylph on a ship would require an enormous amount of power to contain, what with the presence of water everywhere. They would have wanted her nearby.

"You don't make much sense."

I never claimed to. But I do feel a bit cheated about the fireproof bit. When I was in control, I could have been a rather dashing fellow when it came to rushing into dangerous situations. This whole time I could have simply walked through the fire.

Ophaniel doesn't know what to say about the whole walking into a burning boat business. There is so much about being a celestial that he has forgotten. He hoped it wouldn't take long to return, but so long as Worth is around, Ophaniel is never quite right. Never quite back to himself.

He doesn't remember being able to walk into flames. And they look rather terrifying.

I can do it if you don't want to.

But when Ophaniel goes to answer, it isn't as if he has a choice.

ANGELS ON A PINHEAD

L iving inside of an angel for ten years has taken a toll on Worth Goodwin, a condition made no easier by having always been this angel and living a few hundred years of his life blissfully unaware. Thinking he was a Questing Beast—the Glatisant—he enjoyed a relatively acceptable life as a monster, and monster hunter when the world needed it. He fell in love a few times. He enjoyed newspapers. He preferred Bach over Beethoven.

But now he is an echo inside of his true self. Taking over Ophaniel's body is almost impossible when he's in hiding, up there in his apartment overlooking the misery of Shoreditch (and what kind of name is that, anyway?). But out here, in the danger and the heat, Worth is capable of much more. While he has not been the dominant portion of the celestial these ten years, he has been able to do something Ophaniel has not: he has observed. He has walked around the chambers of the angel's heart. He has taken stock. He has been quiet when Ophaniel hoped he was gone.

Worth sometimes wonders if his life has ever been anything but this.

But he remembers a face, one he has not seen in a very long time. And, like a beacon, it guides him forward.

Christabel.

To the task at hand, however. There is a burning ship before him, and there may be remnants of his once paramour, Vivienne du Lac, there. Unlike Ophaniel, Worth understands the sylph better than even she does.

He can smell her in the burning fire, see her footsteps in the curls of smoke. She is not here, but she was before. Though judging by the state of things, it's been some time since she was aboard. It must have returned after taking her to Andalusia, if that's where she truly is.

Worth wonders if he's ever sensed Vivienne like this before or if it's just an added benefit of his being an angel now. Or part of one. He hasn't decided if he's merely a figment of Ophaniel or a legitimate secondary personality. Or, and this is the one he thinks about more often, neither of them is particularly the right being. Worth and Ophaniel are just echoes of someone else.

True to his suspicion, he is undeterred by the flames. It doesn't stop him from reflexively holding up his arms—he once had a body that he presumes was flammable—but all he feels is a light tickling along his forearms. Heat, yes, but it is only bothersome around the tenderest of his skin: his eyes, his lips, the spaces between his toes.

Bursting through the captain's quarters, he wishes someone were there to observe his heroics.

Alas, time is of the essence; as the fire rolls over the ceiling above him like a thousand yellow tongues, he grabs everything he can: Manifests, charred maps, a pile of pens, a small radio. Whoever left the boat to burn did not care to clean up after themselves, and while that is on the one hand rather thrilling—he does love some good evidence—Worth is smart enough these days to know the makings of a potential trap.

They have been seeking Vivienne's captor for twenty years. They were brought here with an anonymous tip. Or at least, a tip from a vampire, which is even worse than anonymous. And what's left of their vampire tour guide is currently a pile of skins on the shore behind him. This whole business reeks.

He has no pockets and immediately realizes that walking around naked clothed in nothing but glory has significant drawbacks. So Worth must simply grab as much as he can before the boat gives way and crumbles beneath him.

Just as Worth is about to depart, the edges of Ophaniel brightening his vision, he spots the curve of a familiar cheek laid upon the writing desk now slipping into fiery oblivion. It is in the form of a sketchbook. Each page flips with the fury of fire, but one drawing is unmistakable. Her face is as perfect as ten thousand marble statues; her neck is long and lean, her shoulders bare and draped and her bones...and on the next page, lace, just a small roundel slipped between the burning pages.

Charred though it may be, there is no doubt whose hands crafted the delicate design.

~

"You really are in there, aren't you?"

They are now inside a cab, one of the underground sort available to them due to Christabel's connections with the Circle of Iapetus. It may be the one useful thing about the Circle. The cab has dark windows and is helmed by a grindylow named Greg.

Nerissa is looking straight across at Worth, as Ophaniel has not yet returned from his brooding depths, into his eyes. Alma has done an excellent job patching her up, but it is unlikely the lamia will heal. And she isn't exactly keeping consciousness consistently.

"It is me," Worth says. "For now."

Kit is there, staring at him measuredly from beneath her curtain of black hair. She has become very possessive of Nerissa, and Worth doesn't think that's a bad thing. If only Nerissa could see what esteem she's got right in front of her.

"We need to talk about the bleaknesses," says Kit, tapping her foot. "And we can't stay here too long, you know. There is a fire out there. And people will be looking for the hands that made the fire. And although we know we didn't do it, we've still got a celestial covered in smoke stains."

"They're tough to get out of feathers," Worth says, reaching back to pull at the useless wings behind him. "And I couldn't figure out how to blink on my way back. I'm sorry it took so long."

"She needs medical attention," says Alma. "More than I can give her. I'm not an expert on globulin-rich creatures. It's just a green mess. Her blood has oxidized copper in it, and it makes me sneeze."

"We have to find Vivienne," Nerissa says. "Forget about me."

"Always the stubborn one," Worth says.

"Hell, I've missed you, Worth." The lamia's eyes are tearing up. Worth watches in utter shock. Though he's seen her through Ophaniel's eyes almost every day for the last ten years, he's never seen her facade so broken. It must be the pain.

Kit gives Worth a very pointed look. It isn't at all subtle and involves waving of her hands and the universal sign for "death and dying" which is a slitting motion across the neck, followed by wild gesturing at Nerissa. He almost laughs. But she is right.

"Nerissa Waldemar," Worth says. "You stubborn monster. We're going to have to pick up this thread when you've stopped bleeding, and we can get you someone better suited."

Nerissa rolls her eyes like a petulant child, but her lids flutter, too. She won't be lucid for long, and at least at that point, they can pull her away bodily. "Very well. But for the record, I was against meeting him again."

~

By "him" Nerissa means a man named Dr. Plover. Worth was briefly a clerk to Dr. Plover ages ago when he and Nerissa lived in London, during the height of their business, long before she and Vivienne escaped to America to avoid him (the story is perhaps more complicated than that but Worth likes to stick to the simpler version). Nerissa has never liked him because she doesn't like nice things. And Dr. Plover is very nice.

Dr. Plover is also a bird. And this bothers Nerissa, Worth suspects, because deep down she hates her own form and thinks that all monsters and beasts should have a proper guise even when interacting among themselves. Though Dr. Plover claims he cannot produce a convincing glamour, Nerissa has always believed he simply does it to be different, and such behavior has always bothered her. Worth sees through this facade, however, and understands that she is just jealous of Dr. Plover as he lives his life without regret and hiding, and that is a price above rubies.

Kit will not leave Nerissa's side, so Worth suggests that Alma be the one to send a message to Christabel, who will be expecting them in Andalusia. The charred remains of the ship manifest confirmed their suspicions: the crew was dropped not far from Gibraltar.

But Alma is the best choice, not simply because she's less emotionally involved with the whole Vivienne business, but also because she's capable of traveling through stone and has remarkable skills tracking down creatures aboveground. Alma has had to give up much of her status among dwarves to work with their motley crew, but Worth suspects she is glad of the distraction. From what he has gathered, family politics among the dwarves are even worse than among angels.

"Worth…" Kit is looking at him with a shocked face. "You're… you."

Worth looks down at his hands and can see that, indeed, he is wearing a glamour very much like the last one he wore for centuries. He wasn't planning on that. He finds himself rather emotional, having been attached to that face, those hands, that pocket watch.

I gather you can't walk around naked.

Ophaniel.

How astute of you. You're helping me, now? I thought you wanted to be rid of me.

I don't know what to do with you. Or with me. I don't like walking through fire. I don't like watching creatures bleed. I shouldn't have left my roost.

Ophaniel has always called the rooftop apartment his roost, and it amuses Worth to hear him use the phrase again.

"Ah, Worth?"

It is perilously tricky to have two conversations at once, especially when one of them is playing out inside your head.

"I cannot account for it right now," Worth says, and it's true.

Nerissa is losing a great deal of blood.

"Greg, my good man," Worth continues to the cabby. "Please telephone the Circle when you can and have an inquest begun into the London coven. If you can find Micheaux, please do. I am not sure how far the infection went, but I suspect it was just these two. Still, he is at risk."

"Of course, sir," says the grindylow.

"And wire Dr. Frye, if you're able to locate her."

"Done, sir."

"Excellent. Thank you, Greg." Worth takes a deep breath. It's a relief and a bit frightening to be back to his old self.

They all look at him, expectantly, so he says, "Kit, please ring the bell."

The bell is in the form of a feather dangling from the middle of a heart and is located halfway down the huge green door. They are in Notting Hill, which is as posh a place as can be, and yet entirely befitting Dr. Plover. Thankfully, the entrance to his office is charmed, and they are in no real danger of being seen. Hopefully.

Someone is watching, still.

This is another strain Ophaniel's been on lately. But he's always on some paranoid delusion or another. It's the celestial sight, he calls it.

We are fine. Stop being such a bother.

Don't say I didn't warn you.

BLOOD OF THE OLD WORLD

Worth, or Ophaniel, or whoever the angel is now, tried to prepare Kit for this Dr. Plover, but she didn't anticipate that the bird would be wearing human clothing. When they open the door, the white bird flies to a ready-made perch roughly the size of an average humanoid. This close, Kit can see the impeccable details about the creature: all the patterns on his tiny suit—arabesque if she's not mistaken—are done in miniature, all the way down to a tiny pocket watch chain coming out of a tiny pocket.

"That is the smallest pocket watch I have ever seen," Kit says, leaning forward and forgetting all appropriate decorum. "And I have seen many pocket watches. I briefly collected them."

"My proportions are somewhat smaller than the average clockmaker might be used to," says Dr. Plover, tilting his head to the side with a gauging glance from his bead black eyes. "But it is functional, I assure you."

The bird, an actual plover, has a white and black pattern across what plumage is visible, so it looks as if he's wearing a little wig. Kit finds him incredibly amusing but knows that she's already been impolite. It's ever difficult to keep her mouth shut in such situations.

Nerissa moans an incoherent phrase about a donkey. Even in the short ride over, she has slipped further away into a place of pain. And the exertion of going up the stairs about did her in.

"All the bantering aside," Worth says. "We have a situation."

Dr. Plover raises his beak, then nods. "The lamia, I see. Bring her into the parlor, and we will begin the examination."

Kit is curious as to how a parlor would be a proper place for a dying lamia—the thought bringing her up short for a moment—but she sees as soon as they get Nerissa through the door that the house is scoured clean save for the entrance. The entirety of the place is either painted white or else tiled brilliantly, and it smells of lavender and antiseptic. The walls that are not whitewashed are lined with shelves upon shelves of items, medical and arcane, all arranged by color across the spectrum.

As she stares as the ochres turning to chartreuse, Kit thinks that this is a kind of art. Not just a healing art, but a visual one as well. She has never seen such an arrangement of scientific items, and it strikes her as a curious contrast to the dark, shattering world around them. For isn't that what's happening?

The bleaknesses. Kit shudders as she helps arrange the lamia on a long metal table in the middle of the parlor, pushing aside the monsters in her memory. Two serving women dressed in nurse's garb come from either side of the room with thick linens, salves, and more modern transfusion devices.

"Annie, fetch me the calcium citrate, if you would," says Dr. Plover, now positioned at another perch, just to the top of Nerissa's head.

Kit notices the further deterioration of her friend. Each scale, once iridescent forest green and gray, is now limned with a touch of orange, like a flower dying at the edges. It makes Kit feel ill to look upon her, as if she is seeing a true marvel of the world falling apart in her hands.

And isn't that what she is seeing?

"Lamias have difficulty processing certain chemicals," Dr. Plover explains. "Common in their species. The calcium citrate works wonders to clot. But that is the least of our problems. Lamias are unique in their blood systems, common in old-world nymphs of her sort."

"Her blood is copper-based," Kit says softly, leaning over to touch the side of Nerissa's face but stopping short. She catches Worth's eye and looks away.

Dr. Plover's ruff fluffs a bit. "Yes, that's correct. She needs oxygen, of course, like most creatures. But in her case, it's hemocyanin that carries the oxygen throughout her body, and it's comprised of two copper atoms and an oxygen atom."

Until this moment, Kit had never considered what her blood is made of at all. She has always assumed it was just blood. But Nerissa always says that she smelled of violets. Perhaps her blood is full of flowers.

"I see," says Kit.

The nurses work quickly to remove what clothing Nerissa has left on her body, gently moving the hair off her shoulders and plaiting it to keep it out of the way. The glamour slipped off somewhere between transit and arrival, but Kit honestly can't remember when.

She's starting to worry. She keeps looking at the stubs at Nerissa's side, hearing the lamia's pained cries, and wondering to herself why she's never been forward with her. Never thanked her. Never said what she felt.

Kit has never been in love before. Or at least, it's been so long that she can't remember. And how should a fox love a lizard? It's as improbable as the moon and sun loving one another. And yet...

"Kit, hold my hand," says Nerissa. It's soft, but Kit hears it and runs to her side to slip her small fingers into Nerissa's long, strong ones. Nerissa's grip is far weaker than it should be, but Kit tries to pour all her strength into assuring her.

"We fought creatures that we think are..." Worth struggles, and it's clear to Kit now that he's fighting off Ophaniel, or exhaustion, or both. He trembles, sweating, brushing his hands through his hair. "We think..."

"Worth, I am quite capable of managing this now that we are with Dr. Plover," Kit says, her voice rising above the din. "I recommend that you see to our other associate and return when you have rested."

Worth nods slowly. "I'm sorry, Dr. Plover...but it's been quite a day. I would try and explain to you exactly what happened, but I fear it currently defies even my understanding."

The bird shakes his head. "No apologies from you, Mr. Goodwin. I always knew you were beyond my realm of understanding, and I am glad that I was not mistaken in my conjecture. But yes, the *kitsune* is correct. Please attend to what you need. I am more than capable of helping Ms. Waldemar, providing I get enough information and we can work quickly. You should go to the kitchen and get something to drink; coffee, perhaps."

Worth's eyes brim suddenly with tears.

"Please, Worth," Kit says. "I can do this. I promise. I need to do this."

Worth retreats toward the kitchen, and Kit is glad of it. There is enough torture between them already that having another conflicted soul in the room feels almost too much to manage.

335

"The creatures. Tell me about them," Dr. Plover says once Worth is gone and the nurses have prepped Nerissa.

The nurses give the lamia a shot from a vial filled with a creamy white fluid, and Nerissa immediately goes slack. Kit feels both relief and worry wash over her in turns.

"Miss?"

"My name is Kamiyama Kumi. I am three hundred years old." She doesn't know why she says that, but it feels essential. There were many times she wanted to tell Nerissa that, and yet, she had always just been "Kit." And that was enough. But no, it wasn't. She should have told her more.

Dr. Plover nods his head. "Then tell me, Miss Kamiyama. Where are the lamia's arms? Because according to my preliminary examination, while they are not on her person, they are living—and in pain—some-where else. Which I think is the reason for her current state and deteri-oration."

The realization of Nerissa's state is shocking to Kit, and she has to hold herself upright by balancing on a small stool. She perches when she's stressed, a habit Nerissa usually finds irritating, but Kit honestly doesn't know how else to deal with such emotions. It comes as natural to her as breathing. Perhaps it's a defense mechanism; that was Christabel's theory, anyway.

Either way, Dr. Plover does not point out that Kit is perching on a stool like a bird, nor that she is letting her tails show. Unlike Nerissa's glamour, which takes constant effort to maintain, Kit's physical forms ebb and flow, as simple as changing facial expressions. But there is no doubt that when she is emotional, she errs toward the fox.

"We fought creatures," Kit says softly. "I cannot describe them to you other than to say that they were not made of matter the way you and I are. And I do not simply mean made of feather or fur. They behaved badly, and at first, took the expression of two vampires we somewhat knew. I have little care for vampires myself, but that has more to do with their general lack of hygiene when it comes to their feet. Did you know that vampires have the ghastliest toenails?"

Dr. Plover lets out a short chirp and then settles on the taller nurse's shoulder. "I do, in fact, Miss Kamiyama. I am sadly, perilously, acquainted with the shortcomings of vampire podiatry. I have been working with the population for years, hoping to help them in this matter, but that is neither here nor there. I cannot say what it is that your friend has fought, but it appears that she is..."

Nerissa moans, and it ends in a whimper. Kit has never heard the lamia sound so small and helpless.

"The body is confused," Dr. Plover says. "Whatever these creatures—what did you call them?"

"I call them 'bleaknesses' because that's the best word I can think of in English. It's a slippery, rubbery language, English. But occasionally I find a decent enough word." Kit sighs, shivering and pulling her knees in even tighter. She likes the feeling when her hair trails down the front of her shins, and she does this for a moment, watching as the nurses and Dr. Plover attend to Nerissa. "It reminds me of an old story."

"Go on," says Dr. Plover.

"You probably think me quaint," Kit replies. "You're trying to save Nerissa's life, and I did nothing to stop the bleaknesses, and now all I can relay to you are stories."

Dr. Plover stops his commands to the nurses—"take the pulse there, no there, you know the lamias don't have the femoral artery placement," or "she is losing blood and if you don't keep pressure on that stump we're going to be in real trouble," or "double-check her other wounds; there may have been something that we missed"—and looks Kit squarely in the face.

His little black eyes are so piercing, so full of wisdom, knowledge, and sadness, that Kit almost feels embarrassed before he speaks.

"We live in a world of gods and monsters, Miss Kamiyama," Dr. Plover says. "And though you are many centuries younger than I, and inexperienced in some ways of this wild world, I can tell you with utmost conviction: stories are just as powerful as any force in heaven or on earth. What moves our hearts, moves our minds. What moves our minds, moves our hands. You and I, Nerissa and Worth, we are all tied together by forces no one truly understands. If something moved in you, please, I beseech you, tell me."

Kit has never heard anyone speak like this before. She feels at once proud of who she is but also stricken with a deep desire to be home, to be in Japan, to climb the mountains of her childhood and eat wild berries in the hillsides.

"When I was a child, they told me a story of the Dread Star," she says, though she calls him by his true name, *Ama-tsu-mika-boshi*. "He was a powerful god, but so far away. My mother told me he was out in the heavens, awaiting revenge from his fall. But that his evil was not evil the way we were taught. It was an evil of nothing. Not the good emptiness that comes of meditation and prayer and fasting, the emptiness that is a sky hunger."

"And there we are, little one; you are moved to the truth, though you know not the facts," Dr. Plover says, and Kit does not argue. Though he is a small creature in current stature, he is much larger than she. But only that his heart has more capacity, she thinks. "I have not shared news with you because I was not sure whom to trust. I have written to Dr. Frye, I have written to the Shah, written to Yer Iyesi. It is not the first outbreak of these bleaknesses, as you call them, but it is the worst."

"What is the cause, then?" Kit is afraid to ask, but does so anyway.

Dr. Plover sighs, hiding his head behind his wing for a moment, the tiny pocket watch clinking inside his vest. "Someone has kidnapped a goddess. A powerful, old goddess. Diana. Artemis. Potnia Theron. She has gone missing, and in her place, these bleaknesses have appeared—if that is what one could call it. And she is not the only supernatural creature to go missing over the last few decades, as I think you are well aware."

"We were headed to Spain," says Kit, slowly putting the pieces together. "To find Vivienne. We'd been searching for years. Then suddenly, we had a lead. But on our way, we were attacked. Nerissa was suspicious that the pieces were falling into place too easily. You don't suspect we're being lured?"

"Lured to kill. You did mostly survive an assassination," says the plover. "But only just. Yet I wonder, would they have let you live? All the clues were laid out for you, it seems."

"Why? I don't understand."

"One must never try to reason with madness," Dr. Plover says sadly, "but accept its repercussions and work to mend them."

"Nerissa will stop at nothing to find Vivienne," Kit says. "She will want us to go to Andalusia, even if she suspects death may follow us."

"I can help, however small. But listen to me: We are going to have to sever Nerissa's body from her missing limb, as I believe it will act as a beacon to you. For now, being hidden from these beasts of nothingness is your only chance. If we do not sever her connection from the missing limb, they will find her. They will find you. They will find London. And we will be part of the bleakness forever. But we will have to capture her, mostly, in her glamour, for it to work."

OLYMPIANS EN MASSE

It always goes back to Hades, Christabel thinks. It isn't that she dislikes his stories; it's that she has grown tired over the years of the Greek pantheon and its trouble. Human beings find them inspiring, amusing, even naming buildings and cities after them. But the more Christabel has studied them, the more she has come to believe that they were really the worst of the divine. Monsters, even. Or more deserving of the name. And she knows this personally, having somewhat unintentionally fallen into a relationship with one of them a while ago.

As Kalum speaks of his grandfather, Christabel finds herself wishing she could have a word with the old rascal.

And that wouldn't be so difficult, as she learns, because according to Kalum, his mother Makaria guards the literal portal to the underworld, a one-way gate to Hades himself, kept safe by generations of their family.

"More properly, *one* of the underworlds," Kalum corrects. They have been talking for over an hour, and Christabel is beginning to wonder how she ever let herself slip into delusions of romance about this man. She must be tired, indeed. "Hades is not as all-powerful as some think, he's merely gotten the bulk of the Western narrative. You know how it goes."

Christabel doesn't exactly, but she nods anyway. Yes, Hermes would agree with that, she thinks, trying very hard not to think about her disastrous romantic fling with the god. She didn't know it was him at the time of course, and well…his eyes were so very alluring.

339

Makaria is making another dinner, despite the fact Christabel insisted she'd had enough food to eat and indeed, she must be on her way. But the woman is having none of it.

Kalum steeples his fingers like a learned professor. "Of course, there shouldn't be portals to the underworld—this or any other—simply open to the general public. It's a danger to every and any creature coming within arm's distance. Present company excluded, of course. And, perhaps that's why your friend's captors took up residence nearby. Though, it's really mortals we must worry about because they are inexplicably drawn toward it. They can't help it. We routinely have to sweep the grounds for wanderers."

He says it almost lovingly.

"And can no one else take turns with you?" Christabel asks. She has decided that being part of the conversation is less painful than trying to swim against the proverbial current.

Makaria laughs her cracked, whistling laugh, banging a spoon on one of the large copper pots she's assembled. The kitchen looks like a raven's roost. "Anyone else? You think that I, a daughter of Hades himself, can simply transfer my powers? No, no. Only my line can preserve the link. Father wouldn't trust anyone else."

"It's an honor, really, though it doesn't always feel that way," Kalum says with a sympathetic look at his mother.

An uncomfortable silence falls upon them.

"So, I suppose that I'll have to visit the villa on my own then. It's not far from here, I'm told," Christabel says.

"No, not far at all," Kalum replies. His dark eyes hold hers for just a moment too long. He's hiding something. Or he's embarrassed. "I can show you the way," he adds.

The realization is not unexpected, but it is still a disappointment. Christabel has spent the better part of the last ten years working to repair the relations between gods and monsters. There is no innocent side, no honorable preservation, among them. If there is anything she's learned, it's that everyone has another motivation. No one is in it for the sheer good of the matter or the betterment of the world.

Everyone wants something.

"I don't have many details," says Christabel. "But I'm told that up until about a month ago the Villa de Valeria was uninhabited."

"Yes," says Kalum. "They are not quite our nearest neighbors, but we had certainly considered the place a few decades away from a ruin. The previous owners were the sorts of people who threw orgies every Wednesday, and to be honest we were quite glad when they finally left town for Luxembourg."

Christabel does not want to ask, but Makaria continues anyway.

"They were worse than vampires," she says in between cracking a long root in half with her hands and then tossing it absently into the boiling pot next to her. "*Mantequero*. Manticores. All those human and animal heads all bobbing up and down and sucking and biting. Quite a mess and a nuisance."

A few decades before, when she hadn't known Hermes, Christabel might have blushed. But now she explores such ribaldry through both an academic lens and a personal one. Though Kalum is delicious to look upon, and he does have the most delicate fingers, she finds herself retreating into her mind to study the facts. Just like Worth, she's learned the hard way that romantic dalliances are dangerous diversions.

"Manticores were not part of the Treaty of Thule," Christabel says, citing her most prized publication to date, if one can call a treaty a publication. "They are infamously difficult to work with and have no notions of propriety, let alone allegiance."

"They weren't always so bad," says Makaria. "But, alas, you're right. We were glad to see them go, and so were the locals. Too many flocks and stragglers ending up dead. You'd think they would have been less brazen about it."

"Regardless of the manticores, my very esteemed hosts, I worry that I am losing time. As I said, a friend of mine has been in possession of this new landlord of the Villa de Valeria a long while, and I am most anxious to see this through," Christabel says. She hopes she cuts an impressive figure, drawing the power of her light around her, but she is doubtful. "I am waiting for my friends, though I fear they are somewhat delayed, so it is up to me to scout the area."

Makaria frowns, drawing her dark hair over her shoulder like a shy maiden. "Of course, of course. We should have considered that you were pressed for time. I will simply have to lend you my Kalum for a while."

For his part, Kalum looks just as shocked as Christabel feels.

"Mother..." He might even be afraid, judging by the tremor in his voice.

"It's not necessary," says Christabel. "He has already been more than kind on the matter. I hadn't anticipated front door service at the airport."

Outside, the wind picks up, bringing with it the heady scent of the ocean churning the refuse of a thousand years. It reminds Christabel of her time with Dr. Frye, and she wishes she were back on that shore with Jenn the Selkie. She also wishes that Nerissa and Ophaniel and whoever else might be on their way would arrive. This was supposed to be their safe house.

With the breeze comes another scent, honeyed and musky, followed by four beautiful butterflies. No, moths. It's nighttime. There would never be butterflies at night.

Christabel knows from her studies that these are *Graesllsia isabellae* and the smell is asphodel. She is about to ask a question about the smell and the unlikely guests when Makaria lets out a gasp.

"Oh, no."

That isn't exactly what she says, for she switches to Greek for her exclamation, and the little butterflies alight on her shoulders, then begin crawling up her face. Christabel realizes it ought to be a pleasant sight, and yet it disturbs her. The smell is too strong, the moths almost frenzied.

"I thought he was just being difficult," Makaria says, as if conversing with the butterflies. "He's always up in arms about some insult or another, and when he said that it was Artemis, well, I simply couldn't..." She groans, talking to the wall, now. "And then she comes in and I can practically see Hermes' hands all over her!"

Instead of making eye contact, or offering any sliver of an explanation, Kalum regards his mother with growing unease. He wrings his hands. His eyes widen. He takes a step forward, gently, as if he were trying to prevent a frightened colt from rearing.

Then words come out of Makaria's mouth. It is a beautiful voice, Christabel cannot deny it, and it rumbles from the very bottom of the worlds.

It is the voice of death.

My sister's daughter is captured. They will take her; they will bleed her. There is no room for her down here. They will leave her to oblivion, undying and unliving.

"Grandfather," says Kalum, falling to his knees before his mother. "What is this?"

I told my daughter, your mother, that there were plots winding their way in the above world. That they would wait until I could not interfere, for it is winter and I cannot travel. My wife lights the other side of the world. But Apollo's sister...she carries the guilt we all do and was brought under false pretenses.

"What do we do?" Christabel has not asked such a question in time out of mind. Typically, people ask her this question, as she has the gift for prioritization and action, a combination she finds most creatures—be they god, human, or monsters—simply do not possess. But she has never been involved in a drama of this magnitude, with true gods and goddesses battling for their survival.

Ah, Monoceros.

She hates that name.

Famed light. You and my niece Artemis are born of a similar light. The same melody of the universe formed eons ago. You will find your answers, and you will find your betrayal there. Your friends hasten toward you.

"I will stay with Mother," Kalum says suddenly, as if it is the most courageous decision of his lifetime. But the words are hardly out of his mouth when Makaria's eyes light up with a deep blue flame, and her teeth glow with the effort of the power coursing through her.

You will help the Monoceros. She is your opposite. She is bright. She is brave. But she will need measures of the other to survive. You do not fight a creature of blood and bone, nor of ichor and bramble.

The enemy of the stars comes to us now.

～

The "enemy of the stars" makes little sense to Christabel, but then again, she long ago realized that sense does not equal her reality. Nothing about her friends, nothing about her existence, makes a great deal of logic. She is forever a living conflict, drawn to desire, and yet prevented from sating herself. A human form and an animal form, living together in harmony, yet always lingering like an unresolved chord...

She has done brave things before. She has put herself before a great beast consuming the souls of supernatural beings. She has tried to sacrifice herself for the love of her life—she can say that now, if only to herself —and then she walked away from him because she knew it was the only way toward a semblance of happiness.

Now the brumal expanse of her heart quivers with anticipation and worry, and again with the thundering chorus of joy that comes with impending battle.

The pieces begin to arrange themselves in her mind as she follows Kalum down a moonlit path toward the famed Villa de Valeria. Vivienne is most certainly more than what she seems, for her part in this strange conjunction cannot be mere chance. If the powers that be wanted her dead, it most certainly would have happened sooner. And why involve Artemis? And now, Hades? This location could not have been an accident.

How long had the orchestration gone on? And how old, exactly, was Vivienne?

"You know, I don't think there's much of a difference between lamias and sylphs," Christabel says out loud to Kalum. She has been silent until now, mostly out of respect for his trembling and muttering, but she cannot take it any longer. So she turns to the subject of some of their academic correspondence. "From a mythological perspective, anyway. They'd both be classified as quite similar."

"There are a dozen other topics we could cover, but I'll allow it. I'd always chalked up lamias as daughters of Medusa, or some such," says Kalum. "But I suppose you may be correct."

"Certainly you have read Ovid," Christabel says, the entirety of her opinion of this man resting on his reply.

"Of course, I have."

"Good. Then I will permit you to stay."

She realizes how flirtatious she sounds, and so she barrels through the conversation.

"I'm trying to bring the story here. This 'enemy of the stars' you mentioned. Why would they want Vivienne? Well, Vivienne calls herself a night sylph, which is a rather vague term. She is, more precisely, a *nymph*. Likely the product of a god and or goddess and a mortal being, I had just not considered that she was of Greek origin. She could even be a lesser demigod. Her power appears centered around the cold, and frost in particular, which is made of water. So she could certainly be a *naiad*."

"But your friend Nerissa is a snake, is she not? A gorgon?"

Christabel sees his logic and knows it is in error, but it is still fun to watch him squirm after the clues. "Her middle name is *Melusine*. Which isn't even clever if she was trying to *hide*, now that I think about it. Nerissa is a character from *The Merchant of Venice*, which has no significance other than the character pretends to be a man named Stephano at once point, but the etymology of the name is of Greek derivation and means 'sea nymph.'"

"But she's a lamia. A scaly thing."

"Scales do not make a snake. She bleeds blueish green, like an octopus. And Nymphs don't have to be beautiful by human standards, Kalum. When they do not follow such shapes, they are labeled monsters. But I spent a good deal of my life researching these very situations. Vivienne—

whose name is laughingly a reference to Arthur's Lady of the Lake and, I should say, well after her time—is only considered a monster for her past. She lived a life of sorrow and blood for a long while before beginning... although there is a good deal of wind to her work, as well. Which is odd, considering it is something most often observed in demigods and the like and she is very powerful. Or at least, I recall her being so. I was so young at the time, you understand, having very little in the way of notes."

Sorrow and blood. "They are powerful, connected beings, Vivienne and Nerissa. And if Artemis, and Hades are involved, then it makes me think of what your grandfather said – something about being guilty for misdeeds. There are so many, though. So, so many."

Another moth crosses Christabel's path, and she stares at it.

Artemis. Leda.

Enemy of the stars.

Cygna.

Ophaniel sits at the top of his roof and complains that the Cygna constellation is out of line...

A letter from Nerissa.

"What is it?" Kalum stops and turns, looking Christabel in the eyes.

"The enemy of the stars. Cygna...but I had thought...and it would mean...oh, heavens, Kalum, we've got to hurry up."

A PROMISE FROM A BUTTERFLY

Artemis is beautiful in the way a mountain is beautiful. Cold like the ocean is cold. Vengeful like a bubbling pit of lava. When the gods first realized Vivienne, albeit by another name, into the world, it was only Artemis for whom she lived. Her entire life revolved around the goddess's compass.

Unlike her own wispy figure, the goddess was all thickness and roundness and power. She towered over everyone else, dwarfed even her brother Apollo. Artemis was a hunter, the power of a trained predator deep in her bones and her every movement. Vivienne—though then they called her Aura—always felt that Artemis kept her around as a point of contrast. Look at Aura; she is so thin and underfed, her breasts so small, her bones so sharp. For the child of a Titan, she should be grand, but she is only frail and full of breezes.

Vivienne can't remember why she said what she did, or what drew her to boast of her own beauty. She knows she was happy with Artemis, that she never wanted for anything. The hunt was her life, and she knew only contentment as she drifted upon the winds and chased the fleetest prey.

But she spoke the words. She had too much to drink. She was soaking herself in the water, naked with the hunting party, and she teased Artemis for her large breasts, teased her for the thickness of her limbs. "It would be difficult for a lover to encircle an oak when they can have a willow."

Artemis did not laugh.

She was furious. But Aura felt as if she had a right to challenge the goddess. Aura was, after all, the daughter of a Titan, too. Why should she not have her fun?

Then Artemis spoke.

And Nemesis listened.

"Behold your goddess," Bastille says, holding out his arms like a circus conductor. "Oh, Aura. It took so long to bring all of this together. Ages and ages, my dear. But you remember, don't you? You remember Cygna? This makes so much sense now, doesn't it?"

Artemis hangs her head, dark hair coiling down her bare chest. They have made her a mockery. And even Vivienne, who has plenty of distaste for the goddess, feels the pain of it. The wrongness of it.

She had told Nadine the story, mostly. As if Aura had been her mother. Because it was safer to have that distance. For centuries, Vivienne supposes, she even began to believe it. Separating herself from the pain was a way of enduring.

Vivienne is trying hard to put the pieces together, working even harder to dredge up the right memories and not the worst memories. Because there was a time when she was...not Aura, not Vivienne, but a creature much worse and baser. A justified monster, perhaps, but a horrific one. Her eyes stream with tears.

She feels clammy. She is frozen, though. And the metal at her wrists bites into her skin, and she can feel that it is cold, which is so strange. All her life, the cold and the wind have been her friends; but now, when she could use them most, they are outside of her grasp.

Bastille is looking at her through his strange, hooded orange eyes.

"Why am I here?" Vivienne asks at last, finding it the best of her options. Not for the first time she wishes Nerissa was here with her. She would have a clever phrase. Hell, even the unicorn would be preferable to being alone.

Then she appears. Out of nothing. Cygna. A mortal, yes. But cut into the world as if in glass. She wears rings on all her fingers, bright silvery trinkets that match what Bastille carries on his person. Her hair is shorn short, square, at her chin, her clothes practical. If not for her strange sharpness, and that she stepped into the room from a black hole in the wall, she would be almost unremarkable.

Cygna looks disappointed, puffing out her bottom lip. "Come now, it hasn't been that long, Aura, has it? Am I that forgettable? Aside from you, I may have been a true competitor if not for my pestilent sister."

Vivienne stares at Cygna's face; tries to remove the modern trappings. Longer hair, a lighter shade. Homespun, perhaps. A diadem on her head. Long, red-tipped fingers...

"Philonoe," Vivienne says, reaching back through the scarred lines of her mind, the compartments she'd burned away for centuries. "But how are...how are you *alive?*"

Philonoe was a daughter of Leda and King Tyndareus, sister to Helen, Clytemnestra, Pollux, and Castor. A footnote in history, but a devoted priestess of Artemis. A mortal.

Yes, they had been together as friends. Vivienne used to plait her hair.

"Ah, but that is the crux of the matter, isn't it?" Cygna smiles widely, showing her even teeth. She is remarkably well-preserved for someone so old, a mortal thousands of years in the making. "Do you remember that night? When I found you? What I said to you?"

Vivienne does not remember the words, no. But she knows the night that Cygna speaks of. The name makes more sense now; she is a daughter of Leda. She should have made the connection.

"Artemis remembers."

Artemis struggles in her alabaster prison, and Vivienne notices that even her hands are bound. Clever. Gypsum, alabaster, the prized component of the Titans. The only thing that might keep an Olympian down. In immense measures, of course. Which Vivienne suspects is below her, as well.

"Tell her, Artemis. Tell her what happened," Cygna presses.

"I do not need to hear it," Vivienne says, fingers shaking, aching. Her body, bereft of its magic, is like an open wound. "I know what happened. I remember Dionysus. I remember the horror. I remember..."

"After you killed your child," Cygna says lightly, to Vivienne, "I came to you in your sickbed, and I promised you we would give Artemis her due. After spiriting your son away, of course. I promised you and promised you and promised you."

That part, Vivienne does not recall. Truth be told she remembers only the barest of glimmers of Cygna, of Philonoe, at all. She was mortal, then. And mortals, at that point in her long life, did little to impress her. They were like shadows, little butterflies flitting in and out of existence. How could she remember a promise from a butterfly?

But she remembers her sons. And the blood of her child on her lips. And the feeling of Dionysus ravaging her body, the blood flowing between her legs, and the chill wind that took her heart.

"By then," Cygna continues, "Artemis had given me her gift. As she did to my sister Bolina, her gift at the hand of Apollo. *Immortality.* It seemed like such a boon at first. But time went on and, oh, I tried so hard to kill myself. I flayed myself; I burned myself; I threw my body to snakes and manticores and beasts of any kind, and still, nothing."

"Until she found me," Bastille says. He has been so quiet that Vivienne starts at his voice. There is warmth in his tone now. "Until she met another who had been wronged by the Olympians."

There was no doubt that the Olympians were wretched, warped, disturbed individuals. It was no surprise they made enemies along the way. But Cygna and Bastille weren't just looking for revenge; they were looking for utter annihilation.

"I'm surprised it took you that long to find someone else," Vivienne says, finding her inner calm. "The list is long and exhaustive. You must have had certain criteria to narrow your options so. And a very, very long time wasted."

Bastille grins. "Oh, but you weren't easy to find, Aura. And we had our minds on a particular Olympian, and you had reinvented yourself so many times we weren't sure it was still you. Besides, we needed to try the magic dampening on someone powerful enough. The metals we found," he holds up his hand, "protect and preserve, depending on the form and function."

"But you've captured me," Vivienne says. "You've brought me here. And there. And everywhere in between. You bargained with Barqan, you ordered me to perplex the streets of Cairo with death masks, and now you've kept me chained for another decade. Why? If you wanted my help, why didn't you merely ask?" As if she would have agreed.

Cygna gives Vivienne a pitying look. "What is a decade or two to you, my dear? But a blip on the radar of life. A mere gadfly on the back of an enormous wildebeest. In Cairo, your powers proved too strong. You made contact with the lamia and your other friends. I couldn't bring you in on the plan until you were somewhat cowed. So you could understand where the power truly lay now."

There are nearly one million words in the English language, and over the millennia Vivienne du Lac has learned a great many of them. She has spoken Greek, Etruscan, Scythian, Phoenician, and every Latinate language known to man, as well as a sprinkling of Basque, Old Norse, and Finnish, her personal favorite. But there is one word that particularly bothers her. And Cygna uses it with the precision of a woman who knows a great deal more information about Vivienne than she had expected. *Cowed.* For the first time in an age, she imagines pulling out Cygna's heart, freezing it and laughing as it shatters into little flecks of red snow.

"You were *extremely* powerful," Bastille corrects, taking out his glasses and cleaning the lenses of one and then the other. "And quite devoted to your friends and the mortal world. But as you can see, they are a comedy of errors. We've been keeping an eye on them, to make sure, and they're still in London caring for that winged thing. And even if they do reach us, we have a variety of protections in place. As you have learned, we've refined our approach."

Winged thing?

Vivienne keeps her face impassive. Never has Bastille given her news. Not even a whisper. She hasn't even known for certain if her friends are alive.

"What the basilisk is trying to say," Cygna says, leaning on the alabaster plinth grown around the goddess, "is that we want your help yes, perhaps. You weren't just given the gifts of your progenitors, the power of wind, but in Zeus's curse, you were given another. Water. Though, thankfully it doesn't seep out of your breasts like in the stories. What a ridiculous notion."

Artemis won't look at her. Vivienne wonders if she knows what happened; she must. But what of the other part? How after her rape, after Vivienne devoured her own children, Zeus came to her and cursed her.

Or so he said.

So everyone thought.

Yes, Zeus stood before her and shouted his decree. He banished her from Greece, he threw down thunder from Olympus and made her drink a rank potion that tasted of salt and brine because she had dared to challenge Artemis.

When Zeus left, and Aura felt nothing, she remained rooted to the ground, shaking, bewildered. Still mad, yes, but with a clarity that only the fear of a god such as he could engender.

Hermes appeared out of the brush with a ram by his side. He explained that he had switched the draught from Zeus, and what she had sipped was only a mixture he'd concocted from saltwater and ram's blood.

He brought her to a shallow pool. He soothed her skin with salves; he combed the blood and burrs from her hair. He sang softly the whole time but said nothing more for a long while.

The sun was rising again when Aura began to untangle the webs of her own heart, and Hermes sat with her while she wept. He gathered her tears in a vial and said quiet words over it, and then told her to drink of it. Her stomach burned with the power of the drink, but then it cooled her mind and soul.

"You will never be whole again," he said, "as so many of us who are ruined by my family. But I will give you something new. I like to change the threads of our story when I can, and I see in you a fellow wanderer, and a conveyor of souls, though perhaps in a different way. Sleep, Aura, sleep, and awake knowing you have as many chances in life as you can imagine. You can rise anew, make for yourself a new name, a new life, a new purpose. It may take a thousand years, but you will find it."

And now Vivienne sits at the crux of a chance in life.

She knows what is coming next.

These sorts of beings—whether they are gods or not, and whether they see themselves as good or not—want something from her. Want her power. Want her mind. Want her experience. It's one of the reasons she struck out on her own so long ago, why she turned her work toward more mortal goals along with monster rehabilitation.

If they were ever really monsters to begin with.

She thinks, not for the first or last time, that they should reconsider the meaning of the word.

Vivienne does not deny she harbors anger toward Artemis; more than anger. She holds a deep, soul-aching fury. But she has healed it with time, though the scar still stands. And she is not alone. Cygna is not wrong that the Olympians left nothing but death in their wake. But this? Were they real allies, they would never have resorted to making her stoop.

They are afraid of her, just as she was fearful of Barqan without his shackles.

"We want your help," Cygna says. "You can help us banish Artemis forever. And then, one by one, her brothers and sisters. To the Void. To the endless nothing. They will not sleep. They will not breathe. But they will be surrounded by blackness and know every agonizing minute."

FIRE AND FURY

Nerissa lives in a world built on overextended neurons, adrenaline gone mad, and the constant sensation that the very fabric of her physical and arcane self is being pulled to the edge of consciousness, reason, and madness.

She is keenly aware that she is as close to death as she will ever be—or has been, for that matter. And that is no small task. She can recall dozens of fights, altercations, blemishes, and even wars that have left her broken and bruised, but none of them felt like this.

It is as if she is on two planes of existence.

No, maybe three.

There is the corporeal world of Earth that she knows well. Her body, writhing and wriggling in Dr. Plover's office, remains there save for two left arms. They are clasped together—she can feel her phantom fingers grasping in a death grip—somewhere colder and darker and emptier than any oblivion she has ever dreamed of, and somehow it seeps through her consciousness into this third world.

A dream world.

Not the Fae. She would know that. She has run from it so many times that it's almost as familiar as London by now, though, perhaps, easier to navigate.

And she cannot explain it for the life of her, but in this in-between place, she feels closer to Vivienne than she's ever been. She can almost smell the myrtle and honeysuckle that always seems to cling to her; she keeps half expecting to see a shadow of her or hear her voice.

But where is Nerissa now?

She has no eyes to close or open, no body to feel directly. It is as if she lives inside of the pain, inhabiting the pathways and doorways woven together in her very being.

Perhaps that isn't so off. Nerissa imagines Kit might have a similar explanation—she is either coping with the pain by creating a sub-stratum inside her consciousness or else she has truly gone mad.

Though, and not for the first time in her life, Nerissa feels as if madness is merely a moniker for what dull minds cannot understand. And that it might be a relief.

The pain moves through her like lightning, over and over again, but does not increase in its severity. Nerissa wonders if it's possible to increase in severity at this point.

It is then, just as she feels closer to the answer to her current state of consciousness, that she becomes aware of a sharp smell. It's spicy and vegetal and reminds her of Cairo. It takes her a moment to realize what it is since she isn't smelling through her nose or any other discernible orifice.

Then she *sees* for the first time since leaving her physical body. But it feels more like a projection. Nerissa knows what dreams feel like, understands the meanderings of her own subconscious; this is not such an occurrence.

She is in a glade, surrounded by bay laurel on every side. Clusters of the plant grow what she would assume would be waist-high if she had such a vantage point. It's difficult to tell.

The sky is a strange shade of robin's egg blue, shifting from a greener version to a more azure hue the longer she lingers on it. The ground is covered in moss and birds fly overhead.

And there is a man.

No, not a man.

A god.

Nerissa is tired of gods by now, but at least she's got the wherewithal to know she's in the presence of one. It has caused some amount of distress and embarrassment in the past to think of them as anything other. But to her credit, they do have a habit of concealing their power and wreaking havoc on the general public.

However, this god is unlike any of the gods she's seen before. He is not concealed in an underworld as Serket and Heqet were. He springs out of this strange Earth—and she is sure it is still Earth, somehow, or at least a strong projection of one—and she sees that he is *indeed* the sun.

Apollo. He stands in perfect, pure nudity, every muscle and vein carved with precision across his body, every golden hair placed with expert care. His hair curls over his bronzed forehead then falls in longer locks down his back. Somehow, though he wears absolutely no adornment, he seems gaudy in his presence; too much gold and glitter for Nerissa. For the first time since vanishing from the pain, she is glad her real eyes aren't looking. She might feel nauseated.

"Daughter of Titans," he says, and his voice is not anywhere near as impressive as Nerissa expects. Perhaps it's the transference. He sounds quite ordinary, but by the cadence of his words, she suspects he thinks the effect is much grander. So is the plight of many a naked man, she imagines.

"Nerissa is good enough," she responds, though she's not sure how. Her voice comes from behind her. Or below her. It's hard to tell without ears.

Apollo looks confused, his glimmering exterior turning oddly wooden as he takes a step closer. "You're a nymph," he says. "You're the daughter of Titans."

"I never thought of it that way," she says. The conversation is a welcome change from constant pain. "I just figured I was the unwanted chaff of some ill-informed coupling."

"You don't know your parentage?"

"It's never really come up, but you're not the first one to ask. If it weren't for my friend Vivienne, I'd still be stalking the English Moors and sucking on anything with a pulse. It wasn't a pleasant life. It's more difficult now to get a decent meal, but it's significantly less exhausting."

"You befuddle me, creature."

"I befuddle myself on most days. But, as you say, I grew up without a family, and so I've had to make my own. How is that so strange? I am no monster, really; I am no worse than you."

Apollo stops and runs a hand through his shimmering golden hair. He appears most frustrated with Nerissa, but she is fatigued and in a great deal of pain.

"I think I'm dying," she says, "so unless you have something to help me through this, I'd prefer to be left alone rather than made to feel guilty about a family genealogy that is irrelevant to my present situation."

"I am the god of healing."

"I'm aware."

"I can help you."

"My arms are severed from the rest of me, and I think they're in a void somewhere."

"That isn't terribly specific."

"I'm afraid in my current state being specific is difficult."

"You really don't want to know?"

"Know what?"

"Your parentage."

Apollo doesn't seem to want to let this go, and Nerissa is losing patience, if patience can exist in mere consciousness. Or dreaming. Or both.

Give a little sweetness if you want something in return. It was one of Vivienne's better pieces of advice, along with making sure one's underpinnings were always clean and to avoid licking people's hands when proffered.

Since Nerissa hasn't yet decided if she's dreaming or not but has accepted that she is probably dying, she figures that Apollo really wants to tell her. He's a gossip, as she has always suspected. One who shines on everyone and sees everything, after all. He probably revels in bringing light to dark places.

"I am Nerissa Melusine Waldemar, or at least that is what I have called myself since I could form a coherent thought," she says at last. "I don't see how knowing my parents could change anything."

Apollo looks absolutely elated. He presses his delicate fingertips together just below his nose, accentuating just how shockingly symmetrical his features are. It is alarming, Nerissa thinks, looking into a face without flaw. Nothing about him can be improved. And that is almost sad.

"How delightful," Apollo says. "It's as if you knew all along."

"Pardon? I'm dying."

"Doubtful."

"What?"

The god sighs dismissively. "I knew you for a chthonic the moment I saw you. *Dying* isn't in your vocabulary, so you can stop blubbering about that. Your mother's name was Melinoë. Melusine is so very close, isn't it? Regardless, she had a tryst with one of those flighty river gods, and along you came. I believe there was some discussion as to what to do. You do realize Melinoë is a daughter of Persephone, so we're practically cousins."

He says this in a manner that does not indicate any such familial relations but rather him trying mightily to make the situation brighter than it is. Or more fascinating. It is neither.

"I'm a snake," says Nerissa.

"Of course you are. Your father was probably Archeron; at least that is my guess. So he flowed through the mortal realm and into the Underworld, which would explain how he met your mother, I suppose. I never asked. It is ever difficult to keep the Potamoi apart from one another. It's likely that you get your...ah, looks from him."

"Why are you saying I can't die?"

"Because you were born of the rivers of the Underworld and a nymph steeped in the River Styx. A mad bird, really, but a friendly one. I suppose you ended up lost in the shuffle at some point. It happens. I wouldn't take it personally."

"I don't."

This new information feels like bubbles inside of Nerissa's consciousness. Or like bees buzzing. She doesn't wish to show that it has somehow changed her, but she knows it has. She feels it in her marrow.

"Not that you aren't still a monster, by some definition," Apollo says with a yawn. "But aren't we all?"

"Can you heal me? I'm in a great deal of pain."

"I can heal anything I can put my hands on, and some things I can't. But first, we must locate those missing appendages of yours, which may prove difficult. But now that you're here, I should be able to trace them back. Give me a moment."

Apollo claps his hands, and a white raven careens from the flock in the sky and lands on his shoulder. He leans back and whispers in its ear, and the thing tilts its head side to side as if listening. Nerissa has always liked ravens and birds in general, feeling a kind of kinship to them, but she is distracted and doesn't ask any more questions.

What would Vivienne say? Nerissa has built a whole story for herself, a place in the cosmos: a lonely monster on the Moors rescued by a gallant nymph, noble of mind and soul who turned from her dark ways.

It still smells of honeysuckle. Why does it smell of honeysuckle?

The white raven flies off, and Nerissa stays for an indeterminate amount of time as Apollo goes stiff as a statue, eyes closed, hands pressed to his ears, brow furrowed in concentration. She tries to push out the questions and concerns from her thoughts, but all she is currently is thoughts, and it is therefore impossible to run from them.

So she thinks of Vivienne. And she wonders that she has never asked about her background. What is a sylph, anyway? As Christabel believes, all monsters stem from the divine, regardless of the pantheon. They have never belonged, not really. And Worth, least of all. And Ophaniel...

Apollo shudders and straightens up, his eyes shooting open. They are white through and through, no sign of an iris or a pupil, but the look of surprise is unmistakable.

"You cannot kill a god," he whispers. "But you can trap it indefinitely."

"What's that?"

Apollo begins to pace back and forth, pulling in his bottom lip. It makes him look like a toddler. A gleaming, naked, physically perfect toddler. "You said a void."

"I did. But then you had to go and drag up all the sordid details of my chthonic past, didn't you?"

"I am going to have to...oh, I hate this part. I can't believe Artemis would be this stupid...I can't believe...Cygna! That goat."

There is a good deal more muttering, but Nerissa doesn't have time to process it because Apollo bull rushes her. That's the only explanation she can give. Whatever presence of hers exists is suddenly thrust out and squeezed into a thin membrane of being and then stretched, pulled, and popped back into consciousness.

She feels warm hands on her face, feels the sun's first rays of morning melting her cold heart, casting its light on her skin. Her skin! She can feel her skin! Something wet touches her lips, and it is sweet, and she usually is more of a savory person, but drinks it down to the dregs.

"Nerissa, it's time to wake up."

It's Apollo's voice, but calmer this time. Grounded. Muffled.

She opens her eyes and sees Apollo, or at least a version of him, standing beside her in Dr. Plover's townhouse. He is a little taller than Kit and wears clothing that was fashionable half a century ago. But it's classic enough that she supposes it passes.

In the light of the mortal world Apollo's hair is dark brown shot with copper, and his skin is a rich olive tone. His eyes are blue rimmed with green, and his teeth are so startlingly white that they are disturbing when he smiles.

Still, Nerissa is not dead. And she is in a manageable amount of pain. And she is incredibly hungry.

Those in the room gasp at his appearance and Nerissa's sudden awakening.

"Hello, everyone," says Apollo. "I'm Apollo. I'm here to help you save the world."

OF TINY, WELL-DRESSED BEINGS

When Worth returns to the living room, a cup of coffee in his hand, still thinking about Christabel, Nerissa is sleeping. But she is not quiet for long, yet in the short time she's unconscious, Worth observes the lamia as her eyes glow from beneath her lids. It's an ungodly sight—or perhaps a godly one, he is still trying to figure those sorts of things out—and it leaks down her cheeks like golden rain. Then comes a heady smell like Mediterranean cooking, that spicy bite of bay leaf he's always associated with such cuisine.

Dr. Plover tilts his head this way and that, and says, "This was not what I had anticipated."

"I thought you were a good doctor," Kit says, heat in her voice turning it almost to a growl. She's going a bit feral, and Worth can't blame her. He'd felt the same about someone else before.

Don't think about her. I don't like it when you think about her.

Well, I can't very well help it. I think she's the only thing keeping me here, old chap. Christabel is very likely the only thing preventing me from going the way of a half-remembered melody in your head, and I'm not particularly keen on all those loose ends.

You were *you* for a long time. Not long in angel years, but long in immortal years, to be sure. I suppose it'll wear off eventually.

Worth is surprised that Ophaniel sounds almost sad about that. But now there is a great deal of screaming, and the presence of Ophaniel rears back within Worth, and he staggers into a buffet table, knocking glass-ware off. He doesn't have time to react, however, because Nerissa sits up bolt straight with a blast of light, her arms out before her as if preparing for a blow.

Arms. Two arms. She is back in her glamour.

One arm is quite familiar. The other is made of some metal material. Bronze, perhaps?

Oh, and there is also a man standing before them. He's wearing the strangest conglomeration of clothes Worth has ever seen, so bizarre that even his limited sartorial taste is offended. It isn't that the man isn't handsome—he is that and then some. Worth is quite positive the man standing before them is the most attractive person of human form he has ever beheld. The eyes could be no more almandine; the hair no more perfectly curled; the skin no more sweetly curved and kissed by the sun.

But the uninvited guest is wearing a toga. And over the toga, a Regency-era jacket in vivid puce, tied with a thick red kerchief about the neck. He also has a crown of ornately twisted leaves in his hair, studded now and again with stones of varying shades.

And a cape. He is wearing a velvet cape. It is green. And it appears formed from moss. And not in a good way.

The man has omitted shoes.

Nerissa is coughing and hacking now, however, and that takes the attention away from the guest. She is shivering from foot to fang, and Kit is putting her arms around her and is she crying?

Worth is feeling a bit off at the moment. Ten years mostly shoved to the back of Ophaniel's mind like an afterthought, and now he's thrust again into this emotional torrent. Usually, Nerissa would be there to comfort him in such a situation, bastion of unfeeling frigidity that she often is. But now she is holding Kit back, and letting the *kitsune* stroke her hair, and Dr. Plover is hopping around them, trying to get questions in.

But then the guest speaks, and everyone falls silent.

"HELLO!"

His voice is musical, arresting, in the way French horns come unbidden in an ill-conceived symphony.

"MY NAME IS APOLLO. I HAVE-"

"Not so loud," Nerissa says through gritted teeth. "You'll wake the whole neighborhood."

Apollo looks around, though Worth doesn't think he is in any way concerned about his behavior. Still, rolling his eyes, he takes a deep breath and tries again.

"Greetings, you of mortal derivation."

"We're not mortals," Dr. Plover says. "Sir? Lord? I'm…"

"Not mortals?" Apollo tries, but he does not seem prepared for such an occasion.

"I'm a celestial," Worth says, adding, "Mostly. Most days. For much of the day. Right now."

"It isn't very straightforward," Nerissa adds. "But these are my friends, and they are here to help you."

"We are?" Kit and Worth and Dr. Plover say this all at once.

Nerissa holds out a calming hand. Not the shining one, the regular one. "Apollo found me wandering around. I was being torn apart after those *things* got to me."

"The bleaknesses," says Kit with a jut of her chin. No one will argue the point, Worth is quite certain.

"Yes. *Those.* I was wandering around, likely headed to the Underworld. My Underworld. You see—"

"You're one of Styx's progeny," Dr. Plover says lightly. "I could have told you that. A lamia doesn't simply appear out of nowhere; nor does Medusa. We all begin as something. Well, except for me. I have always been a bird."

"And a fine bird," says Apollo.

Worth is worried for a moment that this will devolve into a long flirtation before anyone understands what is happening.

Thankfully, Kit, as usual, retrieves the conversational reins.

"Why does Nerissa have a metal arm?" The *kitsune* is cradling the metal contraption, examining it, and the lamia isn't concerned with this overt show of affection. "It's very bright and doesn't match the rest of her."

Your friends confuse me.

You are not alone, Ophaniel.

Apollo takes a deep breath, but Worth can tell this is simply an affectation. The god doesn't need to breathe.

"Your friend Nerissa came to me. Rather, I found her, ambling her way down to the River Styx to cross that final border. Her pain was so great it enveloped her like thick silk, nay, like a feathered corona of raven wings, prepared to escort her—"

"I almost died. He found me. He fixed my arms with this contraption.

It's confusing." She takes a sharp breath, wincing. "The bleaknesses are from a bitch named Cygna who has Artemis. And probably Vivienne."

Nerissa's interruption makes Worth stifle a grin. It is good to see her again.

～

K it is suffering. And yet it is sweet. She felt the last wisps of doubt leave, that thin veil between amusement and slight repulsion for the lamia, replaced with love, but now she sits at its precipice of this veritable cliff. Kit was positive Nerissa was going to die, or else be sundered from her forever, and that thought sent her agile mind into a thousand dark alleyways.

She resigned herself to it.

But now, Kit stares directly into Nerissa's eyes and the lamia does not look away. She also does not move Kit's hand from her own. Cold though it is, the mechanism is a wonder, but Kit isn't pretending that she's holding on to Nerissa for rational reasons.

The bird doctor is trying fiercely to talk to the man-boy god. What kind of god looks like that, Kit can't help but wonder. He should be at least a foot taller. As it is, he looks like an overgrown prepubescent boy, with distractingly chiseled features. And clothing that even Kit knows is out of place.

"We've known for some time that Cygna was a threat," says the man-god, brushing his unnaturally perfect curls from his abnormally smooth brow. If he's trying to pass for human, he's doing a miserable job of it. "She has written scathing notes to we Olympians for a while now, but after a time one gets rather immune to the charms of a mortal threat."

"This must tie back to Cairo," Nerissa says, and Kit feels her lean into her touch, half-thinking. It makes Kit so glad she wants to yip. But she does not. Generally speaking, even the most progressive among immortals don't appreciate such animal responses. "Vivienne was being used to craft masks, masks that granted people visages and powers often attributed to them—and paying for items not in coin but with stones. But then they found something they needed, and they were gone. We lost track of them."

"Christabel thought they had gone aquatic," Kit said. "You know, on the seas. As a rule, most of us struggle to keep our gifts about us on a good day. But having them afloat would mean it was even more difficult to track them using normal means."

"And you have all been preoccupied with Ophaniel. And me," says Worth, looking timid.

Kit doesn't like the idea of figuring out this puzzle. But then, she has sat on this problem for ages now. Christabel wrote to her on the matter once or twice, encouraging the *kistune* to tell Nerissa of her true feelings. But Kit has never really been in love before. She has never trusted people long enough for it.

And now they're closer to finding Vivienne than they have ever been.

And Nerissa loves Vivienne. And has loved her for centuries.

Kit feels herself pulling away. And Nerissa does not notice or does not seem to react when Kit is no longer holding the lamia's hand.

"What is so dangerous about this Cygna?" Dr. Plover lands across from the man-god, as if he wants a better look. "She's the source of this black magic?"

"She named herself after the constellation. After the place in the constellation where time itself folds in and vanishes. Where magic and life cease to exist in time. She had spoken of a desire to give us eternal damnation, in utter blackness—but sustained consciousness—forever." The boy man-god speaks the words as if he's giving a decree.

"Then why send the bleaknesses to us?" Nerissa asks.

"Because you have something she wants. Or someone. Or she's just ready to destroy you." The boy man-god looks dubiously from face to face. "My guess is the one with the wings," he says at last, almost dismissively. "But you all have potential."

"Why bother with us at all? Even presuming that Vivienne is alive, there are dozens of other more powerful, far cleverer, beings out there."

"Perhaps you underestimate her. Vivienne…yes, the other one. Your friend. The one making the masks." The boy god's face darkens, mirth evaporating from his features. He looks terrifying. She cannot explain it other than that. In the absence of joy, his face is a horror.

The man-boy god sighs deeply. "Oh, Artemis. Oh, sister mine. You jealous twat."

They decide to retire for the evening, and Dr. Plover graciously offers his home. Of course, given his lavish, and expansive residence—large for a single man let alone a single bird—it shouldn't come as a surprise. But Kit gets the sense that it's a grander gesture than she can comprehend. One more of many odd social cues beyond her general understanding. These foreigners forever baffle her, even after almost a decade in London.

Kit is given a small room with a wide window, and she spends most of the dark hours looking outside while Nerissa speaks with Apollo and Dr. Plover about Vivienne.

Like most immortals, sleep is voluntary for her. Unlike most immortals, she has learned to like sleeping. It is a deep meditation for her, a time to reorder her often cluttered mind and rearrange her mental furniture.

But tonight, the furniture is too cluttered and heavy to move.

She worries about Nerissa so much that her chest hurts with it. She starts to write a note to her, to send across the house, but then she cannot find the right words. Everything comes out upside down.

Kit is half considering a nighttime walk when someone knocks softly on the door. Two steps toward it and she knows it's Worth. He smells of lavender with a hint of citrus.

"I saw the light," he says somewhat apologetically.

"You've got regular clothing on," she says. "I suppose the other one is resting?"

"I think the 'other one' is afraid of us."

"I do not blame him. We're a rather curious bunch. I never imagined a group of people would keep me among their ranks, but here I am. And no one asks me to leave anymore." She pauses and says, "I haven't had a chance to say, but it's quite nice having you here again. I must admit, I determined that the chance of seeing you again was closer to zero than a positive number. But here you are."

Worth's face pinches into a regretful, strained smile. "I don't know how long I'll have. Ophaniel has every capability of taking me over again. And I suppose we're one and the same, so I shouldn't be sad. And yet I am."

"Some people wish for reincarnation. I suppose you get two lives at once. In some ways that's lucky, you could say."

"You always have a way of phrasing things, my dear," Worth says, and there is genuine warmth in it. "But I'm not here to play philosopher.

Tonight, I'd like to talk about a simpler matter. Well, two matters. And neither is simple. I'm trying to be polite, and I'm afraid I'm terrible at this whole business."

"You're even harder to follow than when you were Worth most of the time," she says to him. In times past she would have playfully hit him on the shoulder, but he is too angelic for that now. "But I assume you want to talk to me about Nerissa."

Worth, as ever, is surprised by her candor. "How did you know?"

"You were looking at me quite intently during today's events. I had a feeling you were thinking about Christabel, and how you haven't seen her in the longest time, but you clearly can't be with her—though Ophaniel does like to talk about her—and you were looking at me the way you looked at her, once. Or at least her from a distance."

"I suppose I was a little jealous. Wistful. But also, in such matters, I like to think I have good experience to share with you."

"I know I should speak with her."

"You should. Why haven't you?"

"Because… because…" Kit tries to make the words come out sensical. But it's ever the struggle when the lamia is involved. "I can't even start to imagine what our lives would be like…together. I'm not the type of person to feel this way. I'm mercurial. I'm unpredictable. I don't like what it does to my narrative."

Worth laughs and Kit remembers just how much she used to like hearing that sound. Vibrant and low and boisterous. "Oh, Kit. Love isn't about fitting a narrative."

"I suppose you have all the answers to love, then."

"I most certainly do not. But I hypothesize that it's love that's kept me here, within Ophaniel, for this long. And love that has made me stronger. Love for Christabel, certainly. For Vivienne, too. And for Nerissa. And Alma. And yes, even you."

"Love feels like a complication none of us can afford right now."

"Love plays by its own rules. If a bleakness were to appear right now and swallow you whole, and cast you into the forever darkness it promises…what would you do?"

"I'd find Nerissa's arms and bring them back."

"Kit."

She relents and finds herself biting back tears. This time the only words she has to say are not in Worth's language at all but in a tongue far older than even London itself.

Worth sighs and embraces her. She lets him. Though she also wants to bite him. When he speaks, it's in a low, lovely voice, that feels like silk on her soul.

"I know Nerissa might seem like she isn't the warmest of individuals, and if we're considering the temperature of her blood, I'm quite certain that would be true. But I've known her long enough to recognize when someone means more than a simple acquaintance. But I also know that in the centuries we've known one another, I've never seen her...well, happy. Despite everything, despite losing Vivienne, she is happy now. I think she has moved on."

"I'm afraid of what happens if we find Vivienne."

Saying it, finally, brings a weight off Kit's shoulders. She's been biting down on that fear since she first met Nerissa ten years ago.

Worth opens his arms again and Kit accepts the embrace. Outside the window, the sounds of late-night London rise, muffled against the pane.

They stand there for a while, listening to the noise around them, until Worth finally says, "So am I, Kit. So am I. That's what I came here to talk to you about."

"But I don't know Vivienne. I've never met her. I only know of her through Nerissa, and while she has kept some secrets to herself, it's abundantly clear that Vivienne is Nerissa's savior."

"In some ways, I suppose; but I do think it's also the other way around. Vivienne needs Nerissa, just as Nerissa needs Vivienne. But when Nerissa told Vivienne her true feelings, well, it didn't go so well. You said before that the heart wants what it wants, and sometimes we cannot control things. I think Vivienne is likely sad that she never loved Nerissa in that way; guilty, perhaps, too."

"She has terrible taste," Kit says.

Worth's lips lengthen into a radiant smile. "Well, she was my paramour for quite some time, so I'll have to agree."

Kit almost laughs. Not quite. But she's open to the possibility that she might laugh again sometime soon. "But now?"

"My heart may never love again the way I love Christabel."

"And you're worried about seeing her again? And Vivienne? At the same time?"

Judging by the look of horror on Worth's face, it's just that. "Yes. Well, and I have a letter. For Christabel. If you'd give it to her...in case I'm not, well, me, by the time I see her. Or if things go south. There's just no way of knowing now."

He hands her a slim scroll, tied with a piece of white ribbon. It smells of fresh rain.

Kit nods. "I'd be happy to give it to her."

"I just hope it isn't too late."

"For what?"

Worth frowns. "For everything."

CRUISING

The Wolesley Hornet takes the curves toward the Villa de Valeria with ease. It's nighttime now, and Makaria is at home, but Kalum is in the driver's seat. Christabel notes how nervous he is, how he drums his fingers on the steering wheel in no discernable pattern at all, just a constant percussive inconvenience. She has clearly frightened him. Or the situation has. But then, seeing your mother channel Hades, your grandfather, with blue lights going out of her brain, can't have been easy.

"You didn't have to come," says Christabel, gently. She doesn't want to offend Kalum, but given the circumstances, she's not averse to it if it comes down to it. Dead weight on a mission like this isn't a good idea. "I could have driven myself or walked."

"Grandfather insisted," Kalum says. "And so do I."

"My friends are...well, they ought to have met us by now," she says. "Something has to have stopped them. So that means it might be just left to the two of us to interfere."

"I gathered as much," Kalum says.

The night air is soft on Christabel's skin, mildly humid and smelling of salt. It makes her wish she could visit this place without the threat of obliteration hanging above her head. And that Kalum was a little less dim. He is impossibly handsome in that chthonic way she can't resist. The polar opposite of what lay inside Worth all those years...

"We don't have to talk," she says, half to herself.

"I don't know what to say, Christabel," Kalum explains. He slows the car down and turns onto a back road. Pebbles grind under the tires, crunching as he comes to a stop. "I think I just wish we had met under different circumstances. I've been here with Mother so long I've started to forget that there are other people like us. And once this is over, we'll go back to guarding the pit of Hades, just like always."

Christabel has never entirely understood what it is about her that inspires men to pour out their souls. What she used to find charming she now finds irritating and, truth be told, quite tiresome. But now is not the time for yawning.

"Kalum, I need you to focus on the matter at hand. We don't even know if life will ever get back to normal."

He sighs. "You're right."

"From our conversations, I'm assuming the villa itself is about a half a mile up that hill and toward the seaside," she says, summoning as much sweetness as she can muster.

He looks confused a moment and then nods.

Guilt-stricken, she adds, "We can talk about your family inheritance after this is done, yes? Presuming we're not all sucked into the endless void and suffering for eternity?"

Kalum nods. "I see your point."

"Good," Christabel says. "Now, you've got a job to do."

When they come to a stop at the base of a hill, she doesn't wait for him to open the door for her. Instead, she hops out of the car and stretches in the riding pants she acquired for the trip. It still feels rebellious wearing them, but she started doing so ten years ago, and she isn't about to stop.

"Now, let's go over the plan again," she says, not unkindly.

Kalum grins, a little brightness in his eyes despite the dark. "I wait here until I see you come back or see your friends. And then I give them instructions and tell them what's going on if they don't already know. But...how will they know where to find you?"

"Alma can always find me," says Christabel, tapping her forehead. "And I suspect Kit can, as well. I've got a distinct olfactory imprint."

I t's been some time since Christabel took a physical role in their business, having preferred the academic slant for the last decade or so. She worries at first that she'll be incapable of scaling the side of the hill, but once she gets moving, it's easier to recall her abilities. She had, after all, traveled the Egyptian underworld with Worth, so long ago, before he had transfigured. It had been ages of walking, and at one point she had found herself in full unicorn form.

Christabel takes a break just before rounding the last corner. She can see the back pathway now, to the south side of the villa and barely in view of the sea. Not much further now. She takes a deep breath and closes her eyes, wondering just what it is she's up against. And if she sees Vivienne, then what? Do they talk about Worth? How would she even begin to explain what happened...

"Monoceros."

Of course, he would show up.

Of course.

Turning slowly, she isn't surprised to see him. She didn't heard him approach; she never does. Another Olympian. A *certain* Olympian. He smells of aged wine and olives.

Hermes.

"Why do you all insist on calling me that?" Christabel tries to make light, but it is just in the hope of delaying the inevitable.

"Because it makes your nose crinkle and it's *adorable*."

"Hermes, please."

"Come now, Christabel, have you entirely lost your sense of humor? You were never so frigid with me."

"We are at war. *You're* at war, and you have time for teasing." She is glad of the dim light because her cheeks are on fire.

"Oh, my darling, I have been at war for so long I scarcely know the difference," he says, his voice deep and sad. It makes Christabel want to be in his arms again, to smell his rich scent, and bury her head...

She coughs. "I ah, well, regardless. I need to be on my way, and I don't want any distractions."

"I'm a distraction now, am I? How delightful."

"Hermes. Please."

"Ah, well. If we are all business, I suppose I ought to at least do my duty. I've got a message." He says it proudly, coming more fully into the sparse moonlight. Not that he needs it. Christabel is reasonably certain, and her research supports the hypothesis, that Olympians don't need a light source to be visible. They each have their own inner network of filaments, of sorts, that illuminate or dim their visages at will.

They have met before, and she observed that light very closely. Very, very closely.

Hermes nods, a look of merriment in his eyes. All of him is merriment. Somehow, he is composed of lines of joy, angles of ecstatic motion. He is at once handsome and beautiful, his dark hair falling into his eyes just below a thick band of leather. His body is pleasing, tastefully robed, dark hair on his forearms, chest, legs. And a dark shadow on his strong, fine jaw. She'd kissed it before, and it *was* delightful.

He pauses before speaking, drawing a long breath. "Ah, darling, I forget you are indeed the most beautiful of your kind."

"It's a certainty when I'm the *only* one of my kind," Christabel says, trying to stall while she considers the what the message might be. "Flattery will get you nowhere."

"A god can hope."

"Not if there is no god."

"Yes, Artemis is up there, isn't she? Ah, well, serves her right. I won't be risking my life and limb," Hermes says, sounding almost bored. "I wasn't even planning on coming here, of course, but then Apollo was so up in arms and, well, I can't very well avoid my duty. And he is so insufferably annoying when he's in a snit."

"Apollo sent you?"

Hermes laughs, and it's like a rushing stream. Christabel thinks for a moment that she would like to bathe in that river water, surrounding herself with his undulating laugh, and then she chides herself at the scandalous thought.

"Apollo? No, he doesn't care about you, darling Christabel. No offense."

"None taken."

"It's from the *celestial*. He's with Apollo now."

Damn, then Hermes didn't come of his own volition. It stings a little. She thought she'd gotten over Hermes years ago, after the incident on the Seine, but apparently not. Curse her hot blood and her cold heart.

"I don't...I don't want to read the message."

"No worries, love. No reading necessary. It is merely a message. No print. No scribblings. The good, old-fashioned way."

371

Christabel frowns deep enough that she can feel it twisting toward tears. Not now. Not now. Not now.

"I am trying to save a goddess. I don't have time for Ophaniel."

"You think *I* do? The last thing I wanted was to visit *you* after being so entirely rejected last time."

"Hermes, this is serious."

"It's *always* serious in my family."

She wants to hit him. And kiss him. And it's very confusing. "You don't seem terribly bothered that your cousin, or sister, or whoever she is, might be just moments from destruction."

Hermes scratches the side of his face in a very human gesture, as if his scruff is itching him. Then he shrugs. "I've been around awhile, little *Monoceros*, and while it may surprise you that I'm not rushing to my niece's aide, remember that we're all quite monstrous in our own right. Remember? You fought to prove it. Artemis plays the blushing virgin, whether by necessity or choice, but she's made a lot of enemies. I warned her against this. I even cleaned up after her a few times. I believe you know Vivienne du Lac? That nymph and I have a history. Not like our history, mind you, but, well, if I'm doing this for anyone—as if I had a choice in delivering messages—it would be on account of her. And you, of course."

"So she *is* a nymph," Christabel says, the delight of being correct welling up in her, almost making her laugh.

"Of course, Vivienne du Lac is a nymph. 'Night sylph'? How laughable. I once gave her the chance for another life. Better than going tits up in a fountain like Ovid claimed, don't you think?"

"You mean... *Aura*..."

"You do remember your Ovid."

"My goodness, I presumed she was of god stock, given her age and her astounding abilities, but I've not had a chance to observe her, and while I had about ten candidates I didn't think that she could be *Aura*, of all people. Gods..." The ramifications of what happened to her...

"As delightful as your epiphany is, I suspect that Cygna and her cronies are attempting to win Aura—Vivienne—to their side because they need her for something. I've no idea if she'll take the bait. And your friends aren't too far away. Apollo is bringing them by chariot, if you'd believe it. It's a rickety old thing, but it gets the job done."

"Chariot? That will take too much time. I can't wait."

Hermes shakes his head, looking over his shoulder. "Ah, darling. Apollo's chariot does not go overland." He squints up at the sky, then nods to himself. "You've got at least an hour. Some of us can flit in and out of space; others cannot, especially with a chariot full of riffraff. The dwarf will arrive shortly, though. I can feel her rumbling."

"Well... thank you. I think. I suppose I should be going now."

"The message?"

"I don't want to hear it. Not if it's from Ophaniel. You know about the two of us, Hermes. There are just some things too painful to face head-on."

"I have to deliver it before I go," he says, and he does sound sad, remorseful. He holds out his hand and touches the side of her arm gently.

"No..."

Christabel starts to run, not certain that she's fleeing from the message or Hermes. As if running would matter! Fear of knowing courses through her body, and for the first time since Worth's transfiguring, she feels her form expanding and filling up new space. Her face elongates, her legs lengthen. She feels her chest swell and her hair streaming down her neck. She is on all fours, but then all fours is all she has.

Still, unicorn or no, she cannot escape the words of the god.

"'When I fall asleep, I still see you smiling behind your coffee at El Fishawy.'"

It was a thousand years ago. No, ten years ago. Yet it was so long ago. Across a table, hands brushing, hot coffee streaming up into her nose. His face. Her eyes. She buried it so deep that it felt like it would fossilize. But those words, those places. Cairo conjures up around her in dazzling beauty, a confluence of sounds and smells and the feeling of promise.

That love was possible.

That maybe...

Christabel collides with a rocky outcropping that appears out of nowhere.

But wait.

"Whoa, whoa, Christabel!"

It's Alma.

~

Alma has been waiting because that's what she was told to do. Though, she isn't waiting simply because she was told to do it; she agrees that it's the right call. She can travel distances far faster than those around her, save maybe that celestial, but that doesn't mean she would put herself in danger storming into an unknown situation.

She's dealt with gods before. They were enemies, mostly. Except for Loki. He has always understood her kind better than the rest of the haughty pantheon.

Regardless, she is not dealing with Loki or Freyr or any of the gods she's met personally. It's been so long that she's felt a proper dwarf, but that's not what's bothering her.

What bothers her is that the earth itself feels wrong here.

Finding her friends was far more difficult than it should have been. Usually, she can sense their individual reverberations above her head as she's traveling through the rock veins. But once she arrived about one hundred miles below this actual location, the signals became very difficult to read.

Thankfully, and for the first time in at least ten years, Christabel shed her human visage and went full unicorn. That is strong enough, at least, to pinpoint where Alma should be. And so, as she feels it happening, half sleeping-below the rock, she shudders as the thermal energy of unicorn power careens down through the Earth, and Alma finally has a guide star.

Coming up through the layers of soil is not an easy task this time, however. The ground itself resists Alma as she presses up and through. Usually, the energy exerted is primarily mental, ensuring that she geolocates correctly. But now the resistance burns her skin and makes her eyes see double.

When she finally emerges, Christabel— more or less in her unicorn form, though she's got some stripes this time and her horn is striated—is barreling toward her at top speed and Alma has to shout to get her attention.

"Christabel!"

Christabel rears back, shaking her silver-grey locks, her oversized dark eyes reflecting like glittering stones. To Alma, in comparison to the rest of her horrid friends, this form of Christabel's is the only one worth writing home about.

But it's still terrifying, too. She isn't big, but Christabel possesses an absurdly heinous amount of power when she's in unicorn form. Alma doesn't think she quite understands that.

"Well, at least I found one of you." Alma crosses her arms and levels the unicorn with an even glance. "I thought you weren't looking like that any longer."

"I... didn't know if I could." Christabel shakes her head as if trying to dispel a fly. "It's off around here. I started running away from Hermes, and I just felt my guard slip."

"Hermes again?"

"I don't want to talk about it."

"Very well, but where are the others? I tried to find them, but it's as if they've lost touch with the earth entirely."

"That's because they have. Hermes told me that Apollo let them use his chariot."

Alma blinks and looks toward the starry sky streaked with fog. "That'll make for an entrance."

"If they get here soon enough. But we must hurry. It's not far from here."

It's a good deal more difficult for Christabel to scale the side of the villa due to her hooves and all the gravel. Alma has to pace herself in order to keep the unicorn from falling to the bottom and having to start the whole climb again.

She still doesn't feel right. If there are more bleaknesses about, perhaps that's the trouble. But it is a great deal of sensation for such little creatures. Well, presuming they're still little. Could they be larger?

For once, Alma wishes she was chattier. But she says nothing as they make the ascent together, just looking over her shoulder now and again to Christabel, who does not meet her eyes.

At last, they reach the side of one of the buildings. It's overgrown with vines, and certainly not naturally. From where Alma sees it, the vines are a latticework of art, a filigree of most delicate craft. They twine up and through one another, a dizzying knotwork that recalls old Celtic jewelry. Yet sharper. Purposeful.

It takes just a moment, but Alma sees a flicker at the top of the vines where there's a small window. From all directions little moths fly around, converging at the pinnacle.

"It's beautiful," Christabel says, finally catching her breath. The moths float about in their own dizzying cadence, back and forth, back and forth, making a wild dance of intertwined movement. "It's...Vivienne!"

A silhouette in the window. The smooth brow, a sharp nose, a neck carved as if with a sculptor's hands. The moths are all trying to get to her, through to her, as are the vines.

But someone is there with her. Someone looming over her. Someone making her scream.

A SIMPLE SUPPLICATION

Vivienne didn't give them an answer. How could she? Now she sits by her small, moonlit window, stroking Nadine's warm brown hair, letting the strands slip through her fingers repeatedly. Nadine fell asleep weeping, and Vivienne wishes she had it in her to cry again. She feels sorrow all around her, like wings unfurling behind, wrapping her in a cold, impossible future. Tears do not come, though. Just a simmering rage.

The metal on her wrists prevents her from truly feeling; from touching that power inside herself.

Cygna is not wrong, Vivienne thinks. And that makes her plight all the more complex. The Olympians have always been monsters—but they have also changed. Perhaps not Artemis. But Hermes, certainly. And Hades, who was ever given the wrong side of things, Vivienne felt. To say nothing of Aphrodite. The few times they met, she was kind, gracious, a kindred spirit. She almost felt like family.

And now Vivienne remembers because she must. She remembers everything. She digs through the permafrost of her memory, the one power the shackles cannot contain. It is painful, like breathing fire, but it must be.

Nadine stirs, eyes flickering open, as if sensing the shift in Vivienne. Her brows are like smudges of smoke on her dark face, and Vivienne gives her a reassuring look.

"I'm afraid," Nadine whispers. "I'm afraid of what they'll do. Now I know what they're capable of."

Cygna and Bastille made an offer to Nadine, as well. And revealed the location of Nadine's prime antagonist, a ghoul named Crad. He had been one of the first consumed and put into the void, as they hoped such revenge would endear Nadine to them. But they could not have anticipated the ifrit's fury at having her own revenge stolen.

"They could have just told us to begin with," Vivienne says, the train of thought resting again on the same point.

"Would you have listened?"

"Probably not. I'd forgotten who I was before. They reminded me. And now, well, I cannot exactly go back."

"I wish I had that talent, to forget," Nadine says. "I remember all too well. How did you manage?"

Vivienne closes her eyes and goes back to the day she had told Nerissa the same thing. Hundreds of years ago, when she was leaving another life. She wanted to start anew, with Nerissa.

"I would tell myself a story," Vivienne says. "I would do it every morning and every night. I would tell myself the story of my new life so many times that eventually it would come true."

"What about your old story?"

"I locked her away. I locked away her pain, her grief, her monstrousness. I see now, that she was just caged. We may be horrors that walk the earth, capable of destruction and power, but I know we are only these marvelous beasts forced in cages again and again. It is no surprise we lash out."

"So, who are you now?"

It wasn't a question Vivienne knew how to answer. "I think my methods are fraying, my dear. Now that I see what I've become, who Vivienne is as a slave, I begin to wonder if all the baubles and details I fashioned for myself were nothing but lies. I wanted to be better, to value human life and mortal existence. I wanted to use my powers for the betterment of the world. Now all of that has been taken."

"Mortals deserve what's coming to them," Nadine says softly.

"Perhaps. But I do not think we are to judge. If we rip apart their deities, if we obliterate everything they believe in, where does that leave us? We are less monstrous because we know better, I think. I find some comfort in that. In our capacity to love, to grow, to move through our mistakes and become..."

Vivienne does not finish. The door swings open to reveal Bastille, dressed in a red smoking jacket and preening. Although Vivienne is no longer what she'd consider at the height or center of fashion, she still knows poor style when she saw it. Bastille is a handsome fellow, gifted with all the strengths a masculine form could wish. But he always pushes his sartorial volume just a little too high.

He is obviously proud of himself. He only wears red when he's feeling sure of things.

Bastille doesn't look at Nadine; he's been ignoring her as of late. "Ah, there's our nymph of the hour," he says. "Have you had time to think over our proposition?"

Vivienne feels that ache at the base of her skull, reminding her that her power is dampened, not stopped. It leaves her breathless. Reminding her that she is Aura. That she is rage. That she is a child of Titans.

But she summons up her brightest smile and keeps her teeth to herself. "I still need some time."

It's worse than usual, the dampening. But as one might worry away a thread in a great tapestry with care and precision, Vivienne feels her own memories slipping through the vice of her shackles' power.

She feels her own magic flicker, feels the pull of a familiar soul…if she cannot escape from here, she can at least let herself be known.

But it takes a great deal of energy. Once Nadine sits up, and the heat dissipates from her lap, Vivienne has to force herself to stand. She does not like letting Bastille lord over her.

He smiles, teeth flashing. "There are many things I can give you, darling. I can give you the finest silks; I can arrange for the best music this side of the Atlantic; I can set a meal for you that would make your toes curl just to smell. I can even let you free of those shackles. But I'm afraid time is the only thing we don't have."

Vivienne does not want any of this. She only wishes that she'd had a chance to explain better to Nerissa. Perhaps it is better, for all of them, if she simply rolls over and does what they ask. They need her power, her magic, to strengthen the connection to the Silence, that great center of negative energy in the cosmos from which Cygna draws her power.

"It isn't so simple," Vivienne says, trying to bring a diplomatic tone to her voice, but finding it sounds frail to her ears. "I am all for revenge, you know. Except, in this case, I feel as if I am being threatened rather than asked."

"We couldn't be sure who you were until Cygna returned, and until

Artemis confirmed," Bastille said. "It was no easy task bringing her here; it took centuries of planning. You wouldn't understand, I don't think, the sacrifices she had to make in order to evade the eye of the Olympians."

"I don't blame her. Unlike me, no one took pity on her. And those who are bereft of pity often fester," Vivienne says.

"And you defend the Olympians?"

"No, I do not. But nor am I certain that casting them into the Silence, or whatever clever name you've deemed for your doom and gloom, is the best method for revenge. I'm still not even certain how you came by her in the first place."

Bastille grins again, his fangs lengthening. "Oh, well, that's a delightful story I believe you'll find a rather fitting irony. You had a connection to a certain Christabel Crane, did you not?"

It's hard for Vivienne to forget the woman who stole Worth Goodwin's heart for good. But she tries not to let the sound of the name impact her expressions. "I did."

"Well, in the last twenty years she's been quite busy. Publishing material, traveling the world, and most recently, working on a truce between the deities and the monstrosities. The legal proceedings were lengthy and, to most, rather boring. But we found a fascinating pattern among the testimonies, and enough to lead us back to the Olympians. Artemis was just the first. While she was not directly involved in the treaties, Hermes, Hades, and Hestia featured considerably. It did not take long to trace the paths."

It does not sound like Christabel. But then, what does Vivienne know? It has been the longest twenty years of her lifetime, and Christabel is so young.

"I would like a chance to speak to Artemis, tête à tête, as it were. Would that be possible?"

"Alone, no. But I would be happy to accompany you if you believe speaking to that shameful creature would aid you in your decision. Because, and I truly don't mean to drag things out, darling, but we'll be able to channel your powers one way or another, you know. The bleaknesses can take what we ask; we believe that your ultimate cooperation will be less...messy. We did just get the mosaics clean."

"The vines…" Christabel whispers. The vines are moving up toward Vivienne's window. They can see her speaking to a tall man wearing red, the lamplight limning his dark, oiled hair. Vivienne's voice carries, and Christabel cannot hear the words, exactly, yet she knows…

They spoke her name.

"Shh…" Alma is not in a mood to speak.

"But if Vivienne is truly powerless, how is it that the vines are…"

"Shh!"

Christabel settles down, huffing. She can't very well climb the vines from where she is, but watching Vivienne gives Christabel a sense of calm, even as fear trembles through her.

What would she tell her? How would she tell her? Worth is dead. The man they both loved was never real to begin with. He was a trapped angel, trapped for his protection by a woman who may be some kind of Ur goddess—Christabel is convinced that Dr. Frye is beyond a deity—because an Egyptian goddess wanted him dead for falling in love with a moon god.

The moon, as if in mockery, slips away behind a cloud and Christabel closes her eyes. Her tears sting, and it's harder to control them in this form. It's been so long since she stood on all fours again; her body feels muddled, confused, and the inner workings are catching up with her consciousness.

"It's alabaster," says Alma, and Christabel hastily clears her throat.

"What is alabaster?"

"Underground," says Alma. "Well, gypsum. And selenite. Massive quantities. It's been hewn into the ground of the villa, sprinkled into the soil. Big, heavy crystals. They're…confusing me."

"*Now* you're confused? I crossed that bridge a while ago," Christabel says.

"It's got a strange property, but I can't remember what exactly."

"The Titans used it on their faces in the war against the Olympians, if I recall. Perhaps that has something to do with it."

There is not, however, time to answer, for an immense explosion above their heads and a sound like shattering wood draws their attention upwards.

A chariot is falling from the sky.

~

Nerissa doesn't like the idea of flying any more than she likes the idea of driving an automobile, but she steels herself knowing that Apollo's chariot predates even boats, and there is some comfort in that.

The god speaks of his chariot in all manner of glowing terms, and always with a loving, sweet tone to his voice, as one might boast of a favored child. He glides his hands over the golden sides, traces the laurels carved into the ivory, and enumerates a dozen different rules. None of them, however, seem to predicate any safety, for there are no restraints in the chariot, nor are there doors. In the Greek fashion, it is forward-leaning, though certainly large enough for their small cadre, and Nerissa cannot help but notice how perilously easy it would be to fall backward and into oblivion.

There are horses—of course, there are horses—but Apollo glosses over them quickly, returning to the construction of the chariot rather than the living beings attached to and contained within.

Kit keeps close to Nerissa during the proceedings, asking a thousand questions with her eyes, yet speaking little.

"I feel better, I promise," Nerissa says as they take their seats. "I wouldn't be going if I was feeling ill. You don't have to keep after me like a mother hen."

Kit frowns into the scarf she's wearing. "I am not a chicken," the *kitsune* says with a half growl. "I am concerned."

"I know you are. I'm sorry about that."

"Why are you sorry? There is nothing to be sorry about, Nerissa." It's more words than Kit has said in hours. Nerissa is both elated and a bit disappointed; she was enjoying the quiet, but not the lack of communication. She does enjoy it when Kit gets animated.

"You seem upset?" Nerissa doesn't mean to ask the question, but feelings have never been her forté.

Kit crosses her arms and looks away. "I'm not."

"You look like a petulant child."

"I look like a petulant *kitsune*." When Kit looks again at Nerissa, her eyes are flashing, and her teeth are out.

She is magnificent. Nerissa has never told her this directly, of course, but it's true.

Worth is speaking with Apollo in a low voice, and they have not yet taken off, so Nerissa decides it's as good a time as any to try and bring things out in the open, as much as possible.

"That was not fair of me. I'm still recovering. The arms don't hurt, exactly, but it's a dull ache. And I get confused. The new arm isn't a permanent replacement, or at least it won't feel that way until the rest of me is officially gone. I know my true form is wounded, that those two arms are frozen, painful, but…"

Kit looks terrified. "You…oh! I suppose it doesn't matter. When this is over, and when we've finally gotten Vivienne to a safe place and hopefully not plunged the entire planet into permanent darkness, you'll finally be happy."

"Happy? My dear, happy is not a feeling I strive for."

"But losing Vivienne made you sad."

"You never met her, Kit. It's hard to explain. But yes. It has made me very sad."

"You loved her."

"I did."

"You do still?"

Nerissa sighs, looking down at the nails on her good hand. She has not bothered to cast her glamour fully; in fact, she cannot. To preserve Dr. Plover's work, and keep the pain at bay, she must exist in this half stage, preserving power she would otherwise use in disguising herself. Letting the glamour slip helps keep her own power from waning. There are no mortals around, anyway, and she believes, here on this rooftop in Notting Hill, that she would be incapable of a full glamour in her current state of exhaustion.

"I will always love Vivienne, Kit. She was the one who dragged me out of the swamp and showed me that I didn't have to thirst after human blood."

"You haven't had *implet* in days," Kit points out.

Nerissa hasn't even considered that. She frowns, looking over at Kit. "I can't explain that. I am different from when I entered the in-between place. I know things now that I didn't know before. I am not just a simple lamia."

"And I am not a simple *kitsune*."

"I never said you were."

"But you are not happy with me."

"Kit…how could you…"

Her hearts. Oh, they're beating fast now. When did that happen? Well, Nerissa can't pinpoint exactly when she started thinking about the *kitsune* as more than a business companion. She chose to stay, even when Nerissa gave her freedom. And though Kit talks about three thousand percent more than even Vivienne ever did, Nerissa knew they had a natural kind of companionship.

Kit has the most glorious eyes, and Nerissa has rarely seen them this close. In the lines of her round face, they cut a clever, wild arc beneath her sparse brows. They have no discernible iris most times, but when she is very excited, they flash a kind of amber red. A fox's eyes.

Nerissa takes a deep breath. "We are about to take a god's chariot up into the sky and make a daring rescue to attempt to prevent a goddess from being thrown into the abyss. And not because she has that many redeeming qualities, but because people like Christabel have taught me that such sweeping judgements are evil. Life that seeks to cause pain and torment to other life, to rob it of its innocence and wonder, is worth fighting against, tooth and nail."

"I don't see what that—"

"Kit, hush. Listen. What I'm trying to say is that over the many centuries of my long and storied life, I have encountered some truly incredible creatures—gods, monsters, and everything in between. I'm not sure which category I've always fallen into, but I have made a good show of it, anyway. I count myself very lucky to know so many arcane beings all around the world. But then, I met you."

Those fox eyes kindle. Kit looks as if she is ready to bolt and so Nerissa reaches out and takes the *kitsune* by her arms, wrapping her fingers—metal and flesh—around the meat of Kit's shoulders.

"And I've held you back from all that," Kit says in a half-whisper.

"What? No! Kit. There is no one else I'd rather have by my side."

"But what about Vivi—"

Nerissa leans forward and pauses just a breath before her lips touch Kit's. In the back of her mind, she wonders what a truly baffling couple they would make—a fox and a snake—and yet, as they make contact, it is the sweetest of matches, the most perfect of melodies. Kit does not resist; she presses back until Nerissa feels her own tongue sweep across Kit's canines.

"Oh, god, finally," says Apollo, pushing past the two of them to get at the front of the chariot. "I couldn't bear another moment of that twisting sexual frustration between you two. It was making me nauseated."

Kit is laughing now, and Nerissa is smiling—as close to a laugh as she gets—and then they sit closer together. Nerissa takes Kit's hands in hers and they settle in as the chariot shudders and rises into the sky. And they kiss once more.

WHO ARE WE, AGAIN?

This isn't going to end well.

You are such a killjoy.

I'm not speaking narrowly. I mean, I'm quite aware that we can't live out this situation for too much longer. Whatever we are together, which I haven't quite figured out yet, is...unsustainable.

Thank you for the reminder, Ophaniel.

That Apollo fellow is familiar, but I can't think of where we've met.

I don't think our mythologies crossed too often.

Perhaps not.

You were saying something about inevitable doom.

They are following the chariot, the very one steered by the aforementioned Apollo, not just because they have a pair of wings but also because they simply would not fit. Or at least, at the moment Worth is quite certain Kit and Nerissa need time alone considering that kiss.

Worth is feeling sorry for himself, and so Ophaniel is at the helm in terms of steering, at least.

Oh, yes, and they have figured out how to fly again.

Worth isn't particularly sure when that happened, but he suspects it has to do with his time as the primary consciousness in the body. After all, even though his Glatisant self was merely an enchantment, he was far more familiar with flying.

But he thinks there is something else at play, as well.

They are headed toward Christabel. Ophaniel is loath to admit it, but he, like Worth, is rather besotted with the unicorn. Though they'd only crossed paths a handful of times, the angel is most likely along for this ride primarily so he may see her again. She confuses him.

She is so easy to find. Is she like that for everyone?

Worth doesn't need to ask who "she" is.

Christabel is a unicorn. What that means, precisely, no one exactly knows. I was there, in the room, when she transfigured for the first time, and I can honestly say it was one of the most incredible moments in my existence.

So I was there, too.

Technically, I suppose; you were always there, weren't you?

Maybe that's it. Because I can sense her closer with every mile we close in on Andalusia. That's what it's called, correct? Andalusia?

Yes.

They fly on a while longer through the dark, the whispering whoosh of the wings punctuating the quiet. Now and again, when the wind is right, Worth can hear Nerissa and Kit speak in low voices, or Apollo giving a command to the four flying horses at the front of the chariot. They aren't easy to see; you have to look just right to get a handle on their size. It occurs to him that Nerissa and Kit might not even be aware they're there at all.

Helios, I think. He used to be Helios.

Clearly, this is bothering you. But finding the historical and/or mythological analog for Apollo is probably not something we have the time for right now.

I don't like this Cygna person and her cohorts. We're close to her. And Christabel. Not long now.

You are disjointed, even for you.

I'm having a crisis. I'm not supposed to care for mortals or... anyone other than celestials. My lover is gone from the world, and I am...

You're lonely. You can say it.

I think I was hoping that when I was revealed someone would come for me. One of my celestial siblings, or perhaps a seraph. That there would be a welcoming party for me...that someone missed me. But, Worth, I feel entirely disconnected from the family I once had, from the worship I once had.

Ophaniel, as much as I'm glad you're opening up to me—to yourself?—well, at all, I suppose, I don't think this is necessarily the best time.

There is no best time. I'm a shattered creature speaking to myself as I fly over the Atlantic Ocean in search for a—

The lightning strike—if lightning is the right word for it, Worth cannot say — comes out of nothing and hits the chariot directly in front of where Apollo sits. It's not natural lightning, of that much Worth is certain, because it makes Apollo shout and seems to derail the chariot's trajectory.

And light it on fire.

Also, Ophaniel's wings are aflame.

Except Worth is also on fire because they're sharing a body, and the angel conveniently decides that now is a good time for him to take a back seat.

Steering is a whole lot harder than guiding, Worth decides, especially when wreathed in magical flame; burning is not something he's used to. Thankfully, the altitude is enough that with a few sharp movements, Worth is free of the worst of the burning. And it's nothing more than a few blisters here and there; given the quickness of his healing capabilities, it won't last long.

Alas, the same is not true for the chariot. The lightning strike—or whatever it was—sundered the connection between Apollo and his horses. Two of them are nowhere in sight; one is frothing at the mouth with a strange oil-slick fluid that Worth is sure he's the only one capable of seeing, and the other is trying to turn the entire contraption around in the opposite direction.

And Apollo is not helping whatsoever.

"They cannot fly!" Worth shouts at him, indicating Nerissa and Kit. "You're a gods-damned god! Do something!"

Apollo shakes his head as if dispelling a charm. In the dark, his eyes glow a dim gold hue. He is angry. But he also appears confused.

Thankfully, the god eventually gets his wits about him; even more thankfully, Kit and Nerissa are seasoned monsters, capable of incredible feats. Kit's preferred orientation is generally upside-down, and so she takes this to her advantage as the chariot bucks and begins to lose altitude. Her tails spring out from behind her, a fan of fur and movement, and she uses this as a kind of rudder for the chariot, slowing its flipping and twisting, at least momentarily.

Apollo jumps lightly from the front of the chariot onto the back of one of his steeds which, once connecting with him, comes into more vibrant focus. Worth understands why he had cloaked them before. They're posi-tively radiant, the horses, and also some kind of flying hippocampi.

Another lightning strike, however, hits more directly now, and sunders the chariot from Apollo. His horse, spooked and as bright as a lighthouse beam, begins a furious descent into the shadowy mountains below.

"What a useless assemblage of arcane mass!" Nerissa shouts as Apollo's bright streak begins its sharp descent.

"Grab my hand, Nerissa!" Worth shouts toward her, but his voice is swallowed up with all the whooshing air. "We've—oh!"

He sees her. Christabel. She is far below them, but there is no mistaking the illumination; not just Christabel, but Christabel as a unicorn. As the ground rushes up to meet them, Worth manages to get a firm grasp under Nerissa's uninjured arm, and Kit—unusually light for someone of her build and size, no doubt a *kitsune* feature—wraps her arms around Nerissa's middle.

Just in time, too. A third lightning strike destroys the chariot, flecks of the wood and metal ricocheting out in a dozen directions.

Now it is truly just the three of them and the rushing wind.

It's hard enough to fly on his own, and the wings strain against the resistance, but Worth manages to slow their mad descent now that his wings are not on fire. And Kit continues using her tails to steer them and prevent them from losing complete control.

But it is not going end well. And Christabel is glowing more brightly. And down they go…

~

Christabel is thinking about how they are going to get Vivienne du Lac out from under the thumb of her captors when a flaming, falling chariot coming toward her and Alma disturbs her concentration. At first, she chalks it up to a strange side effect of her recent transfigura-tion back into her unicorn form, but as the sky lights up with lightning—there had not been a storm moments ago, but stranger things have happened—she sees the shapes of her friends up there.

Most clearly, she sees Ophaniel. And she doesn't like that her heart skips in her chest; she doesn't like that she part hopes that he dies from the fall, and also that he finds his way to her so she can look into his face for signs of Worth.

But no, that shouldn't be her focus right now. The focus should be on *helping them* and hopefully without drawing too much attention.

"This isn't going to be pretty," Christabel says, trying to better position herself under the falling forms of her friends. "I'm know I have flying capabilities, somewhere, but I haven't been able to figure them out."

"I've got this," Alma says, and she almost sounds bored. She reaches down and puts her white fingers into the dark, loamy earth. Grunting, the dwarf mutters words in a language that makes Christabel's skin prickle.

But then, immediately, the ground is softer underfoot. Squishy, almost.

"Won't last long," Alma says, wiping her brow with a dirt-stained hand. "But judging by my calculations..."

Any mortals hitting the ground with the force of her friends would have perished upon entry. And Ophaniel is still trailing fire. But thankfully, they are not mortals, and between Alma's groundwork and their own cunning, it's mostly a matter of losing their breaths and having to get their feet under them again.

Kit lands perched on top of Nerissa, her dark hair falling across her face. And there is a smile there. And...Nerissa returns it?

"Well, I hadn't expected to run into you like this, my dear," says the angel. And it is not Ophaniel's voice; it is Worth's.

Christabel's reply catches in her throat as the angel approaches, still clapping out smoldering patches of fire on his wings. His face is not the blank slate of Ophaniel's, that unreadable monolith. It's Worth, with lighter hair but the same broad brow, the same curving lips, the same...

She is delighted she is not in her human form right now. Because she's quite certain she would run into Worth's arms and make a fool of herself, and this is neither the time nor place for such foolishness.

Someone is crashing up the path, and inside voices rise. Of course, they heard it.

There isn't time!

It's Kalum, and he's looking from face to face. "They were supposed to meet us by the road," he says.

"Pardon the intrusion," Worth says, hand to his heart. He is unclothed from the waist up. It is very distracting. "But you haven't happened to see the god Apollo, have you? We lost track of him in the fray."

∽

V ivienne has only time to see her friends for a scant moment before Bastille clasps her around the wrists and draws her closer.

"I see what this is about now," he says, as if he's gotten an answer to a question that's been bothering him for days. "You're drawing it out. Hoping for rescue."

"I didn't call them," Vivienne says. Was there an angel among them? And something with tails? How much had changed since she'd been away? "Please, let me speak to them. I'll send them away."

The words sound brave, she supposes, but they're not what she feels. For the first time, she feels real hope. That thread is almost free as she pushes down through another layer of her memories, of her true self.

"I thought that twenty years would be enough for you to learn," Bastille says.

It doesn't feel right. Her hands don't feel right. Or rather, they feel *right* when they have felt so *wrong* for so long. They feel cold. They feel strong. Not entirely free from their bonds, but still…

Vivienne risks a glance to the side and sees Nadine there, a look of fear mingled with gladness on her face. And a silver key in her hand, glittering in the cold light of the moon.

That clever ifrit.

Bastille does not have time to react. Vivienne pulls back from him so violently that the shackles fall from her, staying in pieces in his hands. That whole time, Nadine had not been asleep. She had been waiting to free her.

Vivienne does not ask, because outside the window, the cacophony rises, but she knows she must do her best to teach Bastille a lesson.

In years past, she'd stolen the power she needed from others, from those who had loved and trusted her. Like Nerissa, she'd learn to feed on energy that wasn't her primary food, but it worked. Here, there is little of that fuel, but there are plenty of other emotions. Betrayal, memory, the pent-up fury of thousands of years wandering in the wilderness, never quite capable of dying but wishing for it all the same.

She does not mean to change what she wears, but Vivienne transforms quite smoothly before the ifrit and the basilisk. Her hair unties itself, falling in a dark line down her back; a rising tide of silk and frost cling to her body, melting away the old rage and bringing to light the pleasing form beneath. Her eyes go bright, her cheeks flush.

She is Vivienne. She is Aura. She is a daughter of Titans. A monster. A lover. A fighter.

Bastille tries to speak, but Vivienne presses cold into his mouth. Pure, beautiful cold. Ice and air and all, the deepest chill of her soul in a precise and shockingly effective weapon. And then he is on the ground, writhing, unable to scream.

The foundations shudder.

"Nadine," says Vivienne, turning to her friend, seeing her as if for the first time, now that magic is no longer siphoned from her. She is so beautiful, the ifrit. Her dark brows smudged like newly made soot, her eyes fathomless and black as night. Her skin is an impossible hue to guess for it is continually dancing with the light of deep flue flames like one might see in refracted water. "How…"

Nadine stands, holding up a small phial, that glittering slender sliver that Vivienne had seen before. "He was monologuing," she says softly.

"You brilliant beast," Vivienne whispers.

The ifrit has that look in her eyes; the one Vivienne knows well: awe.

Vivienne shudders, running her fingers down her pale arms. She feels grounded for the first time in two decades, as if the earth beneath her welcomes her rather than wants to cast her away.

And again, her eyes are drawn to Nadine. Nadine as she should be. Nadine of flame and smoke and power.

"Now I truly see you," Vivienne says. "Come to me."

Vivienne goes to Nadine and pulls her to her feet. Before the ifrit can say anything more, Vivienne pulls her body flush with her own and kisses her deeply. Vivienne traces the lines of Nadine's shoulder blades with her narrow fingertips, feels the delicate lapping of the fire on her skin. Kisses her more. Again. Better. With promises of what they will be once they can come together in their full forms.

A crash from outside. A cry.

"Nadine," Vivienne says. "At last. Freedom is nigh."

"Yes, but I'm afraid your friends…and Artemis…"

Nadine's collar is like a blight on her body. Vivienne's fingers stop there. "I wish we had time," she says, and she does not mean just to remove the collar.

It is a strange feeling, this love. Before gaining her freedom, Vivienne never thought her attachment to Nadine was this deep. But now she realizes that the intensity was dampened, like all her emotions. If she could freeze time, she knows precisely the matter by which she would attend to the ifrit, and what lines of poetry she might recite, and what cut of cloth she would find...

From below, a shuddering sound.

The ground belches a sulfurous stink.

Hungry, but sated for the first time in a thousand years, Vivienne cups Nadine's cheeks in her hand and kisses her lightly on her surprised lips. "There will be time. Providing we manage to thwart the whole world-ending situation, yes? Then no feat of gods or monsters will keep me from you."

FOUR HEARTS OR MORE

Falling to the ground was considerably worse than hitting it. Nerissa had never had the occasion to go careening toward earth like some deranged meteorite, and as she falls, it occurs to her that it's a sensation she does not like. It reminds her of rollercoasters—horrid human contraptions she's only seen from distances—and how not once in her life she has wondered what it would feel like to put herself under such a distressful situation.

And it is even worse than she imagined.

Her hearts beat out of sync, and though she knows she is nigh immortal, given the fact of her recent run-ins with the Void, she wonders if it's possible to explode upon impact. Perhaps it's the pressure change that has so discombobulated her.

Truly the only thing keeping Nerissa from screaming like a flayed banshee on the way down is that Kit has managed to keep her arms about the lamia's waist. It is not as distracting as it might be if they had found their way into this arrangement without the death-defying preamble, but it helps Nerissa to play over that kiss in her mind a few times before striking the ground.

Nerissa ensures, however, that she takes the brunt of the force. She isn't yet familiar enough with the *kitsune* body to know its weaknesses, and she does not want to take any risks.

Anything for another kiss like that.

Kit lands on top of Nerissa with a breathtaking whoosh, her tails still moving around them, soft fur on her face. She smells like fresh rainwater.

Nerissa looks up at Kit, those amber eyes flashing under her curtain of hair.

"Hello," Nerissa says, her voice huskier than usual. Everything aches.

"Nerissa," Kit says, and how had Nerissa never noticed how perfect her name sounds the *kitsune's* mouth? She could listen to it all day.

"Nerissa!"

Stronger this time, and Nerissa realizes she was falling asleep.

Nothing feels quite right.

Except for the pressure of Kit on top of her; that feels very right.

~

In one brilliant moment, the vines twining their way up toward Vivienne turn to ice and Christabel comes face to face with Worth Goodwin.

From her vantage point, the effect is mostly a physical one; where she was warm moments before she is now frigid. The little ice crystals made it onto her hair and her eyelashes, and she stands staring down at Worth, trying to blink and rearrange his body so it makes more sense.

But no. It is his face. Plus wings. And an unearthly light that reminds her of her sweetest dreams come to life.

"Christabel."

She is shaking. Shaking! What an embarrassment. A woman of breeding and intellect falling weak at the knees—all four of them at the moment—in the presence of her once paramour.

"Hello, Worth."

Christabel is quite proud of herself. She sounds calm, reserved, unbothered. There is a great deal of chaos happening all around them, including the appearance of someone who most certainly must be of Hades itself, and yet she can do nothing else but look at Worth.

This new Worth.

But his eyes are the same. How many nights did she try and bring him back out of Ophaniel, until the damned angel infuriated her so much? Until he told her that he found her disgusting and disquieting, and she finally had to leave London altogether.

"It took me a while to find my way back to you," Worth says. He takes a step toward her, but his feet don't disturb the ground. "I'm sorry."

"I gave up on you," Christabel says. She had hoped to take a step backward but somehow ended up a little closer to Worth.

"I know," Worth says.

There are so many other things she wants to tell him. About Hermes. About love. About her research. About the works she's done with Dr. Frye. About the fact that no matter what she's done, no matter who she's met, she always comes back to Worth. And losing him the way she did, outside the realm of mortality and immorality, has continually driven her to the brink of despair.

How she hasn't been able to turn herself back into her unicorn form until now.

But he's looking at her, and he sees her. Christabel. Not the many forms she takes or the masks she wears, but her. Entirely. Laid bare. And she sees him, the Worth she loved from the moment they met.

Though, truth be told, the frothy blood that sprays across her face interrupts the romantic atmosphere somewhat.

The bleaknesses are far more energized this time, breaking through the ground in a dozen places, and spinning around Alma too fast for her to follow. It's nighttime, and that means their darkness is significantly more difficult to spot.

Alma starts throwing up cascades of dirt around her, and that works for a short amount of time until it's clear that the bleaknesses are splitting up around the particles, even as fast as Alma is throwing it at them.

She doesn't like this. And why is everything so cold?

A deep buzzing sound draws her attention out toward the road, and she sees the figure of a man approaching. He is walking determinedly, fists balled at his sides, and he's exuding a particular geological scent: sulfur. Deep sulfur. And then another, more vegetal smell. Alma has a hard time detecting such things, but she senses that it's floral.

Green flame surrounds the man's form; that much is clear as he gets closer. And as human men go, he is rather unimpressive, though he wears a rather fetching leather jacket. Alma decides that if she makes it out of this situation all in one piece, she'd like to get herself one. Christabel shouts his name: Kalum. But that isn't his name. He's of the Underworld, and that is a language Alma knows well.

Alma has spent most of her life away from these sorts of people, but she's quite certain she's looking at Hades. Or at least, an extension of him. There is just too much power there.

And she's happy, because the moment Hades—or Kalum—appears, he begins blowing green smoke across what has now become the battlefield. It makes spotting the bleaknesses much easier.

But also much more difficult. Because there are so many more than a dozen of them, and they seem to be growing, coalescing. Too many for this group. She will have to distract them, lead them somewhere with more stone.

∽

W orth doesn't feel the bleakness crest his shoulder until it's too late. It saws through his flesh hard enough that Ophaniel rises, taking momentary control.

Not these things again. I'm going to get us out of here.

No! Not now!

This is not your body.

It's not entirely yours, either!

I don't have to stay here.

Look at her and tell me you don't love her.

The pain comes again, and it's impossible to make a coherent sentence internally or externally. But with it comes a fury, too, and Worth is glad of it. Of all the emotions he and Ophaniel share, that is one far more familiar to him and one he can more easily wrest control of.

Christabel rears, and she is such a glorious sight. There is a streak of blood—his blood, he now realizes—across her perfectly white muzzle. She begins to emit a bright light, a clear shimmer refracted along her body in a spectrum of color. She stomps her foot three times on the ground and then begins to move forward, slashing the air with her horn.

Worth is initially terrified. He just wants to hold her. But he sees that the bleaknesses do not like her. They shy from her. And on the other side, the new arrival, the one that Christabel called Kalum, is making the little monsters easier to see.

Buffeting his wings as best he can, though he's almost certain he would not manage flight even if he wanted to, he's able to keep redirecting the green smoke from Kalum toward Christabel, and time and again she slashes at the air.

"Be careful!" It's Nerissa, her voice hoarse. She survived the fall, but she does not look well. She looks confused, her face lit by the green light, her hair down around her in a nest. Worth realizes that she's not in her glamoured form and has not been for quite some time. Likely longer than he's ever seen her.

Which is unusual.

And there is Kit. And she is entirely covered in hair, her mouth elongated and her teeth flashing. She is furious, Worth can tell, but he can't quite understand why.

Except, well, now *that* makes sense.

A bleakness appears from the assembled smaller ones, large and ominous, a gaping maw in the center of them all. It absorbs all light and looking at it makes Worth feel dizzy.

Then a woman emerges from it, stretching her arms lightly as if she's just taken a good nap. She wears white leather, and she brings with her a burnt smell, like after a lightning strike. A beautiful woman, to be certain, but cool. Too cool.

"I'm sorry to interrupt this little revolt going on here," says the woman. "But if you don't settle down, I'm afraid I'm going to have to throw your friends in with the others I was planning on destroying tonight. And really, all I was hoping for was a little conversation."

It shouldn't be a threat, and yet it is.

No.

Ophaniel, what is this?

She has seen the blackness of the center of the stars. She has named the unnamed. She has made it hers.

And then Worth can see nothing but the faint glow of Christabel's horn in the distance.

V ivienne walks over Bastille, floating as she used to, and takes a moment to crunch her icy heel into his pretty face. It won't last, and she hasn't had the courage to kill him, yet. But it feels good.

She takes the ring from his finger, and he whines.

"It protects me...it's holy..."

"Holy? Hardly. It's a fluke of physics. But for now, the bleaknesses will leave Nadine alone." Vivienne gives the ring to Nadine, and the ifrit slips it on. She shudders.

"You should wear it," Nadine says.

"No, you are not yet whole."

Nadine blazes behind her and Vivienne turns, putting her fingers softly on the collar again.

"What else can I do?" Vivienne wants nothing more than to free Nadine, but the collar does not budge.

"Only the hand that placed it can remove it," she says. "And my first owner was not Bastille. Nor Cygna. It was done long ago when another you know was similarly bound."

"Barqan." Vivienne knows without needing to ask, and she closes her eyes against the memory. Once, she was the slaver. Barqan, she thought, was a mere djinni butler, a clever parlor trick for her amusement. But he was never hers; he was Nerissa's. And for all the decades of his imprisonment, he sought to undo her.

She does not like to think that Barqan knew what would befall her. That eventually she would find herself in the hands of Cygna and Bastille.

A thought for another time.

"We've never spoken of my father," Nadine says softly, and Vivienne cannot help but make a sharp gasp.

"I should have suspected. You are of his ilk."

"I should hate you," Nadine says. "I used to hate you. And then…"

"Shh, I know. It is not the time, love."

And saying that word, *love,* fills Vivienne with an ebullient hope, and with that hope a power she has not tasted in two decades. Reaching a hand out to the solid door, she presses the pent up energy into it, and it turns to frost just for a moment before it shatters.

The house is madness, with the attackers at the gate, and while Vivienne and Nadine are no doubt an incongruous sight, they know every turn of the villa in ways the others do not. It is the blessing of a servant, Vivienne realizes suddenly, a gift she had never anticipated needing.

She must quell her frostiness a bit, and it pains her to do so. But her concern is short-lived. A sulfurous mass belches outside, and the very foundations of the villa shake.

"I do believe that Artemis should pay for her crimes," Vivienne adds, almost off-handedly as they make their way toward the basement. "Just not this way. Right now, she is a significant hazard."

Getting to Artemis is not as simple as merely going through a door, regardless of how much frost power is behind it. There are locks. And guards. And mechanisms in place. Vivienne remembers most of them from her time following Bastille around, but she's afraid to encounter something outside her realm of capabilities.

She is cautiously pressing toward one of the doors on the way to the basement, however, when the wall around it begins to crumble. Another quake. This time enough to set her teeth on edge. Where is that coming from? And what on earth is it?

Holding up her hands as debris rains down, Vivienne is able to make a kind of shield for them, pebbles pattering over the solid ice.

Nadine looks up, and Vivienne would normally be glad to see the look of wonder on her face, but in the unfortunate impending doom of the universe, there is little she can do other than make a mental note for the off-chance they escape with their lives.

Without her shackles, Vivienne wonders how she missed Artemis's presence the first time. She couldn't consider her a mother, not in the technical sense, but as Vivienne descends into the villa basement, her senses flood with memories of Aura, of who she was before.

What kind of creature are you?

But then the memory that comes isn't of Aura at all. Or Artemis.

It is Nerissa. Bedraggled and sitting in filth, the remnants of a dozen beasts and men around her like a carnivorous magpie's nest.

Perhaps we met in another life.

Vivienne is blinking back tears, unable to focus for a moment. The room is shaking again, and that is no pleasantness. They reach the lower landing and through the dust and refuse of the basement—lit the old-fashioned way with torches—Vivienne spies the mass of gypsum where Artemis had been.

It's almost covered her entirely. She's impressive, even as a malformed statue that looks more like a lump of clay than a goddess. One dark eye peers out from glittering scales of alabaster and mica. She wouldn't need to breathe, of course. Gods never do. They are not made of flesh, not in the strictest sense.

But Artemis is afraid.

Too quiet. No guards. It reeks of a trap.

Vivienne has, despite her rather wispy appearance, managed quite well in terms of physical fights in her past, though she gave up fisticuffs a few hundred years ago. It's been a while since she's practiced, and she is keen enough to sense her own power flickering unpredictably. But she's willing to try.

A muffled noise from Artemis, and then the ground opens in an impressive geyser of chalk and dirt, covering almost everything that wasn't already alarmingly dirty in a fine white powder.

Two things emerge from the ground: one is a dwarf woman. She is of the Nith, Vivienne believes, a reclusive ground-dwelling creature from the wild North with no pigment and no manners. She thought they wouldn't deign to spend time around creatures of her ilk, but here she is.

And the dwarf woman is certainly helping Vivienne, as she's attacking the thing that comes behind her with gusto. It's a creature of negativity. A void being. Vivienne had seen smaller ones before, pets that Bastille was training up. This one is much larger. Its borders appear erratic, unstable. But all light and feeling vanish upon contact.

Except the dwarf has a method to the madness. She is casting chunks of stone—which she seemingly lifts from the ground as if they are naught but marshmallows—and throws them toward the void creature. It slows it, though it doesn't stall it enough to neutralize the threat.

"My fire won't work well, but we haven't tried your ice," Nadine whispers. She backs up, eyes wild. Vivienne knows the damage those bleaknesses left on Nadine's body—the torture it took to make her speak—and understands why the ifrit wouldn't rush into the fray.

"See to those outside. Then come back to me," Vivienne says.

The ifrit can walk through walls, so this is no difficult task for her. Vivienne watches as Nadine's figure phases away, trails of blue smoke lingering a breath before the first attack takes her off-guard.

The ringing pain in her body awakens her instincts, though, so Vivienne cannot be altogether ungrateful. She fought with Nerissa many times. And in other lifetimes, besides. Many times, she fought demons in her mind; other times, actual demons.

The void creatures are worse, though. They are harnessed neutral chaos. It's only the rings her captors wear that keep them from devouring their masters. Vivienne was never much for magic rings, having thought them fairy tales and dull superstition. But these rings are something else. A kind of fusion between science and the arcane, and they are powerful, indeed.

When the dwarf woman makes eye contact with Vivienne, she nods in return and calls another ice wall, this time up and at an angle that throws the void creature—now heavy with stones—off balance. The abrupt change in temperature does the trick. But it also encourages attention in her direction.

Vivienne closes her eyes a moment, whispering her apologies to Nerissa, to Worth, and to her friends. If it ends here, in the dark basement with a Nith dwarf and the imprisoned goddess of the hunt, then so be it.

JOIE DE BATAILLE

What good is this battle joy without Nerissa? Kit struggles to keep a protective stance before the lamia, her own body shocked from the fall and jittering all over. There are also nerves. Because there was kissing. And it was perfect kissing.

But also, everything in the world is about to be swallowed up into absolutely nothing. So regardless of how good the kisses might have been, Kit understands that daydreaming right now is likely not the most effective strategy. Unless she never wants a kiss again.

The trees around them sway together then, a strange dance orchestrated by the darkness of the bleaknesses. It's hot. Then it's cold. Then it feels as if the center of Kit's chest is beckoning her forward into the nothing that reaches up, up and toward the moon. Smaller bleaknesses rise from the ground all around them, continuing to feed the growing monstrosity. Implacable. Immovable.

Through the nothingness Kit sees stars. Not her stars. Just the nothing stars of nothing worlds grown cold on nothing life; a churning center, a roiling miasma of power.

Cygna stands nearby, unaffected. She is laughing with her head tilted back.

The shiny god-man joins them, looking even more ridiculous in gilded armor and a bright scarlet plume on his head. He glows, at least, though even so, the light is not enough.

Another joins him, and Kit doesn't know the name until someone shouts it: Hades. Except he's not Hades, not really. He's got a body on, like a puppet. And on a regular day Kit might have questioned it, but right now she's more focused on Cygna and a glittering quality in the air behind her.

The shiny man-boy god is not a very good warrior. For all the ornate armor, he is clearly out of practice. Perhaps, she thinks, he is better at inspiring fighters than being one? It doesn't matter.

Nerissa is screaming in pain behind her, suddenly. Kit wheels around, ready to protect her.

"My... arms!" Nerissa groans, clasping at the metal arm with her remaining ones.

But there is no assault. Indeed, the gods are circling Cygna, fending off the bleaknesses; but outside their circle it's relatively safe.

"Your arms?" Kit knows it sounds stupid, and that's the last thing she wants to come across as, but it's hard to think with so much movement happening everywhere.

Nerissa's face, shiny in the moonlight, scales glittering, turns toward Nerissa. "It's...in there..." she says, gasping. "They're..."

But the lamia can say no more.

And Kit understands. Oh, how she understands. The arms are not entirely gone. They are somehow suspended, roiling in that void gathering behind Cygna. And Nerissa's brain is receiving signals from them, except they are no longer attached to her. The pain must be beyond bearing, and that speaks volumes for Nerissa. She is a creature accustomed to pain, numbed to it, perhaps, over the years. Kit thinks sometimes she even welcomes the pain.

Ophaniel and Christabel are fighting, back-to-back, against a kind of bleakness beast that looks roughly like a jaguar full of stars. From the looks of things, Kit doesn't think they'll hold on much longer, even with Christabel's better defense.

They're going to die this time.

And Nerissa is going to die in excruciating pain.

"I came to punish one god," Cygna is saying, "and now it looks like I've got three. Really, I didn't think the family bond extended so far. Especially to you, Hades. You typically stay out of this business."

"This is my holy place," Hades says, the body moving but the lips staying still. Kit finds that makes her even more uncomfortable than the thought of Nerissa's disembodied arms. "You threaten my kin; so I threaten you."

Cygna shakes her head, crossing her arms as if schooling a little child. "Oh, Hades. They always get you so wrong. You're such a delicate soul. I'm sorry for bringing you into this, but you see it's all about the topography, the geological makeup. It turns out that the Titans left behind little clues. It's gypsum you don't like. It's gypsum that will rise and take you; then I will break you and cast you away."

A deep, roiling moan comes from the direction of the house. Cygna's face drops a moment before regaining composure.

"On second thought," she says, looking behind her. "I had thought that I would cast you away, but perhaps you'll be less perishable than the vampires. Voidlings—make them your hosts."

Kit stumbles back as she sees a dozen little bleaknesses break from the enormous void behind Cygna. And straight toward the gods.

~

Christabel knows she is a creature of contradictions, but it still surprises her just how much she enjoys the fight. For a relatively small person, and one with a limited arsenal of attacks, it's not usually difficult to get the upper hand. And though her friends Kit and Nerissa are screaming—she will have to do something about that shortly, she knows—she is rather adept at keeping the little void creatures at bay.

They do not like her horn.

And they do not like Worth's voice.

In all honesty, the sounds he's making wouldn't be appealing to almost anyone, but they do have a certain celestial ring to them. If the voidlings sound like a dissonant reverberation, Worth adds a layer of high, never quite resolving chords. He can make more than one note at the same time. He's always had a variety of mouths, all talented in a variety of ways, whether he was a Questing Beast or a cherub. And she's always been glad, and a little sad, about that. She's never quite put them to use...

But it is exhausting.

She and Worth—or Ophaniel...or both—are naturals together. She doesn't have to worry about his form or style when it comes to the fight. His wings buffet the air enough to confuse the voidlings, who don't seem to have a sentience that Christabel can tell. She's good at sussing that sort of thing out. They are, as she expected, a kind of chaotic nothing. But in that chaos, there is a great deal of unpredictability. Fighting something that *thinks* is considerably easier because there are only so many thoughts one can have when engaged in combat.

Nerissa won't stop screaming, and Christabel tries to get a better look at what's happening across the way, through the blue and gold glow of the gods facing down Cygna.

That scream tells Christabel what her eyes could not.

They are losing.

The gods are struggling against the power of the void. And the void is growing.

Cygna is surprisingly calm through all of this. Though she delivers something of a villain's monologue, she isn't frightened in the least. Christabel senses a calm inevitability about her.

"Worth, this isn't going well," Christabel whispers over her shoulder as she dodges yet another onslaught, the voiding just grazing her ear and making the hair singe and sizzle a moment. "Worth...this is a good time..."

"Not Worth."

"Ophaniel."

"Worth is tired."

"Convenient."

"Worth doesn't know how to fight in this body."

"What do you mean, he—"

Christabel feels the change more than she sees anything, mostly because the light coming from Ophaniel is suddenly so bright that she is momentarily blinded. But she remembers. The first time he transfigured it was no small thing. No elegant angel as he usually presents. It was a creature of flame and horror, mouths and feathers and fury. There are no words to truly assemble his appearance.

Ophaniel is mad radiance, distilled arcana from a profound, celestial realm.

And he is furious.

~

Artemis cannot speak, and in many ways, this is an improvement on her person. Unbeknownst to most, she is not a shy, demure goddess. She is a well of stories, and often can't tell when to stop telling her story and allow the flow of general conversation. It's for this reason,

Vivienne learned millennia ago, that she had such a revolving door of attendants. Not many can manage more than a few decades around her, regardless of the perks.

But looking upon Artemis now, Vivienne is struck by how terrified she appears. That's not an expression she has ever encountered before, not in her long years as the goddess's attendant. That state of fear is not diminished by the alabaster growing steadily over her neck and face. It has already covered her mouth—thank goodness for little favors—and is almost to her nose. But her eyes remain intact.

Alma dispensed with the bleaknesses with methodical ease, but now they are left with a larger problem.

"I can't move the stone," Vivienne says, shaking her hands. They burn from the effort. She had thought enough cold and moisture would impact the growing cocoon of stone, but she was mistaken.

"I can't shake it," says Alma, her low voice tinged with disbelief. "I can't even *feel* it."

Nadine is the one who hasn't tried yet, having re-materialized after getting a good look around the house, but she seems hesitant to do so. She is not necessarily the lesser of the beings—among monsters, such rank would be difficult to determine, not to mention tacky—but she is nowhere near as predictable. Her collar doesn't dampen her skill entirely, but it does strip away her agency. If Bastille were to wake from his bloody mess, or Cygna to think of it, she could call Nadine to her. And the power that flows from her kind is at its most potent when it is natural, from the self, not directed.

"Let me at least shed a little light," Nadine says softly.

Alma takes up the rear, watching the exit. The high windows flicker with light from outside, and Vivienne tries to focus on the task at hand.

Nadine walks up to the goddess and puts one hand, limned in blue flame, upon the alabaster. She immediately sucks in her breath as if wounded but presses on.

"Nadine..." Vivienne tries.

"Shh...please, let me concentrate," Nadine says.

Vivienne waits what feels like a half of eternity, tracking the ragged edges as they continue up Artemis's face, the sounds of the battle rising outside.

Finally, shivering, Nadine slips her hand from the alabaster cocoon, nearly falling over. Vivienne is there to catch her, smoothing the hair at the ifrit's brow, feeling her heart ache with the shared pain.

"It's infused with the void," Nadine whispers. "On a molecular level."

"I couldn't see that," Alma says, and Vivienne detects a note of offense in her voice.

Nadine explains. "It's energy. My energy. For what is flame other than that? I can press into spaces with it, explore around. You wouldn't be able to detect the voids because they are…hiding, I suppose, is the right word, in the very structure of the alabaster." She shudders and then seems to regain a bit of strength, her flame rekindling. "It's a cross. Or at least, a structure much like one. And imagine the little spaces between each corner…"

Vivienne gazes at Artemis. The goddess's eyes are full of tears.

"I bet you feel quite terrible now, don't you, Artemis?" Vivienne says, addressing the goddess for the first time. The words almost catch in her throat. "If the world were truly fair, I would be with Cygna in this matter, and I would leave you to a fate of doom. But as it is, I don't think you're going anywhere. The void may be pressing in around you, but Cygna is out there. And that is where I must go."

"Vivienne, that thing is out there," says Nadine.

"Yes, and its primary focus is Artemis, is it not?"

Nadine nods slowly.

"I think I know how to distract it. Nadine, I need you to stay here. Rest. I'd say to make sure that Artemis isn't going anywhere, but I don't think that's going to be a problem."

Nadine almost looks relieved.

"But I'm going to need you with me, dwarf," Vivienne says to the dwarf.

"Alma," the dwarf says. "If you don't mind."

"Very well, Alma. Show me where my friends are," Vivienne says. "I will have to put on something more appropriate, though."

She glares at Artemis before exiting through the cellar steps. "And don't think that you'll simply get away once we free you. *If* we free you. There will be conversations."

As she departs, Vivienne is pleased to see the recognition and horror in Artemis's face.

∾

Nerissa's life is a long line of pain. She cannot pinpoint exactly when she started feeling this way, but now it is the only thing she is capable of feeling—endless pain, colder than the harshest London wind, deeper than her self-revulsion.

She knows that Dr. Plover isn't really there with her, and yet she finds herself, between moments of absolute madness, having a conversation with him.

"You know, I loved Vivienne for so long that I forgot how to love anything else. And you know, she didn't love me. Not like I loved her. I don't even think she liked me, most of the time. She pitied me, for certain. She wanted to protect me. She feared for me..."

In the in-between world of the void and her dwindling life, Dr. Plover is the size of an elephant. It would bother Nerissa if she thought the bird was real. But clearly, she's in that strange place again, though this time the pain is more insistent.

"You know I haven't had any *implet* in quite some time. Perhaps that's why the pain's so bad."

"No, that can't be it. I honestly don't know what I should be eating, though. I'm not even sure I'm a lamia, through and through."

"Yes, that's a fascinating thought. But I simply don't have enough time."

Then cold. Real cold. Cold on her skin. Her entire body douses in a chill, a familiar, beautiful chill that smells of sea salt and the wandering past. Her world flips upside down, and Nerissa has the strange sensation she's being pulled inside-out, like a sock puppet. So, when she finds herself looking up into a flickering night, the sound of fighting loud in her ears, and the face of Vivienne du Lac looking into her eyes, she does the only sensible thing she can manage: she vomits profusely.

When she rights herself again—taking Vivienne's hand to stand, not because the circumstance makes any sense whatsoever, but because it seems as though it's the right thing to do in the given moment—the wood by the villa is on fire. And imploding. And the villa now boasts a most impressive hole the size of a London omnibus. It looks like a giant doll-house, Nerissa thinks groggily, through spikes of pain and the occasional rational thought. And she can see Artemis, she presumes, encased on the other side of what must have once been a formidable jail cell, glittering in gypsum.

Apollo sees it, too, and Nerissa imagines that this progress must be relatively new for such a raw, roiling sound to issue forth from the god. He starts to rush toward Artemis, but the Hades man—who bodily cannot be Hades, yet somehow must be Hades—prevents him from doing so.

Christabel and Ophaniel—it must be the angel because Nerissa could never attribute such deft, furious, beautiful fighting form to Worth Goodwin—are keeping Cygna occupied. But they are losing. Christabel has dozens of cuts on her white coat, seeping and staining down her sides like a haphazard zebra. And she is tiring.

Nerissa is about to shout out when she feels Vivienne's hand grip her shoulder. She turns to her friend and looks her full in the face. Twenty years she's been waiting to speak to her again, to apologize and to beg forgiveness for a thousand things. To promise her undying friendship. To thank her for all she had done.

But they do not need words, it turns out. Vivienne holds a finger to her lips, little flakes of snow glittering about her like an aura.

Kit is there, breathing hard, a cold mist meeting the air near Vivienne. Nerissa nods.

Vivienne is stronger than she has ever been, Nerissa is sure of it. Her hair is white, crystalline, her fingernails like talons. Her eyes are pupil-less, just endless pools of water. Where her feet meet the ground, little flowers of frost rise around her, leaving a trail like lace in her wake. She holds on to Nerissa's hand a moment longer before squaring herself before Cygna.

It doesn't take long to reach the immortal human. Cygna is wild with knowing, the void creatures around her obeying her every beck and call. They swarm like mad round birds, relentless and untiring.

"Cygna, Cygna, Cygna..." Vivienne's voice comes from the air itself. No echo, yet strangely resonant. Resonant in every drop of moisture.

"Oh, well, there you go with your dramatics," says Cygna, holding up her hands. "I was hoping for a challenge."

The massive bleaknesses and the smaller ones all halt at once. The living world seems to take in a collective breath. The night lingers on, afraid.

Beside her, Kit is growling. Nerissa tries to reach out with her good hand but instead finds the stumps where her arms used to be. They are knit together with ice. Vivienne...

"What can I say? I've always liked to make an entrance," Vivienne says coolly.

The bleaknesses do not move toward her yet.

409

"Oh, Aura. Aura, Aura." Cygna says the name, that other name, in a mocking tone. "I was hoping not to have to swallow you up. I really did think you'd make a lovely conqueror by my side."

"I know you've been hurt. You've been broken," says Vivienne, and Nerissa is surprised to hear a note of pain in her voice. Being genuine has never been the sylph's strong point. But perhaps Vivienne is no longer just a sylph.

What you think, you become, Nerissa dear. If you spend all your time thinking yourself a monster, why, that's what you'll be. But in my long life, I've reinvented myself a thousand times. There is great power in the mind.

A thousand times.

For what are monsters, truly? They are not, Nerissa thinks, merely born out of a broken world. No, they are made in the same way of angels and gods. Necessity forms them. It is only their power and visages that terrify those unable to reconcile or be made comfortable around them.

Vivienne looks at Kit. She is so beautiful, so fierce. In the silvery light of Vivienne's power, the *kitsune* is a painfully perfect monster.

"I have not been broken," says Cygna. "I have been *forged.*"

Cygna holds up her hand, ready to strike.

"Fox woman, *now!*"

It is Vivienne who says the words, and they are so counter to what Nerissa is expecting to hear that she doesn't have time to prevent Kit from running headfirst toward Cygna.

PRECIOUS

Until Vivienne arrived on the scene, literally forming out of a mist behind her, Kit had been prepared to kill Nerissa herself. Not out of any sense of hatred, but out of love. She could not allow Nerissa to endure any more pain. And even if she could, they were losing the fight. There was no chance they would win; for what is magic good for against the void?

But then, there was Vivienne. Kit didn't need to ask the nymph's name. Perhaps she was a daughter of Benzaiten; maybe she was a goddess in her own land. But it is clear to Kit that, watching Vivienne emerge from a mist before her, that she is more powerful and grand than Nerissa even knew. And Nerissa loved Vivienne. So much so that Kit knows without a doubt whom she is seeing

"Hello, Vivienne," says Kit. She has lost a good deal of her blood and energy, but she is preparing herself for a final fight. And there are tears all over her face. She would have preferred a better introduction. And she would have had more to say. But for once, Kit finds that she has nothing more. The energy required to make words is beyond her.

Vivienne's face is like a carved statue, the lines and curves so precisely made they are at once beautiful and terrifying. She is not very big, and yet her presence extends meters beyond her in every direction. And it is snowing, too. Kit feels the flakes on her lashes.

Kit looks up. The flakes are moving slowly. Too slowly. And beyond

411

them, the other players in the battle are doing the same. Christabel's horn is a blur, arcing as she rears back; Ophaniel's wings unfurl one feather at a time. All but the bleaknesses are slowed to a fraction of their typical speeds. Hades and Apollo are pushed down to the ground, screaming in pain.

"I only have a moment," Vivienne says, reaching out to touch's Kit's cheek. The *kitsune* feels her tears freeze before evaporating. "But you need to listen very carefully. I cannot hold this for long."

Kit nods.

"I cannot do this alone. First, I will take away Nerissa's pain. Then, I will help to trap Cygna in her own game. Can you help me?"

"Yes, I am always prepared," says Kit.

"Good," Vivienne says, her lips spreading in a smile so beautiful that Kit's heart knows why Nerissa fell so deep in love for so long. "I'm going to need your teeth."

~

This is the scene before you.

A woman, arms raised, her eyes filled with emptiness, raising her voice in victory. Time hitched, just a moment before, but she was unaware. She is too entrenched in the goings-on about her to notice such a small thing. And there are so many little voidlings to command; so many that she has not quite realized that she is losing control over them. Bastille is no help and might be dead. Her groundlings ran away when the angel arrived, to say nothing of the unicorn.

But Cygna is a woman driven by a desire for vengeance. And yes, she is most assuredly justified in her fury. She, like Aura and Melinoe, our Vivienne and Nerissa, did nothing other than attempt to write lines in her own story.

Is she evil? She certainly looks it. Even her veins are pulsing. She has waited thousands of years as an immortal soul in a mortal body. Unlike Aura and Melinoe, she has never had power, per se. Her metamorphosis was one solely of her own energy. She tried to kill herself, dozens of times, but eventually realized it was of no use.

So, you can perhaps excuse her if, in this moment of near triumph, hoped for in the dark for so many long seasons, she overlooks one of the monsters. It's easy to do so.

For Cygna is looking directly at Vivienne, the one she knew as Aura, and she is outraged and dead set on punishing her. And, to Cygna's eyes at least, Vivienne is the most whole and, therefore, the greatest threat to her. But also full of promise. If Cygna could tap into that power, siphon it for herself...

Cygna does not see the fox woman slink up behind Vivienne, paws frosting in the lacy trail behind her. Cygna does not hear the *kitsune* scurry to the edges, darting around the voidlings.

Vivienne's voice is as cold as the frost of midwinter, merciless. It doesn't matter the words she says; you likely know the sort of thing she is saying. She is a hero, after all. But Vivienne, for once in her life, is not seeking attention for power. She is seeking attention as a *distraction*, and that makes all the difference. For if Cygna truly knew Vivienne in any way, this alone would be enough of a tell. She has made the mistake of thinking that Vivienne is still Aura, but that name and that life died thousands of years before. For Cygna, even her new name did not change her heart.

Nerissa realizes too late that Vivienne is going into the fray.

Ophaniel falls to his side, exhausted, eyes dimming.

Christabel's form flickers back to that of a diminutive woman, her long hair pale down her back covering most of her nakedness. Her tears fall to Ophaniel's wings, but he stirs not.

Hades rages in a green light of fury; Apollo falls when he reaches the border of what used to the villa's wall, seeing his trapped sister.

But Kit goes forward as if she moves in another time altogether.

The frost emanating from Vivienne is about to cross into the negative sphere around Cygna when Kit launches herself. Her tails propel her at an unusual angle, unexpected and impossible to block.

Kit's teeth slice cleanly through Cygna's hand, ripping it off in a smooth motion. She takes one look back over her shoulder and sees Nerissa, arm reaching out helplessly, before she hops into the circle of the abyss.

"Get her! Get her!" Cygna is screaming, but she hasn't realized that the voidlings aren't interested in her any longer.

The ring is not here.

The ring is their commander.

The ring is a circle of bone from a Titan's tooth.

A giant cracking sound shocks everyone to their feet as Artemis finally bursts from the gypsum prison, the minuscule void infusion following the ring to the depths.

The great void grows and grows, calling all the little voidlings home, even the microscopic ones woven into the gypsum. Vivienne helps it along with great sheets of frost and ice, and soon Alma, the dwarf, is doing the same, casting frozen stones into its gaping maw.

The *kitsune* jumps into the void.

"Kit!"

Nerissa tries to scream the name, but there is nothing left of her voice. She has shrieked herself mute.

"Shh," someone is saying, holding her up—all fire and fury.

Then another being comes by her, dark and blurred and familiar. Nerissa feels hot tears on her face, scrambling forward on her knees.

"You must let her go. You must let this be."

She breaks from the hands holding her back—Hades, it was *Hades*— and closes her eyes and searches, searches. The land is ice and fire all around her, and Nerissa is certain that this life is not worth the effort if Kit is not in it. How cruel to have found something so rare, so beautiful, only to see it...

"Do not despair," Hades whispers. "Think!"

Nerissa remembers that voice. From *before*. Before the time she went mad, when she was someone else altogether. Except before she did not think. She despaired, and that despair turned to madness; if Vivienne had never found her...

Kit feels the stifling end around her. She no longer breathes. She does not need to. She no longer sees, and she is glad of it. She spat out the finger and the ring as she entered, but her momentum was such that she could not stop herself from going *through*, not with all the chaos about her.

There is no time here.

Only thought.

Only madness.

She sings a low song she remembers from before she was herself. She hums the words softly. Or does she? It does not matter. What is Kit is quickly dissipating. She will be in this ever-nothing for eternity. She will not die. She will not dwindle. She will wait, aware...always...

If she had tears to cry, she would fill up the void with them. But she has left Nerissa alive. And the world itself...

But there is yet a little light.

Kit tries to move in the strange space, that which has no laws when it comes to physical movement. She sees a dim light, dwindling, but not far. It shouldn't be difficult to make her way there—

Smack!

A hand slaps her across the face, nails rending at her skin. It's a cold, dead hand, but when Kit puts out her fingers to touch it, she understands. She knows. There, there is the other arm, fingers encircling the other's wrist like bracelet.

And the hands know her, too.

～

"Pull her to you," Hades says.

"Bring me closer, grandfather," Nerissa says to Hades.

The god nods. In the distance, Artemis cradles her brother like a baby. She is three times his size, and her tears bathe his small head. He keeps asking her not to fuss, but fuss she does, holding him to her breast and sobbing.

Vivienne restrains Cygna, lashing her to the ground with ice. Vivienne needs only hold up a single hand to keep the spell intact, and Cygna bangs against the walls of her icy prison to no avail. Until the void closes, none of them are safe.

"There we go," Hades says, putting Nerissa gently down before the slowly closing void. It smells like burning, like the ever-present asphodel of the Underworld, but singed.

Nerissa reaches. She closes her eyes and reaches. Not with her good arm. But with the other ones.

～

Christabel cradles Ophaniel on her lap and watches, overcome with wonder and sadness. Her angel is cut from shoulder to navel, a great gash that will not bind no matter how many tears she applies. The void has sundered him, and he will not open his eyes. She has already wept for Worth. But now she cries for him again, and for Ophaniel, and for every unuttered word.

"I used to think that my love for you was a kind of curse, you know," she says softly, moving the golden curls from Ophaniel's pale face. His chest rises and falls. Slower and slower. "But now I realize that perhaps it was not a curse at all, that it was a blessing. For who would Christabel be without a heart? Just a blind monster, raging in the dark…"

∾

The void is all but a sliver, wind still whipping from every angle, when Vivienne finally sees a hint of the *kitsune*. It was a gamble. All of this was. But when the weight of the world and the very concept of existence hang in the balance, one must make some sacrifices.

She just hoped that it wouldn't be so final.

And then…yes. There she is! It is barely perceptible at first, but the void shudders for a moment, and just as it quickens its pace, a clawed hand appears. Then a face, smeared with blood. It is like watching the birth of a great god, Vivienne thinks, and the symbolism is not lost on her.

Nerissa screams, blood-curdling and fearsome, and then Kit is out, pulled by a pair of disembodied arms that, as soon as they appear on the right side of the void, fall limp to the ground, dead.

The lamia rushes forward to the *kitsune*, draping her body over Kit's protectively.

And it is over.

Inasmuch as these sorts of stories are ever over.

The righteous triumph; the wretched fall.

Just in time for tea.

OUT OF THE VOID, LIFE

Morgan watches Christabel from across the fire, gauging the young unicorn. She has not been the same since returning from Andalusia, but the old dragon has lived long enough that she's come to expect such changes. All these stories of metamorphoses leave out the fact that we are continually changing, and this is especially true for monsters.

Her story is a good one, of course. Christabel always tells good stories.

"And what happened to them all?" Morgan asks. She knows some of it from Christabel's letters, but due to the sensitive nature of what happened—including the eventual involvement of local communities as well as the Circle of Iapetus—some details were left out.

Christabel leans forward, her eyes glistening in the firelight. Morgan thinks, not for the first time, that Christabel is not a creature of flame or ice, but somewhere in between. A balance. And that must be difficult. For maintaining equilibrium all the time...well, the thought of it makes her uncomfortable.

"Nerissa and Kit returned to London for a time. Dr. Plover was able to form new limbs for her, though I doubt she will ever fully recover," Christabel says softly. "The last I heard they decided to take a tour of Indochine. Then perhaps, to Japan. I warned them that the situation was difficult there, politically, but they are both ever stubborn. But they have each other."

"Well, time will tell," Morgan says. "I'm sure their services will be most appreciated." She pours another cup of tea from the service, adding three cubes of sugar for Christabel.

"I suppose it will. And I suppose we will be around to see it," says Christabel softly. "Not all of us, though. Vivienne and Nadine were last in France. I believe they are opening a kind of parlor there, you know, a salon. So like-minded monsters can find one another. We located Micheaux and his coven; he was frightened, but unharmed by Cygna. Ah, and Cygna. Her trial is due in two months, just after Artemis's. And they will all meet me there. In Prague."

"Prague. What a lovely city."

"Indeed," Christabel says, but there is no joy in her voice.

"Dare I ask about your friend the angel…"

"He did not die," Christabel says. "At least, I don't think so. He diminished. I did not find evidence of his death."

"Well, at least there is that. I don't think it would have been bearable to see an angel die."

"Bearable, yes, where I once imagined I could not withstand such a thing. I have learned that there is much beyond my capabilities. But, Dr. Frye, I am so very tired."

"You are in Scotland. It is a full moon. There is good whisky and a fair wind. My dear, you are due a rest. Why don't you stay here instead of going to Prague? Surely they can do the hearing without you."

But Morgan knows there is no telling Christabel anything. She has made up her mind.

~

When Christabel takes the short path back to her cottage, the wind is indeed coming from the west. It smells of loam and good earth and the salty sea, and though it lifts her spirits momentarily it is not enough to last the short walk.

Ophaniel vanished that night of the battle. He asked her to help him up the hill; not with words, but with hand motions and guttural sounds. It was a long struggle up that half-demolished landscape, but they made the ascent at last and stood in the starlight.

She reached over to touch him, but he was gone. Perhaps angels did not die the same way as other monsters…

Happy endings are for the weak, she decides, though she believes quite the opposite if she really thinks about it. It is difficult not to feel sorry for herself after everything. It is not that she thinks she deserves the happiness, but she hoped that love would be enough.

Perhaps not. Perhaps love is the mortar that keeps the wall together, and one must reinforce it with justice, with righteousness, with truth. It is not the love that is the wall; it is the vast sum of it all.

Christabel is just about to turn the latch on her door when she hears a soft, familiar sound. Her heart leaps into her chest, and she does not need to ask who it is when she turns slowly to see him.

Ophaniel. Worth. This being she has loved above all else.

"Hello, Christabel," says Ophaniel.

The angel is smaller than he was before, it seems to her. Somehow diminished. There is a great scar down the side of his body, across his chest and down almost to his navel. And, beside that, speckles over his skin almost like the spots on a cat. Burn marks, she knows, from the voidlings. A deadly reminder of what almost happened.

"Hello, Ophaniel."

"I've come to say goodbye," the angel says.

"I know," she replies. His face, ever still and difficult to read, said nothing of love.

"And to thank you. Your tears kept me from death, from true death. I found my LORD, you know, and he healed me and sent me back."

"But you must go now," Christabel says.

Ophaniel takes a step closer to her and holds out a hand, so delicate and finely wrought.

Her hand slides over his gently, cautiously.

"I must," Ophaniel says. "For a while. I don't know how long. I need to rest. My body is twisted inside out after casting out the darkness, and I need to sleep a long while."

"I'll miss you," Christabel says.

"I know."

"I would tell you to write, but I know it's not your fashion."

"It is not."

"I will think of you often."

Ophaniel kisses her before there is time to wonder at it; before Christabel can say if she had been thinking about it at all. But when their lips meet, she is certain this kiss has been waiting for her all her life. It is so full of love, of understanding, of an unearthly knowledge, that her entire spirit soars.

I have loved an angel, she thinks. *And that is enough.*

The kiss fades, and Christabel sees, through the closed lids of her eyes, the radiance disappear.

Ophaniel is gone.

She is afraid to open her eyes again, to see that blank space. Her hands are balled into fists, and she takes a half step back, steeling herself.

But then there is a hand, warm and welcome, wrapping around one of her own, gently teasing the fingers open.

"I am still here," Worth says. "If you'll have me."

Christabel gasps and opens her eyes. It is no mirage. It is no dream. It is Worth Goodwin, as foppish and darling as he ever was.

"Worth!"

"Perhaps, if you have loved the angel, you can love the man, as well?"

She looks at him, drawing his fingers to her lips, kissing them. He does feel... different. "You're not..."

"A monster. No, I'm not at present."

"But how?"

Worth sighs, shaking his head. "It's a kind of truce. Ophaniel will take a long time to heal. But he is weary. And we both agreed that...well, living as two beings isn't necessarily a bad thing. You are a unicorn. I am a facet of an angel. We both agree that we love you. And so, on the full moon, I am Ophaniel. But the rest of the time, I will be yours. If you will have me."

"As Worth."

"More or less. Certainly, this form only. But who knows? We shall see, shan't we? I can't imagine that Waldemar, Goodwin, and Crane can lie dormant forever."

"Of course not," Christabel says, with a laugh. She takes a step closer and puts her hand on Worth's cheek. It is so warm; so flushed. "We have many questions, and many answers, and many dark roads ahead."

Worth leans forward and wraps his arms firmly around her, letting Christabel sink into him. "I will be here. I promise. As long as you provide newspapers and tea, of course. I cannot live on affection alone."

"Of course, darling. Of course. I shall make you a house of newspapers and tea."

∾

Dear Vivienne,

Thank you so very much for the lovely hat and trinkets. Kit is quite enamored of the belt; she says the print is from one of the nearby towns where she lived in Japan. How ever did you know? No, don't answer that. I am quite glad that you are using your newfound power for artistic purposes rather than freezing time and crazed monsters.

We have delayed our trip to Cambodia and instead are visiting Bali for a little while. It is a beautiful place, you know, full of the resplendence of the tropics.

No, I no longer need implet. *I no longer need blood. I just need food. Not much of it, but now and again I like a good rare steak if I can get it. Dr. Plover has given me plenty in the way of supplements, mostly copper-based, providing all the nutrients I need without resorting to the darker pathways.*

For all that Bali is lovely, we have heard of a mountain dragon that is currently dining on villagers twice a year. While I do not consider twice a year to be egregious, Kit is insistent that we take a look. So, we shall do.

I have promised to return to Prague, that great city of my heart, in July, and so we will. The tropics aren't exactly delightful during summer, of course, but it's also simply the right thing to do to support our Ms. Crane. Did you hear about Worth? Strangest thing, isn't it? The girl deserves a little brightness, don't you think?

I also plan to visit cousin Kalum and Makaria, as well as grandfather, before I get back to Prague. I don't relish the idea of being back in Andalusia, but those two need company. And it's good to know that I have family...I hope you are reconnecting with yours, if you wish.

Alma tells me of some strange business involving Loki up north. I do not think we have heard the last of Barqan. And Kit wonders if Cygna was, perhaps, just a diversion...

It seems our adventures continue on.

Oh, Vivienne. What adventures we have had. I keep the sight of you, bright and encrusted with frost, holding back the void, every day. And I know that we are as we ought to be. I love you, and I will always love you, but now that I have found Kit...well, you know. I think we were always searching. You will forever be my sister. And I suppose, in some ways, we truly are sisters. Cygna was our sister, too. But we must all hold ourselves accountable. I will look forward to seeing Artemis on the stand, as well, though her trial will be considerably more challenging due to the intervention of Olympus. Who knew they had their own barristers?

Be well, my dear. Say hello to Nadine for me.

I look forward to seeing you in Prague.

Your Nerissa

FIN

ACKNOWLEDGMENTS

In particular, for this book (and this series as a whole), I would like to thank the magical women in my life. I am a skeptic by nature, but having these remarkable humans around me makes me believe in destiny, fate, and the power of divine friendship.

To Olga Alfonsova and Roshi Khalilian and eternal Zug sky theatre, Hamilton singalongs, and raclette; to Kayt Leonard and getting lost in Vienna, almost; to Susan Griffith for twin souls and palates; to Jennifer Hansen, my harmonizing Scandinavian sister who knows my heart; to Carrie and Audrey, who made me an eccentric aunt; and to Jackie Reeve, Andrea Stolz, Marziah Karch, Fran Wilde, Melissa Wiley, and Ruth Suehle, my glittering gals.

ABOUT THE AUTHOR

Natania Barron is often preoccupied with teacup patterns, illuminated manuscript grotesques, and long vocabulary lists of dead languages, but she promises it all makes sense in her head. Her novels and short stories often explore the subjects of monsters, old houses, complicated wardrobes, and unrequited love. Her lifelong love of the fantastic means she generally gravitates toward all things magical, lush, and eerie, but has also been known to meander toward the Gothic and horrific side of things when she's feeling especially cheeky. When not venturing into the worlds she's made up in her head, she spends her time drinking tea, obsessing over fountain pens, discussing the complexities and wonders of octopodes and cephalopods, hiking in the woods, and baking more than is probably considered acceptable. She lives with her husband, two children, and a pair of rescue dogs, in Chapel Hill, North Carolina.

FALSTAFF BOOKS

**Want to know what's new
And coming soon from
Falstaff Books?**

Try This Free Ebook Sampler

https://www.instafreebie.com/free/bsZnl

**Follow the link.
Download the file.
Transfer to your e-reader, phone, tablet, watch, computer, whatever.
Enjoy.**

Made in the USA
Columbia, SC
24 September 2021